BETWEEN THE ROCKS

A Novel

Barbara Hawes

COPYRIGHT

ISBN-13: 979-8656127608
ASIN: B08BVSVCD1

Cover design by: Barbara Hawes
Library of Congress Control Number: 2018675309
Printed in the United States of America

DEDICATION

To my beloved sister and best friend, Susan Hawes Smith

ACKNOWLEDGMENTS

First and foremost, thank you to Bernadette Barone who talked me into writing a book. I never would have considered such an adventure without her idea for the two of us to write our own books. Her persistence to forge ahead along with some storyline and character suggestions were very important in bringing all the elements together.

Thank you to my sister, Susan Hawes Smith who was one of the first ones to read my book, critique it, and offer important suggestions.

Thank you to my sister-in-law, Bonnie Hawes who was also one of the first ones to read my book and give me a lot of positive feedback.

Thank you to my dear friend, Mary Cosenza who read it, gave me great feedback, and then offered to proofread it and write the synopsis. Her professional abilities turned out to be invaluable.

CHAPTER 1

The long stretch of road between Misquamicut and Weekapaug would be desolate if not for the companionship of the Atlantic Ocean. The wind dispensed constant conversation, albeit hushed and secret.

A girl walked down the road, alone, seemingly without purpose, away from the bar down by the wharf. No one noticed her leave. The straightness of the road acted as her guide.

Eventually a bend in the road made her stop and take notice, as if she needed to make a decision. There, by her feet, was a narrow path that led to the beach. Her right hand was free to lean on a boulder for support while her left hand, clutching a bottle of wine, went up into the air for balance. The path wound down and around to the water's edge. High grass and large boulders created a secluded area below the road's surface.

She sat down between two boulders holding the bottle of wine in her lap. She raised the bottle to her lips and took a swig and then wiped her mouth on her sleeve. Looking up at the tiny sliver of moon, she cursed it for smiling at her.

Night had pulled the temperature down from the forty-five degree high of the day to a bone-chilling thirty-two. A northeast wind raced off the ocean in a punishing onslaught. A shiver traveled through the girl's body. She drew her knees up to her chest and hugged them for warmth. Her teeth chattered.

She took a pill bottle out of the pocket of her jeans and looked at it, and then looked over her shoulder to see if she was being watched. One of the houses up and across the street had a sign in the front yard. A small, add-on sign that said *Vacancy* was swinging gently with the breeze below the larger sign. She nodded her head and mumbled, "Vacancy. Good word for it."

The process began. She took a big gulp from the bottle of wine and then twisted it into the sand. With her eyes closed, she rested her head on the rock and waited for the moment that would enable her to proceed. Her thoughts merged with dreams as she dozed off into a drunken sleep. Waking slightly, she moaned, "Jess."

The sound of the wind whistling between the rocks brought her to. She opened the pill bottle and shook a few capsules into her hand and stared at them for several minutes. She squeezed shut the hand that held her fate, and squeezed her eyes shut trying to find the nerve.

Now or never, she thought. She shoveled the pills into her mouth not allowing herself to overthink what she was doing. They sat on her tongue for a few moments. Holding the bottle up against her lips she told herself, *this is it*. With tears running down her cheeks she raised the bottle and drank, swallowing the pills. "Fuck you! Dad," she yelled. Another swallow. "Fuck you, Mom!" She put her hand up to her neck and yanked off a necklace. "Fuck you, Kevin!" With a tearful sob she threw the necklace. She poured the rest of the pills into her hand, brought them to her mouth and quickly pushed them in, swallowing them with the last of the wine. She threw the empty bottle and it rolled down to where the ebb and flow of the incoming tide could play with it. She watched the water rock the bottle and it lulled her into a trance. Her eyes became heavy and they eventually closed. She slumped over onto her side. The pill bottle lay near her head. She felt nothing except a plausible end to her life.

JACKIE WOKE UP IN the hospital without any recollection of how she got there. A nurse was standing beside her when she awoke. The sun was shining through a window. Jackie squinted and recoiled. *Death is a sunny day*, she thought. *Am I alive?* The light was blinding. Her head throbbed. Jackie looked around the room. She shook her head in disbelief, and looked up at the nurse and asked, "How did I get here?"

"Someone found you down at the beach and called an ambulance," she answered.

Jackie looked at her I.V. and then noticed her wrists were strapped to the bed. She looked up at the nurse and asked, "What's this?"

"It's for your protection. We'll take them off soon. I'll be right back." She left quickly before she had to answer more questions.

Jackie started to doze off again. A woman came in and pulled up a chair beside her bed. Jackie stirred and turned to look at the woman. She was not familiar.

The woman was not dressed in a uniform but had a name tag on her shirt. "Hi, my name is Susan Connors and I am the social worker here at the hospital. How are you feeling?"

Jackie looked at her as if to say, "How do you think I feel?"

"Well, I'm sure you're tired and I won't take up much of your time. We don't know your name, hon. You didn't have any ID on you. Would you like to tell me your name?"

"Not really," she said.

"Could I call someone for you?"

Jackie laughed and turned her head away.

"Well the fact of the matter is that you will probably be sent to a psychiatric ward. I just want to warn you. If you are under eighteen, you'll be placed in foster care. It would be better if you cooperate. We want you to get the help you need. This is a tough enough time and I want you to be as comfortable as possible."

Jackie finally looked back at the woman letting what she said sink in. She finally said, "I'm eighteen, so you can forget about foster care. Been there, done that. No thank you!"

"Ok, that's a start. Would you like to tell me a little more? How about your name?" Susan had a sweet and pleasant face with a trusting smile that got Jackie to talk.

"Jackie, Jackie Furth, but I was thinking of changing my last name to Bonet (bow-nay)."

"Why were you thinking of changing your name?"

"'Cause I hate my father that's why. I don't want his stinkin' name no more."

"Do you want to talk about that?"

"No!"

"Is Bonet your mother's name?"

Jackie shot a look at the woman as if the statement was ridiculous. "No! I just *like* the name, *okay*?" She snapped impatiently.

"Where do you live Jackie?"

"Nowhere."

"Would you like to talk about anything, Jackie?" Susan said her name each time, now that she had the information.

"I'd like to talk about getting these shackles off my wrists!" Jackie said, lifting her arms an inch off the bed, straining under the straps.

"We'll do that, just as soon as we know that you are cooperating and don't try to harm yourself again."

"Whatever!" Jackie turned her head away.

"Well, I think that's enough for now, Jackie. You rest. If you want to talk to me later just tell the nurse and they'll call me, okay Jackie? I'm here to help you. I'll come by later."

Susan Connors left her room.

CHAPTER 2

There would be guests to feed and two kids to prod out of bed to get ready for school when Leena returned to her inn after her early morning jog. Before she went inside, she would routinely stand at the end of her property as she caught her breath and look out at the ocean. The inn sat on a tiny bump-out of land on the coastline of Rhode Island which allowed residents and visitors to enjoy sunsets as well as sunrises. It was here, standing on the edge of the continent, facing the profound strength of the ocean where Leena connected to the rhythm of life and found her inspiration.

On this chilly April morning something caught Leena's eye between the rocks below. She crossed the street to get a better look. Her heart sank when she thought it was a beached seal. She strained to discern what it was. She looked at her watch and decided she had a little more time. She walked down the narrow path to the water to get a better look. As she got closer, she was startled and horrified to see it was a human being, a young woman lying motionless on the sand. She gasped and fell to her knees near the girl's head. Leena yelled, "Oh my God!" She moved her long, brown hair off her face with trembling hands and put her ear up to her mouth to listen for breathing, but the wind didn't permit it. She felt for a pulse on her neck. Leena's own heart was beating so strongly, she couldn't tell. She took a deep breath and closed her eyes to concentrate. She felt a pulse. Leena popped her head up, turning left and then right, to see if there were any people around to help her. There was no one. She felt panicked. The waves were washing up and under the girl's legs. Leena saw the pill bottle on the sand and picked it up. She saw the wine bottle a few feet away. "Suicide!"

Leena scurried back up the embankment and back to the inn and called 911. She woke Bruce and he accompanied her back to the girl while they waited for the ambulance and police to arrive. Jason and Becky stood at the edge of the street looking down at their parents as they fussed over her with a blanket and a towel they had grabbed in haste. They yelled questions to them like, "Who is she?" and "Is she dead?"

"Do you know this girl?" the officer asked as the ambulance attendant placed her onto a stretcher. Her arm dangled off the edge as dead weight. Leena and Bruce cringed.

"No, I was jogging this morning, like I usually do, and found her here," Leena said. "Here, this pill bottle was next to her." She handed the bottle to the attendant. "And that wine bottle was next to her too." She pointed to the bottle. "Is she going to be okay?" Leena asked the man.

"Don't know yet." He took the pill bottle from Leena and looked at the label, then put the girl into the back of the ambulance.

Leena answered as many of the police officer's questions as she could. By this time some of their neighbors had come out and were standing on their lawns to see what the commotion was about. Their neighbors Gloria and Ashton Miller came over to the Frazers to find out firsthand what had happened.

"Kathleen dear, who is that girl? What happened?" Gloria asked.

"I don't know, I found her by those rocks," Leena replied, pointing down to the spot.

Gloria looked in the direction Leena had pointed to. She observed the wine bottle on the sand. She shook her head in a disapproving way and said, "I keep telling Ashton that the riff-raff from that amusement park down at the wharf is spilling into our community. That's why we got a new security system last year. Cost us a fortune. Why, just last week someone came tearing through here so fast I thought they'd drive right into the water. I wish they had. Would have served them right."

Leena kept her eyes on the ambulance as it drove away. She didn't bother to tell Gloria that it appeared to be a suicide attempt. Gloria would have put her own spin on it eventually, so telling her would do no good, Leena learned over the years. "Good bye Gloria. Have a nice day." Leena said.

Bruce gave her a polite smile with the corner of his mouth. "Gloria, Ashton." Bruce acknowledged his neighbors as he turned his back to them. Bruce gently placed his hand on the small of his wife's back, guiding her back to the inn.

"Call me later if you find out she had anything to do with that robbery over in Charlestown," Gloria called out to the Frazers.

Becky and Jason followed their parents inside, asking lots of questions.

Their guests had been watching the drama unfold: from the window inside, and from the front lawn. Leena offered the explanation about the girl's suicide attempt, which was certainly less off-putting than letting them think she was a victim of an assault.

THROUGHOUT THE REST OF the day Leena couldn't stop thinking about the girl. Her curiosity got the better of her and she called the hospital that afternoon to check on her. She was told that she was alive, but didn't get any more information.

The second Becky and Jason got home from school they asked their mother if she found out who the girl was.

"I have no idea, Beck. Did you hear anything at school? Anyone not show up?"

"No, pretty sure she wasn't from our high school. I think I would have heard something about it if she had been from around here," Becky said.

"You saved her life, Mom," Jason said.

"Oh, I don't know," Leena started to say.

"You totally did, Mom," Becky added. "I mean, who would have ever seen her down there? She was dressed all in black and she was, like, hidden behind the rocks."

"Maybe she'll be mad at you for saving her," Jason said.

Becky added, "Maybe she wanted to die for a good reason, like she only had a month to live or something."

"That's enough. Let's not speculate, okay?" Leena laughed lightly. "It is what it is. I did the right thing."

"It's pretty cool. My mom saved someone. You're the best." Jason said.

"Thanks honey, that's sweet."

WHEN BRUCE GOT HOME from work Leena charged right into a conversation about the girl. "I keep thinking about that girl, Bruce. I called the hospital and they said she was alive. I think I'll call again tomorrow."

"If it makes you feel better. Just don't get too involved."

"I know, I just want to know if she's okay," Leena said. "I mean, if I hadn't been out so early..." Leena shook her head in disbelief at the thought of how different the outcome might have been.

Bruce walked up to his wife and kissed her forehead. "You saved her, no doubt. That's my girl."

THE NEXT DAY LEENA kept to her routine and went on her early morning jog. Right before returning to the inn, she stood on the spot where she usually stood and looked down where she saw the girl the day before. She relived the scene in her mind. Leena felt proud to have been the one to save her life. She tried to imagine what could have been so awful that she would decide to end her life - a life that had not even begun yet. Leena stood there, shaking her head. She noted how secluded the spot was the girl chose. It was a miracle that she had seen her at all. She was about to leave when something glistening in the sun caught her eye. Leena climbed down as she did the day before and bent over and picked up a necklace from between the rocks. "This must be hers," Leena said. It was an all gold, heart-shaped charm hanging from a chain. She turned it over and saw an inscription that read, *To Jackie Love, Kevin*. "Don't tell me she tried to kill herself because of a boy!" Leena said. She put it into her pocket and returned to the inn.

She finished her morning chores, fed guests, and saw her family go off in different directions. Leena sat down with her cup of tea on the front room's window seat, took out the necklace, and looked at it again. Leena decided at that moment to bring it to the hospital and have it returned to the girl. It was just the excuse she was looking for.

THE SMELL OF DISINFECTANT was the first thing that hit Leena when she entered the hospital in Westerly. She instantly had a flashback of visiting her mother in the hospice unit at this very hospital only seven months before.

At the front desk, the receptionist gave Leena the proper information about what ward to go to. Leena took the elevator to the second floor and followed the instructions she had been given. When she got to the nurses' station, she explained why she was there and showed a nurse the necklace.

"Oh, so you're the one who found her," a nurse said to her. "Let me call the woman from Social Services, she'll want to see this. Just have a seat if you don't mind."

She watched as the nurse made a phone call. She could not hear what she was saying but she saw her looking at her as she spoke. Leena sat and waited. She watched nurses and orderlies pushing patients down the hallway. Leena picked up a People magazine and started to flip through it, trying to kill time. After fifteen minutes a woman with a confident step and hair that was firmly in place approached her holding a clipboard. She offered her outstretched hand to Leena. "Hello, I'm Susan Connors with Social Services."

Leena jumped to her feet and accepted her gesture. Leena said, "Hi, I'm Kathleen Frazer. I live down on the beach in Weekapaug. I'm the one who found that girl yesterday."

"It's very nice to meet you," She said with firm eye contact.

"I came to bring this. That's why I came," Leena said nervously, handing her the necklace. "Maybe it's something she wants back. Or maybe not, if she did what she did for this 'Kevin' person."

Susan looked at the charm and its inscription and nodded her head, then said, "Yes." Giving it more thought she said, "Maybe this will give me a lead."

"I'd love to know how she's doing if that's alright," Leena asked.

"Of course," Susan said as she looked up from the necklace. She continued, "It looks as though she's going to be fine. It might have been a different story if you hadn't found her when you did." Susan smiled at Leena. "I wasn't able to learn too much about the girl, but I did learn that her name is Jackie Furth, she's eighteen and I think she lived in Connecticut at one time. I don't know where she's been living lately. I couldn't get her to say much."

Leena asked, "What happens to her when she is well enough to be released?"

Susan's pleasant face changed for the first time since she met her. As she tilted her head and frowned, she said, "I'm setting up some state-run counseling sessions for her. She has no insurance so it's not much, but we don't want to throw her to the wolves. She may decide not to go, and legally that's her decision. She will be on her own if that is what she chooses to do. We can't find any family, and she won't give us any information. I'm trying to find out if she has any friends she could call. Unless she is deemed crazy, and that doesn't appear to be the case, Jackie will be free to go."

"I hope she takes you up on that offer of help," Leena stated.

As the two women talked Jackie had been up and walking, pushing her I.V. cart. She heard her name and stopped to listen to the two women down the hallway. They didn't notice her.

"Where did you say you lived?"

"The Weekapaug area. My husband and I own a bed and breakfast there called *Sunset Inn*. I go for my jog every morning around sunrise. Anyway, that's how I found her."

"Well she's one lucky girl," Susan said.

Leena said, "I have a daughter who is seventeen, well, she'll be eighteen soon. I couldn't help wondering why she would want to kill herself. It's so sad."

"Unfortunately, suicides and suicide attempts are not completely uncommon, especially for girls," Susan said.

"How sad to think a young person like her would feel she has no one to turn to in a crisis. When I found this necklace and realized she may have done this because of a boy my heart sank. I guess at this age it seems like the end of the world when a boy breaks up with you. I went through that same thing at her age. The break-up, I mean, not the suicide attempt." Leena laughed. Susan was nodding her head as she listened. "Well, I better get going. I don't want to take up any more of your time," Leena said. "So, she's going to be okay, right?"

"Yes, physically she will be. She's out of the woods. We can only hope for the best. Thank you for this, by the way. It might be helpful," Susan said holding up the necklace.

Jackie saw her necklace dangling from Susan Connor's hand. She was tempted to walk over and snatch it but she stayed put.

"Call me if you'd like an update. Here's my card." Susan handed her a card. They shook hands and parted company.

CHAPTER 3

A mountain of paperwork hid the surface of the desk upstairs in Leena's office. She shuffled one stack of papers to one side and stacked another pile on a chair. Leena ran her fingers through her hair and let her forehead come to rest in her hands.

Becky walked into the room and looked at the mess. "What's all this?" she asked pointing to the chair.

Leena looked up at her daughter giving her a look with raised eyebrows, which showed her frustration. "What do you want? Can't you see I'm busy?"

"I can see this room is a mess," Becky said.

"Thanks, I hadn't noticed," she said sarcastically. "You wanna help me look through all this crap to find a musician's contract?"

"What? No. I just came in to ask you something."

"Pray tell, let me guess. 'Can I have the car today, Mom?' Am I close?"

Becky stood and stared at her mother with her arms crossed. It was obvious Leena was right. "So can I?"

"Oh my God, Becky, you haven't even touched that room of yours."

"I'll touch it later, I promise. Tina and I…"

"Tell you what, you go to the store and pick up the items on my list and you can have the car," Leena said as she dug into her pocket and pulled out her shopping list and handed it to her. "I'm sort of on a deadline here. That engagement party is tomorrow, and some guests are coming later today."

"Oh come on! Can't you go?"

"If I had time to do it I would do it. I'm asking *you* to do it."

"Can't Dad do it?"

"He's out at the hardware store getting a part for a bathroom." She sighed and dipped her head down. Her forehead almost touched the desk. Lifting it again she looked at her daughter. "Why am I explaining this to you? Will you go or won't you? Just tell me yes or no."

"Alright, but can I go to Tina's after?" Becky asked, changing her expression from put-upon to pleading.

"Alright, but only after you clean up that room of yours," Leena said sternly.

"But how can I clean it if you want me to go to the store?"

"I meant *after* you come back here and *before* you go to Tina's."

"Mom, I can't do…"

"Sure you can. Now go!" Leena said as she went back to searching through her pile of papers.

Forty-five minutes later, Becky came back with the items on the list and she cleaned up her room.

"Be home by midnight. Who else is going to be there?"

"Chris of course, and Tina's boyfriend Josh."

"I see," Leena said holding a small stack of papers.

"You find what you were looking for?"

"I found it, but now I'm looking for the list of musicians I had. Need to book something for a party for next month."

"Try Googling it."

"What?"

"You know, look for bands on the Internet."

"Oh. I hadn't thought of that. I have that list around here somewhere," Leena said as she sorted through more papers.

"Suit yourself. I'll see ya later. Thanks Mom, love ya." Becky leaned down and kissed her mother on her cheek.

"Love you too, honey. Be careful!"

She turned and left, passing her father in the hallway. "Bye Dad."

"Where's she going?" Bruce came into Leena's office.

"She's going to a friend's house, Tina's."

"I just wanted you to know I'm home. I'll be in room six. I found the part for the sink. I'm pretty sure I can have it ready by tomorrow," Bruce said.

"Pretty sure? It's gonna have to be, Bruce! The guests are arriving today *and* tomorrow and they've reserved *all* the rooms!"

"It will, it will. I better go to work then. Did you have any luck booking the entertainment for that party?"

"No, not yet. I'll have to do some research on that. That group I got for the New Years thing was good. What was their name?" Leena asked as she went back to searching through the papers on her desk.

"*Smooth Blues*, right?" Bruce helped.

"Right! They were good. But they were more jazz."

"Didn't this party ask for rock music?"

"Yeah they did. I'll have to try someone new, that's all."

Bruce turned to leave and then turned back around and said, "Did you try searching online for a band?"

"Not yet. Becky just said the same thing. You think that's a good idea? I mean, how do you know how good they are?"

Bruce shrugged and said, "Never know 'til you try 'em, I guess." Then he left.

THE INTERCOM BEEPED AND Jason spoke to his mother from downstairs. "Some guests are coming, Mom."

"Thanks honey. I'll be right down." Leena hurried down the hallway and down the stairwell. She relieved Jason who had been stationed in the lobby area. "You're the best!" Leena whispered to him. Jason left and Leena took his place.

Leena greeted a couple from Ohio. She handed them a card key and, as she walked them down the hallway to their room, she explained how their key worked for the front door and their room. She handed them a packet which included information about the inn, a menu, prices for special services, a map of the area, a list of local shops and eateries with various coupons included. "Dinner is served between six and eight. It's all in the brochure."

Leena went to the kitchen and went over the menu with Hal. Michelle emerged from the bathroom in her black skirt and white shirt. Leena looked around the room. "Michelle, where's Carly?"

"She said she'd be here in a little while. She can't come tomorrow though."

"What? I thought we were all set with that." Leena heard the doorbell ring again. "More guests, excuse me."

A young woman was standing in the entryway. She was dressed all in black and wore heavy black eye make-up. Leena approached her. "Hello. May I help you?"

The woman stood silently for a few seconds, then took a step forward. Leena waited for her to speak.

"I'm looking for the owner of this place, a Mrs. Frazer?" she said timidly, avoiding eye contact.

"You found her. What can I do for you? I'm afraid there is no vacancy tonight." Leena explained.

She paused again and finally looked right at Leena. "I'm not looking for a room, ma'am. I'm, my name is Jackie. I think you're the person who found me last month, you know, down by the water?" She looked down at the floor half way through her query.

Leena looked at the girl more closely. Her eyes widened as she started to recognize her. She remembered the long, brown hair that covered her face. "Oh my God! You're *her*?" Leena stepped forward toward the girl. She looked up at Leena again. Upon closer inspection, Leena observed her brown eyes, the color of her hair, surrounded by gobs of black eyeliner which created two black holes. "How are you?" Leena asked as a big smile lit up her face.

"I'm okay now. I wanted to meet you. I wanted to thank you, I guess." She maintained eye contact and then the floor pulled her eyes back down once again.

"I am delighted to meet you, Jackie. I'm Kathleen Frazer. Well, most people call me Leena. I am so thrilled you're okay. I called the hospital to check on you. They said you were doing fine. I was so relieved!"

"I found out you brought my necklace to me." Jackie put her hand up to her neck as if to show the necklace but it was absent. Leena noticed her short fingernails were painted black.

"Oh, yes, well, I was out for my morning jog, I mean, my usual route I take in the morning, and I noticed it in the sand the next day. So I figured it was yours." There was an awkward pause and Leena found herself staring at the girl. "So come in, come back to the kitchen and have some tea or hot chocolate and a bite to eat."

Jackie followed her through the library to the kitchen, looking around as she walked. "This is a nice inn you got here," Jackie said.

"Thank you. We've been here for going on eight years now. My husband and I renovated it and turned a regular house into an inn. Boy, if I knew then what I know now, I don't know…" Leena turned to Jackie and led her to a seat at the kitchen table and took some cookies out of a canister and put them onto a plate. She placed them down on the table. Jackie sat down. Hal stopped chopping and looked over at the girl seated at the table.

"Hal, this is Jackie, Jackie, Hal. He's my chef. He's wonderful."

"Hi, Jackie," Hal said. Jackie nodded at him.

Leena put a kettle on the stove to boil water. The doorbell rang again. "Will you excuse me?"

Michelle walked into the kitchen. "You here to work?" she asked Jackie.

"Me? No, I'm just, I'm here to see Mrs. Frazer."

Leena came back in and took two mugs out of the cabinet. "Tea or hot cocoa?"

"Oh, nothing, really."

"I insist." Leena stood holding the mugs, one in each hand. Her expression said, "Well?"

"Tea," she said shyly.

"Tea it is." Leena put a teabag into each mug, poured the water and brought them to the table. She offered cream and sugar which Jackie partook of liberally.

"This is a very nice surprise, Jackie. I'm glad you came." Leena sat down. She took a cautious sip of her tea, making a slight slurping sound. She brought the mug down to the table. She ran her fingers through her fine strawberry blonde hair as she formulated her next question. "Where do you live?"

"I live up in Westerly with a friend. She's letting me stay there."

"Well, that's good," Leena felt awkward but asked anyway. "So everything is okay with you?"

"I'm fine." She looked down into her mug. "It was pretty stupid what I did. I know that now. I mean, my boyfriend, Kevin, he was cheating on me. I should have known. He's a Scorpio and all."

"I see." Leena let her talk.

"But hey, things are great, and, thanks to you, I have a second chance." A hint of a smile appeared turning her lips heart-shaped for a moment.

"I think you'll do just fine," Leena didn't know what to say. "Cookie?"

"Thanks." Jackie took a cookie off the plate and ate it slowly.

They sipped their tea and endured an awkward pause which was broken by Bruce entering the kitchen. He stopped when he saw the girl at the table. "Oh, Bruce, you'll never guess who this is. This is the girl I found at the beach last month, you know the one that went to the hospital? This is Jackie. Jackie, this is my husband Bruce." Leena avoided the word suicide.

Bruce stared for a moment and then smiled courteously and held out his hand. "Well, what a surprise. How are you doing?"

Jackie strained to look up at Bruce's face directly above her from her seated position. "Fine, thank you." Jackie replied, taking his hand and shaking it. Her hand disappeared in his.

"Good, good. Good to hear that." Bruce continued to look at her and then broke his stare and looked at Leena and said, "I'm done up in the bathroom. It's working great. We're all set. I'll be upstairs if you need me. Nice to meet you, Jackie."

"Same here," Jackie said.

"Thanks. Appreciate it, hon," Leena said as Bruce walked over to the door which led to their private home upstairs. He punched in a code, the door buzzed and a green light came on. Jackie watched with curiosity. He opened it and disappeared behind the door.

"He's pretty handy for a lawyer," Leena said.

"He's a lawyer for the inn?" Jackie asked, a bit confused.

"No. Well, yes he's a lawyer, but not for the inn. His firm is up in Westerly. This inn is more my business than it is his. But he helps a lot. Like today, a pipe under a sink was leaking. He fixed it. It can get crazy sometimes. All the rooms are booked this weekend, so they all had to be working." Leena gabbed on. "Last month it was a hole in one of the walls. A guest's kid was monkeying around. He puttied it and painted over it and, voila, good as new."

"I see. Did you do the decorating yourself? It's awful pretty everywhere." Jackie asked. "Real high class."

"I did. That's the part I love so much. I thought we'd never finish the renovations. Come. I'll show you around. Take your tea." Leena got up and Jackie followed her into the main dining room where there was a fireplace with a high mantle. Jackie observed all the personal detail as Leena commented on some of her favorite items she had added over the years. She pointed out the hallway leading to four guest rooms. Then they walked across to the front room which was decorated in a Victorian-era motif. She pointed up a staircase and explained how there were five more guest rooms upstairs. They walked into the library, the room they initially passed through on the way to the kitchen.

"Wow," Jackie said. "This place is awesome!"

"Thanks." Leena's phone rang and she answered it. She talked to someone about booking a room for a week in August. She walked over to her reservation book. When she hung up she said, "It's coming up on the busy season. School will be out soon and the vacationers will be on their way. We're booked for almost every day between now and Labor Day, believe it or not."

"Awesome," Jackie said. "So where do you and your husband live?"

"Oh, we live upstairs. It's all separate," Leena explained. She led her to the stairwell door in the kitchen, where Bruce had exited a few minutes before. "Our living area is right above this kitchen, the dining room, lobby, and library. This is how we get to our home." Leena pointed to the door.

"I see. Just the two of you live here?"

"No, I have a son who's fourteen, Jason, and a daughter, Becky, who is seventeen, well almost eighteen, and she's a senior at the high school. Maybe you can meet her someday. She's not home right now, though. You're about that age?"

"I'm turning nineteen next month."

The doorbell announced another guest. "I should go," Jackie said. She placed her mug back down on the kitchen table.

Leena and Jackie walked to the lobby where new arrivals had just entered the inn. Jackie watched as Leena greeted the guests. "Wait here," Leena said to Jackie. She escorted the guests down the hallway and returned a few minutes later.

"You come and visit anytime you want, really, anytime. I mean it," Leena told her.

"I appreciate that. I hope to find a job, and I'm trying to get my life together. I just wanted to meet you and let you know I was okay, and to thank you."

"You are very welcome. I am so pleased to see you are doing well."

"Well, it was nice to meet you, Mrs. Frazer."

"It's Leena. And it was very nice to meet you, Jackie." Leena walked her out onto the front porch. They both stopped and let the beautiful sea breeze distract them for a moment. Jackie stepped down the three steps and onto the walkway.

"Thanks for the tea and everything, Leena," She forced herself to call her by her first name.

"Don't mention it. Take care now." Jackie started to walk away toward the street when Leena had an idea. "Jackie. Did you say you're looking for a job?" Jackie turned back and nodded her head. "I could use a waitress this weekend, and well, maybe for other times too. You interested?"

Jackie walked back toward Leena and her face lit up. Leena saw just how naturally beautiful the girl was. "You mean it? Really? I'd *love* to. Sure! When?"

"The guests have been arriving for the weekend, as you can see, and their anniversary party is tomorrow afternoon. I think I might be a little shorthanded. As a matter of fact, I am sure I could use more help. You want to come tomorrow?"

"I could do that! Tomorrow's fine."

"Great! I'll have an outfit for you. How does that sound?"

"It sounds *great* Mrs. Frazer, I mean Leena. I'll be here. Thanks."

"I look forward to it. Why don't you come at two. Oh and Jackie," Leena said.

"Yes?"

"If you wouldn't mind, could you not wear such heavy eye makeup? And would you consider getting rid of the black nail polish?" Leena was feeling confident she was not asking too much.

"Sure thing, no problem," Jackie said without the slightest sign of disapproval about her new requirements. "I'll be here. Thanks again!"

"I'll see you tomorrow, then." Leena watched as she walked away. Jackie had a bounce to her step. Shyly, Jackie looked back at Leena, her hair partially covering her face. She gave Leena and the inn one more glance, waved, and then she turned back around and kept walking.

SELLING THE IDEA TO Bruce would come later. Leena had the final say in the decisions regarding the inn, but she usually passed her ideas or plans by Bruce. He had his doubts about Jackie.

"You hired that girl?"

"Yes, I hired her. It was an impulse I admit. It's a trial basis and she knows that. If she doesn't fit the bill this will be the last time."

"If she's terrible are you going to be tough enough, you know, have the nerve to tell her that she didn't make the cut and she's out?" Bruce was always her voice of reason.

"I would do that, of course. I have to, Bruce. I can't run this place correctly if there's a weak link. Remember the girl that I hired last year? She was awful. I fired her right away." Leena said.

"You have selective memory, Leena. Yes, you did fire her but you let her work three more times. Didn't she drop soup on someone?" Bruce's eyebrows emphasized his point.

Leena's face acknowledged his point. "You're right. If she's no good I will not let the situation linger."

"You make the decisions. That's what being a boss is all about," he said a bit condescendingly. "You can be too soft sometimes," Bruce said.

"I know, but I have a good feeling about her," Leena defended.

"Leena, she just tried to *kill* herself! You can't expect her to be completely stable!"

"I still think she needs a chance and a break, that's all." She said, gesturing with her hands. She paused and said, "I will be tough if I have to."

AS PROMISED, JACKIE RETURNED the next day. Preparations were in full swing and Leena was moving in all different directions. Jackie felt like a spectator at a tennis match. Finally, Leena came over to Jackie and greeted her warmly. She led her back to the kitchen and handed her a few pairs of black pants and skirts and a white shirt.

"Try these. Pants or a skirt, you decide. I'm sure one of them will fit you. Okay? Michelle, could you come here?"

Michelle had been working for Leena for over two years and Leena trusted many details to her. She introduced her to Jackie.

Jackie went into the bathroom next to the kitchen and got dressed.

"Michelle, could you let her do some serving? I'm not sure if she's ever done it before but let's see how she does, okay?"

"Sure thing Leena, no problem." Michelle went into the back yard where a tent was set up as a precaution to bad weather, but due to lovely weather, it would act as a shield from the sun.

Jackie came out of the bathroom and Leena explained the arrangement. "So, here's how it works. I'll pay you fourteen dollars an hour. They won't be tipping because it's a party. If this works today and you are still interested you might want to help me out with other stuff. So, if you work when guests come just for dinner, then I'll pay you twelve dollars an hour but you keep your tips. And they usually tip very well. Sound good?"

"Sounds great," Jackie said.

"Oh, wait." Leena went into a kitchen drawer and pulled out a scrunchie for her hair. "If you don't mind wearing your hair back." Leena handed it to her.

"No problem."

"If you have any questions about where things are or whatever, come find me or Michelle."

Becky appeared in the same outfit and walked over to her mother. "Beck, hon, this is Jackie, Jackie this is Becky, my daughter. She's working today too. Jackie, Becky can help you with anything as well."

The two girls smiled and said hello. Leena decided not to tell Becky at that moment what the connection was to Jackie. The two girls walked away. Leena could see them chatting with each other and laughing. Leena smiled. She had a sense of pride and accomplishment.

CHAPTER 4

Leena only had two hours before Wendy's visit to finish as much work as possible. Leena tied up many loose ends such as her online banking, arranging for flower deliveries, and scheduling lawn maintenance. She still had to book a rock band.

Jason came into the room and asked, "When's Andrew gonna be here?"

Leena looked at the clock and saw it was almost eleven o'clock. "They should be here by about one."

"Where's Dad? I'm bored."

"He's down at Fred's watching some game, remember?"

"Oh," Jason said.

"Why don't you go down to the kitchen and see if Hal or Michelle need help," Leena suggested.

Jason looked at her like she was crazy. "Nah," he said, and left.

Leena decided to take Becky's and Bruce's advice and search for a rock band online. One band she found was called *Backlash*. Their description simply read: *For the most rockinest retro sound in Rhode Island.* Their song list was impressive. Another band called *Time Travelers* from New London, Connecticut also fits the bill. They described themselves: *We play a wide variety of 60's & 70's music. Our three-part harmonies and groovin' beat make it impossible to sit still. We are a four-piece band currently performing at many clubs and private parties.* Leena gathered information on both. She found another Connecticut band called *Many Miles Away*. She noticed that they played *The Police, Beatles, Steely Dan, Rolling Stones, Pink Floyd and Led Zeppelin and more.* The description went on to say, *Many Miles Away have earned a reputation as one of Connecticut's most true-to-the-source cover bands with one of the largest lists of cover songs by all the most popular bands of the 60s, 70s, 80s and the 90s. Many Miles Away perform in Connecticut, Rhode Island, Massachusetts, and New York.*

Leena liked the description. She found a picture of the band performing and the caption below it that read, *Many Miles Away recently played at "The Club" in Hartford, Connecticut.* Leena looked at the photo again. The lead singer caught her eye. He looked familiar. Leena looked at the picture again, scrutinizing the lead singer. The microphone was in front of his face and his eyes were squinting as he sang. Then Leena finished reading the caption below. *Pictured from the left: Dave Jenkins on bass guitar, Carl Zawkowski on drums, Pete Spangella on keyboard, and vocals, and Michael Everly on guitar and vocals.*

Leena let out a yelp and held her hand up to her mouth. She quickly looked over her shoulder and down the hall to see if Jason was around. She turned back to the computer and said, "Michael!" She thought, *Could it be my Michael Everly?* It had been twenty-two years since she last saw him. His hair was shorter but he still had a beard. "This *is* Michael!" Leena whispered to herself. Her eyes filled with tears as she sat and stared at his picture for many minutes. "Oh my God, Michael!" Leena stood up and went to the window and looked out without really seeing. She went back and sat down at the computer. She took a deep breath and scrutinized the website further. She gathered all the information she could about them and jotted down the upcoming dates and locations where they would be performing. Her heart was pounding and she couldn't take her eyes off the computer screen. She searched other sites and got a little more information about his group, but their website was the only one that had the photograph. "Wait until Wendy sees this." *This is so bizarre,* she thought. She stared at the photo some more. "Michael," she said out loud. "That's Dave. Oh my God!" She sat in total disbelief, staring at the screen in a trance.

Leena was so distracted that she gave up everything else on her to-do list. When one o'clock was approaching, she jumped in the shower and got ready for Wendy's arrival. As she showered, she thought about Michael. Ever since high school, she wondered about him, her first love, her high school sweetheart, her first lover. They had the real thing.

Across the room in her study hall sat the boy of her dreams. The only studying Leena did was memorizing everything about Michael Everly she could in a forty-five minute time period. He had long brown hair, parted in the middle, tucked behind his ears just the same way she wore hers. He wore jeans, a t-shirt and an old pair of sneakers. She wondered how he got a tiny scar at the corner of his left eye. He slouched as he sat with one leg propped up on the other at the ankle.

She could never get up the nerve to talk to him. He was a senior, she, a junior. They exchanged looks from across the room but up until that time they had never spoken to each other. After a month of study halls, it happened. He walked down the hallway to his locker after study hall as he usually did. Leena approached. He watched her walk toward him. A big smile gradually changed his face. His big blue eyes seemed to sparkle. Leena swooned for an entire week when he finally spoke to her: "Hey, how ya doin?"

Eventually, they sat next to each other during study hall and chatted

when they could get away with it. A few times he helped her with her math
homework. Walking her to class afterward became the new routine.

THE DOORBELL RANG IN the kitchen and Jason ran to let Wendy
and Andrew in. "Hello, Jason. How's it going?" Wendy greeted him.

"Fine. Where's Andrew?"

"He's coming, he's coming. He's getting his stuff out of the car. Why
don't you go help him?"

Jason ran out to greet Andrew and helped unload his two backpacks
full of video games.

"Where's your mom, Jason?" Wendy asked.

"She's upstairs. You can go up."

"Hi Hal, how's it going?" Wendy asked as she passed through the
kitchen.

"Very well, and yourself?" he answered back.

"Good. Everything smells divine as usual, Hal."

"Thanks."

Wendy and the two boys climbed the back staircase and entered the
Frazer's home. The boys went straight to Jason's room and shut the door.

"Hello? Leena? I'm here." Wendy yelled.

Leena came out of the office with a towel on her head. "Hey," Leena
said as the two old friends hugged.

"Come on in."

"Where's Bruce?"

"He should be back later. He went down to Fred's to watch a game."
Leena had a strange look on her face as she looked at Wendy.

"What? Why are you looking at me that way?" Wendy observed
Leena's shifting brown eyes.

"You won't believe what I just found on the Internet!" Leena said in a
whisper as she headed into the office pulling Wendy by the hand. She
revealed her hidden treasure with a few clicks of the mouse. "Look. It's
Michael! You could have knocked me over with a feather, Wendy. Can
you believe this?"

Wendy sat down in front of the computer and stared at the picture on
the website. She read the caption. She looked up at Leena and said, "This
is amazing!" She looked back at the web page. "It's him! It is Michael.
And that's Dave!" Wendy pointed to the bass player. "He played in a band
in high school."

"How *cool* is this? It's my Michael!" Leena's eyes were sparkling with
excitement as she admired the picture.

Wendy watched Leena look at the computer screen. She had not seen
Leena so excited since she had contemplated buying the inn years ago.
Wendy and Leena stared at each other for a few seconds before Wendy

spoke. "How did you find him? Were you Googling him?"

"No, not exactly. I was searching for bands for an event I'm having here in June. They requested a rock cover band. Anyway, I found this site. I mean, how weird is that? Isn't the Internet great!?"

"I thought you hated the Internet. You were complaining about it the other day."

"I know. It's a love-hate relationship. I don't have to tell you how evil it can be when you have to worry about the kids using it. But isn't this *great*?" Leena was smiling from ear to ear.

"I know. So would you hire him for your thing at the inn?" Wendy asked.

"Oh, God, no! I hadn't even thought of that. That would be way too weird, don't you think?"

"It would be," Wendy said still staring at the screen.

Leena had a glint in her eye, "What do you think about going to see him perform? Look he's going to be at this festival in June, in Connecticut."

"I suppose. You want to contact him?"

"No. I don't know. I haven't even processed this yet. But maybe we could just go see him perform. I doubt I would talk to him. I would just want to *see* him again."

"I'm game. You mean you just want to 'see' him? You really wouldn't go up to him and say 'hi'?" Wendy was puzzled.

"Oh!" Leena let out a big sigh at the thought. "How could I? I mean after all these years? I don't look like I did in high school!" Leena said as she opened up her arms in a gesture and her eyes widened at the mere notion of Michael seeing what time had done to her. "I weigh fifteen pounds more than I did in high school. Please!"

"And you don't think he's aged a day since then?" Wendy asked sarcastically.

"Well, yeah! I mean, of course, I know he's aged. That's silly. Look, age is only a good thing for wine and cheese." Leena chuckled. "It couldn't be a good thing for two old lovers. I mean, we have these images in our mind when we think back about old flames."

"And you want him to remember you as you were then?"

"I guess that's what I'm saying. I don't know, Wen. I can't think straight."

"You had it *bad* for him. I remember that. You were pretty upset when it ended."

"He broke my heart. But it's been twenty-two years. I think I'm over it now."

"So let's make some plans to go. What the hell? Unless you think this would stir up some old feelings. You are married you know."

"Thank you for reminding me. I had forgotten," Leena said sarcastically.

"Do you even know if he's married?" Wendy asked.

"I have no idea."

"Maybe he's still waiting for you?" Wendy said smiling.

"Right, that must be it." Leena laughed.

THE BOYS CAME INTO the kitchen when hunger drove them out of Jason's room. Leena and Wendy were preparing dinner.

"So how has your first year of high school been, Jason?" Wendy asked.

"It's okay. Harder classes. My science class has been cool. We get to do labs and stuff."

"He adjusted well," Leena added. "And you started middle this year, Andrew?"

"Yeah. I'm not in the same school where my mom teaches anymore."

"That's right," Leena said. "She can't check up on you now." She smiled at Wendy.

"He's at that magical age where he's embarrassed to be with his mother," Wendy said.

"You guys are getting so grown up," Leena said. "We've been in that phase for years around here. Feels like there's not much more parenting left. They'd be happy if I didn't care anymore."

"I don't need you telling me what to do anymore, Mom," Jason said.

"Yes, dear," Leena said giving him a look. "Dinner's not ready, guys. Grab an apple or something, but don't fill up. We'll call you when it's ready."

Discouraged, they went back to Jason's room empty-handed.

"So Andrew gets along with Frank's boy?"

"So far. I thought I was going to bring Jeremy with me today but his mother took him to something. But we haven't run into anything major. The worst thing we deal with is his ex-wife wants Jeremy to eat certain things. She's a bit of a health nut. She and Frank have squabbled over those types of things, like her not wanting him to eat candy or cookies and stuff. It could be worse. That's what I tell myself."

"You're brave to move forward and get married with both of you having kids."

"We all get along. Hey, who's minding the inn down there? You working tonight?" Wendy asked.

"No, I've given myself the night off to be with my friend. Hal, Michelle and Jackie are running the show tonight. I trusted them to handle it without me. I give myself a break more than I used to. I had to stop being so anal about it. It was driving me mad."

"Glad to hear it."

"I'm learning, the hard way I suppose, that I can't do it all myself. I mean, it's less income and that bothers me, but at the same time, I'm able to concentrate on booking it for special events. Before I was just chasing my tail. I can't go full speed every day. Besides, I really had to put Michelle on a more regular basis. No one's gonna stay with a job that they only get called once or twice a week. I tell myself that I don't want to be a waitress and chambermaid. I want to be an innkeeper and manager."

"Now you're talking."

BRUCE CAME BACK FROM his afternoon of watching football and drinking beer with his buddies. It wasn't apparent to Wendy but Leena knew he was drunk. He took a beer out of the refrigerator as he passed through.

"Wendy, hey, good to see you. How's what's his name?" he struggled to remember his name.

"Frank? He's fine." Wendy answered.

"You guys still engaged?"

"Yep."

"You ready for dinner?" Leena asked him.

"Sure." He left and went to the TV room.

Everyone converged at the dining room table for dinner around six.

"Where's Becky?" Bruce asked in a demanding way.

"She's out with Chris."

"She should be home. This is a family meal."

"Well I said she could go."

Bruce kept his scowl for several minutes. "Wendy, how are the wedding plans going?"

"They're going great. We're set with September 28th, here at the inn. I'm thinking I might use one of the bands that Leena found online. She's got quite a few good possibilities for some of her guests." Wendy looked at Leena and smiled.

Leena looked at her and gave her a warning glance with a question on her face about what she might reveal. But she knew that her friend would keep mum.

"How's that going?" Bruce directed the question to Leena. "Aren't you cutting it a bit close?"

"I'm working on it."

"You save things like this until you have no time left, then you run around and complain that you have too much to do."

"Thanks for the vote of confidence, Bruce."

"I'm just stating that if you organized yourself a little better these things…"

"Alright, Bruce. Not all of us can be as organized as you are. You're the champ."

"It's a fact of life for someone like me."

"You worry about your office and I'll worry about the inn."

"It's our investment, Leena," Bruce didn't drop it.

"I know! And things have been working out pretty well for the last eight years," she defended herself. "Seven of which have been in the black, not the red." Leena looked over at Wendy and she could tell her friend felt embarrassed about the way Bruce was talking to her.

"It's been going smoothly because I am here as your safety net. This inn would have gone belly up if it hadn't been for me," Bruce boasted.

Leena was disgusted. "You can shut your mouth any time now."

"Well, it's true, you…"

"Enough! It hasn't been all smooth sailing for you either. Need I remind you about the time you were sued for malpractice?" Leena looked at Wendy to continue. Jason and Andrew watched their back and forth jousting. "Remember when that client decided you didn't handle the selling of his business correctly and sued you?" She was settling the score.

"That suit was dropped, don't you remember?" Bruce was almost yelling.

"Not before you dragged this whole family through hell for *four months*!" Leena was losing her temper, and her voice went up.

Wendy tried to steer the conversation in a different direction. "Bruce, so tell me, how is Rita? Does she practice law anymore? It's been ages since I've heard about her."

"Yeah, she's still practicing, but up in Providence." He answered Wendy, but he was still riled up at Leena. "Did Leena tell you about the girl she hired?"

"Yes, the girl she saved. How nice of her to do that."

"She's some suicidal punk rocker who doesn't give you eye contact when you speak to her."

"Can you say anything nice, Bruce?" Leena said. "She's working out just fine."

Jason said, "I like her. She's way cool. She's got a pierced belly button." Jason and Andrew both laughed out loud with mouths full of food.

Bruce nodded. "See? That's what I'm talking about. Do we need that type around here? She could be a bad influence on the children."

"Oh please!" Leena scolded.

"Hasn't she been showing up late? Weren't you complaining about that the other night?"

"Complaining? No. She was late once and I addressed it and everything is fine," Leena said.

"I'm going on record as saying she's trouble," Bruce said.

"Duly noted. Court is now in recess." Leena threw her napkin on the table, got up and stormed into the kitchen.

"She's white trash," Bruce said, loud enough for Leena to hear him.

"Bruce," Wendy pleaded. "Would you do me a favor and drop this subject?" Then she leaned into him closer and whispered, "Not in front of the kids, okay?"

Bruce took his beer bottle and tipped it upside down and emptied the rest of its contents into his mouth. He looked over at Andrew and Jason who were staring right at him. "Fine," he finally said.

Leena returned to the table and they ate the rest of their meal in total silence.

CHAPTER 5

Bruce walked through the kitchen while Leena prepared for a luncheon. The staff had the day off. He maintained his silence from the night before, playing the martyr once again. Leena stopped what she was doing and watched him pass through. Her eyes bored holes into the back of his head. He turned around and glared at her.

"What? What?" he snapped.

"I'm just looking at the man I chose to marry. A man that picks on his wife and finds fault with pretty much everything she does and every decision she makes."

"I'm very supportive of anything you want to do and you know it. I can't even give my opinion without getting my head bitten off."

"And you can't let one day go by without a drink!"

"Is that what this is about? I can't have two beers with friends? I get bitched at the minute I come home."

"Two?" She laughed. "I didn't bitch at you the minute..." Leena stopped. "Look I don't want to go into it. Just go. What is it today? Golf?"

"Yes, you know I'm playing golf with Cam today." He turned to walk out the door and almost bumped into Jackie as she was coming in.

"Hi, Mr. Frazer."

He looked at her and did not return the greeting. He left.

Jackie walked into the kitchen.

"You weren't scheduled to work today, Jackie."

"I know. I just wanted to come and help. I wasn't doing anything so I figured I'd help you out with your luncheon."

"You sure?" Leena asked.

"I'm sure. And you don't have to pay me or nothing."

"I'll pay you, that's no problem," Leena said. Jackie shrugged.

They worked together one-on-one for the first time. Leena had been organizing the food and putting cold cuts onto platters. Hot dishes were in the oven. Leena found she could tell Jackie to do something and she followed through with very little coaching. The girl worked hard. They communicated well. Leena was starting to take a shine to this girl.

"Thanks so much for your help, Jackie. I appreciate it. This sure went a lot smoother with some help." Leena said as they finished the cleanup. "I wasn't looking forward to this today. With my friend visiting, we didn't get enough sleep." Leena wiped the counter and removed her apron.

"No problem. I don't mind. It gave me something to do, besides." Jackie said.

"Jackie," Leena said, "I don't want to get personal, so if I am stepping over my boundaries you let me know, okay?" Leena started.

"Okay." Leena had Jackie's full attention.

"You've been late quite a few times and you've shown up in the same clothes. I guess I want to ask you about your living arrangements and if everything is alright."

"Well," Jackie started slowly. "I have been living with a friend up in Westerly but last week she let her boyfriend move in. I think she wants me to move out but hasn't really said it. I've been sleeping on the couch. He's kind of a jerk and they argue sometimes. I leave sometimes and sleep out in her car. I mean, they let me stay inside, but sometimes I don't want to. I don't know, I think I need to figure something else out. I'm sorry about being late and all."

"I see. I had a feeling something had changed. You seem a little down and I'm just concerned."

"I'm not going to try and kill myself again, if that's what you're thinking."

"No, I wasn't thinking that," Leena said

"I started looking in the paper for apartments but most of them are so expensive," Jackie said. "I'm trying to save up. I'll need to find a roommate too."

Leena paused and walked across the kitchen gathering her thoughts. "I have an idea, Jackie. I have that room off the kitchen, here in the back." Leena gestured toward the room behind the laundry room. It's an apartment, basically. My mother stayed here for a year when she became too infirmed to live alone. She died last fall. Anyway, how would you like to live there?"

Jackie's eyes lit up. "Really? That would be awesome!" She paused and then said, "I'm sorry about your mom."

"Thanks. I've been thinking that you have been working out very well and perhaps in return for room and board you could take on a few more responsibilities, like greeting people in the lobby when you hear the bell ring, you could take calls, and perhaps doing some of the cleaning of the guest rooms. You could still waitress. Does this interest you?"

"Does it ever! Yes, it sounds great!"

"Let's not waste any more time. I'll show you the room. Wait here. I have to go get the key." Leena went upstairs and came back down with the key. She led the way through the laundry room to the apartment and unlocked the door. "As you can see this room has its own entrance to the outside, over there." She pointed. "It has its own bathroom too. You would have to use the kitchen here for any meals you might want to prepare for yourself. And the laundry room is at your disposal too. Other than that, you can pretty much be on your own."

"This is wonderful, Leena. I don't know how to thank you!" Jackie was on the verge of tears. "It's a dream come true!"

"I would ask that you not use the laundry room at peak times when they're in full swing, though, but any other time is fine." Leena paused and looked at Jackie as she took everything in. She continued. "I would have to set down one rule. One condition, really. If you had any friends over, I would ask that they not hang out inside the inn. I mean they could come in but they couldn't just hang out in the library or the front room. That kind of thing. Does that make sense?" Leena tried to justify what she was saying. "I don't mean to say you can't have friends come over but I do need to keep these rooms available to my guests and I want to maintain the level of, sort of, solitude and privacy that people who come here enjoy."

"I understand what you're saying. I don't really have any friends that I would invite over anyway. I know where you're coming from."

"Okay, great. So, it's all furnished as you can see. Check to make sure there are plenty of towels and sheets, soap and all that stuff. You know where the supply closet is. Just help yourself to whatever you need." Jackie followed her listening to every word. "You are also welcome to food here in the kitchen but as you already know that these cabinets are off-limits," Leena pointed to a row of cabinets. "They have supplies for the guests and Hal has all that arranged and inventoried. That's his domain. But these two cabinets contain stuff you are welcome to. Just check with Hal first because I may be wrong." Leena smiled at her own inconsistency. "As far as the refrigerator goes, again, check with Hal about what's what. You are welcome to use it for your own stuff. We have our own kitchen upstairs so I really don't stock much down here."

"I don't know how to thank you. This is too much. Are you an Aries?"

"Uh, yes, yes I am," Leena replied, a little surprised she guessed correctly.

"That's what I thought." Jackie donned a smug smile.

Leena nodded. "Anyway, you can stay here tonight if you like. Do you have stuff you need to get from your friend's place?"

"A few things," Jackie said.

"Why don't we take a ride over there later to pick them up."

"Sounds awesome Leena. Thanks!"

There was a long pause and Jackie started to cry. Before Leena got a word out Jackie threw her arms around Leena's neck and hugged her. She sniffed and said, "Thank you so much, Leena. You're a lifesaver!" Jackie laughed and wiped her nose with her index finger. They parted and Jackie continued on that thought, "In more ways than one."

Leena was at a loss for words. Tears filled her eyes too. She took

Jackie's hands and gave them a squeeze. Leena turned and left, allowing Jackie to look over her new home.

LEENA AND JACKIE RETURNED to the inn with one box of worldly possessions and an armful of clothing. Jackie spent the rest of the day rearranging her new apartment.

Leena had some time to herself that Sunday afternoon. She grabbed a book and a cup of tea and went out on the front porch to read. Jasper, the family cat, jumped up in her lap. There was a warm breeze coming through. She lifted her head and chin to catch the breeze on her face and hair. She drew a long, deep breath as if the fresh air was pure oxygen. She petted Jasper, scratching him behind his ears. He purred with contentment. She had yet to open up her book at the bookmark. She felt a small twinge in her stomach as she thought of Michael and the possibility of seeing him again. Her mind went back to high school.

It was September of 1978. Leena had met up with her friend Abby at a school dance on a Friday night. They, along with about six other girls, crammed themselves into the bathroom down the hall from the gymnasium. They worked on their hair and makeup as if they were getting ready for their movie debut. The clatter of their conversations echoed in the small space, escaping into the hallway. "Is he here?" "Did he look at me when I walked by?" "How does my hair look?" Abby fired off her questions in quick succession. Leena had hardly finished telling her that her hair looked fine when Abby threw out the next question designed to boomerang back to satisfy her ego. "Does this make me look fat?" She knew it didn't. Eventually, Abby and the other girls left in a pack, on the prowl for boys.

Leena left the bathroom after they did and stood near the back of the gym and looked around. The room was starting to fill up with students. She watched Abby flipping her hair in a flirty manner in an attempt to maintain the attention she was receiving from a male classmate. Abby suddenly dashed out of the gym with a girlfriend, laughing; the boy followed her. When Abby was out of sight Leena turned to watch the band set up their equipment. That was when she saw him. Michael was squatting on the floor untangling wires, organizing their placement. Apparently, he was helping the band set up their equipment. Leena didn't expect to see Michael that night: He didn't usually go to dances. She watched him for several minutes.

Abby came bouncing back inside the gymnasium and came over to Leena. "Wanna go outside? Jeff's got a few doobies."

"No thanks. You go." Leena was still watching Michael.

Abby looked in the direction of Leena's gaze. "Oh, gotcha. Say no more. See you later." Abby left and exited with Jeff.

Leena got up the nerve to walk over to Michael. She stood a few feet away and looked down at him crawling around on the floor. His hair swept the floor when he reached underneath the makeshift stage for something. When he got what he was reaching for he stood up. He saw Leena and stopped.

"Hey, what's up?" A big grin lit up his face.

"I came to hear the band tonight. I came with Abby. She went outside and so I was just watching you guys. Anyway, I saw you working and thought I'd come over and say hi." Leena justified her every move out of nervousness.

"Glad you did. You gonna stay around?"

"Yeah, I was planning on it."

"So stay here, I won't be much longer."

"Oh, sure, you finish. I don't want to interrupt. Pretend I'm not here."

Michael smiled, only this time with his lips closed. He said, "That'll be hard to do, but I'll try." They stared for a moment without speaking, then Michael turned and went back to the jumble of wires.

About half an hour later the band started their set. Michael watched and tinkered with a few knobs on the amp. Leena had moved back from the stage, to the side. She listened to the band and bobbed her head. She had lost sight of him.

Someone touched her right arm. She turned quickly to see. It was Michael.

"So what do you think?" Michael yelled above the music.

"They're very good," Leena yelled back. Michael nodded in agreement.

"I'm playing with them next week. Pat's going to visit a college so I'm gonna fill in."

"You play guitar? I didn't know."

"Yeah."

"Where are you playing?"

"Some relative of Alan's, a bar mitzvah." Michael laughed. "The Big Time."

"Gotta start somewhere."

Michael nodded and smiled.

By the third song, Michael had moved closer: their arms were touching. Still looking forward at the band he blindly took her hand and held it. Leena turned toward him the second he took her hand. Michael turned toward Leena and took her other hand in his. They stood, eye to eye, staring at each other. They didn't speak. They put their arms around each other and anchored their hands into each other's back pockets and moved slowly to the music, maintaining eye contact. Michael leaned into Leena and kissed her. After the kiss, she rested her head on his shoulder.

Michael stroked her hair.

A few songs later they sat together on the floor behind the makeshift stage, leaning against the wall. The gym was filled with students. The music was unrelenting. The lights were low. They kissed some more.

Leena was enjoying the memory of that night long ago. *Making out,* she thought, *that's what we called it.* She laughed at the term.

Jason brought Leena back to reality by letting the screen door slam as he went out. Jasper's head popped up simultaneously and looked at him. "I'm going to Ryan's house for a while, okay?"

"Sure, hon. Be back by six."

"Okay," Jason said as he jumped off the porch avoiding the stairs completely. Leena watched him run down the street and the same smile returned to her face. She thought, *There are so many different types of love.* Leena petted Jasper. He yawned and stretched and put his head back down to continue his nap.

CHAPTER 6

Leena entered Becky's room with a laundry basket under her arm. She put it gently down on her bed and observed Becky standing at her easel, painting. Becky continued to paint without acknowledging her mother's presence.

"That's beautiful, Beck, absolutely breathtaking."

Becky stopped the motion of her paintbrush momentarily to look Leena's way and gave her a smile. "Thanks. Do you recognize it?"

"No. Should I?" Leena scrutinized the painting.

"It's the wharf down on Atlantic Ave. Remember the painting I did last year with all the people at the wharf? Well, this is a similar view, only at off-season."

"Oh, I see it now. It's just wonderful. I wish I had your talent."

Becky shrugged and said, "You're good at other stuff, like decorating the inn. That's an art you know."

"That's sweet, honey. I don't see that as an 'art,' it's just business, well sometimes it's a hobby." Leena removed Becky's clean clothes from the basket and placed them on her bed.

Becky shrugged again and continued her application of oil paint. "Have you seen Jackie's drawings? She was sketching at the kitchen table the other day. She's not bad."

"No, I didn't. Really? I didn't know she could draw. She's good?" Leena asked.

"I think so. We're going to go down to Watch Hill later and do some sketches. She said she's never tried to paint." Becky stopped and looked at her mother. "Can you believe that?"

"Remember, she hasn't had the advantages you've had. That's nice you're going to bring her with you," Leena said. "I'm sure you could teach her some stuff."

"I suppose, if she wants." Becky changed the subject. "Chris and I are going out later so I won't be home for dinner."

"You're seeing a lot of that boy. How serious is this?"

"It's serious."

"Maybe you shouldn't put all your eggs in one basket. Maybe…"

Becky cut her off. "You're not going to start *that* conversation again are you?"

"I just worry that…" Leena couldn't finish a sentence.

"Don't go there, mother. Just 'cause you were hurt at my age doesn't mean I will be."

"Alright, I hope you're right." She got up and left.

Becky had found her true love. Her words. Chris Felton: a tall, slender, and athletic young man who had just been accepted to Notre Dame on a partial scholarship. Becky had been accepted into Rhode Island School of Design. They would soon be parting, facing college life without each other, and they had vowed to stay true to each other.

Leena saw many similarities to the relationship she had with Michael back in high school and her daughter's relationship with Chris. She had already given her daughter the gloom and doom report of how most relationships do not survive the separation after high school.

Leena went to her bedroom to put her and Bruce's laundry away. She slowly folded items and carefully placed them into drawers. She worried about Becky's heart being broken. She recalled her own heartbreak.

Dad sat in his chair in front of the football game, oblivious to the clatter of dishes and conversation. Everyone's belly was full, and new stories and new arguments unfolded. Leena had trouble concentrating. She deliberately averted her eyes away from the phone which she had anticipated ringing for the last two hours. At 8:23 it finally rang. "We need to talk," Michael said. Thanksgiving dinner felt like a lump in Leena's stomach as she hung up and waited for Michael to arrive.

Leena tapped her foot nervously as she looked out the window. Headlights from the driveway lit up the ceiling of the dining room signaling his arrival. She jumped from her chair to get to the door before anyone else could. Michael walked in and Leena threw her arms around his neck and kissed him on the cheek. He hugged her back then pulled away. Michael was greeted by Leena's mother and sister with much enthusiasm and questions about college life. Leena's foot started tapping again. When the questioning was over, and the offer of pumpkin pie was turned down, Leena left with Michael to go for a ride.

She followed him to the car with anticipation, marred by mood, charted by foreboding. She didn't like the vibe.

They pulled out of the driveway. A curtain moved, then quickly back – her nosy sister. Fingers clasped tightly together to ward off the evil spirit of bad news. Silence, intolerable, the radio breaks the surface tension, playing a familiar song.

Where was he taking me? *She thought,* Say something, anything.

They pulled into an empty parking lot. He cut the engine and the lights. Turning toward her, he took her hands, cold as they were, in his and swiveled in his seat to speak directly.

Her mind began to race. Aren't we just two reunited lovers picking up

where we left off? *she thought. "Michael, what are we doing here?" she
asked aloud. He stared at her blankly. "You've changed."*

"You're right, I have changed."

*She waited, dreading the news, she shut her eyes to endure the
execution.*

He continued on an even keel. "School has been quite an experience."

*She listened as her life as she knew it sank into a miry pit where
gravity increased tenfold. "Just say it, Michael!"*

*That's when the bottom dropped out. "I don't know how to tell you this
so I am just going to tell you," he said, just as serious as he could be.
Leena gripped the sides of the seat and steadied herself. "I met someone at
school. Her name is Sybil. I didn't mean to meet anyone, it just happened."*

*Leena stared straight ahead. "Did you sleep with her?" she asked. She
slowly turned her head for the answer. They looked straight at each other.
He didn't have to say a word, his body told the tale all too well.*

*A blindness came over her, mute, deafness and denial followed, self-
preservation shutting her down entirely. Capsizing, a way to defend as her
world was falling apart, she stumbled out of the car. She didn't remember
the door handle, the open door, the slam, the plea to "get back in the car,
please."*

*A light rain had been falling as she walked. "Come on, get in the car."
She walked on. The rain increased. Coming down in sheets of sadness and
loss, future dreams of long walks together and longer gazes vanished. The
rain washed them away. Walking with purpose and intent, hugging herself
in an attempt to remove the chill.*

*"I won't ask again, Leena, would you please get back in the car?"
Michael asked, leaning to the right talking out the open window as his
Chevy Nova crawled beside her. Her head snapped around and shot him a
look that, as they say, could kill.*

*She turned into her street and headed toward her house. Michael gave
up the pursuit. She was soaking wet, shivering cold by the time she opened
her front door. Her family's expressions shifted from surprise to concern at
the sight of this wet girl.*

*Leena went to her room, shut the door, and sat on the floor, staring at
the wall. The sobs came, at first, quietly with a sniff, and then louder sobs
from a deeper place anyone would dread going.*

Leena finished her chore and picked up her empty laundry basket and
went over to the window. She thought about the fate of that Thanksgiving
evening and wondered if she had been too hard on Michael. She had
refused to take his calls, which were numerous at first. She refused to see
him at his Christmas break. By January his calls had dried up. She finished
her senior year in a fog and she was officially getting on with the rest of

her life.

CHAPTER 7

A warm breeze blew Jackie's long, brown hair off her face one minute and covered her face the next with a move of her head. "Man, it's windy. Good thing you brought those clips," Jackie said to Becky as she looked down into the satchel, seeing the clips along with pads, pencils, and Cray pas.

"I learned that the hard way, believe me," Becky said as she shifted her weight from one haunch to the other, taking supplies out of the bag.

"You come down here a lot?" Jackie asked.

"Once in a while." Becky wrestled with her folding chair. "Put your chair this way, into the wind, so your hair won't drive you mad," Becky suggested. Jackie unfolded her chair and lined it up with Becky's. She handed Jackie a large sketch pad, clips, and different weight drawing pencils. Jackie sat and contemplated what to draw. Becky only took a few seconds to compare her blank paper to the scene in front of her before commencing. She let her graphite fly around the page. Like a Ouija board, her pencil moved across the paper: the picture seemed to draw itself. Furiously she sketched a distant house and a boat tethered to the dock.

Jackie marveled at her instant inspiration. "How did you decide what to draw so fast?"

"I didn't really. I don't let myself think too much. It's best to just start sketching and let the scene put itself down on paper. Just draw the first thing you see."

"This is different than the stuff I normally draw. It's like, landscapes are too much information," Jackie commented, "or maybe that the information is too far away. I don't know."

Becky was quiet as she rubbed her number six pencil sideways to create shadow. Jackie observed her technique. She decided on a nearby fence. Slowly and cautiously Jackie drew. Within a few minutes, she had made a decent start.

"You like high school?" Jackie asked.

"Eh, it's ok. I'm glad it's almost over." She rubbed the pencil some more and then used the side of her hand to smudge her clouds. "I'm really looking forward to this summer and going to college but I am *not* looking forward to being away from Chris," Becky said as she looked up at her scene and down to the page again.

"You're lucky to have him," Jackie said. "Where are you going to go to college?"

"Risdee."

"Where's that? *What's* Rizzee?"

"Ris-dee," Becky pronounced it slowly. "Rhode Island School of Design. I got accepted, miracle of miracles. I'll be dorming there, even though it's not all that far from here. Chris is going to Notre Dame on a partial scholarship. That's way out in Indiana!" Becky let out an audible sigh. "It's *so* far away!"

"Indiana, wow, that is far."

"I worry about being away from him. My mother, oh my mother!" Becky sounded annoyed but contradicted herself by laughing. "She keeps telling me I'm too young to settle on one boy. I guess she got her heart stomped on at my age and she never hesitates to tell me how foolish Chris and I are being."

"I thought Kevin was 'the one' and he turned out to be a two-timing cheater," Jackie said, clearly still hurt by recent events.

"Well, it's not that way for Chris and me. We're committed to each other."

Jackie thought, *so were we,* but kept the comment to herself.

Becky stopped sketching and looked over at Jackie's work. "Not bad, not bad. You've got the knack. So what's your story? Where'd you grow up?"

"Mostly in Connecticut. We moved around quite a few times. Spent time in foster homes in my teens."

"Really? How come?" Becky asked.

"My asshole father was a drunk and smacked me around too much. Showed up at school with some interesting bruises that I couldn't explain and they took me outta the house."

"That's horrible," Becky said. "I can't imagine. Where was your mother? Did she like, die or something?"

Jackie didn't answer right away. Becky looked over at her. Jackie looked at Becky and said, "No she didn't die."

Becky left it alone. "Hey, that's good. I like how you zeroed in on the detail of the wood. You have a different technique. It's good."

"Yeah?"

They sketched quietly without conversation. Becky blurted out minutes later, "So why'd you do it?"

"Do what?"

"You know, why'd you try to kill yourself?"

Jackie stopped drawing and looked down at her paper. Her long hair hung on both sides of her face. She lifted her head and swung her hair over her left shoulder, looked at Becky, and said, "I really don't know. I was pissed at the world, pissed at myself. My boyfriend, Kevin, cheated on me, so I left. My parents *sucked*. So, I got real drunk and went on a tear. I went to that bar and…" She stopped, feeling embarrassed.

Becky stopped sketching. "Go on, I'm listening."

"I hitched down to this area. Some creep gave me a ride. We went to that bar down at the wharf and I, uh, it's embarrassing, but I let him have sex with me. Or I was too drunk to care. I'm not sure which. I guess I wanted to get back at Kevin, so I did it with the first guy who came along." Jackie laughed. "Like Kevin even knew, or cared!" She sighed loudly, "What a jerk I was. I was so disgusted with myself. I got myself a bottle of wine and left, and eventually ended up where your mother found me."

She had Becky's undivided attention. "Where'd you get the pills?"

"I had them from when I was living with Kevin and I had trouble falling asleep. Living with him was stressful. So, when I went down to the beach to 'end it all,'" Jackie said, as she used both hands to gesture the air quote marks, "I was newly homeless and decided I was nothing but a slut and a loser. I didn't *have* no family to turn to," she said angrily. "I hit a dead end."

Becky held her pencils in her closed fist. "Wow. You don't seem like some kind of loser to me. I can't imagine what it must be like to think you can't go on anymore."

"I still have my doubts. I mean, what's life all about? But, thanks to your mother, I feel like I have a second chance at something. Not sure what though." Jackie said. "Do you get along okay with your parents?"

"Pretty much," Becky said. "I'm pretty close to my mother. But she's trying, I think, to find out if Chris and I are having sex. We are, but I haven't told her. I would feel funny telling her that. Maybe I will eventually. She asks stuff like, 'How serious is this relationship with Chris?' and 'Have you reached a new level?' Stuff like that."

"She cares, it sounds like."

"I know." Becky went back to her drawing again.

"How about you and your dad?" Jackie asked.

"We get along okay. He's sort of distant. He stays out of the way more than anything. I don't tell him any of my personal shit, no way! Good thing for him he had a son. I think he likes Jason better. He's the one he does stuff with. They surf together and ski, basketball, stuff like that. I'm not into sports so, I don't know, we just sort of pass in the hallway."

"Fathers suck!" Jackie proclaimed.

Becky laughed. "I wouldn't say he sucks, but I guess I wished things were different."

"I don't think he likes me," Jackie stated.

"You don't?" Becky said.

"No. I get a vibe from him like I'm in his way, or I shouldn't be there or something."

"I wouldn't take it personally. He just isn't Mr. Friendly, that's all."

"Maybe. You're lucky to have your parents together. This country is fucked up. Most homes are broken. If it's not cheatin' it's drugs and booze tearing it apart."

"I know. I have a few friends from divorced parents. Where are your parents now?" Becky asked.

"I don't know. I don't think I care neither," Jackie said as she reloaded her mind with some bad memories. "My mother left me and my sister when I was twelve and Jesse was fifteen. My father was a drunk and he beat my mother when he felt like it. He knocked us around sometimes too, just for kicks. I guess that's why my mother left. One too many smacks upside her head. That, and the musician guy she was seeing - she ran off with him."

Becky turned right around and looked at Jackie. "Really? Wow. That's cold. So your mother never came back for you and your sister after that?"

"Nope. I think she figured that coming back to her kids meant coming back to our father. I can't even try to figure her out."

"My mother would never do that."

"Never say never. I never thought my mother would leave, and I never thought she'd stay away for good." Jackie's voice cracked with emotion. "But she did. Anyway, can't go back. It can't change nothin'." Jackie's tone was angry. She picked up her pencils again and continued her drawing. "Thanks to my mother I ended up in a foster home. It was after my sister left for good. She was seventeen and I was my father's only punching bag by then. So I got placed with a foster family. I ran away from them, and when they finally found me living in an abandoned building, I was put into a group home for girls until I turned eighteen." Jackie looked down at her paper but didn't draw. She held her pencils still and then lifted her head up into the wind again to refresh her thoughts.

"That sucks. No wonder you thought your life was over." Becky said. Jackie's head nodded and she looked over at Becky and smiled at her new friend.

"It was kind of like 'what came first, the chicken or the egg?' My father would drink, so my mother went out catting around. I think this made him drink more which made her go out more, and so on, and so on."

"I hope my parents never get that bad. They can have humdinger fights sometimes, and it's usually fueled by my father drinking too much. He can be a jerk sometimes, but it's never come to blows, you know, never physical," Becky explained.

Becky looked at Jackie and said, "Let's go down there and do a new sketch, ok?" She pointed to a new location.

They gathered their stuff and walked over to the pier. They sat down on the pier, cross-legged. Jackie sketched some seagulls. Becky sketched a boat with a store behind it.

"Maybe I can fix you up with a guy," Becky suggested.

"Please! I'm off guys for a while."

"Well, say the word. Chris has a few nice friends. Ya can't stay off them for good."

"I can try," Jackie said. They both looked at each other and laughed.

"I think I'll use this one for a painting," Becky said. "I'm gonna have to teach you to paint."

"I'd love to try that," Jackie said.

The sun changed the shadows and the wind was murder on their hair. They packed up the car with all their supplies and headed back to the inn.

BECKY ENTERED THE CODE on the touchpad near the stairwell, the door buzzed and she motioned to Jackie to come upstairs with her. It was the first time Jackie had been upstairs in the Frazer's home.

"Nice place," Jackie said. "So, this is your home?"

"That's right," Becky said. "It's totally separate from the inn. My mother sort of designed it, and when it got renovated, they made it so no guests can accidentally wander into our home. Clever, huh?"

"I'll say. You mean I can't get to the rooms from up here?" Jackie asked as she looked down the hallway.

"Well, there is another door. You can see it down there." Becky pointed to the end of the hallway. "It's just there as a fire escape door. We don't use it. Guests can't open it." Becky showed her around. "This is Jason's room. This is the TV room. And right here is my mother's office." Becky led the way back down the hall "See? Living room here."

"Nice. It's so… I don't know, rich?"

"My mom decorated everything. Here's their bedroom," Becky pointed as they walked back down the hallway again. "The kitchen. And alas, my room." Jackie followed her into her room. Becky put on some music. "Let's get something to drink."

Becky and Jackie went to the kitchen and poured themselves some juice. They heard the sound of the stairwell door open and then shut with a distinctive click. Bruce entered the kitchen, stopping abruptly when he saw Jackie. The girls looked at Bruce.

"Hi Dad."

"Hi honey."

"Hi Mr. Frazer."

"Jackie."

Jackie and Bruce stared at each other for a few seconds. He observed her long, straight hair that covered half her face like an open curtain. Becky poured juice. Jackie leaned against the counter and looked down at the floor. She slowly turned around and faced the counter and watched Becky pour.

As Bruce continued to look at Jackie from the back he spoke to Becky. "Where's your mother?"

"I don't know. We just got here."

The girls walked past him carrying their glasses. Becky smiled and shrugged as she passed him. Bruce watched them walk away. Right before they went back into Becky's room Jackie turned around to see Bruce watching her. She turned quickly and followed Becky into her room. Becky closed her door.

"See what I mean?" Jackie asked Becky in a whisper.

"See what you mean about what?" Becky had no idea.

"Your father. He hates me."

"He doesn't hate you."

"Maybe I better go downstairs to my room."

"Don't worry about it. Stay!"

They stayed and chatted until Chris called to say he'd be out front in fifteen minutes. Becky left and Jackie went downstairs to her new apartment.

CHAPTER 8

In an attempt to ward off bad luck Leena decided to agree with everything anyone said three days prior to her weekend with Wendy. Bruce couldn't drink too much; Jason couldn't get to her when he called Becky stupid three times in one day. If Becky wanted to spend as much time as humanly possible with her boyfriend, Chris, it was a damn good idea to Leena. She didn't want to tempt fate by creating any conflict, any reason to stay behind, right before departing for adventures unknown.

Then she feared she was being too obvious. She was going off to see Michael Everly perform with his band. At the last minute, before walking out the door, Leena stirred it up by reminding Bruce about the back light that didn't work. He hated it when she reminded him of a chore. Her "nagging," as he called it, usually resulted in, at the very least, a look of disgust and annoyance on Bruce's part. Sure enough, he gave Leena a look when she said, "It's not just a bulb that's out, it's something else." She heard him mutter as he walked away, "I know."

Leena put her overnight bag into her car, and put a handful of CDs, most custom burned, on the front seat. She started the engine and looked up. Jackie was standing there waving goodbye to Leena before she pulled out. Through the windshield, and through a light mist, she looked at Jackie standing there in her black jeans and a gray t-shirt. Her hair hung down like a sheet, partially obscuring her pretty face. She looked as gloomy as the weather. *Is she going to miss me?* Leena thought.

She put the window down and poked her head out. "You're all set with everything, Jackie?" Leena asked, not really knowing what to say. She had already gone over specific instructions with Jackie, Becky, and Michelle that morning.

"Oh, sure Leena. No problem. Have fun."

"Well, thanks for seeing me off. At least someone cares."

Jackie shrugged and smiled. She brought her arms up from where they were crossed over her stomach to her ears, simultaneously placing her hair behind them with all of her fingers in a quick rotation of her wrists. Her arms went back to her stomach. "See ya." One hand quickly rose to wave goodbye.

"I'll see ya," Leena backed out. She was off to Connecticut.

BEFORE SHE EVEN REACHED the highway, she was singing along

to some of her favorite songs. Most every song reminded her of Michael. Music, such a big part of their lives, cemented the memories of the past.

An old Cat Stevens song came on. Tears pricked her eyes as a flood of emotion washed over her. It was nothing short of time travel.

Leena sat on the edge of Michael's bed while he showed her his impressive album collection, all organized alphabetically, stored in egg crates stacked three high. Leena pointed to a Cat Stevens album. Michael pulled it out and put it on the turntable. He took his guitar out of the case and played along with the record. Leena was impressed. He was dead on. Every note and every word penetrated her soul. He captured her heart forever on that day, but not just with a song.

His parents were at work. They had hours to let love follow the path of least resistance. They had already had their first kiss months earlier at the dance in the gym. They had already fogged up the windows of his Chevy Nova on a few occasions.

This day was different. Leena thought she'd be nervous when, with just a look, they decided to make love for the first time. How did her eyes say "yes"? Inevitably they were lying horizontally. Inexperience was just a faint whisper in her ear: a voice which did not tell her to hold back, but to go with it.

Michael's breathing was audibly louder and his expression told of his anticipation. Somehow Leena knew he'd be gentle and knew he'd go slowly. He embraced her as he had before, only closer, without a barrier of clothing.

Leena's best memories of her days with Michael flooded back as she realized she'd be seeing Michael again. The ride to Wendy's house went by in a flash.

"The eagle has landed," Leena said as she got out of her car and greeted her friend by giving her a big hug.

The mist and the threat of rain were gone. The air was fresh and the leaves were a young and nubile green. Leena was feeling reborn. Wendy saw a change in her friend.

"You look great," Wendy started out. "Something looks different."

Leena had a childish grin on her face that she couldn't seem to hide. "Thanks. This is a new outfit." She looked down at herself.

"That's not what I meant."

Leena feigned puzzlement as if to say, *Whatever do you mean?*

"Come on inside," Wendy said as she turned toward the front door. Leena followed her inside.

Wendy got right to the point. "What's our game plan for this festival?"

"It's an all-day thing. We could go whenever you want. I guess it's one of those things that has a little of everything, I imagine: Arts and crafts, food vendors, sidewalk sales, et cetera."

"And Michael's band, lest you forgot?"

"Yes, Michael's band. I didn't forget. They go on at eight."

"I think there's more to this than just curiosity," Wendy said.

"There's nothing more, Wen. Am I excited about seeing him again? Yes. I can't really think beyond that." Leena suddenly got choked up.

"What's wrong?"

"I just can't believe that I'm going to see him."

"Come on, let's sit out back. Iced tea?"

"Sure."

They took their tea and went outside. "Your garden, Wen, is so awesome." Leena said. "I mean someone should feature this in a magazine."

"Right."

They walked along a tiny path lined with flowers with a similar color scheme: pink. Taller perennials stood behind them. A babbling stream, powered by an electric pump, ran through the garden at an angle.

"Seriously?" Leena said. "You should have your wedding here. It's so lovely."

"I thought about that, as you know, but my house, with its one bathroom, is the size of a shoebox. It just didn't make sense. Your inn makes a lot more sense."

"I wish we could clone this garden into my yard," Leena said.

"Your grounds are beautiful."

"It doesn't compare." They walked slowly along the path.

"I appreciate the compliment." Wendy did some show and tell as Leena pointed and asked questions. They came around again and took a seat on the back deck under an umbrella. The sun was now out, full force.

"So when do you want to leave?" Wendy asked.

"Oh," Leena sounded startled. "What time is it?"

"It's going on two."

"Three, I guess? What do you think?"

"Three is fine."

"I feel nervous," Leena admitted.

"That's understandable. We'll make this all about having *fun*! If you decide to go up and talk to him that's fine, if not, that's fine too." Wendy said to try to alleviate her anxiety.

Leena tried to imagine what would unfold if she walked up to him. "It's been so many years I don't think he'd recognize me!"

Wendy made a frown. "What, you grew a hump and a third eye?"

Leena laughed.

"So do you have any feeling one way or the other whether you'll talk to him or not?" Wendy asked.

"I don't think I will. As of right now, I am only going to go out of curiosity to see his band and to see what he looks like, *that's all*. I don't need the pressure of meeting him and all the small talk and all that." Leena paused and tried to reorganize her thoughts. "We'll make this about having fun like you said. We'll shop and stroll."

"And see your old flame. Very normal day out," Wendy said.

AFTER SPENDING A FRUSTRATING ten minutes looking for a place to park, they snagged a newly vacated spot next to the curb, right in the center of town.

Leena kept looking at her watch telling Wendy just how much more time it would be until Michael's band performed. Wendy had the patience of a saint. She smiled and acted as if she had no idea that only five minutes had passed since Leena's last report.

"I'm being unbearably silly, aren't I?" Leena asked not really wanting the truth.

"Well, sort of, but I can't say I blame you. Hey, this is your day! You hungry?"

"I'm a little too nervous to be hungry. You want to get something?"

Sure, why don't we get a bite to eat at that place right down there," Wendy pointed. "Otherwise we'll be starving later."

They walked down the sidewalk without talking and just observed all the people. As they walked, they had to give a wide berth to parents with strollers and the elderly. They observed young people congregating, wearing clothes that should have covered more bellies, and pants that should have covered more underwear. An elderly couple sat on a bench eating ice cream together outside the ice cream shop. Leena imagined that perhaps this was a couple who were high school sweethearts and they spent their entire life together, and would stick it out right to the end, through thick and thin.

As they approached the restaurant they had to stop quickly when a dog ran right across their feet almost knocking them down. Wendy screamed and dropped her purse. They looked at each other and laughed. Wendy bent over retrieving items that spilled from her purse. Leena, who was standing next to a telephone pole, saw a Day-Glo green poster advertising the festival's entertainment for the evening. There were two pictures with two band's names: *Many Miles Away* and *Jill and the Beanstalk*.

Wendy stood up, still putting items back into her purse. She looked at Leena who stood unusually still: sort of in a trance. Wendy turned her head to see what had caught her attention. It was a picture of Michael and his band mates. "My word," Wendy exclaimed. "That's him right there isn't it?" She pointed to the guy in the middle. "I recognize him."

"Yes." Leena looked pale. "Oh my God, Wen, this is really going to happen isn't it?"

"Yes, it is," Wendy said. "And I think you're going to get up the nerve to talk to him after it's over."

"No absolutely not!" She said, still insisting, as she shook her head, keeping her eyes fixed on the poster. Leena looked at Wendy quickly and then yanked the poster off the pole, folded it and stuffed it into her purse.

Wendy's eyes widened. "Leena!"

"There's more on other poles. Look." Leena waved her hand and Wendy looked down the street. The posters were easy to see. They dotted the street, every other pole.

They went to the restaurant and got seated. They tried to read the menu but they kept talking. They had to tell the waitress to come back twice. Leena looked around the restaurant like it was a museum, while Wendy tinkered with a knickknack she bought for her mother from a vendor.

Leena removed the folded poster from her purse, flattened it out and put it on the table. She stared at the picture of the band. He was more recognizable than the picture on their website. The four members of the band stood together with their arms on each other's shoulders. Two were smiling and two were not. Michael's smile was unforgettable. Wendy watched Leena.

"Can I see that again?" Wendy asked.

Leena slid the paper toward Wendy. Wendy turned it around and picked it up. "Wow, that's him alright. He doesn't look that much different. His hair's shorter."

"A lot shorter," Leena said.

The waitress returned. Leena took the poster out of Wendy's hands and put it back into her purse. The waitress took their order and left.

From across the restaurant Leena spotted a guy with a familiar face. She stared intently and said, "Wendy, don't look now, but that guy looks like Kenny Peterson! No, don't look I said," as Wendy looked anyway.

"For crying out loud, you're right! At least I think you're right. He looks so, ah," she trailed off and Leena finished the thought for her.

"Bald and fat?"

"Well, yeah I suppose." They both giggled.

"He really let himself go, didn't he?" Leena observed. "Oh shit, do you think that I would dismiss Michael if he has 'let himself go'?"

"I don't think so. I think you would love him even if he had an arrow going straight through his head." They laughed loudly. A few customers turned toward them, including Kenny.

Leena became straight-faced when she saw Kenny looking at them. She put her head down. She positioned her elbow on the table and put her hand up to her forehead, obscuring her face. "I don't want him to see me, he's Michael's old friend, remember?" Wendy was snickering. "What's so funny?" Leena asked.

"Don't look now," Wendy, laughing, could hardly get the same words out Leena had just spoken minutes before, "but Kenny is working on his physique." Leena looked anyway and noticed Kenny shoveling French fries into his mouth. She burst out laughing, making a snorting sound. She picked up a wine list menu and covered her face, pretending to read it.

"We should talk to him," Wendy said.

"Are you *nuts*?" Leena scolded. "He might tell Michael I'm here. Or he'll figure out why I'm here. How embarrassing!"

"You're over thinking it. It might be fun to talk to him. He can give us the skinny on what Michael's up to. Maybe he's here to see his band too."

"Maybe. I don't want to talk to him."

"Fine."

They finished their lunch and went back out to the sidewalks among the street merchants. One booth had glass-blown earrings. Another sold note paper with sketches of the sea. There was no shortage of paintings and photographs. The artists sat under light canopies reading a book or sipping a beverage waiting to make a sale.

They stopped to watch a horse-drawn carriage moving down the street in no hurry, filled with hay and people. The clip-clop of the hooves echoed down the tiny alleyways between the stores.

Further down, up on a grassy area, there was a clown twisting and tying squeaky balloons into animals for fascinated on-lookers. The clown's partner was juggling pins and telling jokes at the same time.

Nearby, two women who had flowers and birds painted on their cheeks, painted flowers and birds and other things onto the cheeks of squinting children.

The smell of fried dough, hamburgers, hot dogs and sausage and peppers filled the air, quite possibly tempting even a vegetarian. Cotton candy and taffy were still popular items. The only healthy thing for miles around was fresh-squeezed orange juice and lemonade.

After several purchases of unnecessary things Leena and Wendy sat down on the grass to listen to a guitar and mandolin duo sing unfamiliar songs. It was a welcome relief to their tired feet. They took the opportunity to organize their purchases into one easy-to-carry bag. Leena had found a small print of children playing on a beach. She knew just the spot at the inn to hang it. She found yet another cookbook to add to her already large collection. Leena leafed through the cookbook quietly.

"You're not thinking of trying to do it all yourself again, are you?" Wendy asked. "You still leave that to Hal?"

"Hal's great. But no, I wouldn't take that on again." Leena said lifting her head out of the book and looking at Wendy. "Been there, done that, as they say. Besides it was like Mutiny on the Bounty for a week. Remember?"

"I certainly do. You called me in tears more than a few times. You were in over your head."

"I was madder than a wet hen at everyone. Looking back, I don't blame them. I was impossible to live with. Like it was their duty to be my slave for that inn? But things happen for a reason, I always say, and that chaos forced me to hire some help. It worked out for the best. Like I said, Hal is wonderful!" Leena concluded. She went back to the cookbook. "I'm always looking for a new recipe, but mainly for the family. Actually, I still do most of the baking for the guests."

"You're very good at that."

"I've been teaching Jackie how to bake. She seems to like it a lot. She's my new apprentice. And Michelle has been great. I can give her a lot of responsibility. I wouldn't have been able to come here today if I hadn't delegated the work to them all."

"Does Jackie clean too?"

"She cleans the rooms and waitresses. She's been pretty agreeable, I must say."

"She strikes me as a little odd if you don't mind me saying it."

"Odd? In what way? You're sounding like Bruce now."

"I don't know, really. She talks to you without eye contact and stares at the floor. She sort of mumbles," Wendy said. "Not odd. I shouldn't have said that. She doesn't seem comfortable with socializing, that's all."

"She's young. Her self-esteem is undoubtedly low. She'll come around."

"You did a nice thing taking her in."

"I like the girl. What can I say?" Leena concluded.

IT WAS GETTING LATE. They decided to go back to the car and put their stuff away and get out their sweaters and folding chairs.

When they got to the green, they saw a large white van that hadn't been there before, parked near the curb. It said "Jenkins Appliances" on the side. There were six or seven guys milling around a make-shift stage. Amplifiers came out of the appliance truck along with guitar cases and a drum kit.

"Wendy, look! That *must* be them!" Leena almost jumped and twirled around. "Jenkins, that's one of the band mates."

"What do you want to do? Stay here and set up our chairs, or go over and ..."

"Don't even *say* it," Leena insisted.

"Alright, I'll follow your lead."

A fairly large crowd had gathered on the green and Leena was thankful for the camouflage of people. She got very quiet and hardly spoke. Wendy tried to chat about things but she was faced with yes and no answers or "huh?"

Leena's eyes were fixed on the stage and surrounding area. "There he is, Wen!" Leena spotted him. Perhaps if he had been clean-shaven with a neat haircut, she would not have recognized him so quickly. Leena started to cry. She dug inside her purse for a tissue.

"Hey, you okay?" Wendy asked.

Leena dabbed her eyes and blew her nose. She tried to speak, but couldn't. She dabbed her eyes again. She finally broke her gaze and looked directly at Wendy. With a sigh, she said, "I simply can't believe that my eyes are finally seeing Michael." Her chin quivered and more tears flowed. She mopped them up again.

Wendy leaned over and gave her a hug. Leena put her head down on Wendy's shoulder, sniffing. Wendy didn't need to say anything. She let Leena have her moment.

Leena composed herself and sat like a statue as *Many Miles Away* took the stage and prepared to play. It was ten after eight. After a few sound check problems got worked out, Michael took the microphone and addressed the crowd. "We're *Many Miles Away* and we just want to thank you all for coming tonight. We're gonna start off with a *Beatle* song. You all know it. This is *Day Tripper*." He planted his fingers on the fret board and played. The familiar bass-driven riff was instantly recognizable. The crowd cheered and clapped.

They played straight through for thirty minutes before he spoke again. They were surprisingly good. They did a wide variety of classic rock tunes besides The Beatles: Stones, Beach Boys, Eagles, Steely Dan, U2, Police and Nirvana. She thought of Becky when they played a Dave Matthews Band song, Becky's favorite band.

"We're gonna take a very short break and we'll be back. Stick around," Michael said as he and the others left the stage and walked behind it.

"Let's get up and stretch," Wendy suggested.

"Hmm? Ok." As they walked among the crowd Leena watched as Michael and his band mates went behind the van. She saw smoke rising up from where they were. She hoped it wasn't from Michael.

"Well?"

"Well, what?" Leena asked.

"So you're not going to go say hi?"

"I told you. No! This is fine. I'm enjoying him from a distance."

The girls went back to their chairs and sat down. The band came back and Michael spoke to the crowd again. "I'd like to introduce the band." With one hand at his side the other arm outstretched he presented the boys: "On bass guitar is Dave Jenkins, on drums Carl Zawkowski, and on keyboard Pete Spangella, and me, I'm Michael Everly."

The crowd gave them an enthusiastic round of applause. After they finished the first song of the second set a man up near the front yelled out "*Sympathy for the Devil*, man."

Michael laughed, pointed and made a face. "We don't do that one. You all know what happened when the Stones did it?" Michael laughed again. "I don't want a riot. How 'bout this one instead?" They broke into *Gimme Shelter*. The crowd was jazzed.

The applause was followed by a momentary silence. Impulsively, Leena stood and yelled out, "How about *Brown-eyed Girl* for a brown-eyed girl?" Some people in the crowd turned toward her. Wendy not only looked up at her incredulously, but her eyes almost popped out of her head. Her jaw was hanging.

Michael looked in the general direction of the request. "I think we can do that one, right Pete? That's a …" He looked right at Leena. She was a fair distance from the stage and it was dark, but there seemed to be a question in his mind about the voice and the figure standing up in the crowd. He forced himself to finish his sentence and fumbled to remember what he was saying. "So, um, that's a crowd-pleaser." Leena sat down. Michael looked over at Dave, on bass. They nodded at each other and started to play.

"This was our song, Wen. Remember?" Leena said watching Michael in a trance.

Wendy was still astonished but managed to say, "Yes, I remember." Wendy looked at Leena and then at Michael, and back at Leena with her mouth partially open.

Leena dabbed her eyes with a tissue through the entire song. There was something a little different about Michael at that point. He looked over in Leena's direction many times.

"What made you do that?" Wendy asked.

"I don't know. I just did it. It was sort of out-of-body. Freaky huh?"

"I think he recognized you, don't you? Look! He keeps looking over here."

"No!" Leena denied it. "I doubt it."

Michael looked in their direction off and on through the rest of their set. Around 9:15 they were done. They came out for an encore doing *Twist and Shout*. The crowd stood up and cheered and everyone was dancing and clapping.

"Thanks a lot for coming out tonight. See you next time. If you want any more information about us come talk to us after the show or visit our website at www dot many miles away dot com. Good night." Michael turned to leave the stage. He looked their way one more time.

Wendy looked at Leena and said, "He *so* saw you, Leena! I'm sure of it."

Leena was silent. She felt the same way but ignored it.

The other band started setting up their equipment just as soon as Michael's band cleared their equipment off the stage. Some people in the crowd left while others were just arriving. Some stayed. Leena and Wendy stood up.

"I do want to get up the nerve to go over there. I suppose I will never forgive myself if I leave and go home and I don't say hi to him."

"It's true. I think it's something you should do," Wendy advised.

"My feet feel like cement, Wen. Oh God, what should I do?"

"I'll go with you. That'll make it easier."

But before Leena moved, the decision was taken out of her hands when a figure appeared, standing right next to her in a shadow. Leena sensed something in the corner of her eye and turned. It was Michael. There they were face to face: the first time in twenty-two years. They stared at each other, transfixed. Wendy was speechless. Her jaw dropped again. As she observed them, she backed away about ten feet, giving them space.

"Leena?" Michael asked as they engaged in a trance-like stare.

"Yes, Michael it's me."

"So that *was* you," Michael stated.

"Yeah," was all Leena could manage.

"It's been… how long has it been? I can't believe this."

"Twenty-two years."

"Well, how the hell are you? Wow, what a cool surprise!"

"I'm good. How you doing?"

He didn't answer her question but asked his own. "Are you just here, or," he fumbled to say it right. "Did you know I was here?"

"I found your band on the Internet, so I thought I would have a look-see. I was just curious, that's all. Wendy here…" She looked for her friend and noticed she had been left to fend for herself. She saw her in the distance. "We came together." Leena didn't know what she was saying.

"Wow, this is awesome. I'm glad you found me. You look great!"

"No, you look great. It's great to see you. Your hair's not quite as long," Leena said.

"Neither is yours." They laughed.

"And you still have the beard." Leena blushed. She quickly remembered how it scratched her cheeks. She examined his face. Time had been good to him. He wore his forty years well. His hairline receded slightly but he was far from bald. She saw the scar near the corner of his left eye and instantly remembered the story behind it: A schoolyard fight with a notorious bully at the age of twelve.

There was an awkward pause, then Leena remembered to say, "Your band is *great*, Michael!"

"Thanks. We all enjoy it. I've been playing since way back when. Formed the band a few years outta high school actually. You remember Dave, don't you?"

"Yes I do!"

"The other guys, I've known them for years and years." He paused and then repeated himself. "You look great."

Leena motioned to Wendy to come over. "Oh Michael, this is my old friend Wendy Lassiter. You'd remember her as Wendy Pulford."

Wendy stepped forward from the background. "Hi Michael, it's good to see you again. You guys were awesome." Wendy said.

"Wendy. Well, I'll be. Sure I remember you. How are you?" Michael said, but didn't wait for Wendy's response. "This is a great surprise seeing the two of you. What a blast from the past!"

"Do you play often?" Wendy asked.

Michael had shifted his gaze back toward Leena and answered, "We do this pretty much every weekend during the summer. A little less often the rest of the year." Michael changed gears as if he had just come to. "Listen, I've got some packing up to do. Can you stick around?"

"Sure," Leena said.

"Okay then. I'll meet you on the curb over there," Michael pointed to the street. "We'll get a drink. He started to walk away. He was still looking at Leena as he walked.

"Sure," Leena said again.

He turned toward the stage and broke into a light jog. Leena watched as he helped his friends load the rest of the equipment into the van.

Wendy waved her hand in front of her face. "Earth to Leena, hello."

"What just happened? Pinch me."

"I'd say you just had a close encounter of some kind. I was feeling sparks."

"He asked me to stick around. He has to pack up." Leena told Wendy as if she had not been listening. Then Leena quickly turned her head to her old friend and said, "What the hell am I doing? This is crazy! I'm acting like a schoolgirl. I'm married with children for crying out loud!"

"You haven't done anything wrong. Relax."

An interruption of feedback from the microphone made the two women turn and pay attention to the stage. The next band had just come out and were fiddling with the equipment, not unlike what Michael had done before starting. The lead singer, a young woman, came on stage and started tapping the microphone, attempting to talk. After much torturing of ears, she managed to get out her announcement. "Hello Connecticut. We're *Jill and the Beanstalk* and we're here to rock you! I'm Jill. One, two, three, four…" And they were off and running. They were punk rock. Even from a distance they could see multiple piercings, gobs of make-up and black sneakers. Their clothing was black too. Leena imagined Jackie would have loved this band, but it was starting to wear thin for Leena and Wendy. The lead guitarist was as skinny as a beanpole. Suddenly the band's name made sense.

Leena and Wendy walked over to the curb where Michael had pointed. After another ten minutes, Michael finally walked toward them. "Come on," Michael motioned with his hand. They followed Michael. Leena watched Michael from behind. She had it in her mind that she wanted to remember every move he made and everything he said. She didn't want this meeting to become a blur. *It has to last for the rest of my life,* she thought.

"You guys were awesome," Wendy said again as they arrived in front of a pub.

"Thanks." Michael pushed the door open and held it for them. Michael's head moved as he watched Leena enter the establishment. She felt his eyes on her.

They found their way to a booth. Michael and Wendy ordered a beer and Leena ordered a glass of wine. They talked about old times and people they knew: who was dead and who was still around.

"You know who we saw today?" Leena said. She looked at Wendy. They both smiled. "Kenny Peterson. At least I think it was Kenny. He looked kinda… different."

"Oh, Kenny, he's around. I ran into him a few months ago. He's kinda weird now. Well, he was weird in high school too. I think he sells insurance now."

"Is that right?" Wendy said.

As the conversation flowed Michael and Leena shot each other glances that lingered. Leena stared at him, but would then look down at the table. She didn't want to be caught staring. She wove her fingers tightly together in an effort to control any nervous ticks. Maybe she was hiding her wedding ring. At that moment, Leena observed a wedding band on Michael. Her stomach flip-flopped.

"Oh, remember the time you and me and, yes Wendy, you were there, and George went to that park, and we got so stoned, then we got lost?" Michael said, laughing as he recalled it, revealing his big smile which was still the same, only one back molar was now missing.

"Oh my God, yes! How funny was that?" Leena chuckled.

"Remember George threw his underwear up onto the statue of General Whatshisname and he was holding his underwear in his outstretched hand?" Michael said. They all laughed together. "George was streaking, running around the statue?"

"We all ended up running out of there when we heard a police siren," Wendy added. "The siren had nothing to do with us, but we were stoned and paranoid."

"George mooned the cop!" Leena added, laughing hard. "Remember? Before he fell into the bushes trying to put his pants back on."

"Right!" Michael laughed. "I've never laughed so hard."

"Those were the days," Leena said, still laughing.

The laughter died down and there was a long pause.

"So is the band what you do for a living?" Wendy asked.

"Not exactly," Michael was still laughing. "I haven't quit my day job. I own an antique store over in North Stonington called *Ever More Antiques*. It's a pretty good living. It's not a desk job. I meet with other dealers from time to time. The band and I, we make a few bucks with the gigs too."

"Antiques?" Leena sounded surprised. "I never figured you'd be an antique dealer."

"You never know what life has in store, I guess," he said.

"Are you married?" Wendy asked. Leena's head snapped in her direction. She was shocked at the question. Wendy knew Leena would chicken out, avoiding the tougher questions, and she would regret not knowing in the long run.

"Ah, I'm married." Michael sounded reluctant. "Got married about eight years ago. We live in Voluntown, next town over from North Stonington."

"Kids?" Wendy asked.

"I've got a son, Tommy, he's six. He's going into first grade this fall." Michael said. "So spill. What are you both up to? Married, divorced, kids?" He took turns looking at them.

Leena and Wendy looked at each other as if to say, "Who should go first?" Wendy took the lead. "All of the above. I'm divorced, but I'm engaged. The wedding is coming up this September. I also have a son, Andrew, and he's twelve. And I'm a fourth-grade teacher in Groton. I live in Gales Ferry."

"No kidding! My wife is a teacher too. She teaches second grade in Voluntown." Michael looked at Leena and asked, "Don't tell me you're a teacher too?"

"No, far from it," Leena answered.

Michael looked back at Wendy. "What a small world." He was shaking his head. He turned toward Leena and asked, "So what's your story, Leen?"

Leena got a twinge in her stomach when she heard him call her "Leen." He used to call her that often, especially when he was pleading with her for one reason or another.

"I live in Rhode Island now. Moved there about eight years ago from Waterford, Connecticut, and opened up a bed and breakfast." Leena explained. She avoided mentioning her husband.

"No kidding?" Michael jumped in. "That is so cool. By yourself?"

"No, we, my husband and I, live there. We've got two kids, Jason who just turned fifteen and Becky who'll be eighteen real soon."

"Wow. Eighteen! So you both run the bed and breakfast?" Michael asked.

"I run it mostly. Bruce is a lawyer up in Westerly. We live down in Weekapaug. That's where the inn is, which is part of Westerly. We live there too, at the inn, I mean."

"It's gorgeous," Wendy added. "It's right on the water. It's called *Sunset Inn*. You should see it! Leena's done an exquisite job decorating it herself. It's wildly popular."

"Wendy!" Leena was embarrassed.

"It is!" Wendy reiterated.

"You married a lawyer?" Michael asked.

"Yes."

"I wouldn't picture you marrying a lawyer. So suit and tie."

"You never know what life has in store, like you said."

"So you found me on the internet?" Michael asked Leena directly.

"I was looking for a band to hire for my inn, as it turns out. I've hired live music before, like classical music quartets, or someone strumming a guitar doing James Taylor type stuff. I've sort of stayed away from louder type music. The inn is in a close-knit community. But someone specifically asked for a rock band, a band that played classic rock to be exact. I thought 'what the heck.' Gotta expand. So anyway, there you were. You can't imagine how shocked I was to see you."

"I bet. We just got that website going about a year or so ago. What a difference. We've increased our business quite a bit. But I love it. I like the store, but I just love that band. Can't imagine not playing."

"You should be proud of it," Wendy added. "It definitely shows that you've been at it for a long time. You're polished. Confident."

"Well thanks, Wendy. It keeps me out of trouble, you know?" Michael said, laughing at himself.

"I feel that way about the inn." Leena said. "I love that old place. It's a pain to run at times. I bite off more than I can chew, but it's all worth it. The first year we didn't see a profit, but now we've got a good reputation and it's a good business."

The three old friends talked and reminisced until eleven o'clock. Michael announced he had to leave. Leena felt a moment of panic with the thought of never seeing Michael again.

They left the pub and strolled down the sidewalk to Wendy's car. Leena felt like she was taking a chance but she felt she had to do it. "So, Michael, do you want to keep in touch? You know, like email? Do you have an email address?"

"That's a great idea. I was thinking that," Michael said, sounding a bit nervous for the first time that evening.

Leena started to dig through her purse looking for her business cards. Michael took out two business cards for the band from his wallet which had the website and his email address.

"Here, let me write down my personal email address for you. This one is the one that's on the website that we all can read. Well Carl reads them mostly. He's the 'webmaster.' Here's mine." Michael wrote the address on both cards and handed them to both women. Leena handed him her *Sunset Inn* business card and did the same by writing down her personal email address on the card.

"I don't have a card," Wendy said, laughing.

"That's okay," Leena blurted out. "I've got the info." She put Michael's card into her purse.

"*Jill and the Beanstalk* must be done," Leena said. "It's so quiet."

"Must be," Michael said.

"Clever name," Leena said nervously, stalling. Michael nodded.

They all stood by the side of Wendy's car. Leaving was the next thing to do. There was much hesitation.

"It was really great seeing you Michael. I had a great time," Wendy said.

"Oh thanks. It was great seeing you too." They shook hands.

Wendy walked around and got into the driver's side and waited. She gave them some time to themselves.

"Well," they both said at the same time. They both laughed nervously.

"You first," Michael said.

"Well," Leena repeated, and then she was at a loss for words.

"This was quite a surprise for me, Leen, Miss Kathleen!"

"Please, no one calls me that. My mother did when she was mad at me." Leena said.

"Geez, how *is* your mother?"

"She died last year."

"Oh no! I'm really sorry to hear that. I always liked your mom so much."

"Thanks. She always liked you too. How are your folks?"

"My mom's okay, my dad isn't doing all that well. He had a heart attack a while ago, but he's hanging in there. I mean, he's okay. He had to have bypass and everything. But he's good!"

"Oh dear," Leena mumbled.

"Yeah." Michael looked down at the curb.

There was another awkward moment. They both realized they were ending their conversation on a downer.

"So email me," Michael said, staring directly into Leena's eyes.

"Okay," Leena promised. Their eyes were locked. Neither moved to leave.

At that moment Michael leaned forward and took Leena's hands into his without breaking his stare. Leena felt a surge of nervousness and elation. She looked down at their joined hands. Michael pulled her toward him and they embraced. Leena heard a very faint moan come from Michael. Leena turned her head and kissed his cheek on top of his beard. They parted slightly and Michael kissed her cheek in return.

"Leen," he said. He tilted his head, still staring at her. Their hands were still together. "I'll see ya."

Wendy waited patiently. She looked over a few times, trying not to be obvious.

Leena's eyes filled with tears. "I'll see ya, Michael." She turned away and blinked. The tears ran down her cheeks. She got into the car and quickly wiped her cheeks, looking at Wendy as she did. She put the window down.

Michael placed the palms of both hands on the open car window as if to hold the car down. "Take care. Night Wendy." He looked at Leena again. "Night Leen."

Leena could just get out "Night," and with a signal to Wendy that it was alright to drive away, they left. Leena looked back and stared at Michael as the car drove away. They stared at each other until they couldn't any longer when the car turned at an intersection. Leena turned back around in silence. She fished a tissue out of her purse. Wendy left it alone.

CHAPTER 9

The sound of footsteps and jingling change could be heard in the hallway. Leena's attention was taken away from a TV show as she listened to Bruce mumbling to himself. She knew he had been drinking.

"Well, well ladies," Bruce said. He leaned heavily against the door jam. "Look who's living upstairs now."

Jackie turned her head away, trying to minimize her presence. Leena and Becky looked up at him. Leena shot him a disapproving look and said, "You're drunk, aren't you?"

"Me? No. I had only a few with Cam and Charlie." His slur was unmistakable.

"You liar!" Leena said. "Good thing you're a lawyer so if you kill someone in your car on the way home you can get yourself off!"

"Whoa, what crawled up your ass?" He looked over at Jackie. She had looked up at him. "What are you looking at?"

Jackie got up without answering him and said, "Good night Leena, night Becky, see you in the morning." She quickly walked around Bruce.

"Don't you even say good night to me?" Bruce asked.

"Good night Mr. Frazer." Jackie said from the hallway.

"Oh, I'm *Mr.* Frazer but *she's* Leena. I see."

"Jackie, you don't have to leave," Leena said, and then directed her comment to Bruce, "I said you're drunk. I don't like it. Go to bed Bruce!"

"That's okay." Jackie rushed down to the stairwell and went to her room.

Bruce turned back around and said, "I suppose she knows the code now? That's just great!"

Leena got up and walked to the kitchen bringing three mugs. Bruce followed her. "What was Jackie doing upstairs?"

"What did it look like she was doing, Bruce? We *were* watching a show together. Now, thanks to you, we're not."

"It's getting pretty chummy chummy around here lately."

"What do you care? If I want to invite her upstairs that's my prerogative."

"I live here too," Bruce argued.

"Hardly. You're always out, usually getting loaded. I wonder where you go sometimes." Leena was fuming.

"Where I am? I always tell you where I am. Whas your problem?" He slurred.

"I don't really care if you're out. I don't like the getting *drunk* part. You're an ass! Go to bed and sleep it off."

"I'll go to bed when I get damn good and ready. Maybe I want to watch TV too." Jason came out of his room to use the bathroom and saw his father. "Jason kiddo."

"Hi Dad," Jason said. He and Leena watched as Bruce walked to the bedroom and shut the door. Leena looked at Jason. Jason shrugged and went to the bathroom and closed the door.

Leena went back to the TV room to finish watching what was left of the show with Becky. Within minutes they heard snoring coming down the hall from the bedroom.

"I'm gonna tell him off tomorrow," Becky said.

"Just let it go," Leena said.

"I think it *sucks* the way he treats her!" Becky started to cry and stood up. "It's not fair!"

"Becky, wait, let's finish the show. Stay."

"That's okay. I lost interest." She went to her room.

Leena sat and stared straight ahead. She didn't pay attention to the television. The local news came on. She barely noticed. Leena was already feeling the let-down after her weekend with Wendy and her meeting with Michael, and even more let down with her marriage of late. This incident made it worse.

Leena got up and shut off the television and went to the office. She had wanted to write Michael a note but didn't know if she should. Her encounter with him had stirred up emotions that turned out to be more powerful than she had expected. She fought the urge to write to him up until this night.

Leena sat and thought for several minutes, trying to decide on just the right tone.

She Wrote, *Dear Michael, It was so lovely to see you the other night. It was such a treat to see you perform in your band. You are very good.*

Delete. *That was awful, you sound like you're writing to the Queen of England*, she thought.

Dear Michael, The longing for you all these years was too much and I am so glad that I finally got a chance to see you after so many years. I didn't like the way things ended for us...

Delete. *Horrendous. That was worse than the first one*, she thought. "How about something in between," she said out loud.

Dear Michael, Thanks for being so hospitable last weekend. I know it must have been a bit of a shock to have me just show up out of the blue like that. Wendy and I had a wonderful time and we enjoyed the show. It was fun chatting afterward. Feel free to write anytime. Regards, Leena.

She had to think long and hard whether to write "regards" or "love." She left "Regards." Sitting with her right hand on the mouse positioned to click "send" she couldn't quite get up the nerve and decided to sleep on it, leaving the note as a draft.

Leena got spare sheets and blankets out of the linen closet and made up the futon in the office. The thought of sleeping next to Bruce, or waking up next to him, was unpleasant.

LEENA FINISHED HER MORNING jog and returned to the inn. She showered, fed her guests and said goodbye to the kids before Becky drove to school with Jason. She climbed the stairwell up to her own kitchen. Bruce was sitting at the table quietly sipping his coffee, nursing his inevitable hangover.

Leena tossed the morning newspaper onto the table where it landed next to his elbow. Startled, he looked up at her. She stood facing him, staring at him.

He stared back and then finally said, "What?"

"You know very well 'what.'"

"No, I don't."

"So you were that drunk that you don't recall what you said or did?"

"I told you I wasn't drunk."

"Right," she said sarcastically. "You come home after drinking, or you come home and do your drinking. Either way, it's gotta stop!"

"I don't need a lecture from you!" Bruce stood up to leave.

"There's no excuse for the way you're treating Jackie."

"So, that's what this is about?"

"That and your drunken behavior! That's not enough?"

"Look, just because I don't approve of the hired help being in our home, doesn't make me a bad person. We got that expensive security system for a reason."

Leena looked down at the floor and realized he had a point. The reason the system was installed stemmed from an incident with one of Leena's first employees: a girl named Beth she hired and befriended. They went grocery shopping together and baked together, not unlike the relationship Leena has with Jackie. Sometimes Leena invited her upstairs for tea. Leena suspected that food was missing once or twice. Days later, she and Bruce realized that some cash that had been left on their dresser was missing. She had been seen by Hal coming down the stairs from their home when Leena wasn't around on the day in question. Bruce and Leena put two and two together. Beth denied it when Bruce confronted her. Leena didn't have the guts to fire her but Bruce did. He had their elaborate security system installed after that.

"I know we had one bad experience, but that doesn't mean Jackie…"

"I know, but why take the risk? She comes from nothing and now she's put into the lap of luxury. It's only a matter of time before she…"

"So paint everyone like her with the same brush. That's just like you. Can you give her the benefit of the doubt?"

He was quiet for a moment. "She isn't exactly of high caliber breeding. You have a tendency to hire any ol' stray alley cat that wanders in."

"Now you're being mean! And such a snob!"

"It's the truth. That Beth girl was a derelict. I think I have a say who enters my house, my home! You agree?"

"Yes." Leena paused and thought about it. "I didn't give Jackie the code, by the way. Neither did Becky. She came up with Becky. Tell you what, we won't give her the code. Fair enough? That's a compromise."

"Thank you. I gotta go." He stood up.

"You've conveniently skirted the original issue: your drinking."

Bruce glared at her. He refused to discuss it. "See ya later." He left.

Leena went to the computer as soon as she was alone. She opened up her email and there waiting for her was a note from Michael. She couldn't believe her eyes. *I should have sent my note. We must have written them at the same time. No, I'm glad I didn't send the note*, her thoughts were a swarm of bees. Taking a deep breath, she opened the note.

Hey Leena, It was a blast seeing you guys last week. You planning any more trips this way? Your visit seemed to erase 22 years, if just for a little while. Cool. Michael.

Leena decided to send the note she prepared, but replacing the *feel free to write* line with *It was like a trip back in time*. She changed *Regards* to *Way cool*, then clicked send. She also sent copies of both notes to Wendy. *That's a start*, she thought. "The start of what?"

A RAY OF LIGHT shone on the cloud of flour that hung in the air above Leena's work area as she rolled out dough for a pie. Jackie, Leena's new apprentice, stood next to her with her own dough. "See, this is about how thick it should be. Any thinner and it'll tear," Leena instructed. The ingredients were lined up on the counter: Canned cherries for Leena's pie; a bowl of cut up apples, sugar, flour, nutmeg and cinnamon for Jackie's.

"Why don't you make the pecan pie? I hate cherry," Becky said, sitting at the kitchen table, thumbing through a fashion magazine.

"I might, maybe later. These pies are for the guests, hon," Leena said. She placed her dough into the pie pan and Jackie followed suit.

Wanna go to the mall, Jackie?"

"Sure, when?"

"When you're done. I'm bored." Becky sat with her legs crossed, one leg swinging. She flipped through the magazine impatiently. She came to an ad for lipstick. "I like this color. What do you think?" She held up the magazine for them to see.

Leena nodded. Jackie said, "There's a new place at the mall we could try. They have cool lip glosses there."

"Yeah." Becky's cell phone rang. She looked at it and said, "It's Chris. Hello?" She trotted out to the front porch to take the call in private. Her voice trailed behind her.

"While you're at the mall why don't you and Becky go get yourself some tubes of paint, my treat."

Jackie looked at Leena and said, "Really? I couldn't..."

"I insist. I think you have a real knack for art, Jackie. I saw some of your sketches. Who knows, maybe someday I'll be able to say, 'I knew her when.'"

"Yeah right." Jackie laughed at the thought.

Jackie and Leena put their fruit into their pie pans and covered the apple pie with the top layer of dough. Leena showed her how to cut slits in the dough for it to vent. For her own pie she cut the dough in strips and made a crisscross pattern. Then she placed the pies in the oven. She pointed to the oven that she had preheated and pointed to the dial. "You set the oven at 350 degrees and they'll cook about an hour. You can tell they're done when the liquid starts to seep through the holes. Also, the crust will get golden brown when it's done." Leena and Jackie placed all the dirty dishes in the sink and wiped the counters down. "You can't go wrong with the apple pie. It's pretty popular. Using Macintosh apples is probably..."

The phone rang in mid-sentence.

"You want to get that, Jackie?" Leena asked. Jackie was standing right next to the phone. Leena's hands were in the water.

"Sure. Hello? okay." Jackie held the phone out toward Leena. "It's for you."

Leena whispered while making an inquisitive face, "Who is it?"

Jackie shrugged, indicating she had no idea.

Leena lipped, "Ask."

She put the phone back to her ear and asked "Who is this?" She put the phone on her hip and said, "He said he's calling about hiring his band for one of your things." Jackie put the receiver on the table.

Leena nodded and wiped her hands on a dish towel. "Oh good. Hello?"

"Leena? It's Michael. Can you talk?"

"Hi." Leena swung around and looked at Jackie, inadvertently getting her full attention. She proceeded to turn her back to Jackie, and then fixed her hair as if Michael could see her. Jackie noticed the change in her demeanor.

"Was that your daughter?" Michael asked.

"No, it's, ah," she paused and didn't want to talk about Jackie in front of her. She felt a wave of nervousness flow over her as if she had just been caught stealing.

"I thought they'd be in school. If this isn't a good time to talk, then I'll email you," He said.

"Um, no it's fine. Let me get that information for you. I wanted to talk to you about that. Just hold on a minute. I need to get my date book." She put Michael on hold and told Jackie, "I need to go upstairs."

Leena picked up the phone upstairs in her bedroom and closed the door. "Hi. I'm surprised to hear from you."

"I'm sorry. I thought the kids would still be in school."

"Jason is still in school. Becky got out early today. That was Jackie who answered the phone."

"Is she your daughter? I thought you said you had two kids."

"No, Becky is my daughter. Jackie is a girl who works for me and she lives here. It's a long story."

"Oh. It was nice seeing you the other night. I felt like we had just scratched the surface. I figure you went to the trouble to find me and came all that way to see me, so I thought I'd call you," Michael said. There was a long pause. "Okay, say something."

"I am happy you called. It just took me by surprise. I don't know what to say. I don't know what to think," Leena replied breathlessly.

"I was thinking about you and... Is it okay I called?"

"It's more than okay."

"So, I was thinking. I sometimes go out of town to meet with antique dealers and I, um," Michael stumbled.

"Oh, really? Where do you go?"

"Well, as a matter of fact I'll be down in Mystic tomorrow and," Michael paused hoping Leena would finish his idea, which she did accordingly.

"Maybe I could meet you there, after you finish with your business."

"I'll be done around ten o'clock, give or take. Let's see. Where could we meet?"

"How about meeting in the parking lot of the Mystic Aquarium? Everyone knows where that is." Leena said.

"That's a good idea. Okay, it's," Michael stopped himself from saying "it's a date," and said, "it's settled then. Ten o'clock tomorrow at the aquarium. See you then."

"Okay, see you then. Bye." Leena placed the phone down on the hook and sat there for a minute just staring. She got up to go back down to the kitchen, stopping in front of the mirror to look at her reflection to see if she could spot how she was feeling by the way she looked on the outside. With a pivot and a sigh, she headed back downstairs. Jackie was sitting at the table looking through the same magazine Becky had been looking at.

Leena said nervously, "I'm booking a band for that anniversary next month and I wanted to find out more about them."

"You gonna hire that one?" Jackie said.

"Oh that one? That one was busy on that particular date. I need to keep looking. I'll keep that one on my list, though."

Becky returned to the kitchen and announced she was going to the mall with Chris. "You coming Jackie?"

"Sure. Let me get my purse. Am I done here?"

"Oh sure. I'll watch the oven."

"Hey Mom, guess what? Chris was voted MVP from his basketball team. He's amazing." Becky's face lit up when she talked about him.

Leena smiled, "That's great, honey." Leena got her purse and took out some cash. "Here, this is some money for Jackie to buy some paint, okay? Help her pick out what she needs."

"Sure." She took the money.

"And for you too, of course."

"Thanks."

Chris knocked on the front door. Becky ran to open it. Leena quietly followed her and peered around the corner to see her greet him. She seemed transformed by his presence. They said a few things Leena couldn't quite hear, and then they headed for the kitchen holding hands. Leena quickly went back to the kitchen.

"Hi Christopher. How are you?" Leena was polite and friendly. "I hear you're MVP."

"Hey, Mrs. Frazer, it's cool. What an honor." He smiled widely. "I've got practice at five. I'll have her back before that."

"Can Jackie come with us? She has some stuff she wants to get too." Becky asked.

"Sure," Chris agreed.

Becky ran across to Jackie's room and knocked. After hearing a faint "come in" she disappeared into her room.

Leena and Chris endured a few awkward moments together alone in the kitchen waiting for Becky to come out with Jackie. She wanted to talk about something, just to break the ice. "Don't you also play baseball?" Leena asked as she continued her clean up.

"I do that too. I've got practice for that tomorrow."

"They sure do keep you busy. Practice makes perfect, as they say. I hear you've been accepted to Notre Dame. Talk about exciting."

"I'm stoked."

Becky and Jackie came back into the room. "We'll be back before five. See ya," Becky said to her mother.

"See ya," Jackie said.

"See ya," Leena copied.

"Good bye Mrs. Frazer," Chris said.

BEFORE DINNER, LEENA CALLED Wendy. "Pick up, pick up," she said impatiently. Finally, she answered. "Wendy?"

"Yeah, Hey Leena. How's it goin'? I read your email. Are you surprised he wrote?" Wendy asked.

"No, not now, I'm not. You'll never guess who called." Leena stated.

"Who? Michael?"

"Yes!" Leena squealed with delight in a half-whisper.

"*Really?*" Wendy yelled into the phone. "Oh, My, God," She said separating each word. "So tell me everything."

Leena proceeded to tell her how Jackie was there and had answered the phone. "I had to lie to her. She kind of looked at me funny. I felt so nervous. It really threw me. I went upstairs to talk to him."

"Kinda risky calling you at the inn, don't you think?"

"He figured the kids were in school. Becky was home early. Normally she would have been in school."

"So what did he want?"

"We're meeting tomorrow in Mystic at the aquarium at ten o'clock. He's meeting some person in the morning about some antiques first, though."

"Wow. What do you think is going to happen? I mean, this sounds like something is going on. Is that what you want?"

"I don't know! I really don't. I can only play this out one *minute* at a time. I have to admit that I do want something to happen and yet I don't. I mean, I didn't mean to complicate my life. It was going along just fine."

"You know you say that now. You and Bruce have not exactly been 'just fine.'"

"We have our ups and downs and I figure that's all normal. But I wonder if I would have gone to see Michael like that if my marriage were running on all cylinders."

"If you were in married bliss, if you ask me, you probably wouldn't have gone at all. Seeing him on that website would have been enough. I think something's been missing from your marriage for years. Remember, you tell me *everything*." Wendy laughed.

"Right, I know." Leena nodded, acknowledging the truth. "He came home drunk again the other night and humiliated poor Jackie. She and I and Becky were watching TV and he questioned why she was upstairs. I could have killed him."

"What did Jackie do?"

"She left politely and went downstairs to her room. He can be such a jerk."

"Well, I hope you do a lot of soul-searching before you dive into anything with Michael. Take it slow. Don't be too impulsive. He's married too!"

"I know. That's why I think this is just a very innocent meeting. Two old friends, that's all."

"I don't know about that! Promise you'll call me right away after you see him," Wendy said.

They talked for a few more minutes about what she was going to wear. At this stage of the game Leena described it as an adventure and nothing more. With a promise to call her as soon as humanly possible they hung up.

WHEN BRUCE CAME HOME he brought with him his typical "poor me, I had a long day" look, a look that Leena had gotten used to. Bruce had never been one to open up to Leena about his business or much of anything. She didn't like it but learned to live with it.

Anticipating meeting Michael in Mystic the next day, Leena was feeling anxious and a bit guilty about her decision to go. Leena tried to have a meaningful conversation with Bruce. Perhaps she wanted to alleviate some of her guilt. Or perhaps she was trying to justify seeing another man by forcing Bruce to react to her in his usual indifferent way. In any event, Bruce was true to form.

"How was work? You look down, what's going on?" Leena asked.

"Hm? Nothing," Bruce said.

"Want to talk about it?"

"Not really. What's for dinner?"

"Pork chops, rice. You seem quiet. I just thought I would ask."

"I'm just tired and I'm hungry." He said with more indifference than Leena expected.

Leena was determined to crack this stubborn shell open. "How's June working out?"

He waited several seconds before responding. "She went to the hospital last week for some shortness of breath thing. She was back to work on Monday," he said not even looking at her.

"You're kidding!" Leena exclaimed. "Why didn't you tell me?"

Bruce finally looked at Leena as if she were hysterical. Her raised voice startled him. "I thought I told you. Sorry."

"No, you didn't." Leena had had enough cracking. She left the room and finished preparing dinner.

The family dinner was very quiet. Only Leena made an attempt to make conversation. The response she got from Jason to "How was school today?" was simply, "Fine."

While Bruce was watching the evening news after dinner Leena decided to try again. "Did you ever settle that Halpern case?"

"No, not yet." Bruce kept his answers short.

"You think it will go to trial?"

"Hard to say. It'll probably settle."

"How's Charlene?"

"She's fine. You're full of questions tonight. How come?

"I was thinking we don't talk much. Maybe if we did things would be better."

"Better?"

"You know, we don't talk much."

"What do you want to talk about?"

Leena sighed loudly. "Never mind." She sat with her arms crossed and watched the news with him and waited to see if he'd ask her about her day or about the kids. Nothing. He never broke his gaze at the television. A report about an Israeli car bomb took Leena's desire away to stay. She had had enough. She was feeling annoyed beyond belief and she left the room. Her plan worked.

Leena walked down the hall, passing Jason's and Becky's doors, pausing briefly to hear what they were doing. Jason was humming along to a song, presumably with his headphones. Becky was on the phone talking a mile a minute.

Leena sat on the edge of her bed and started to cry. Her plans to see Michael the following day had become a wake-up call about her own marriage. She concluded she had been pushed into it by Bruce's indifference.

CHAPTER 10

Even with all the busywork she did beforehand, Leena got to the aquarium fifteen minutes early. Michael was not there. When she got sick of waiting in her car she got out and walked around on the sidewalk next to the building. Just like the night after his show at the festival he appeared behind her, almost magically, she turned when she sensed his presence. "Oh, Michael, you startled me. Hi."

"Hi. You been here long?"

"Not really, about ten minutes." Leena stared at Michael. There was a long pause as an awkward moment played out.

Michael finally said. "You look great."

"Thanks. You do too."

"What do you want to do first?" Michael asked. "We could find a place for lunch, or we could go into the aquarium, or we could go downtown to the village and go shopping."

"Yes to all those things," Leena smiled. "But let's go inside the aquarium first since we're here. Besides, it's too early for lunch."

"Have you ever been here before?"

"Oh sure. It's been quite a while but yeah, twice I think."

"I was here last year with my son, Tommy."

"Oh really. Would you rather not go in?"

"No, I want to go. It'll be fun," Michael said as he motioned to walk by waving his hand in a forward motion.

"You said you're down this way on business?" Leena asked.

"Yeah, I know a few people in this area. We have a pretty good deal worked out with each other. But I go all over the place. I was in New York last week."

"Oh, you don't say."

"So how far is your inn from here?" Michael asked.

"It isn't all that far. It took me about twenty minutes to get here. How about you?"

"About fifteen."

After paying separately they entered the building. From the sunlight into the darkness, it took a minute for their eyes to adjust to the lack of light. The tanks supplied what light there was. They walked around looking in each tank and did very little talking at first.

They stopped in front of an octopus tank. "Interesting creature,"

Michael said. His hands were behind his back.

"Hmm, yes. Is it true they squirt ink?"

"Yes, I think so," Michael said. "They're very intelligent, you know."

"Really?" Leena looked more closely at the creature.

They moved on to the tank where many good-sized sharks were swimming in a circle. "They've got to keep moving forward or they'll die," Michael said.

"Isn't that true for everyone?" Leena joked.

Michael looked at her and they both laughed. Their stare lingered. "It's true for me." Michael moved closer.

They were feeling each other's presence in a different way. Their stares said more than their spoken words. They moved along slowly from tank to tank and stopped in front of a school of brightly colored fish. Without looking at Leena, Michael felt for Leena's hand and took it. Leena turned her head and looked at Michael. He turned his head and then his body to face her. They were eye to eye. At five feet five, Leena was only a few inches shorter than Michael. She liked the fact that there was no neck straining when it came to Michael. Bruce's height, at six feet five, always made standing together awkward. There was nothing awkward about being with Michael. He took both of her hands, leaned toward Leena and kissed her on the lips. It was a gentle kiss, electric. The desire she once had for him came flooding back. They separated and looked at each other for a moment and then went back to looking at a tank. Michael put his arm around her waist. Leena nervously held her own hands in front of herself. They both stared ahead not knowing what to do next. They eventually continued to walk through the darkness of the aquarium, tank by tank.

They came upon a large tank that at first seemed empty. Suddenly a sea lion swam by. "I think this is the tank that has the show up above in the auditorium. You want to go see it?" Leena asked.

"Sure. Let's find out what time it will be." They learned the next show would not begin until eleven-thirty at the information booth. "That's not too long." Michael consulted his watch. "A little more than an hour."

"We can go see that Titanic exhibit. That wasn't here last time I came."

"Ok." They walked around looking at the rest of the indoor displays and tanks.

Leena said, "I remember coming here on a field trip with my son a few years ago. I was one of the chaperones. Each parent was assigned to a group. Ever try keeping your eye on eight kids all at once, in the *dark*?"

"No!" Michael feigned horror, raising the palms of his hands near his face. He then smiled.

"It was quite a challenge. I really wasn't able to enjoy this place since I was so busy watching kids. I'm enjoying it today a lot more." Leena said.

The Titanic exhibit opened up a new conversation.

"My grandmother's cousin survived Titanic, you know," Leena said.

"Really! You ever get to talk to her about it?"

"No. I never met her but my father used to tell us that she was in a lifeboat with very few people in it. The story goes that her mother, who was with her in the lifeboat, had a hard time living with the guilt of surviving and dealing with the death of her husband. Their family was never the same. It was such a sad story."

"I'll say. Family is everything."

Leena nodded.

THEY WENT OUTSIDE AND observed the beluga whales from above the water and then below through the glass. They strolled around the outside perimeter of the tank to the seal and sea lion tanks in the back. They found a bench and sat down.

Michael spoke first. "Leena, I really didn't plan on kissing you. It just sort of happened."

Leena looked Michael in the eye. "I'm glad you did."

Michael took her hand with his left hand and put his right arm around her shoulder. They sat in silence for a full minute. Their eyes met again and Michael kissed her again. This time it was longer and deeper. Leena felt Michael squeeze her hand. He stopped. He moved away from her face only a few inches and stared. It seemed they had an entire conversation with just their eyes.

Finally, Michael looked forward. "I don't know, I didn't mean for this to happen. I mean, I'm just here seeing an old friend." Michael turned to look at Leena again and smiled.

"Me too. I just wanted to catch up. I am not regretting it, though, are you?" Leena asked.

"No, not a bit!" he said, wide-eyed, selling his conviction. "I wanted to kiss you last week when you were standing by Wendy's car. God, it was *so* weird seeing you! It was like no time had passed."

Leena nodded. "I know. I wanted to kiss you too, right there."

Michael continued to look at Leena. His stare went deep. He studied her face. He took his hand from their lap, letting go of her hand, and raised it up to Leena's face and brushed her hair from her forehead. His hand skimmed her cheek and chin before he brought it back down to her knee. Leena reached over and took his hand again and rubbed the top of it. "Are you happy Michael? I mean with your life?" Leena looked into his eyes.

"Yes, I guess. I do okay. Business is good and I love the band and…"

"You know what I mean."

Michael paused. "My life is good. So you want to know what I am doing here with you, kissing you, if I am happily married? Fair enough."

He sighed loudly. "I really don't know. When I saw you, the old feelings returned as if, like I said, no time had gone by. I can't explain it, but I felt I had to see you again and so here I am. What about you?"

"I guess the reasons are similar. My life is good. I enjoy being an innkeeper and I have two great kids. I think my marriage has been stale for a while and we have some issues – nothing major, but enough to put a wedge in the middle of everything. Wendy said that if I had a great marriage, I probably would have been content to just find your website and I wouldn't have gone to see you in person. Maybe she's right."

"You're here, I'm here. All I can say is I am happy to be here with you." Michael said.

"I am very happy to be here with you too, Michael."

They took each other's hands and leaned into each other and kissed again. Leena put her hand on Michael's leg.

"Let's go see the show," Michael said.

MICHAEL HAD A VAN. The back was full of what looked like junk. Michael informed Leena all the items were valuable antiques. Michael pointed out the new items he had just acquired and he explained what made them valuable.

They went downtown. After being seated in a restaurant they quietly studied the menu with very little talk. When the waitress came over, they ordered their meals.

"So, tell me about your bed and breakfast." What made you decide to do that?"

"I really don't know. I like to decorate and fix up. I did that with our house in Waterford. It was always in the back of my mind to have a B&B. When we decided to move closer to Bruce's firm in Westerly, we found the inn, only it wasn't an inn. It was just a worn-out, old house. It was really too big for the four of us. But something about it I loved. The location of course was perfect – it's right on the water. The price was very reasonable, mainly because it was in disrepair. We couldn't justify buying it until I suggested making it into an inn."

"That sounded like quite a risk."

"It was sort of. We had the luxury of having a pretty good income from Bruce's law practice, and we had some inheritance from my parents' estate, so we could afford the renovations. Bruce set it up as a business and a residence and that was that. The first year we were in the red but by the end of the second year, we started to break even. We made a separate living area upstairs for our home."

"I see." Michael sat straight up with his elbows on the table making his shoulders hunch up, his forearms flat on the table. He stared at Leena making her feel uncomfortable.

"What?" Leena finally asked.

"You, that's what." He smiled a sweet smile without breaking his gaze. He reached across and took one of Leena's hands in his.

"I think I was more comfortable in the darkness of the aquarium," she said shyly.

"We could go back!" Michael kidded.

Leena laughed lightly and they stared at each other. Leena asked, "So tell me how you got into antiques, of all things."

"Now that was *not* in the back of my mind at all. I figured I would be a musician as my profession, which I am, actually, but it wasn't enough. It was enough when I was a bachelor. I lived simply. I didn't require much. Then I met Alice and things got serious and, you know, wedding bells and responsibilities and then a *kid*! Actually, she got me into it. She used to drag me to go 'antiquing' every weekend. I wasn't thrilled but I used to drag her to my gigs in some dingy places and she wasn't thrilled with that. So anyway... What? You're laughing."

Leena was laughing behind her hand. "I'm picturing you both doing things you didn't like all 'in the name of love.'"

Michael blushed. "I guess. Seems silly now that I'm saying it."

"So how did the store come about?"

"It started with placing a few ads in the papers to sell some antique stuff we had accumulated. We got pretty good money for them. I went to the garage one day and after digging around and finding stuff we both had forgotten about I suggested opening a store. So we did. Kind of like your inn, the store is more my business. Alice minds it once in a while, like on weekends, but she's a teacher so that takes up a lot of her time. With my band, I had all day because we'd play at night, mostly on weekends. I had a mortgage to pay. It worked out better than I thought it would, actually."

"Life can get expensive," Leena said.

"You got that right. So tell me about Bruce." Michael asked.

"Bruce? Really?"

"Really. I want to know."

"Well, he's honest, and he's hard-working. He's a lawyer. I told you that already. His firm is called *Frazer & Churchill*. He's a smart guy. He can practice law in Rhode Island, Connecticut or Massachusetts. He passed all three bars. His partner, he's younger. He's only Rhode Island." Leena looked at him and smiled. "He has his world and I have mine, I guess. That's what it has come to. We pass each other and do our own thing. I mean, he's into watching sports. I hate that. My interests are not his. Probably not an uncommon complaint for most married couples."

"True. How'd you two meet?" Michael asked.

"We met in college. He was three years ahead of me and we hung out together with a bunch of other people at school. It wasn't any whirlwind relationship. It was more gradual. It's almost like we didn't date because we had already been going out with friends, as a group." She looked down at her plate and continued. Her tone had changed. "Then I got pregnant in my junior year. He just finished law school and was working for his father. We got married when I was three months along with Becky. It wasn't shotgun or anything but it seemed like the right thing to do."

"I see." Michael seemed sad to hear her story. "Didn't you graduate?"

Leena reluctantly said, "No. I became a stay-at-home mom. I don't regret that though."

"Okay, so what's Alice like. How did you meet Alice?" Leena asked.

"Well, like I told you, I was living the bachelor life and at thirty-two met Alice at a friend's wedding. We started going out and she pretty much shamed me into leaving my old life behind and we got married. We had Tommy six years ago."

"Were you madly in love?" Leena asked not really wanting to hear the answer.

"Yes, I guess you could say that. I had my doubts at first. I felt like a cradle robber. Well, her parents made me feel like I was some lecherous 'older man.'"

"Why? What's the age difference?"

"She's thirty-one. She was twenty-three when we got hitched. I was thirty-two."

"You said she's a teacher, didn't you?"

"Yep. She teaches second grade. She loves it. Loves kids. She has a good heart."

Leena picked up her soda and said, "Here's to us. Here's to today." They clinked their glasses and finished their food.

After lunch, they walked down to an area where they could watch the boaters and fishermen. There was a grassy area behind some stores where a stone wall separated the lawn from a very narrow beach area. Without much conversation, they sat down on the ground where the sand came up against the wall. The water was just a few feet away. There was a light and gentle breeze blowing; seagulls hung in mid-air. The sounds and the smells of the sea were intoxicating. A small barge blew its loud whistle like a bellowing baritone.

Michael and Leena sat with their legs outstretched; Leena laid her head on his shoulder and her hand on his leg. Michael stroked her hair. They enjoyed the silence. There was no need to fill each moment with talk. Feeling each other's presence was enough.

"Why don't we pretend it's 1980. I'm serious." Michael said.

Leena took her head off his shoulder and looked up at his face. She stared. *That face*, she thought, *that's the face I remember like it was yesterday.*

"What are you thinking?" Michael asked.

She took her hand off his leg and brought it up and placed it on his face. "I'm just looking," she smiled, "and I'm remembering what this felt like." She stroked his beard.

Michael leaned down and kissed her. Without feeling as self-conscious as they did at the aquarium they gave in to their feelings. Seagulls laughed and car horns honked but Leena and Michael's involvement would not be easily interrupted. They knew without even saying a word that they would limit their activities, as much as desire was pulling them in another direction. A relationship so old was really just brand new. Leena found his shoulder again for her head. They took each other's hands.

Leena broke the silence. "I've got to get going. I don't want any questions about where I've been if I can help it. Let's head back. I'm sorry." Leena said reluctantly.

"No, don't be. We should get going, you're right."

Wiping sand off their backsides they stepped up onto the wall and headed back to where Michael's van was parked. With both hands on the wheel, he froze to say something. Leena looked over for a reason why the vehicle was not moving.

"What's the matter, Michael?"

"All I know is we need to see each other again. Please say you will."

Leena looked straight ahead as she spoke and said, "Yes."

They drove back to where Leena's car was parked at the aquarium. Michael pulled up beside Leena's car and shut off the engine. He leaned over to kiss her again before she had a chance to get out. He moved down her neck and to her collarbone. Leena closed her eyes getting lost in a deep desire she had not remembered feeling this intensely before. It took every bit of effort, on both their parts, to stop again. Leena fixed her hair, found her purse, and got ready to get out.

Michael fumbled for a scrap of paper and a pen in the glove box. "Here's my cell phone number. I don't think I gave it to you," Michael said.

Leena did the same, writing her cell number on a receipt in her purse. "Email me later," she said.

"Okay."

She started to get out and he reached over and lightly kissed her on the cheek. They both nodded their heads as she got out, and he watched her walk to her car.

On the drive home, she went over the events of the day to cement them into her mind. She never wanted to forget. She also went over what she would tell anyone who asked where she had been. She realized she had no groceries or packages. She decided to stop by a convenience store to pick up juice, milk, eggs and bread. There was a fabric store down the street so she went inside and quickly picked out some fabric for some pillows. Now she had items from her "errands." She was going to have to learn how to lie.

Leena was glad for the time it took to drive home. She needed time to decompress. She pulled into her driveway at about a quarter to three, a half-hour later than she had planned to return. Becky and Jason had just gotten home from school. There was loud music coming from Jason's room. Leena, carrying her packages, hurried inside to take her post as a parent of two teenagers.

"Jason, turn that down!" Leena yelled.

"Oh come on, Mom, you have to hear this music loud!"

"Now!"

"Where were you?" Becky said when she heard her yelling at Jason.

"I just went out to do a few errands."

"Dad called looking for you. He said you didn't have your cell phone on."

"Oh, yeah, I forgot to turn it on. When did he call?" Leena said.

"A few minutes ago."

Dinner got made quickly with the help of some leftovers. Bruce called back and Leena was ready to tell him how she had been out doing errands, but he didn't ask.

"I'm going to be late tonight. I've got some loose ends to tie up before court tomorrow. Then I'm gonna grab a bite with Al and Marcus. Okay?"

"Sure. That's fine," Leena said waiting for some kind of question.

"Alright then. I won't be too late. I'll see you later."

Leena hung up and was relieved about not having to lie, but annoyed that he was so disconnected that he simply called to tell her he wasn't coming home. "Maybe he's having an affair," Leena laughed at the thought.

CHAPTER 11

The inn was purring along like a machine. An engagement party was on the docket. Hal had the refrigerator organized like Gap pants on a shelf. Containers filled with the three meal choices, chicken, fish, and beef, were stacked and labeled; salad, appetizers and side dishes, the same treatment, waiting for their call of duty.

A delivery truck had arrived at the kitchen door entrance with flower arrangements. Michelle directed the man into the library and instructed him to line them up on the floor. She and Jackie took it from there and distributed them throughout the dining room, front room and library.

Leena went upstairs to her bedroom to change into her dress to play the part of hostess. Bruce was getting ready to go out with friends for nine holes of golf and then go to a sports bar later.

"Big party tonight?" Bruce said.

"Yep." Leena whipped off her clothes and stood in her closet in her bra and panties, searching for a dress.

Bruce watched her moving the hangers from right to left. "You look good. Have you lost weight?" He went up behind her and put his arms around her bare waist.

"What are you doing? I'm trying to get ready."

"Can't a guy touch his wife?" Bruce said, pulling her up against himself and nibbling her neck. "You've definitely lost weight."

"A little." Leena turned around abruptly and pushed him away and gave him a scolding look and repeated, "I'm trying to get ready?" her inflection rising to a question for emphasis.

"How about a quickie?" Bruce cajoled, ignoring her remark.

"Now?" Leena asked annoyed. "You don't ask me for *months*, then you get a bright idea at a time like this?"

"You used to like to sneak off and make love," Bruce tried to convince her one more time.

"That's too far back to remember. Go. I need to get downstairs!" Leena snapped as she pulled a dress over her head.

Bruce's pleasant face turned sour, transforming into disappointment, then anger. "Fine." He picked up his duffle bag and left with the attitude of a spoiled child.

Leena sat on the corner of the bed and absorbed her guilt and shame. She thought of Bruce as an interloper. She brushed off her feelings, relieved the moment had passed. She found some shoes and jewelry to accessorize. With a little hairspray and makeup, she was good to go.

Another van arrived at the back of the inn and Michelle went outside again to tell three men where to park after they were done unloading their equipment through the front entrance. It was the band Leena hired for the event, the band she decided to take a chance on from the Internet. They called themselves *Backlash*. The lead singer, who was also the lead guitarist, and drummer were both in their forties. The bass player was a handsome twenty-something-year-old man with wispy, dirty-blonde hair - something that did not escape Jackie's or Becky's attention. The two girls buzzed around the band area like two bees around a honey pot. They found out his name was Rick and also found out, in quick succession, he was single, he was from Providence, his favorite band was the Red Hot Chili Peppers and his favorite color was red.

In the hallway, Jackie said to Becky, "You're going out with Chris. Rick's mine."

"Can't a girl just look?" Becky teased. "He's all yours. Chris is coming over later."

"Good," Jackie said smugly, but with a smile. "Tell me if he looks at me when I walk through the room. I'm going to go move those flowers around a little." Jackie pointed to a vase across the room.

"Okay," Becky observed as Rick watched every move Jackie made. The two girls looked at each other from across the room and Becky smiled and nodded. Jackie turned back to the flowers, then glanced over at Rick. Their eyes met. They smiled.

Guests arrived and the volume of voices rose up and out into the kitchen where Leena discussed plans with Hal, Michelle, Jackie, and Becky.

After meeting the young man in the band Jackie's mood elevated tenfold. She found any excuse to walk in the direction of the band throughout the evening by refilling water glasses or checking to see if the guests had everything they needed. Rick smiled at Jackie each time she walked by.

The band took a break and Rick headed straight for Jackie. Her back straightened up and her eyes brightened when she saw him walking toward her. "Hey, Jackie, right?"

"That's right."

"How's it going?" Rick asked.

"Pretty good. You guys sound great. Who are the other guys in the band?"

"Oh that guy's my Dad," Rick said, pointing. "And the other guy, Peter, that's my Dad's friend." He pointed to the drummer. "They used to have another guy who played bass but he died, so I'm filling in."

"Oh, that's awful."

"Yeah, it was kinda sudden. But I'm having fun doing this. It's cool." Jackie was nodding and staring at Rick listening to every word he said. "You live around here?"

"As a matter of fact I do," Jackie said with a big smile. "I live *here* at the inn."

"Really? Sweet. Kinda cuts down on your commute to work, eh?"

"It's a nice deal. I mean, I don't want to waitress forever. I want to be an artist."

"Really?" Rick said. He took his right hand out of his pocket and brushed his hair off his eyebrows. "Like what kind of art do you do?"

"I draw mostly. But I'm getting into painting." Michelle motioned to Jackie to come to her. "I've got to get back to work. I'll see you later." She twisted around, waved, then left.

"He's cute," Leena said to Jackie.

She blushed and dipped her head down with a sheepish grin. "Yeah."

The band finished their set with Stairway to Heaven around eleven. The party broke up and most of the guests that were staying over went to their rooms. Laughter could be heard out front where a few couples lingered on the porch, taking advantage of a full moon.

Jackie had been hanging around the back of the room, watching the band carry their equipment out to the van. Rick saw her and motioned for her to come to him. They walked out onto the front porch. "So, Jackie, anyone ever tell you you're real pretty?" Rick said, standing with a confident footing with his hands in his pockets. He stood under a hanging lantern where the blonde highlights in his shaggy hair were revealed. His blue eyes captured Jackie's full attention.

Jackie didn't know how to respond. She smiled. A moth fluttering against the lantern caught her eye, breaking the intensity of their stares momentarily. She turned back to look at Rick again and he was still staring at her. She watched Rick's father and friend load up the last of the equipment.

"You wanna get together some time?" Rick asked her.

Jackie's eyes widened and a big smile lit up her face. "Sure!"

Rick went over to the van and came back with a pen. "Give me your hand," he said. At first, Jackie was puzzled but then caught on. Rick took her hand in his left and wrote his number on her palm. "There." He handed the pen to Jackie and presented the palm of his left hand to her. Jackie wrote the number of the inn on his palm. She delighted in the opportunity to hold his hand as she wrote.

"There," Jackie mimicked.

"So, I'll see ya," Rick said. His father had been motioning to him to get in the van.

"See ya," Jackie said.

Rick walked away and got into the back of the van. He turned around to look at Jackie, tossing his hair back from his eyes. He gave her a big smile and gave her the thumbs up with one hand and then closed the sliding door with the other hand.

The van pulled out into the night and Jackie watched the taillights. She stood staring at nothing for a minute. The sound of a woman's laughter from the front porch brought her back to reality. She went back inside.

CHAPTER 12

Eating had not been so much of a priority anymore. Fighting the bulge demons had almost seemed like a full-time job. Now Leena had to remind herself to eat. An odd reversal, but she wasn't complaining. Jogging had been the only thing that absolved her sins. Michael was ever-present in her mind. With every thought of his touch a little butterfly would flutter in her stomach, making eating a chore.

Leena had taken up sewing again. What was once a hobby was now a much-needed distraction. There was time to fill before her next meeting with Michael. The inn was the beneficiary of her new obsession. She had made three new pillows for the front room sofas and she put cushion covers on all the dining room chairs, some of which had become stained. She started to make valences for every guest bathroom. Fifty napkins for the dining room were waiting in the queue.

A NEW DISTRACTION CAME to light. Leena found, in the local newspaper, an announcement for a book club at the library which took place every Wednesday morning at ten. The selection for the upcoming meeting was a Toni Morrison book, an author Leena admired, but one she knew was not an easy read. Pleasure reading was another casualty of her infatuation with Michael. She decided to try and change that. She ran out and purchased the book and got through the first two chapters before the meeting.

Leena arrived a few minutes early and found the library's conference room. Other participants, mostly women, started to trickle in. They greeted each other with a smile and a little small talk.

Then Gloria arrived.

Gloria, Leena's next-door neighbor, was rich. She had married well. What Leena had learned over the years was that Gloria was a shallow, self-centered, high-maintenance snob. She did have one talent: a knack for knowing everything about everyone in town. She projected status and breeding so quickly that suspicion and disbelief were the remnants of any encounter with her. Anyone with common sense would see through her façade. Hiding behind an ungodly amount of makeup on her surgically enhanced face and the designer threads on her skeletal frame was more than likely a bored and unfulfilled housewife with too much time on her hands.

Leena lowered her head and put her hand up to her face in an attempt to be overlooked by her neighbor. To Leena's chagrin, Gloria spotted her immediately.

"Kathleen, is that you?" Gloria sat down in the seat next to Leena.

Leena looked up. "Gloria, hi."

"You're joining our book club?" Gloria asked.

"Thought I'd give it a try. You come to these?"

"Every week!" Gloria turned and addressed the woman in the next chair. "Do you know Kathleen Frazer, Sheila? She's my neighbor."

"Yes, we just met," the woman said.

Gloria looked back at Leena. "Did you read the book?"

"I started it. I haven't gotten through much yet, but I hope to. I love Morrison."

"Oh, it's a glorious book. Gloria is reading a glorious book. Oh, I made a funny," Gloria laughed at her own lame joke as she carefully removed her hair from her cheek with just one carefully painted, fake fingernail.

Leena smiled politely. Leena also learned never to ask Gloria a question because she could be stuck for an hour listening to the answer, yet not getting the answer after all. Inevitably the answer would turn into a story about herself or her rich, successful husband.

She proceeded to ask Leena in quick succession about Bruce, Becky and Jason. After learning they were all fine, she asked about "poor" Jackie. Leena didn't want to discuss Jackie. She knew Gloria's mind was already made up. Since Jackie was not related to the Frazers Gloria felt she was fair game.

"I can't believe she's working for you now. I must say, it's very generous of you. But I feel bad for the girl. I doubt she had much of an upbringing. Didn't she look dreadful that day they took her away on the stretcher." She lowered her voice slightly and said, "I heard it was a suicide attempt." She acted as if she was the one to inform Leena of the truth. Gloria shook her head and made the pity sound, "Tsk tsk. She's living with you now, right?"

Leena knew full well that Gloria knew the answer. "Yes. She's working out wonderfully. Thanks for asking," Leena said.

Gloria was not done with the subject. "She seems to advertise her lack of breeding by wearing distasteful clothing." Leena practically had to bite her tongue off to keep from telling her off. Gloria continued her stream of consciousness by saying, "Did you see the outfit she was wearing the other day? Her belly was showing, her belly *ring* was showing, I should say, and her pants were *dragging* on the ground. I hope she doesn't greet your guests in those outfits." Gloria's penciled eyebrows barely moved as her brow fought against Botox.

Leena looked at her watch. It was a few minutes after ten. The instructor had not arrived yet. Leena changed the subject 180 degrees by asking a question Gloria could not resist. "Where did you get that outfit, Gloria? It's very pretty, and flattering."

"Oh, this?" She said, placing both hands up to her chest displaying all ten fake nails. "I got it through the Saks Fifth Avenue catalog. Luckily I can buy clothes that way since I'm a size two." Gloria carefully looked through her purse and found her compact. Leena watched her as she preened, along with the rest of the people sitting at the table.

Leena, still smoldering from Gloria's comments about Jackie, couldn't resist an opportunity to give it right back. She made sure the entire group could hear her comments. "What a pity your daughter wasn't chosen for the cheerleading squad. Becky told me she tried out and failed. I'm sorry to hear that."

Gloria looked quickly at Leena, her compact made a snapping noise when she shut it. She struggled for words. Leena smiled and waited for her response. "Jennifer didn't want to be on that team anyway," she said with a mouth full of sour grapes. "Most of the girls were lower class."

"Becky made the team. Does that make her low class?" Leena challenged her.

"Oh no, not at all. Your Becky is a good girl. I just meant that *some* of the girls just were not Jennifer's type."

"I see."

"Instead Jennifer is enjoying lessons with her personal vocal trainer much more. She's been told that she has a natural ability. 'A gift,' I think her teacher said." Gloria concluded with a victorious smile. She looked around the table.

Leena had doubts about this. To her knowledge, her daughter had never been in any choral groups at school. She had been in the senior play with Becky and had gotten a small part, that of a servant. She sang with the group, not solo.

The acorn didn't fall far from the tree. Jennifer was a clone of her mother: a diva in training. Breaking a nail was cause for a sick day. Leena smiled and nodded at Gloria.

The leader of the book club finally arrived and apologized for being late. She introduced herself as Sally Feldman and passed around a sign-in sheet which asked for a name, address, phone number, and email contact.

"Welcome. I'm glad to see familiar faces and a few new ones. What we do is we go around the table and state our name and where we live. Just a little ice breaker. Kerry, why don't we start with you."

The woman sitting directly to Sally's left started. Of the nine participants, seven women and two men, Gloria and Leena were the last two in the circle. Gloria leaned into Leena's ear and whispered, "Sally's a Jew."

Leena snapped her head around, incredulous. She looked right into Gloria's big brown eyes as she fluttered her false lashes. Leena was speechless. She tried to give her a look of disapproval to no avail.

Randomly people shared their thoughts on the book for the next hour. Sally did a good job keeping the focus. Leena remained quiet throughout most of the discussion. She was not as far along as most of the readers, some had finished the book completely.

When the meeting ended, Leena made it a point to chat with a few of the people. The group slowly dispersed. Leena deliberately prolonged her interaction with one of the other women, making sure Gloria left before her. She made the mistake, only once, seven and a half years ago, of accepting Gloria's invitation to have coffee at her house one afternoon. Never again.

Outside the library, Leena got into her car. She was about to start the engine when she heard a tapping on her window. Startled, Leena turned quickly. Gloria was tapping with one of her fingernails and was motioning for her to put her window down.

"Gloria, you startled me," Leena said as the window went down.

"Kathleen, dear," she started, "Did Bruce tell you about our dinner party next month?"

Leena had to conceal her disappointment by smiling. "Dinner party?"

"Yes, Ashton and I are having a party. I'm sure Ashton mentioned it to Bruce the other day at the club. You'll be getting an invitation soon. It's for a few neighbors and business associates." Ashton had his own business as a financial analyst in Westerly, not far from Bruce's office.

"I'll keep an eye out for the invitation. Thank you, Gloria," Leena said.

"I just wanted to give you the 'heads up' on it. Mark it on your calendar for July 17th! And I'll see *you* next week?" Gloria said, wagging a fingernail in Leena's face.

"Oh, I don't know if I can. I hope so. I need to finish the book." Leena shrugged and smiled. Leena looked down and started the engine. She put the car in reverse to signal their conversation was over.

"Okay, dear. Take care." Gloria's words faded as Leena's car backed up. Leena glanced her way, giving her a smile and a nod before she pulled out. She was already feeling mad at Bruce knowing he probably accepted the invitation. He'd endure anything to hobnob with the social elite and thought nothing of dragging her along.

CHAPTER 13

Tuesday finally arrived. In an attempt to leave nothing to chance Leena had cleaned and organized everything to perfection the day before. More than likely she needed to keep busy. She had labeled all the leftovers in the refrigerator for Becky, Jason and Jackie. She double-checked rooms Jackie had cleaned after guests left.

Leena made some finger sandwiches and packed them into a tote bag with some juice. She put the tote onto the floor of the back seat of her car very early in the morning, before her jog.

"I really *need* to see you again." Those were Michael's words to Leena two weeks ago. She was feeling it too. They made plans to meet, this time in Charlestown at the Ninigret Wildlife Preserve in the next town over from Weekapaug.

Bruce had left for work over an hour ago. She hoped there would be no questions about where she was going. Becky and Jason, now out of school for the summer, slept late, and Jackie usually did too, but on this morning, Jackie emerged from her room rubbing her eyes, looking for the coffee.

"Good morning." Leena watched her examine the coffee maker. "I'm sorry Jackie, I don't have any more coffee. Make some if you want. You know where it is."

Jackie nodded. "What time is it?" She was still squinting.

"Nine."

Jackie became more observant as she became more awake. "You look like you're going out."

"I have a few errands to run. I know of a place I want to look at some wallpaper samples. There are two rooms that don't have wallpaper, and one that needs replacing. I'm thinking it's time to change that. So, we'll see. But I shouldn't be long." Leena was nervous.

Jackie had been half-listening. She nodded and then said, "Becky and I are taking that painting class today, down at the community center near *Parsons Restaurant*, remember?"

"Oh, is that today?" Leena had totally forgotten. "It's not until later, right? What time?"

"Two o'clock. You said you might stop by."

"Oh right, I did. I will try to come by, sure."

"Whatever. I'm probably going to feel like a fish out of water there. What do you bet the class is mostly old geezers."

"I don't think so, hon. I know the instructor and she is very good. She has her own gallery. Becky took her class last year, only it was for portraits. It's not just for 'old geezers.'" Leena mimicked.

"I guess." Jackie shuffled across the kitchen floor and found the coffee can in the cabinet. She held it up to show Leena, to get her approval."

"Of course. Please, make some coffee. I'm gonna get going. I'll see you in a little while." Leena said, breathing a sigh as she closed the door behind her. She was off to meet Michael. She called his cell phone to see if he was on route.

"Michael Everly," he answered.

"Hi, it's me. Where are you?"

"Hey, I just got off 95 and I'm following your directions at this point."

"I can't believe we're doing this."

"Me either. I can't wait to see you again, Leen."

"Me too."

There was a long pause as they both thought of what to say next.

"This was a long two weeks," Michael said.

"You said it. Where were you going today?"

"I'm going to the shoreline in Stonington, Connecticut. I can stop there on the way back. Did you have to answer to anyone?"

"Jackie. She's my tenant slash chambermaid slash waitress. I said I was going to go shopping for wallpaper."

"Wallpaper, huh? Can you buy wallpaper at this refuge?"

"What do you think?" Leena laughed.

"I'll see ya in a few," Michael said.

MICHAEL PULLED IN BESIDE Leena's car. He hopped out and got into her car. They sat in silence for a few moments not knowing what to say or do. He finally leaned over and kissed her straight on the mouth. Leena was surprised at his quickness, but not disappointed. She kissed him right back.

"We're going to get ourselves in quite a pickle, if we don't stop this," Leena said.

"Oh well," was all Michael could say, and he went back to kissing her.

When they stopped Leena asked if he wanted to go for a hike and see the preserve. She started to explain how beautiful it was there and it was one of her favorite spots to come to for hiking or bird watching.

"I'm going to be very honest with you," Michael said. Leena looked at him nervously. He continued in a serious tone. "I really want to be with you today. You know what I mean?" He was staring directly at her, holding both her hands.

"Yes, I do know what you mean," Leena was on the same wavelength. "It's pretty much all I could think about all week. I'm feeling a little nervous, though."

"I don't want you to be nervous. There's nothing to be afraid of. It's just me. We've done this before."

"I know, and I still can't believe it's *you*."

"Where do you want to go? This is your neck of the woods."

"There's a place down the way, it's not very far from here," Leena told him. "It's nothing fancy, I'm sure. But it's convenient." She regretted using the word convenient.

They found the little motel. Michael went in and paid for the room. When he came out, he got back into Leena's car and she drove over and parked in front of their room.

Flowers had been planted in an attempt to create some curb appeal for this old motel. It was a noble effort, but as an innkeeper, Leena saw, all too often, alternative ways to enhance first impressions. *Give them a reason to come back.* Some straggly pachysandra and a few bent over marigolds planted along the walkway would hardly discourage two people determined to find some privacy.

The door opened to a simple but functional room. There was a slight smell of mustiness and a thin layer of dust. The fabric of the curtains was a bit outdated. Hanging above the double bed was the obligatory motel painting of a lighthouse with stormy clouds and breaking surf.

"It's not the Hilton, is it?" Michael asked.

"No, not quite." Leena said as she looked all around.

"I bet your place is nicer."

Leena nodded humbly.

They sat on the end of the bed together. Michael patted it and bounced a little.

Michael talked first. "Leena, I want you to know that I don't take this lightly. I mean I know that sounds like a load of shit coming from a married guy but I," he stopped. He looked choked up. Leena shifted her weight to turn to look at him.

"You what?"

He also turned toward her. He lifted his knee up onto the bed and looked right into her eyes. He took her hands and said, "I still have deep feeling for you Leena. They came flooding back when I saw you. I really had no idea, after all these years." His eyes were so sincere.

Leena broke her stare and looked down. She started to cry.

"Now I've upset you. I didn't want to …"

"No, you haven't upset me. I am very happy." She laughed through the tears and said, "You wouldn't be able to tell I'm happy by looking at me, though." She sniffed and said, "I felt our connection take up right where we left it twenty-two years ago the second I saw you standing beside me on the green. It's weird. I didn't expect that *at all*. I figured if I got the nerve to talk to you, I would just say 'hi,' do some catching-up and then we'd go our separate ways. I was blindsided."

"Same here," he said.

There was a long pause. Michael finally said, "I am glad you came that night." He leaned toward her and kissed her on the mouth. They spent several minutes kissing and holding each other at the edge of the bed.

Michael pulled away. Leena kept her eyes on him. He walked over and drew back the bedspread and blankets. Leena got up and closed the curtains. Michael stood in front of Leena put his hands up to her face and kissed her again. His hands slid down her arms and then moved over to the buttons on her blouse. They stopped kissing. She watched his hands unbutton her blouse. Michael's expression changed as he saw more of her skin. He anticipated seeing it all momentarily.

Michael sat down on the edge of the bed. She got down to her bra and panties and walked toward Michael and stood between his legs. He reached out, put his hands behind her back, and pulled her toward his face and kissed her belly. Leena played with his hair and kissed his forehead. He guided her down to the bed.

There was no reason to stop this time. It wasn't fast like she thought it might be, full of exploding passion, it was slow and deliberate, tender and dreamlike. It had been a very long time since she had been touched like this, and longer still since she had cared. *Something this wonderful could not possibly be wrong,* she thought.

When they were still, they both slept for a short time. Leena was in a half-sleep, Michael was out. Eventually, Leena got up to use the bathroom. Michael stirred and awoke when she returned. "Come back to bed."

Leena slide back under the sheet and cuddled next to him, putting her head on his chest and shoulder. She stroked his chest with her left hand.

"I can't believe we're here together. I wish we had made love more when we were young." Michael said as he stroked her hair.

Leena said, "Remember we did it in your car? Doing it in the back seat of the car was some sort of coming-of-age thing I guess." Leena laughed gently.

"It was sort of exciting that way, wasn't it?"

"Yes, I guess," Leena agreed. "My daughter is seventeen now, the age we were when we…" She didn't want to mention the break-up. "… knew each other. I ask myself, 'Do I want Becky having sex and getting into some serious relationship?' No! But I think she may be having sex with this guy Christopher she's seeing. She looks at him like he's a God."

"Would she tell you?"

"She confides in me but she hasn't come right out and told me they've having sex. I'm not sure. I hope not, and yet I don't regret our decision for one minute to have sex at that age." Leena said.

"I hope you've had *the talk*."

"Oh, yeah. The sex talk. The condom talk. I didn't just sit her down and say, 'We need to have *the talk*.' It's been more gradual than that. When the subject comes up it usually ends with, 'Oh Mom, please, I know!'"

"No one ever talked to me," Michael said.

"Me either."

"You were my first, Michael." Leena reminisced, staring into his eyes. "You know that."

He leaned into her and kissed her. "Same here," he said. "You know that too." He ran his fingers through her strawberry blonde hair. Leena closed her eyes enjoying the moment and the memory. "We gave each other a gift that would cement our fate forever." Leena had almost forgotten how sentimental Michael could be.

"I loved you so," Leena said softly.

"I loved you too. Unfortunately, I hooked up with that *Sybil* when I went off to school. I ruined everything."

"Don't remind me."

"I always figured you'd forgive me. But you didn't!" Michael said sadly. "I always figured you'd take me back. You never returned my calls."

They both got quiet and a little uncomfortable, but it was good to get some of it out in the open.

"But you know," Michael said, "I have to tell you, when we were together at the aquarium, and later downtown, I was having a difficult time controlling myself. It was almost too much. But I wanted the time and place to be right. This is no great place but it's right. Does that make sense?"

"Yes. This place is fine. It's kinda cozy, really. I was feeling the same way. I wanted to rip your clothes off that day." They both laughed.

Leena continued, "Michael, I haven't been this happy in a long time. I know it's complicated and I really don't want to think about all the baggage we have between us."

"It's complicated alright!" There was a pause. "No use worrying about it right now."

Leena nodded and then they snuggled a while longer.

"You hungry?" Leena asked.

"A little, why?"

"I packed some finger sandwiches and some juice. It's in this bag," Leena said, pointing to her tote bag on the floor.

"Well, aren't you a clever girl. Bring it on."

Leena leaned down and picked up her bag. They ate their sandwiches on the bed, naked. Leena surprised herself with her lack of modesty. She was very comfortable with him.

"We still have time, what do you want to do?" Leena asked. Before he had a chance to respond, she said, "We could leave here and go back to Ninigret and hike around."

"I'd love that." Michael smiled slyly at her. "But there's one thing I want to do before we head out."

"What?"

"This." Michael grabbed her by her waist and pulled her back down until she was lying right up against him. They stared into each other's eyes, and then engaged in a long kiss. It took no time for their excitement to reach a full boil again.

THEY HEADED BACK DOWN to Ninigret. There was still time to take the hike Leena had planned. They found a well-traveled path and went for a walk. Holding hands, ducking under limbs and jumping over fallen branches, they went out to a scenic overlook and stopped. It was breathtaking. Finding a place to sit on a rock they huddled together.

"I love it here," Leena said, holding up her head with pride as if she owned part of it.

"You were right, it's lovely."

"I'm glad you were able to see it, or that we made *time* to see it. This really completes my day. I don't know about you."

"I am full up," Michael said, kissing her neck from behind.

"Come on, I'll show you one more spot."

Leena led him by the hand and they hiked a little further into the preserve. They entered a clearing that was in stark contrast to the tall trees. Leena came to an abrupt halt. "You hear that?" She looked up and pointed. "It's a red-tailed hawk!" It screeched and circled over their heads. "I love the sound of the birds early in the morning. It's siesta time now. Except for Mr. Hawk here who's probably looking for lunch, it's dead quiet now."

Michael looked at Leena after he watched the hawk. "I didn't know you were such a nature lover."

She laughed with some embarrassment, and said, "I guess. Next time we'll do what you want to do and see."

"I did exactly what I wanted to do today. And I'm seeing exactly what I want to see too," he said as he stared into her eyes.

They hiked back and Leena was happy to be a tour guide. Back at the parking area, about an hour after the hike began, they stood by their cars and embraced. Michael pushed right up against Leena's body as he kissed her.

"I shouldn't have done that," Michael said.

"Oh dear," Leena laughed.

Michael motioned with his head toward their vehicles. "There's always your car or my van." Michael joked. They both laughed.

"We better go," Leena reasoned. "It's getting late."

"I miss you already," he said.

LEENA CALLED WENDY FROM the car on the way home.

"We did it."

"What? Did what?" Wendy asked, forgetting the protocol of receiving word immediately.

"Michael and I. We met and ended up in Charlestown and, well, we *did* it."

"Leena! Oh my God. You didn't! You did? How are you feeling?"

"Elated. Elevated. My cup runneth over. This was the best day of my *life*!"

"I'm happy if you're happy." Wendy said and then added, "I just want you to be very careful. I don't want you to get hurt." She cautioned Leena "He's married, Hon."

"I *know*! We're in the same boat, Wendy. Michael felt like we had taken up where we left off and that's how I feel. It's weird. It's like time stood still for us," Leena said.

"I know things have not been great with Bruce but are you ready to leave Bruce and end the marriage?"

"I'm not thinking about that, and I don't want to worry about it right now. I am going to take it one day at a time and see where it goes." Leena got quiet. She said with a whimper in her voice, "It happened again for you. You found love a second time. It could happen for me too. Why not?"

"You're right. Why not? No one deserves it more."

"Thanks for being supportive, Wen. You're the best friend a gal could possibly have. You're not being judgmental about it and I appreciate it. I mean I know how you feel about cheating. What Jimmy did to you sucked! I wouldn't blame you if you wanted to scold me for this. I mean how am I any different than Jimmy?"

"You're very different than Jimmy, believe me. Look, every situation is different. You gotta do what you feel you gotta do. I'm here for you."

"Thanks. Love ya."

"Love you too."

CONCENTRATING ON PREPARING DINNER was a challenge. Leena could still feel the touch of Michael's hands on her body, his breath on her neck. This was something that was going to be hard to put aside for the next week.

Leena thought about her own marriage and how it had fallen into disrepair as she chopped up broccoli for chicken divan. *What a shame. It always had the potential to be great*, she thought. *It has come to this. Bruce pushed me to this*, she thought. *This was meant to be. Getting back with Michael was fate.* She convinced herself. *Things happen for a reason.*

Bruce got home early. She had a sudden attack of nerves and guilt. Something she hadn't had until she saw Bruce's face. *Will he see on my face what I've done?* She thought.

"Hi, where were you? I called a few times. Did you get my message?"

"No, I didn't. I forgot to check the machine. I'm sorry."

"Tonight is the night we're having dinner at the Jackson's."

"Oh, for goodness sake, I forgot that completely. I can go get ready. I have time, right?"

"Yes. I told them we'd be there at 6:30. You've got plenty of time."

She avoided his question, she thought.

"So where were you all day?"

Her mind raced. "Well, I went out to look for wallpaper for a while, I ordered some, it should be ready to pick up in about three weeks. You know, I want to paper some rooms. So I finally decided to get paper. I don't know. I was around other than that. Oh, I went for a walk, and if you tried to call, I had the vacuum cleaner going. I think that's why I didn't hear the phone."

Bruce apparently got more information than he needed and simply said, "Oh." He hung around the kitchen while Leena puttered around. He seemed to be in a good mood and chatted with her. He was jazzed up about his win in court. Normally this interaction with him would have been a welcome relief, a long time coming, to the usual indifference, but instead, it made her feel more guilty for what she had done. *Maybe Bruce is not so bad after all*, she thought.

A terrible thought came into her head at that moment. *What if, later, Bruce asks me to have sex?* Their sex life was practically non-existent, but on the rare occasion they did have sex was when he was in a good mood after winning or settling a significant case. She decided she would simply tell him no. Just like all the times he had told her no, or ignored her advances so many times, leaving her feeling ugly and rejected. *Problem solved.*

Just as soon as Leena's concerns over her own situation were averted a wave of nausea came over her when she realized that the same thing would, no doubt, happen to Michael. She couldn't stand the thought of him making love to his wife. Worse yet, *would he be the one initiating it?* She had to put it out of her mind.

Jason and Becky came in to eat. Leena intercommed Jackie downstairs in the kitchen. Leena invited her to join Jason and Becky for dinner upstairs. Jackie was delighted with the invitation. Leena pushed the button to open the security door to let her in.

CHAPTER 14

Leena's concentration was shot. Her head was still in the clouds over her meeting with Michael. If Leena had her druthers she would stay in and watch TV, read a book or fiddle at her computer. She did not want to go to the Jackson's dinner party.

Leena took a shower. The hot water felt wonderful. The solitude gave her another opportunity to think about Michael. As the water flowed over her body where Michael had touched her, she closed her eyes, imagining being in his arms again. She hugged herself and rubbed her arms. She had no regrets whatsoever. Washing him off her body made her feel sad.

The sight of her sweatpants and sweatshirt hanging on the chair tempted her to stay home. She dried her hair. She reluctantly dressed for the dinner party. Leena applied make up at the dresser mirror. Bruce came up behind her to use the mirror to tie his necktie. He looked so happy with himself as he checked his hair. Leena grimaced when she thought of all the years ahead of her, potentially, with him.

GEORGE AND CAROLINE JACKSON were both attorneys and owned a lavish home in Westerly. Bruce's and George's practices were in close proximity to each other.

Leena realized Bruce was a snob: a fact that was especially apparent when she observed him at such functions. He only wanted to hobnob with people of his own ilk.

Leena was unimpressed by the Jacksons' wealth: a spacious entryway laid out in marble showcased a curved staircase and a huge chandelier; their grand piano; and their Mercedes and big SUV in their heated garage. She did, however, manage to feel underdressed and inferior the minute she arrived when she saw the other women. There was always the inevitable feeling of regret over the outfit she had chosen.

After the initial greeting at the door with superficial hugs, George got right to what was important: drink orders. Bruce asked for his usual *Manhattan*, while Leena agreed to a glass of white wine. Caroline directed them both into their large parlor where other guests were mingling.

Then she saw her. Gloria was sitting there in the room sipping on wine, just barely holding onto her glass at the stem with two fingers. Her stick-straight, blonde hair was a carbon copy of Jennifer Aniston's style. Her dress hung from her skeletal frame by spaghetti straps. It was low-cut in the back and front. Leena realized at that moment that Gloria had gotten breast implants. It looked as though someone had put two baseballs under her skin. *This must be their coming out party*, Leena said to herself. Gloria didn't notice Leena right away. She was bending the ear of Carol, Bruce's friend's wife. Carol's head bobbed slowly as she endured Gloria's chatter.

Leena turned to find Bruce who was already in a deep conversation with George about falling interest rates and refinancing. She wanted to scold him for bringing her to the Jacksons' house, and for the inevitable face-to-face she would have with Gloria. But for Bruce to not show up with his wife would be a social faux pas.

Leena managed to steer clear of Gloria for the entire happy hour, engaging instead in a conversation with a man from Providence who was a vice president of a college. He was a bit full of himself, but entertaining nevertheless. Leena did see the advantage of getting out and rubbing elbows with people. Word-of-mouth was a large part of how guests found her inn. *This is a business meeting*, she told herself.

She thought dinner would never be announced. It was well after 7:00 and she was starving. Hors d'oeuvres had been passed around by the hired help but Leena only had one. She didn't want to regain any of her now twelve-pound weight loss.

When dinner was finally announced the guests filed into the dining room. The table was impeccably set and there were name cards beside the bone china and lead crystal water glasses. Leena found her name and Bruce's name. Right next to her setting was Gloria's card. Leena felt trapped and angry again. She looked around to see if it would be possible to exchange her card with someone else but she realized how complicated that would be since the spouses were also assigned to be seated next to their wives. She took her place dutifully.

Leena was startled by Gloria's shrill voice. "Oh Kathleen dear, how lovely to see you again," Gloria said as she waited for her husband to pull her chair out for her. Leena had pulled her own chair without the assistance of a man.

"Nice to see you too, Gloria," Leena returned the salutation.

"Ashton, look we're sitting next to the Frazers," Gloria said to her husband.

"Leena, very nice to see you," Ashton said.

"Ashton, hello," Leena said. Leena thought about how apropos it was for Gloria to have found and married a man with the name Ashton. *Such a snobby sounding name*, she thought.

"The inn is looking marvelous these days. You'll have to give me the name of your gardener. Ours can no longer work for us," Ashton said.

"Is that right?" Leena said, and thought to herself that Gloria probably ran the poor man off with her impossible demands. She made a mental note to tell her lawn maintenance guy to be on the lookout for her.

Bruce found his place setting as he stood next to his chair, still in deep conversation with one of his lawyer friends. They laughed loudly. Leena caught a few words from their conversation. Hearing "birdie," she knew he was discussing golf and not nature.

"So Kathleen," Gloria started, "How did you like the book club meeting? Are you going to come to next Wednesday's meeting?"

"Please, Gloria, call me Leena."

"Alright, *Leena.* I'll try to remember."

"I did like it very much. I'll try to come. Sally Feldman? Is that her name? She did an excellent job. But I'm not sure how often I'll be able to get away with the busy season here. I might have to forgo it, unfortunately."

All of the guests - there were twenty-five in all - were now seated and conversation buzzed around the room. Leena recognized many other couples she wished she had been seated next to. Bruce sat next to Leena but did not attempt to include her in his conversation. More than likely other guests had Gloria's number and did not engage with her. Gloria had Leena all to herself.

Gloria sank her teeth right into some gossip about one of the women at the book club named Debbie who apparently didn't have the presence of mind to curtail her daughter's participation in the tryouts for the school play because she was too fat. Gloria's clone, Jennifer, was lithe, nimble and perky, and just what the directors were looking for, Leena learned.

"Why didn't Jennifer get the lead?" Leena asked, knowing the answer. She remembered Gloria's comment about her daughter's dubious singing ability.

"Nepotism," Gloria proceeded to show her misuse of the word. "She got a good part, but I think that Jenny girl, you know the other Jennifer? I think she knows the director's family well. Either that or they got the two Jennifers mixed up, which would account for why she didn't get the lead."

"Ludicrous!" was what Leena wanted to say to Gloria. If Gloria couldn't embellish, she would out and out lie. Leena did say, "So why didn't you go and complain or go talk to the director?"

"I didn't want to make waves. I didn't want to embarrass Jennifer."

Another ludicrous statement. The year before Gloria made a total fool of herself at the cheerleading tryouts. She tried hard to pull strings, and when that didn't work, she started a major bitch-fest in front of all the mothers and girls. Jennifer didn't seem embarrassed however, according to Becky who made the team that day. Jennifer was used to doing very little while her parents set up her life for her and fought all of her battles.

Leena endured story after story from this woman for the next half hour. The line between truth and fiction was anyone's guess. Each story tore down a person she knew in an attempt to puff herself up. Leena wasn't sure how much more she could stand. Didn't Gloria know how transparent she was? No one was spared. Leena figured she herself must have been fodder for many a story Gloria had told to some other captive listener.

Leena managed to strike up a conversation with the couple across the table and she felt a sense of relief as the main course was served. Bruce had been of no help. By the time a fruit cup with sherbet came for dessert Gloria was trawling for more information.

"*Leena*, dear," Gloria stated proudly, remembering to call her Leena. "Are you going to continue to employ that girl? Will she live there indefinitely? You know, the rumor is that she was living on the street turning tricks before she came to our fair neighborhood. What if she's turning tricks at your inn? Or being indiscreet with your guests? We're concerned for your well-being."

Leena felt anger boiling to the surface. She knew she was not going to engage in, nor corroborate, anything about Jackie to anyone, let alone a piranha like Gloria.

"She is not turning *tricks*, as you so delicately put it."

"I got it from a reliable source that she…"

"I don't want to hear it, Gloria."

"But will she be staying on with you?"

Gloria didn't know how to take a hint. "Gloria, that is quite simply none of your business," Leena said, not knowing what she was going to say until she said it.

Gloria looked at her in disbelief. It showed in her eyes but not in her penciled eyebrows which were not in a natural location. She didn't give up easily. "Surely you're not defending that little scamp?"

Leena remained silent. She was close to causing a scene and she knew it.

Gloria forged ahead, without a clue. "I think you should put her out on her ear. Our neighborhood doesn't need her type. Why, it could drag our property value down!"

"You planning on moving out, Gloria? I didn't know." Leena said with scorn. Her voice was a little louder. Ashton looked at Leena.

"No," she said, puzzled by the question. "I'm just saying…"

"Maybe you should. I mean if you don't like our neighborhood you should move out. Cut your losses."

"That's not my point, dear," Gloria continued. "We neighbors should stick together."

"We neighbors," Leena mimicked, "should not *stick* our noses where they don't belong!" Leena's voice rose above all the rest, getting louder. She got up from her seat and stormed to the bathroom located down the hall. A few of the guests noticed and watched her walk away, then they looked at Gloria's startled eyes. Bruce stopped talking and noticed his wife's abrupt departure.

"Excuse me," Bruce said as he got up from the table and went down the hall to the bathroom. He tapped lightly on the door and said, "Leena, it's me, what's wrong?"

Leena opened the door and took Bruce's arm and dragged him into the room, shutting the door behind him. Bruce looked surprised by her actions. She was crying. "Why did we have to come here tonight? Why didn't you tell me that Gloria woman would be here?" Leena asked angrily.

"I didn't know they'd be here. I only knew about a few couples. What happened?"

Leena blinked, sending tears flowing down her cheeks. She snatched a tissue out of the box behind the toilet and dabbed her face. Bruce was not sympathetic at all. He saw her emotional outburst a as sign of weakness and a possible detriment to his business and his standing in the community. His lack of sympathy made more tears fall. "I want to go home, Bruce."

"What did that woman *say*?"

"She said pretty awful things about Jackie, not that *you* care. She was at that book club the other day too, and she managed to give her a few zingers there too. I just can't stand her. She's a snob and a bigot!" Leena said, sniffing and dabbing her eyes with a tissue. "She accused Jackie of being a prostitute, Bruce!"

"Look, it's unfortunate that you were seated next to her, but can we please get through the rest of the evening without incident? Dinner's over and it will be better. We won't stay much longer, I promise," Bruce compromised. "Come on," he coaxed her, putting his hands on her shoulders.

Leena knew she wouldn't win. Dinner was over, she reasoned. "I'll be out in a minute, okay? Give me a minute." Leena was nodding her head in her own agreement to pull herself together.

Bruce rubbed her arms and squeezed them at the bicep. "Okay, good girl. I'll see you in a few then." He kissed her forehead and left, dreading any questions regarding the incident.

The guests had started to rise from their assigned seats and mingling started anew in some of the other rooms adjacent to the dining room. Most of the guests didn't notice a thing and Bruce was relieved. His pal Marcus came up to him and asked if everything was alright.

"Everything's fine. That Miller woman is a little hard to take, apparently. Can't say that I blame Leena." Bruce said in defense of his wife.

"Tell Leena not to take it to heart. She had Carol cornered earlier and I got an earful that I didn't come rescue her." The two men laughed lightly. Bruce saw Leena approach.

"How are you feeling, hon?" Bruce asked her.

"I'm fine. Hi Marcus, I didn't get a chance to say hi to you earlier, I'm sorry," Leena said.

"I was just telling Bruce that you should not take anything Gloria has to say seriously. She is a well-known busy-body. Carol was cornered earlier and she was *not* happy."

"Thanks, Marcus. I shouldn't have let her get to me like that."

Bruce put his arm around Leena's shoulder and squeezed her toward himself as if to reward her for coming around.

The rest of the evening went smoothly. Leena avoided eye contact with Gloria. Leena enjoyed being included in a circle of people as they discussed the pros and cons of owning their own business. Leena fit right in.

The men, predictably, separated from the women and many of them were in the study smoking cigars and having a nightcap. The women stayed in their klatches discussing tennis, yoga, fashion, dieting, and men. Giggles from the women and guffaws from the men came together in midair with Vivaldi's *Four Seasons*, creating a din.

Gloria and Ashton had left around nine. Leena and Bruce left a little before ten. They said their goodbyes and thanked the hosts for a wonderful evening.

Leena drove home. Bruce had imbibed a bit too much to be trusted behind the wheel. He went straight up to bed and was snoring within minutes. Leena slept on her futon in the office. It seemed like the right thing to do.

CHAPTER 15

"Hello?"

"Hey, it's Rick, remember me?"

"Hell, yeah I remember you. What's up Dog?" Jackie asked.

"You feel like comin' out with me and a few friends tonight? Like, I could swing by and get you? I'm meetin' 'em at *The Vibe* up on Route 1 in Westerly. You heard of it?"

"Sure, I heard of it. I'm game. I'll be done around 9:30? Is that okay?"

"Purr-fect."

"Okay. So like, I'll see ya."

"Yes you will."

Jackie could hardly contain her emotions. She looked at Hal and, in the absence of Leena, went over to him and told him about her date. The biggest smile filled her face. "Remember Rick, Hal? He's coming by later and we're going out!"

"That's wonderful, Jackie," Hal said politely.

"You remember him, well, him and his dad's band? They played here a while ago?"

"Sure, I do."

Leena walked in from the dining room and Jackie ran over to her and hugged her.

"Rick called and he's going to come by later after my shift and we're going out. Isn't this great?" Jackie twirled around. Leena and Hal looked at each other and smiled.

"Where's he taking you?" Leena asked Jackie.

"*The Vibe*, it's not too far from here."

Becky walked into the kitchen and Jackie told her about her plans. Becky said, "He's a hottie. Don't you think he's hot, Mom?"

"I'm too old to think someone that young is 'hot.'" Leena thought about it and smiled and said, "Okay I think he's hot."

The three of them laughed.

"What are your plans, Becky?" Jackie asked.

"Chris'll be here soon. We haven't decided what we're doing yet."

"Come by *The Vibe* later and join us!"

"Wait a minute, she's still only seventeen. You're not going to a bar. And you," Leena looked at Jackie. "You're nineteen, but the drinking age in this state is twenty-one, you know."

Becky rolled her eyes. "I'm not going to drink, Mother. We're not into that."

Jackie didn't mind the warning the way Becky did. She loved the fact that Leena was looking out for her. She said, "I know. I'll be careful. Thank you, *Mother*." Jackie said. She giggled and ran to her room.

RICK'S CAR PULLED UP behind the building near the kitchen entrance. He knocked at the door and Leena let him in. Rick stood in one spot, rocking, with his hands in his pockets. Leena observed what a handsome young man he was, although a bit scruffy. They chatted about his father's band and Leena asked how long his father had been at it. The answer was twenty-eight years.

When Jackie finally emerged from her room, they both couldn't help but notice her beauty. She had let her long brown hair down. She was wearing a shirt that showed her belly ring and her shapely bosom. Her jeans rode low on the hip. There was quite a noticeable transformation from waitress to civilian. Rick couldn't take his eyes off her. Leena watched their attraction.

"Hi," Jackie said timidly.

"Hi, you ready?" Rick said without taking his eyes off her.

"Yup." With a big, wide smile, Jackie hugged Leena goodbye.

"You be careful, young lady," Leena whispered in Jackie's ear.

Jackie looked right at Leena and said, "I will, I promise." She kissed her cheek and they left.

IN THE PARKING LOT of *The Vibe* Rick dug into his pocket and pulled out a license that had someone else's name on it. "Here, you'll need this. They card at the door."

Jackie looked at the card and it had a picture of a woman on it with shorter brown hair. She didn't see the resemblance, but at a quick glance, she'd pass. The name on the card was Dolores Martin and according to her birthday, she was twenty-three. "Dolores? What a geeky name," Jackie laughed.

"If they ask you what year you were born in say what's on the card, so you'd better memorize it," Rick said.

They got in with no problem. The bouncer looked quickly and waved them by. *The Vibe* was hopping. Rick led the way through the crowd and met up with his friends. He yelled above the music, "Jim, Andrea, I'd like you to meet Jackie." They all exchanged pleasantries.

Rick went to the bar and came back with two beers. "Cheers. Here's to us." Rick and Jackie clinked their bottles and drank.

The intense beat of the music pulsed through their bodies. A young man rapped while his DJ spun records and rapped backup vocals.

"He's pretty good… for a white guy," Jackie said to Rick, laughing. Rick nodded.

After a few songs, Rick motioned to Jackie to follow him to a back room where the music was less intense. "Jim, we'll be back here," Rick yelled, pointing. Jim nodded.

There were two pool tables and four pinball machines. Many of the men turned to look when Jackie walked through the room. They found a small table in the corner and sat down. Rick pulled his chair right next to Jackie's chair.

Rick spoke. "I'm really glad you came tonight, Jackie, I mean Dolores." They both laughed.

"I'm glad I came too," she said staring at him.

"What do you do, besides play in that band? Jackie asked.

"I've been in construction mostly. The company I'm working for is putting in a residential development right over the border in Connecticut. I'm really busy. The pay is good. How long you been working at that place?"

"Just since May. Leena's been super nice to me and gave me a pretty good opportunity. She's been like a mother to me."

"Really?"

"She's so nice. She really seems to care about me. She offered to let me live at the inn in my own little apartment, and work there too, of course. You living at home with your parents?"

"No, I moved out last year. Saved up and got out. It was time to go. But they're cool, my parents. I see 'em a lot."

Their conversation stopped. They stared instead. Suddenly Rick leaned over and kissed Jackie. He took hold of Jackie's hand under the table. When they parted he stared at her without blinking. Jackie found his intensity hard to take. She loved it but it made her self-conscious. She looked down as if she was looking into her comfort zone. When she raised her head, he was still staring at her. His head was resting on his hand.

"I kinda liked that," Rick said. He leaned into her across the small table and kissed her again. His eyes were half-closed. "I could get used to this." He opened his eyes and smiled, and kissed her again.

She quickly looked around the bar to see if they were being watched. His kiss was what she wanted, but the last time she was in a similar situation was the night she went down to the bar at the wharf – the night she tried to kill herself. She went cold remembering it.

The music from the jukebox thumped, making conversation close to impossible. Jackie swayed in a mock dance with the man who brought her to the bar. His arms went around her waist, pulling her into him. This man whose name she did not know easily seduced her with compliments and liquor. Jackie put her arms around his neck and dumped her head on his shoulder. She laughed at nothing and lifted her head, grabbing the sides of his face and drawing him to her mouth.

He took her hand and led her outside toward the water and to a place under the wharf. Jackie didn't question where they were going. She sat down heavily on the sand and quickly reclined. He was on top of her, kissing her and putting his hands up under her shirt. He tugged at her shirt and pants. She felt the night air on her exposed breasts. Briefly, she lifted her head but the gravity was too much. She mumbled "No." She grabbed his head to pull him down onto her mouth again. Her signals were mixed. The world was spinning. She dug her fingers into the sand to hold on. Suddenly, she felt him inside of her and she sobered up enough to realize what the sensation meant. She opened her eyes and he was above her. His long, dark hair hung down in her face, swaying with every thrust. He was rough, plunging into her deeply. She whimpered, "Hey!" He didn't stop. "Hmmm," she tried to say something but her head felt disconnected from her body.

"Yeah? You like it? Yeah, yeah?" the man with no name said.

Jackie felt his weight lift off of her. When she opened her eyes, he was kneeling beside her, pulling up his pants. Jackie rolled to her side, away from him, and cried. She heard him say something but she didn't know what. When she turned back over, he was gone and she was lying on the sand alone.

"What's the matter, Jackie," Rick said.

Jackie looked frightened. "Huh?"

"What's wrong? You look like you're somewhere else." He squeezed her hand.

She looked down at his hand and she pulled her hand away.

"Jackie?"

"I'm fine, really. I'm having a terrific time. Hey aren't those your friends over there?" Jackie pointed to the people across the room.

"Yeah. You want I should ask them over?"

"Sure."

Rick signaled to his friends Jim and Andrea and they walked over to their table.

"How 'bout a game of pool, Rickie my boy?" Jim said.

"Let's all play," Rick said. They went to the wall and each chose a cue.

"I'm not good at all," Jackie said.

"So what," Rick said. "I'll show you."

They played teams. Rick and Jackie were stripes. Rick spooned up behind Jackie and put her into position for the next shot. She realized, to her relief, that she was enjoying the lesson. He helped her swing her right forearm bringing the cue stick through in a straight line, sinking the three-ball.

Jackie jumped in the air and gave out a yelp. "Alright!"

"You try it yourself now," Rick said.

With a pouty face, Jackie pretended to be sad without his guidance. She took aim and shot, but her ball missed the pocket. "Next time I'm gonna need more help," she said.

Rick walked over to her and hugged her from behind. He kissed her neck.

They alternated their turns. Their opponents took the win. Another couple came over and asked to play the winner.

"I better get going, Rick. I'm getting up really early to work the morning breakfast shift with Leena," Jackie said.

"We're gonna get goin', Jim," Rick said.

Jim slapped Rick on the back. "Later, dude," Jim said.

"You know it," Rick said.

OUT IN THE PARKING lot Rick put his arm around Jackie's shoulder as they walked to his car. Before getting in he guided Jackie's body up against his car and planted a kiss on her lips.

"I'd like to see you again," Rick said.

"I'd like that too," Jackie said.

They got into his car and headed back to the inn. "My father and I are playing a gig next weekend up in Providence. Maybe you could come see us."

"I'd love that."

"I'll call you about it later this week. Better yet let's do something on Sunday. I don't want to wait an entire week," Rick said.

"Sure, I'm free any time after 10:00 a.m."

They arrived back at the inn and Rick pulled up behind the kitchen next to Jackie's apartment door. He leaned over and kissed her again, only this time for several minutes. Jackie wanted to take it slow. She didn't want another hit and run encounter.

"So call me?" she asked moving away from him slightly.

"I'll come by around one on Sunday," Rick said.

Jackie got out of the car and said, "Okay, see ya, good night."

"Later." He backed out and she watched him drive away.

Once his car was out of sight Jackie started to turn to go into her apartment. Something caught her eye. She looked over at the neighbor's house and saw a curtain moving and a figure behind it in the only room with a light on. Then the room went dark.

AFTER BREAKFAST WAS SERVED to the guests and the kitchen

was returned to its shiny state Jackie and Leena put the second load of laundry into the washer and transferred the previous load to the dryer. Jackie told Leena about her upcoming date. "Rick is coming by around one and we're going to spend the afternoon together."

"That's wonderful. Where are you going?"

"I'm thinking Mystic. I wanted to go to *Mystic Pizza*. I *love* Julia Roberts and that's where they made a film with her in it, you know."

"Yes, I know. It doesn't look like the place in the movie any more. It's been renovated since then."

Bruce walked by in a loud red shirt and announced he'd be back later. He had a golf date with his equally hungover friend, Cam. The two were to commiserate in a golf cart in the midday sun. Leena's eyes glistened and one side of her mouth turned up slightly at the thought of him suffering in the heat. He had embarrassed her again in front of some of the guests the night before. He conveniently forgot about his clumsy and stupid behavior. Leena poked her head outside the laundry room door to watch him leave. She turned to Jackie and made a face that said it all. Jackie laughed out loud. She felt Leena's frustration. "He can be such an ass!" was all Leena said, then returned to the machines.

"So is this serious with Rick?"

"It might be. We really connected the other night at *The Vibe*. That's a cool place. You like hip hop?"

Leena turned to her and made a face as if she had eaten a sour ball. "No, sorry. Why, is that what you went to listen to?"

"Well, it happened to be what was there last night. It changes. He said next week some rock band will be performing. The rapper guy, he was okay but I could hardly understand what he was saying. I like rock and punk rock better. And even some old stuff like Pink Floyd. They're cool."

"Now we're talking. I grew up on Floyd, and the Beatles, Stones, you know. Now it's considered 'old' or 'classic.' Well, it is classic. I don't mind that term. I sometimes feel bad for this generation with the choice of music you have today." Leena added the detergent to the washer and shut the lid. "There. That's done."

"Rick's playing up in Providence next weekend and he invited me to come see him."

"Great. He and his father were pretty good. I was pleased." Leena said.

"You think you'll hire them again?"

"I certainly do. They were better than I thought they'd be. I have a party booked here for the third week in November and they'd be perfect. You want to ask Rick? Or I could give his father a call."

"I'll mention it to him later. Cool."

WHEN RICK ARRIVED, JACKIE floated to the front door on a cloud. She found Leena before they left and told her she'd be back for the dinner shift.

"You're off?" Leena asked her.

"Yes. I'll tell you all about it later."

"Have fun."

In his car, Rick immediately leaned over and kissed Jackie. She felt a little embarrassed but liked it just the same. She smiled and looked down at her lap and put her hand to her mouth. Rick gave her a gentle slap on the knee and drove off. He stared at her more than he should have while driving.

"I had fun the other night," Jackie said, breaking the silence.

"Most fun I had all week," replied Rick. "I don't know what we're doin' today, but I felt like doin' it with you."

"How about Mystic? *Mystic Pizza*?"

"Your wish is my command." Rick turned again and stared at her, alternating between her and the road.

Their conversation was stilted and at times awkward but they found their footing by the time they got to Mystic. Jackie anticipated seeing the restaurant that was in a major motion picture with her favorite movie star, Julia Roberts. She explained most of the movie to Rick, who listened patiently.

"It doesn't look like it did in the movie," Jackie said as she looked around. "Leena was right. She said they renovated it since then." Jackie asked the waitress a few questions about the restaurant but she didn't know anything about it.

Their taste in music was common ground. They had similar stories to tell about attending rock concerts and about their mosh pit bruises. Jackie felt jealous when Rick told her he had seen the Smashing Pumpkins in concert in the mid-90s. They realized they may have been at the same concert the year before last when they both saw Pearl Jam.

AFTER THE DINNER SHIFT at the inn, Jackie unloaded every detail to Leena. She wasn't shy about what she did with Rick. Leena only wished her own daughter was as forthcoming about her relationship with Chris. Jackie didn't leave much to the imagination.

"So we took a detour and we drove through the area where he is working at that construction site." Leena listened while looking in a cabinet. Jackie laughed and confessed, "Of course, being Sunday there wasn't anyone on the site. We were kissing for a while. He's such a good kisser. I mean no one was around!" she giggled. "He's just so awesome, Leena."

"Sounds exciting. New love is very exciting." She turned back around and found the clove jar she had been looking for. She stepped away from the cabinet and sat down at the table with Jackie.

"Things were a little hot and heavy there for a while, there in his car. No one was around. Oh, I said that. Anyway, I almost let him go all the way, but I decided I didn't want to rush things. I did with Kevin, you know, and look where that got me. I really like Rick and I don't want to blow it. Does that make sense?"

"It makes perfect sense, dear," Leena said.

"Rick was very understanding. I like that. He didn't pressure me or nothing." Jackie laughed. "Well, a little. Any guy would, but you know, he wasn't mad or anything."

"Well that's a good sign, don't you think?"

"Yup. He made me feel real at ease and, like, safe. But, I didn't want it to happen in a car. I want it to be more special than that." Jackie looked off in a daze and then turned back, focused on Leena, and asked, "Did you feel this way, you know, like butterflies, when you met Bruce? Is that too personal?" Jackie asked.

"No, that's okay. Um, yes, I suppose I did feel that way, sure. That was a long time ago," Leena said. She and Bruce had been friends for over six months in college and they gradually dated, but usually with others as a double date. By the time they were romantic, they seemed like the oldest of acquaintances. By contrast, her memory of her feelings when she met Michael in high school was very much what Jackie had been describing, and of late, the same emotion, carried over twenty-two years.

Leena related to Jackie's happiness over her new relationship. Leena had to keep hers a secret. Jackie could broadcast hers to the world. She felt some jealousy in the way that Jackie could so talk freely about her new boyfriend. Her light and breezy attitude simply appeared without any reason to hide. *My day will come,* Leena thought.

CHAPTER 16

After leaving their motel room, Leena and Michael went to downtown Mystic and blended into the crowd of tourists. Joining the window shoppers and the young parents pushing their strollers they held hands as they moved with the flow of people. They had no purchases, only ice cream cones which required constant attention.

They could hear the sound of live music coming from around the corner. As they approached there was a young man playing acoustic guitar sitting on a stool in front of a bistro. Green bills piled up like fallen leaves in his open guitar case.

They found an open-air café and stopped to have a bite. Michael and Leena sat across from each other and watched people walk by. The distractions of life all around them quelled their own flow of conversation for the time being.

An abrupt rain shower sent people scrambling for cover. The café had an awning. They watched an elderly couple move a little faster than they suspected they were able to, which made Leena and Michael laugh. The couple stood next to them under their awning for the duration complaining about the downpour. The rain stopped within ten minutes and the sidewalks resumed their orderly chaos.

Michael fished around in his jacket pocket and pulled out a box. "I don't know if you can wear this but I want you to have it."

Leena had been looking in the other direction. She quickly turned around to face Michael. Without saying a word, smiling, she opened the box. Inside was a silver necklace with very intricately designed birds that made up a chain. "Oh, Michael it's beautiful! I'll wear this. I could say I bought it myself. That's what I'm going to do." She proceeded to fasten the clasp behind her neck. Michael helped her.

"It's an antique that I purchased last week," he said.

"Oh Michael, I love it, what do you think?" Leena moved her hair for his opinion. She felt it with her fingertips.

"Gorgeous," Michael said staring into her eyes. "Oh, the necklace, yeah it's nice." They both laughed.

Leena said, "Thanks. It's lovely!" She leaned over and kissed him.

After lunch, Michael suggested taking a walk down by the water. Up to this point it had been a perfect day, rain and all. They walked down to where the water lapped the shore. Leena rolled up the bottoms of her pants to step into the breaking surf. Michael found a shell and gave it to Leena. He grabbed her by the hands and tried to pick her up to throw her into the water. Leena swerved out of the path of this raging bull. The sound of the ocean and the wind drowned out her scream and laughter.

They fell prone on the sand with an exhale. Heaving for their breath, they waited for the proper amount of air to fill their lungs before kissing. A tear clung to the corner of Leena's eye. Her emotions were raw.

"Some of my very fondest memories are of when you and I were together," Leena said.

"Me too. It was the best time," Michael said.

"Remember that dance? Who was the band that night? *The Rain Kings*? Or some silly name like that?" Leena asked.

Michael laughed and corrected her. "No, *The Reigning Kings*. You know, they reign?"

Leena chuckled and said, "Oh, all these years I thought it was *Rain*, like the weather?"

"I think the lead singer, Mike Radkowski, was a history buff or something," Michael said.

"Well, we didn't stick around very long to hear them as I recall," Leena said.

Michael agreed. "No, we didn't."

Folding their arms behind their heads and looking up at the blue sky the memories of their life, long ago, caved in on them, back to that time and place twenty-two years ago.

Behind a scoreboard on the football field was the destination. The music from the gymnasium echoed in the trees and the light from an open side door lit up the embankment. They struggled to get up the hill without slipping. "The spies are not onto us," he said. The chaperones were unaware. Skipping through the misty grass of the football field on their way to seclusion they held hands, guiding each other. The excitement of the moment couldn't be measured in hormones or years of age. No one saw them disappear behind that scoreboard, not the chaperone at the door, nor the one near the band had a clue. "Shhh, come on." The moonlight shone down upon their shoulders creating shadows on the ground that merged. The scoreboard blocked the light from the gym but it didn't block the light from the moon. They lay down in unison with full awareness of the color of each other's eyes. Consent was biding its time: full consent to invite a kiss, and more. Full body contact was not just for football players. A wisp of hair blew across her forehead, momentarily covering her eyes. "That wouldn't do," he thought. He moved her hair and waited for a sign from her. With just a twinkle in her eye and a flicker of an eyebrow, it was understood. Moist and warm kisses, lots of them; leaves in the hair; grass stains on the backs of the jeans. Only later, pulling themselves together, would the crinkling of leaves by their ears alert teenagers in love. They discovered how to fold into each other's thoughts, like a hand in a pocket.

Leena turned her head and looked over at Michael. He was staring up at the clouds. She said, "I wonder what this relationship will cost us." Michael turned to look at her and took her hand, braiding their fingers together. She continued, "My heart won't take it if you leave me again." Leena said. "I love you, Michael. I don't care if that scares you. I had to say it."

Their eyes were locked, hardly blinking. Michael said, "I love you too." His brow furrowed. "Too much I think." He broke the stare and turned back to look up at the sky again. "I don't know where this is going, but let's agree to take it one day at a time and not do anything rash, or anything we would regret later."

"I didn't say anything about that," Leena said.

"I know, but I feel that's where this conversation may be headed. I mean there are kids involved, businesses, spouses, it would be a mess. So let's just enjoy what we have for as long as possible."

"I know Michael, but…"

"We're together now and that's what counts."

Leena was not sure what Michael was telling her but she heard what she wanted to hear and agreed to keep everything under wraps.

They sat up and held their knees with their forearms and looked out on the water, enduring an awkward moment.

"So far there haven't been too many questions about my whereabouts." Leena finally spoke. "I had to go order wallpaper the other day. I told Jackie and Bruce I was re-papering one of the guest rooms. I was thinking of doing it anyway, but now it looks like I have to do it. Well, after the busy season."

"The things we do for love," Michael joked.

Michael stood up and offered his hand to Leena. They walked along the water. They only had another half hour before they had to leave to go back to their normal lives.

At their cars, Leena wiped her feet thoroughly with a towel and banged her shoes together in an attempt to eliminate all the sand. Michael did the same.

CHAPTER 17

Michael told Leena he would not be able to see her during the coming week. He had a lot of post-sale organizing to do and a few new shipments came in that needed attention. He had no choice. Leena understood completely but was sorely disappointed.

"Maybe we can take a chance and call each other at some point. That way I can hear your voice. These emails don't cut it." Leena wrote to Michael. She did not get another response until the day after. He wrote a quick note and didn't respond to Leena's question about calling on the phone.

Sorry about this week. Can't be helped. I'll talk to you in a few days. Love, Michael.

Leena stewed while she stared at his note. She plotted while she cooked. She secretly cried while showering.

She kept busy with errands throughout the week. In addition to her usual inn-related chores, she needed to fill the hours in-between. On Monday she went shopping and bought herself a few new outfits. She went for a walk at Ninigret on Tuesday. She continued her book club on Wednesday even though she was far from done with the selected book, and she subjected herself to Gloria seated across the table. Thursday, she organized cupboards, polished woodwork and cleaned out her refrigerator. On Friday while tending to some of the guest rooms she noticed the faucet in room eight still dripped incessantly. Bruce said he had fixed it.

When Bruce got home that Friday from work, he plunked himself down in front of the television with his usual beer. There on the floor next to the television cabinet was the new DVD player, still in its box. Bruce had promised to install it the week before. There it sat, and there he sat. Leena saw red.

JACKIE AND BECKY RETURNED home from their painting class down at *Parson's*. As they walked up the steps, they met Jason sitting out on the porch with a strange look on his face.

"What are you doing out here, Jason?" Becky asked.

With a worried face, he pointed with his thumb at the house and said, "They are going at it like I've never heard before," he said.

"Mom and Dad are fighting?" About what?" Becky asked.

"I'm not sure, something about a faucet."

"A faucet?" Jackie asked.

"A leaky faucet, I think," Jason said.

Jason stayed outside while Becky and Jackie went inside. They could hear the muffled sounds of yelling above in the kitchen from the inn kitchen. Becky headed toward the door to go up to her home. She gave Jackie a glance before she pressed the code and opened the door. Jackie went to her room. She wanted no part of the turmoil. As Becky opened the stairwell door the volume of voices rose, rising tenfold when she opened the door to their home at the top of the stairs.

"It's fucking annoying, that's what it is, and I am fucking sick of it!" Leena screamed.

"You're just a bitch! Something crawled up your ass and hasn't left for days."

"You want to talk about bugs up the ass? I would LOVE to tell you about how many you have up there!"

"If you don't like the way I fix things then hire a God damn plumber. I didn't go to law school so I could fix pipes!"

"This affects my business, but hey, that's ok, it's not your business is it? You're a *lawyer*, ooh. Watch out, *he's* a *lawyer* and he is *special*," Leena was out of control, unleashing it all. "You've never cared about this place, have you?"

"Get off it, Leena. Get off your rag!"

"Why, so you can watch that TV? What show is so important that you can't fix that fucking bathroom?"

Bruce took a deep breath and calmed himself so he could make a statement. "I'm not going to fix one single thing now. How do you like that? Put that in your *pipe* and smoke it."

Becky had slipped into her room quietly and closed the door. Her arguing parents didn't notice she was home. She heard every word through the wall.

Leena snapped. "You've never given a shit about a thing around here, the kids, this marriage, the house! I'm sick of it!" She screamed at the top of her lungs. "And were you ever going to get around to hooking up that DVD player or were we just going to admire it in its box?"

"Right, that'll get me to do it. You have such an inviting tone." Bruce fought back.

"You're just a drunken idiot," Leena yelled.

Bruce was done. He turned heel and walked down the hallway and into their bedroom and flung open a closet and some drawers. A few minutes later he walked out into the hallway with a small suitcase and said, "When you come to your senses, give me a call. I'm outta here." He walked toward the stairwell. Becky came out of her room and Bruce stopped in his tracks when he realized she had been in the house. He stared at her but didn't know what to say. He looked down at the floor and left without saying another word.

In another world there would have been a white flag. The air was polluted with hostility. *The end won't come soon enough*, Leena thought. She was sabotaging anything that was left of the marriage. It took every bit of energy to keep her secret about Michael. She wanted to throw it in his face and then watch him burst into flames. She had always expected more from him and the marriage – she pushed and pulled but he had never budged more than an inch in eighteen years. Leena had declared war over territory but it was really a war of love. She knew she had pushed him too far. It was intentional in an underhanded way. She wanted to break him loose from his inertia.

Her anger eventually dissipated and she was left with the residual side effects. She suddenly felt like a coward. Avoidance of issues and the clatter of guilt in a head already full of thoughts, unwanted thoughts pushing aside the desired ones. Resentment for Bruce rose again. It was a vicious cycle.

WITHIN AN HOUR BRUCE called the house from his cell phone. Becky answered. "Hello?"

"Hi, honey it's Dad."

"Hi, Dad! Where did you go?"

"I just wanted you to know I'm fine and I'll be back tomorrow, I just needed some air. She needs to cool off without me there. Everything'll be fine. Where's Jason?"

"He's in his room."

"Is that where he was when your mother…" Bruce rethought what he wanted to say. "Where was he when …"

"He was outside. He heard you guys fighting if that's what you want to know. So he went outside. I think you guys scared him," Becky hoped he felt bad.

"We didn't mean to. Would you put Jason on the phone for me? I want to tell him I'll be at his basketball game tomorrow."

"Ok, I'll get him. Hold on." She put him on hold and then intercommed Jason in his room. "Pick up, it's Dad," Becky said.

Jason picked up and Bruce conveyed his apologies. "Hey, kiddo. I'm sorry your mom and I had a big fight."

"That's okay. I've heard it before. No big deal," Jason said, hiding the fact that it scared him this time.

"Well, I just needed to give Mom some space and I wanted you to know that I'll be at your game tomorrow. It's at 2:00, right?"

"Yep, that's right."

"Okay, kiddo. I'll see you then."

"Bye Dad."

JASON FIDDLED WITH THE radio buttons as Leena took him to his basketball game. He found a song he liked and bobbed to the beat.

"Jase, I'm sorry about all that yelling yesterday. I really am," Leena said alternating her head back and forth to watch the road and to see if Jason was reacting to her statement.

He looked at her then back to the radio buttons.

"I feel bad if I scared you. So, I'm sorry," Leena struggled.

"That's okay Mom. I understand. You were mad about the faucet and stuff."

If only it were as simple as plumbing, she thought.

"Well, I shouldn't have been mad about a dumb faucet. It's pretty silly now that I'm thinking about it."

"Did you talk to Dad yet?" Jason asked.

"No, honey not yet. I will though."

"You can talk to him now. He'll be at the game. He called last night and said he'd be here."

"Oh, really? Good, I'll see him there and that'll be good." Leena said.

She pulled in and she saw Bruce's car in the lot. "I'll be in in a minute, honey," Leena said. Jason got out and walked over to Bruce's car. Leena stayed in the car and watched as Bruce got out and gave Jason a pat on the back. He said something to him and Jason went into the gym. Bruce saw Leena and walked over to her car.

"Can I get in?" he asked, through the open window.

Leena nodded.

They both stared straight ahead for a minute without speaking. Finally, Bruce spoke. "Look, I don't know what brought on your outburst yesterday, but I think we can both agree that it is not healthy." He stopped and sighed. "I said some things I wish I hadn't said, and I'm sorry. Do you want to talk about what's really bothering you? It can't possibly be about that faucet?"

Leena felt embarrassed and guilt put a knot in her stomach. She wanted to patch it up the way she usually did, but she wasn't sure if she wanted to ruin the progress, as she saw it, of turning Bruce off.

"I apologize," she said, reluctantly, staring straight ahead. "I was pissed. Things like that just get to me every once in a while. It was wrong of me to scream at you like that. It was about the faucet, but I guess it wasn't. I need stuff done at the inn and I either have to hire someone or you'll do it. So when you say you'll do it and don't, it's like, I don't know, a bomb goes off in my head. And I don't like your drinking. You tune out and fall asleep on the couch. For quite a long time now you have been ignoring me and I've gotten used to it but the resentment rears up in me and it comes to the surface. When you act like an ass when you've had too much to drink, that's when I wish you'd ignore me."

"Look, just 'cause you hardly ever drink and I like a cocktail from time to time…"

Leena cut him off. "From time to time? Try every single night."

"Well, maybe a few drinks would soften you up and not make you so edgy and negative all the time." Bruce's ire was flaring up.

"Are we going to continue our fight right here in the parking lot?" Leena asked.

Bruce sighed and slumped in the seat. "No, of course not. Maybe we should talk later when we're both calm and focused. We need to discuss our options and strike a deal, okay?"

Always the lawyer, she thought. She nodded.

"I will try to pay more attention to you from now on. We should work on our relationship."

Oh God, what have I done? Leena thought. *This is not what I wanted.* "Let's go in and see Jason's game," Leena said.

CHAPTER 18

Anyone witnessing Becky's reaction to Chris's departure for college would have thought he was going off to war. Chris Felton sat like the Lincoln monument on the front porch with Becky sitting on one of his knees with her arms around his neck. Time had run out. Becky couldn't delay the inevitable.

Chris eventually worked his way down to his car where it was parked at the curb. "I'll be back in three months. Now, come on now, lighten up, will ya?" Chris said into her hair. Her arms were around his neck again.

Becky sniffed and wiped tears off her cheeks with the back of her hand. "This is so hard. I didn't think it would be this hard. You're right. Three months. Three *months*! That's too long!" Becky started to cry again and collapsed back onto his shoulder. "Call me when you get there, okay?"

"You know it," Chris said. With their foreheads touching he said, "Love you Becky. You're my girl, you know that."

"Love you too." Becky cried. "Call, and write, and then call some more."

Chris drove off, and as his car turned the corner Becky slowly pivoted, and went inside the inn, through the kitchen, and past everyone without speaking. She went straight up to her room to sulk. Leena knew better than to try to talk to her at that point.

Becky came back down later and walked slowly through the kitchen and approached Hal and lingered to watch him wrapping a fish fillet around a wad of stuffing. She continued to walk along the counter stopping in front of a freshly frosted cake. Leena had her face in her guest book but turned every so often to watch Becky. Becky raised her hand and extended her index finger moving toward the edge of the cake to sample the frosting.

"Don't even think about it," Leena scolded. She had already shifted in her seat to observe.

Becky froze and looked at her mother, then looked at Hal and Michelle, who had also turned to see what Leena was talking about. Becky lowered her hand down to her side and walked away from the counter. She plunked herself down into a chair across from her mother and folded her arms across her stomach. She remained silent as she reached across the table to fiddle with a pen.

"You want to talk about it?" Leena asked.

Becky looked over at Hal and Michelle. They had returned to their tasks. Still silent, Becky shrugged, looking down again at the pen she was twirling on the top of the table.

"Come on. Let's go out on the front porch." They both stood up and Becky followed Leena outside.

Becky picked up Jasper, who was sleeping in the sun on a chair, and put him on her lap. Leena sat down in the chair next to her daughter. "Life is not over. Chris will be back at Thanksgiving. I know it seems like forever but it will pass, you'll see. You've got to concentrate on your life and what's ahead." Leena paused and waited to see if Becky would speak. Leena continued. "You need to start packing for your own college experience. Going to art school has been something you've been talking about for *years*! You'll meet plenty of new…"

"Please, Mom, don't tell me I'll meet some other guys. Chris and I are committed."

"I wasn't going to say you'd meet another guy. Just that you'll meet new *friends*, that's all. And you'll have fun. You'll see."

"I'm afraid, Mom."

"Of what, honey?"

Becky shifted her weight in the chair, putting her foot up under the other leg. "I'm afraid Chris will meet another girl and fall for her. I mean, Chris is so cute, so athletic, the girls will be all over him."

"If it's true love, honey, it will work out. Besides, it's out of your control."

"Yeah, that's what I'm afraid of." Becky looked out at the water. The two of them sat quietly. Becky stroked Jasper's fur and looked down at him. She turned to her mother and said, "Didn't you lose the love of your life after he left for college? Didn't it fall apart when he came back at Thanksgiving?"

Leena looked at Becky. "I can't believe you remember that old story. I shouldn't have told you about that. Look a year or so later I met your father and you and Jason wouldn't be here if it weren't for that. I mean, Fate's a funny thing." Leena was rambling. She was trying to see the positive side of picking Becky's father. "Looking back now I can see that it's difficult to commit to another person at such a young age. I think it's near impossible to commit that young. But, like I said, if this is the real deal with Chris you will both stick it out." Leena felt like a hypocrite. She felt the exact same way Becky did. She saw Michael as the love of her life and she thought they'd end up together forever.

Becky nodded and realized there was nothing she could do about it at that point. "I wanted him to come home for Wendy's wedding, but he can't. They have to budget their airfare and all."

"That makes sense. He doesn't even know Wendy. We're all going to have so much fun, you'll see."

They sat out on the porch for a little while longer talking about their dresses for the wedding. Leena had to return to her duties for the dinner crowd.

A WEEK FOLLOWING CHRIS' departure Becky was packed and ready to leave for college. Becky's mood had lifted considerably. She had been receiving nightly calls from Chris.

"I'm gonna miss this place, my room," Becky looked over at Jason. "I don't think I'm going to miss you, my pain in the ass little brother." Jason stuck his tongue out at her.

"You're not exactly going to be far away from home. You can come home any weekend you want." Leena told her. "Bruce, you ready to go?"

"I'm ready. Let's hit the road." Bruce said. "Jason, let's go."

It had been quite a while since the entire family did something together. The last time they had taken a trip together was four years ago when they all went to Disney World. Jason decided to go along for the ride. Deep down he was going to miss his big sister but he wouldn't admit it.

BECKY'S DORM WAS NICE but very small. Her roommate had not arrived yet. They stayed for an hour chatting with some of the other parents and compared notes on their empty nests. One of the mothers was crying and carrying around a bunch of balled up tissues in her hand.

Leena felt a little sad but at the same time happy for her daughter to move on with the next phase of her life.

Leena remembered her first year at college. She was scared. She didn't know a soul and felt confused about what she was even doing there. She had not declared a major - not unusual for a freshman - so she started with a liberal arts program. By year two, she went into business management. She could only hope that what she learned at college was paying off as a business owner. It was that year she met Bruce.

When it came time to leave, Becky looked a little nervous and was looking for a few hugs that Leena was glad to give to her. Bruce went over to her and put his arm around her shoulder and told her that he was proud of her and that he'd miss her, and then he hugged her. When Becky pulled away, she had a tear rolling down her cheek. Leena watched Bruce's interaction with his daughter and was surprised by his emotions. She knew this was not an easy thing for him. Jason went over to Becky and they gave each other a quick hug. They eventually left the dorm with Becky in it.

The car ride home was quiet. Leena couldn't really miss her. Becky was not very far away from home, only about fifty miles. Leena figured she'd come home often. Becky, the child she had before completing college, was going off to college and would be turning eighteen in October.

How did time slip by so fast? Leena thought. She too would be having a milestone birthday next year: turning forty.

CHAPTER 19

Jackie stood on the porch wearing a long, flowing summer dress. Her shift was over and she had hurried to get ready for Rick. Now she waited for him, leaning against the railing, pushing her face into the warm sea breeze.

They did not have plans to go anywhere special, only plans to get together. Jackie felt she had done enough waiting.

The sound of loud rock music arrived right before Rick's car came around the corner. Jackie straightened up and looked in the direction of the sound. A smile found her face as Rick pulled up to the curb. Jackie motioned for him to park in the back. The music stopped abruptly with the engine. Rick got out and wasted no time, giving Jackie a hug and a kiss. Jackie swooned.

"Where do you want to go tonight?" Rick asked.

"I don't know. I don't care. Wherever you want to go is fine with me."

"We could go get a bite somewhere. Go back to *The Vibe* later? There's a punk rock band playing there tonight."

Jackie didn't want to go there but didn't want to say no. She wanted him to herself. "That's fine, I guess."

"You don't sound too enthused. You suggest." Rick said. He stared at her with his big blue eyes. His straggly, dirty-blonde hair hung down, framing his face. She was addicted to his smile: One front tooth slightly overlapped the other.

"You want to just hang out in my apartment? I've learned some recipes from Leena and Hal. I made some chicken Parmesan."

"A home-cooked meal? Why didn't you say so? Let's go."

They entered the side door into the kitchen. She got her chicken dish out of the refrigerator and put it into the oven to heat up. Then she unlocked the door to her apartment. Jackie rubbed her hand on the wall to find the switch. Rick immediately looked all around.

"Nice. So this is your apartment. Very nice. You work and you get room and board?"

"Yes, that's right. We've worked it out. I keep my tips from waitressing, so I can have spending money and I can save a little. Leena has helped me a lot. She helped me set up a bank account. That was a first for me. She enrolled me in an art class. She's helped…"

"Leena is really something," Rick said. "It sounds like you both have a nice relationship."

"It's been nice. She saved my life." Jackie said, but Rick didn't pay attention to the comment because it didn't sound literal. "She's been like a mother to me," Jackie added.

"That's really great. I like her. I get a good vibe off her. She's not all uptight like some older people."

"I don't like her husband Bruce much."

"I didn't really meet him, did I?"

"I don't think so. He seems mean and kind of snobby. Well, not kind of, he *is* a snob. They fight sometimes. I can hear them yelling down here in my room. They live above me."

"So they work together all day here? No wonder they argue. They're damn sick of each other," Rick said with a laugh.

"No, he works in Westerly. He's a lawyer. I think he thinks that he's better than everyone else 'cause he's so educated and all that. He thinks his shit don't stink."

Rick laughed. "You're funny."

"Let's not talk about him. I'll lose my appetite."

Their conversation stopped for a brief time. Rick walked around the apartment, looking it over.

"It'll be another twenty minutes or so before my dinner is hot. You wanna take a walk outside?"

"Sure." Jackie showed him to the door that led to the outside. He put his hand on the door, preventing her from opening it. He scooped her up and carried her to the couch, gently placing her down on the cushions. He sat next to her, leaned over and kissed her. They lay on the couch for many minutes kissing. Finally Jackie said, "Let's wait." She meant what it sounded like. "Let's take a walk before dinner."

Rick got up. "You're the boss. Lead the way."

They took a slow and meandering stroll down the street along the water. Jackie pointed out how the lay of the land allowed a view of sunrises and sunsets. They chose a large boulder and sat and watched the sun come down to the surface of the water. The reflection, as bright as the sun, broke up into a million pieces. As it touched the ocean, they both said "Ah!" They kissed. They turned and watched the sun sink below the earth. The sky transformed its purples and oranges into muted gray tones.

"I think dinner is ready now," Jackie said.

Back at her apartment Jackie went into the kitchen to get the chicken Parmesan. She served it onto two plates and brought them back to her apartment."

"I don't want to eat in there. I don't want to run into him. You don't mind eating on the sofa?"

"Nope. Just hook up my feed bag anytime any place." He took a fork-full and blew on it and ate it. "This is very good."

"Hal showed me this recipe. I made key lime pie for dessert. Leena taught me that one."

"You're going to spoil me. You got any beer?"

"Sure." Jackie went back to the inn and took two beers out of the refrigerator and brought them back.

After eating they got comfortable on the loveseat. Jackie had turned on the little television which sat on a shelf. Rick had his arms up on the back of the sofa. "That was great. Being here with you is great."

"You want dessert now?"

"I'm stuffed. Later, Okay?"

"Okay."

The TV show was silly. A similar one came on after the first. The bursts of laughter from an unseen audience didn't seem to add up. Maybe it wasn't funny because Jackie was anticipating Rick's next move the whole time.

They sat close together. Rick slid down and put his head on Jackie's shoulder. He turned his head to look at her. She smiled, but kept looking straight ahead at the show. He nibbled her neck and she laughed saying, "That tickles."

Rick sat up straighter and took Jackie's chin in his one curled index finger and guided her to face him. He moved his lips slowly across her cheek and brushed her mouth with his lips. He still had not kissed her. His hair tickled her cheek. She closed her eyes and waited for it, wanting it. He rubbed her nose with his nose, and then just when she thought he'd never kiss her, he did.

Soon the loveseat was too confining. Rick stood up in front of Jackie. He stared at her without speaking and lifted his shirt over his head. He kicked off his sneakers and took Jackie's hand to guide her to a standing position.

"Show me where you sleep," he said.

JACKIE STARED AT RICK'S profile. A tear ran down the side of her cheek and was absorbed by the pillow. Rick looked over at her.

"Hey, why the tears?"

Jackie quickly wiped her cheek with the palm of her hand and said, "It's nothing. I don't know. I'm just feeling a little emotional."

A big grin slowly crept onto Rick's face revealing his overlapping teeth. He said, "Well you're gonna be crying a river from now on because I intend to rock your world as much as possible."

Jackie laughed and then got serious. "I don't think I've ever felt …"

Rick propped his head up onto his hand. "Felt what?"

"That was pretty awesome. How'd you learn to do that?"

Rick laughed out loud. "Like, did I take a class or something?"

Jackie felt embarrassed about her comment.

"Hey, cutie," he lifted her face with his hand, "I don't know what I did right, but it just comes naturally with you. You bring out the best in me, that's for damn sure."

Rick got up, still naked, and went to the bathroom. He came out and went into the living room and got their beers, bringing them back to the bed. He lay back down on the bed, on his side, and propped himself up on his elbow and said, "A toast," he held the bottle up in the air, "to us." They clinked their bottles together and drained their contents.

They lay together in Jackie's bed the rest of the evening, talking and eventually making love again. Rick fell asleep right away. At some point during the night, sleep found Jackie.

THE SOUND OF SOMEONE knocking at her door woke Jackie up. She popped her head up and saw Rick sound asleep next to her. Jackie grabbed her bathrobe and went out to her living room and opened the door.

On the other side of the door in the laundry room was Leena. "Did you forget? You're doing breakfast this morning with me?"

"Oh, Leena I'm so sorry, I forgot. I'll be ready in a minute." Then Jackie motioned to Leena with her head and smiled.

"What?" Leena asked, puzzled.

"He's here."

"Who, Rick?"

"Yes, Rick. He stayed over." Jackie lowered her voice to a whisper. "I'll tell you about it later."

"Look, you stay. I'll manage alone. Don't worry about it, really." Leena said.

"I can be ready in a few…"

"Seriously. Don't worry. I'll talk to you later."

"You sure?"

"I'm sure." Leena gave her a warm smile and turned around and left.

Jackie gently shut the door and went back to the bedroom. Rick was still asleep. Jackie looked at the clock that said 7:07. She yawned. She could hardly keep her eyes open. She got back into bed and fell right back to sleep, not waking until after ten o'clock. It wasn't a knock at the door that woke her this time.

JACKIE'S SMIRK AND RICK'S cowboy demeanor revealed exactly what happened the night before. Sitting at the kitchen table together Jackie had cooked breakfast for the two of them. Leena came through the room.

"Rick, hello. Good to see you again." Leena looked over at Jackie who was having trouble keeping her eyes off her new beau. "This looks like a breakfast fit for a king, and a queen, of course."

"Yeah, we were pretty hungry," Jackie said. They both stared at each other and giggled. Only a videotape of their encounter would have spelled out what she meant more clearly. Rick smeared his toast through his egg yokes and shoved the entire piece into his mouth.

"You're planning on working tonight, right Jackie?" Leena asked.

"Of course. Leena, I'm so sorry about this morning." Rick looked at her, puzzled.

"No problem. It happens." Leena didn't want to burst her bubble. "Tonight is important. I have a full house this weekend and I would need to know right away if you can't work."

"I'll be there, I promise."

"I've got a gig up in Providence with my Dad, tonight," Rick said.

"See? We both have to work," Jackie said, finding joy in their common work schedule.

"I'm going to run down to the garden center. I'll see you later." Leena left.

JACKIE AND RICK RETURNED to her room later in the day after spending time shopping and walking along the water again. Jackie told him she had to get ready for work. She feigned anger when Rick did not facilitate this. "Rick! I have to get ready."

"I'm ready, so let's go." He grabbed her and carried her to the bedroom.

Jackie managed to get herself in the kitchen on time, reporting for duty. Michelle and Hal were already there.

Bruce found Leena in the dining room. "Can I have a word with you," he asked.

Leena had a handful of silverware. She was arranging place settings. "Sure, what's up?" Leena looked up at Bruce and noticed his angry face. His head was tilted to one side. This was never a good sign. "What?"

"It's about Jackie," he said.

"What about Jackie," Leena continued to walk around the room. Bruce followed her.

"I noticed two beers are missing." Bruce assumed this was enough to inflame Leena.

"You're disrupting my busiest time of the day, of the *week,* to talk about *beer*?"

I'm pretty sure Jackie must have helped herself to it, and I want to know what you're going to do about it."

Leena stopped what she was doing and addressed the issue head-on. "You want me to talk to Jackie, is that what you're saying?"

"Oh, I'll talk to Jackie myself, don't you worry. I wanted to check with you first to see if you had taken the beer. It was missing before Hal and Michelle got here."

"Obviously *I* didn't drink it. I hate beer. Maybe Jason took it. You ever think of that?"

"You can't be serious," Bruce defended his son.

"I hope it wasn't Jason, obviously, but I wouldn't go blasting Jackie before you know."

"Look, I don't really trust her, you know that. She's underage for drinking alcohol, you know. We don't want to get into trouble with serving alcohol to a minor!" Bruce lectured.

"Yes, Bruce *I know*." Leena was annoyed now. "Can you *stop* being a lawyer for two minutes? Geez. I'll *talk* to her, okay?" Leena went back to her chores. Bruce walked into the kitchen. Leena watched him leave.

"Jackie, a word," Bruce said and turned and walked toward the front porch. Jackie followed him. Outside he laid into her. "I'll get right to the point. Did you help yourself to the beer in the refrigerator down here?"

Jackie felt a wave of nervousness. She knew she'd have to tell the truth. "Yes, sir, I did."

"Did you know it was not yours to take? Did you know you are still underage?"

"Yes sir," She looked down at her feet. "I'll pay you back for…"

"The money is not the point. I need you to not take it in the first place. We don't need to get in trouble around here for serving alcohol to a minor. We could get shut down, sued, fined, you name it." Bruce's voice was a little louder as he reached the end of his statement.

A couple who were staying at the inn approached the porch, returning for dinner. Jackie stared at the couple as they stared back at her. They didn't know what she had done but it was clear she was being scolded. Jackie was embarrassed.

"I don't know if it's because you didn't have the right upbringing or what, but you need to follow our rules around here if you want to stay. I think my wife has been *pretty* damn good to you so far, so don't bite the hand that feeds you."

"That's *enough!*" Leena walked up behind Bruce, coming to Jackie's rescue once again.

"I'm handling it," Bruce said, with such a smug arrogance that Leena's blood began to boil.

"No, you're not. You're making things worse. You're doing this in front of guests, *again*! Drop it, Bruce. Don't you have a game to watch at a sports bar tonight? Isn't this cutting into your cocktail hour?"

Jackie watched as the fury in both their eyes escalated. She took the opportunity to sneak back to the kitchen. Bruce didn't notice.

"I thought you didn't want to do this in front of guests. Look who's arguing in front of guests now." Bruce said as if he won the point. He sounded like a child.

"You're right. I don't want to stoop to *your* level. We are done. DONE!" Leena stormed away, furious. She went upstairs to their home where she could cool off. She went to their bedroom and stood in front of the window. Below she saw Bruce pull his Mercedes out of the driveway and speed away. Leena had to pace to calm herself down.

Ten minutes later Leena came back down to the kitchen. Jackie looked visibly upset. Leena motioned to Jackie and they went into Jackie's room for privacy. "I don't think I have to scold you any more than Bruce already has. He has a way of humiliating people. I don't mind you helping yourself to food and stuff, but you do need to stay away from the booze."

"I won't ever do that again, Leena, I'm very sorry. Rick was here and …"

"I understand, I really do. If you are going to drink, and I don't think I can stop you, you need to get it yourself, okay?" Leena spoke very calmly. "I mean, it is true that we could get in trouble for serving a minor."

"I guess it was just an impulsive thing I did. It won't happen again."

"Okay then, I think we can get back to work and have a great evening. Come on."

CHAPTER 20

Michael pulled in next to Leena's car. He winked and smiled at her as he walked past her on his way to the front desk to pay for the room, something Leena could not bring herself to do. When he came out with the key Leena followed him to what was now "their room" in the town of Mystic.

"I feel like I can breathe again," Leena said.

Michael held her in his arms and said, "Breathe."

"I lost it last week, Michael." She looked up at him.

"What do you mean, 'lost it.'"

"I went on a rampage. I was yelling at Bruce for stupid stuff. I know it was because of you. Wait, that came out wrong…"

"I know what you mean, you don't have to explain." He hugged her again.

"I couldn't see you last week and it got to me, plain and simple. That didn't make it right."

"I'm sorry we couldn't meet. I missed you like crazy. Alice asked me why I was acting so moody. She wanted to go out to dinner with some friends of hers and I didn't feel like being social. She kept asking why I was acting different. Finally, I said, 'Let's go.' So we went out with them and, it was cool, I guess. Actually, it was good being with other people."

"I hate the people Bruce makes me hang around with. They're all a bunch of snobs. I think I've changed but Bruce hasn't noticed. Well, he noticed the other day when I flew off the handle."

"You should be careful. You could say something when you're angry that you don't want to say."

"I guess. I mean, maybe that would be a good thing."

Michael looked at her with a scolding expression. "Don't do that."

Leena shrugged.

"I had a gig this past weekend in Storrs," Michael changed the subject.

"Oh, really?" Leena said "I wish I had been there. I'd love to see you perform again. Tell me next time and maybe I can make arrangements to stay at Wendy's."

"Alice was there, so, that wouldn't have worked out."

Leena became silent. Her name was like nails on a chalkboard. She got up and paced.

Sensing her discomfort Michael changed the subject again. "What lunch did you pack today? I see your bag here."

Leena looked down at her bag and momentarily forgot what she brought. "Um, I don't, some sandwiches and stuff." She felt a tear roll down her cheek. She quickly wiped it away.

"This is not a day to be sad, Leen. I thought you were happy to see me?"

"I am happy to see you, you know that. I just think that you're not sure about *us,* are you?"

"I'm sure about us, Leena, I just don't think we should do anything on pure emotion. We don't want to hurt anyone, that's all. No one deserves to be hurt by this. I know you'd agree with that."

"Yes."

"Okay," he said

He sat next to her on the bed. Their silence was an invitation to move beyond conversation. No words were needed when it came to their mutual feelings of attraction. A rush to achieve was set in motion by motivation and instinct. Any idea about what should be done or not done was put on hold. Resolution remained hidden beneath the sheets. Their encounters were a way of going back in time, erasing other lives by degree.

"I have a proposition for you," Michael said. "Alice and Tommy are going to go visit her sister in Massachusetts next weekend. What do you say you come and stay at my house?"

Leena's excitement was palpable. "I would *love* that!" She was up on her elbows. "To spend the entire night together? It's what I've dreamed about."

"Well, this is our chance." Michael kissed her forehead.

Leena smiled and snuggled closer to Michael putting her head on his chest. "I'll tell everyone I'm going to Wendy's to help with the last-minute wedding plans."

"You've got all week to decide about what you'll tell people."

"Michael, I love this idea. I can't wait." Leena stretched her neck up and kissed him on the mouth.

They lay together for a while longer. Michael said, "We still have time today. What do you want to do?"

"Let's go shopping. Let's walk around. I want to walk along the sidewalk and hold hands. That's what I want to do."

"Alright then. Let's go."

They left their room and walked along looking in the store windows, holding hands. They stopped in front of a jewelry store. Leena stared at a display of rings. Michael started to walk again but Leena lingered there. Michael went back to her. He stood by her side as she looked in the window. Neither said a word. They continued on.

The leaves on the trees still clung to the color green, but they had lost the vibrancy they once possessed a few months before. September's sun was less intense now but it was still too hot to take as a direct hit. They found a bench in the shade of an old maple tree and ate the lunch Leena had packed.

"Maybe we can attempt to set up a timeline," Leena tried to sound rational, broaching the subject from a new angle.

"What do you mean?"

"You know, like where we want to be at such and such a date."

"I can't really think in those terms. Not before the holidays. Let's seriously talk about this in January. Fair enough?"

Leena nodded reluctantly. They ate in silence.

"We should head back to the cars," Michael said after they finished their sandwiches.

They walked down the sidewalk and Leena stopped again. "Let's go in here," Leena said when she realized they were standing outside the public library.

"Here? What for?"

"Why not. There's a book I want to look for. I'm thinking I might go back to the book club again."

Michael followed her obediently into the library. "Now we must whisper," Leena said with a smile. Michael nodded.

They wound their way in and out of the isles. Leena found the book. "If I borrowed it, I would have to return the book to some Connecticut library. I should wait until I am in my own state." She shut the book and returned it to the shelf.

Michael stood patiently by her side. "You'll be passing through Connecticut next week."

"I better not leave a paper trail. You know, in case it becomes overdue." She continued to walk and look at book titles.

"Remember when we went to the library after school when you had that paper to do? I was helping you with research," Leena asked.

"I remember. I also remember I did this in an isle." He started kissing her neck. Standing behind her he pressed up against her and put his arms around her waist.

"Michael!" Leena whispered. "What are you doing?"

He turned her around and kissed her. "That's what I'm doing." he teased.

She kissed him back. "We shouldn't be doing this here."

"Why not, there's no one around," he whispered.

"Someone could walk by and see us."

"You didn't feel that way back in high school."

"Yes, I did. I was in mortal fear that Mrs. Bidwell would catch us. But that was high school. We're older now," she said.

"Whatever happened to being young at heart?" Michael took her hand and led her to a staircase.

"What's up here?" Leena whispered. Michael shrugged.

There was a program going on in a room. They could see slides flashing on a screen through the window of the door. Down the hall were some empty rooms. Michael smiled wryly and pulled her into a room and shut the door.

"Michael, what are you *doing*?"

"This." He went back to what he started between the bookshelves.

Standing against the wall, they engaged, careful to be quiet. At the point of no return, they got down on the floor. Leena found her rhythm, matching Michael's. When they caught their breath they pulled themselves together. Sitting on the floor leaning against the wall, they both smiled like children who just got away with sampling grandma's pie cooling on the windowsill.

At that moment, outside the room in the hallway, the meeting had broken up. People were walking and talking. The bathroom doors across from the room they occupied opened and closed.

Leena and Michael scrambled to their feet and stood next to the wall near the door, ready to make a clean getaway. They waited until the last person left and the hallway was quiet. Michael opened the door and looked both ways. They left the room, visited the bathrooms first, and then walked down the hallway toward the stairs. An older gentleman came out of the room where the slideshow had taken place.

"That was a great program," Michael said.

The man nodded in agreement. "Yes, it was. He's a great photographer, isn't he?"

Michael nodded, "Yes he is. Well, good day, sir."

They giggled as they descended the stairs and left the library. Out on the sidewalk, Leena burst out laughing. "You're bad!" Leena said.

"That was fun. I'm glad you suggested the library. Who knew!"

They laughed and held hands all the way back to the parking lot. Michael and Leena returned to their vehicles and stared at each other. Their smiles faded.

"I hate for this day to end," Leena finally said. "I had so much fun."

"Me too. They'll be other days just like it," Michael said.

"I know, but I hate to wait so long. I hate to sneak around. I wish…" Leena stopped, not wanting to spoil the mood with a sore subject.

Michael pulled her up close to him and they kissed. "Let's email each other tonight and make plans for the next weekend."

"Ok, I can't wait," she said.

"Miss you already," was Michael's sign off.

CHAPTER 21

A candle flickered in the middle of the table at their favorite restaurant. The reflection of the flame made their eyes like mirrors, seeing themselves in each other's eyes. Under the soft light of night, it wasn't discovery and mystery that brought them together anymore. It was the comfort of routine and the lack of surprise that made their relationship work.

"I suppose you're going to have the prime rib?" Alice asked, looking at her husband over the top of her menu.

"I might, I might not." Michael looked up from his menu and smiled. "Maybe I'll surprise you."

"I doubt it," Alice said smiling back.

The waiter took their orders.

Michael was quiet. Alice picked up on it.

"Why so quiet? What's on your mind?" she asked.

Michael hesitated. He sat up straight and braided his fingers together, placing them squarely in front of himself, looking right at his wife. "I'm concerned about us."

"Why? What are you talking about?"

"Our plans aren't working out. I thought we'd be pregnant by now. It's been over a year. It's changing us, and I don't like that. I mean, we've been arguing more, and I think it's the tension. I wanted to apologize."

"I don't like arguing either. I hate it."

"I'm sorry, babe. Lately, I don't know…"

"You've been sort of moody."

"It's been a bummer. I won't lie," Michael said.

"That's why I said we should just stop trying. If it happens it happens. I don't think I can go through much more disappointment, Mike. And if it's going to ruin our relationship I don't…"

"Maybe we should try a different way. Like, see a fertility specialist."

"We can't afford that. We talked about that. We've already sunk all that money into the addition."

"I thought it would happen quickly, like the first time. I wanted to get the room ready. Now I'm kicking myself. That money could have gone to in-vitro or whatever."

Alice's lip was quivering. "Maybe it's not meant to be. Maybe we were just meant to have one child."

Michael took her hand and squeezed it. "Sweetie, don't cry. It'll happen. The doctor didn't find any reason it won't happen."

"I'm getting old, too old to have another baby."

"Please. You're only thirty-two."

"That's old for having a baby."

"No, it's not. My cousin, for Christ's sake, had her baby at forty-one!" Alice stared at Michael. "What?" Michael asked.

"You, that's 'what.' I love you," Alice said.

"You're my girl. Besides, Tommy needs a sibling. We have siblings." Michael was relentless.

"And your point is? You hardly talk to your brother."

"I got along fine with Gary growing up."

"Whatever," Alice said looking defeated.

Alice and Michael stared at each other in silence for a few moments. A smile crept onto Michael's face. "You know, *trying* to have the baby is the fun part. Are you ready for me later?" he said with a big grin. "Huh?"

"Yes." Alice smiled and shook her head.

Michael stroked the back of her hand, running his fingers over her wedding rings. He took her hand up to his mouth and kissed it.

ALICE WAS UP EARLY getting ready to go to her sister's house for the weekend. She packed like she was going for a week. Michael shuffled into the kitchen where Alice was finishing up her dishes.

"Good morning, sweetie," Alice said. She stepped closer to Michael and kissed him.

Michael slid his feet across the kitchen floor to the coffee pot and poured himself a cup. "Morning. When are you leaving? I thought it wasn't until later?"

"I'm not leaving until later, but I wanted to be ready. It's the school teacher in me. I'm just planning my day."

Michael sat down at the table and watched her putter around the kitchen. "Where's Tommy?"

"He's in his room. He's packing all his dinosaurs."

"That'll be an extra bag," Michael said. "So do you think you might be pregnant?"

"I don't know," Alice said, laughing at Michael.

"Well, you might be."

"And I might not be. I'm not getting my hopes up."

Michael got up carrying his coffee cup toward Alice. He put one arm around her waist and kissed her on the neck. He moved his hand down lower and rubbed her belly. Alice indulged him. She placed her hand on top of Michael's. "You want to try again?" Michael asked pushing up against her from behind. "We've got time."

"Mike! No, Tommy is right in there," she motioned with her head.

"He'll hear us."

"No, he won't. Come on," Michael buried his face in the hair on her neck. "You know how I am in the morning." He kissed her neck and caressed her body.

Alice turned around and faced him. "You're bad!"

"I know. You love it when I'm bad." Michael pulled her into the bedroom.

A few minutes later, Tommy walked toward their bedroom door and saw it was closed. He knew the rule. He went to the television, turned it on and watched cartoons. Harvey, their dog, jumped up onto the couch with him.

About a half-hour later Tommy's father emerged from the bedroom wearing just boxers and headed for the shower. "Hey sport," he said as he passed him, kissing him on top of his head.

"Daddy! Can you go to Aunt Gabby's with us, please?"

"I wish I could honey but you're going with Mommy. Daddy has to get together with his band later. But I'll see you tomorrow afternoon, okay honey?"

Tommy nodded. Michael went into the bathroom and turned on the shower.

AROUND ELEVEN ALICE HAD the car packed. Michael buckled Tommy into a car seat in the back seat. "See you tomorrow, sport." He kissed him on the cheek.

Michael went around to the other side and hugged Alice and kissed her goodbye. "Have fun with your sister. See you tomorrow. Call when you get there. Drive safe!"

"I will. Bye, sweetie. Love you."

"Love you too. Miss you already." Michael said.

CHAPTER 22

From the vantage point of her car, Leena watched customers come and go at a Seven Eleven. She had been there since two. It was two-thirty. Finally, Michael pulled in next to her. He smiled and motioned for her to get in his van.

Leena got in. Michael said, "Sorry I'm late." He leaned over and kissed her. "You look great," Michael said.

Leena usually dressed casually in jeans and hiking boots, but this day she wore a long skirt with boots and a sweater that was a little tighter than she normally wore. "Thanks."

, Michael didn't linger in the parking lot, fearing he'd be seen by someone he knew. He headed toward his house. He wound his way down many side streets lined with trees and rock ledge on the way to Voluntown. As beautiful as Leena's dream spot was in Rhode Island she envied the residents who had so many trees. The smell of the sea was gone but the fresh smell of forest was just as inviting.

As they neared Michael's street, he requested that she duck down. Humiliating though it was, she agreed. Pine needles gently crackled under the tires going up his driveway. When Leena felt the van come to a stop she sat up and looked around.

She noticed that Michael's property was fairly private and secluded. Neighboring houses could be seen through the woods but not clearly. His house was a small saltbox-style. There was a shed on the side of the property for lawn equipment and bicycles. There was no garage.

"So this is the place. Not much to it, but it's comfortable," Michael said.

They both got out and slowly walked around the property. Leena said nothing, just observed. There was a large boulder in the front near the street. The front lawn was open and sunny; the backyard had more trees and shade. There were a bird feeder and a birdbath on the side. As they walked behind the house there were folded lawn chairs leaning against a rickety back porch. A few toys and a small bicycle cluttered the yard.

Leena looked at the house from the back. It was apparent that a new addition had been recently added. The shingles and the roof didn't quite match the rest of the house.

"It's lovely, Michael. What a nice spot you've got here. Is this something new?"

"Yes, I put an addition on. It's a tiny house, so this was a long time coming. Anyway, I did the construction myself."

"You did? I didn't know you were a carpenter too."

"I like working with my hands. There's a lot of satisfaction to it. I hired a buddy of mine to help too. Once you cut a gaping hole into the side of your house, time is of the essence. I started it last April. It's almost finished." Michael stood proudly with his hands on his hips looking at his handy work. Then he turned to see if Leena was impressed.

"Wonderful. You didn't tell me you were working on your house." Leena said, noting an aspect of his life not revealed. "I can't wait to see the inside."

"Come on," he said.

Opening the door, a big, friendly yellow lab greeted them. His tail wagged so hard Leena thought it would break the leg on a table.

"This is Harvey, Harvey, this is Leena." Michael bent down and rubbed the side of his belly. "Good boy, yeah, that's my boy." Michael looked up at Leena.

Leena bent down and petted the top of his head. Harvey accepted the new friend gladly. He circled Leena and sat in front of her. His tail swept the hardwood floor. He handed her his paw.

"Aww, how sweet!" Leena said accepting his paw as a gesture of friendship. "You didn't tell me you had a dog."

"Come on, Harvey, come on boy." Michael let him outside and he ran all over the yard sniffing and searching. He marked a few trees and then came prancing back with an old tennis ball in his mouth. He dropped the ball and barked at Michael through the storm door. Michael stepped out onto the front step. "Ok, boy, there you go." Michael threw the ball and he ran like a racehorse to get it. "Come on, let's go before he gets back."

Inside was cute and cozy and each room contained plenty of antiques. The motif had an old country farm quality, a style Leena appreciated but never went for herself. He continued the tour through the house. It didn't take long to get to the bedroom. A cold chill came over Leena suddenly. Her happy mood shifted. She stood in one spot. Michael started to walk away.

He noticed she was not following him. "Leena?"

She stared at the bed. "Why didn't I think of this? I'm so stupid!" Leena scolded herself.

"What are you talking about?"

"This is your bedroom with, *her*. I mean, this is *her* house." She stopped and looked at Michael. "It's lovely. She did a nice job. It feels like a real home, Michael, but ... " Leena backed up into the living room and turned around. She looked around and she knew right away that most of the decorating ideas were hers. Maybe Michael found some of the antiques, but she placed them. She looked around and saw a basket full of craft items and needlepoint. The table in the corner had small Matchbox cars on it. The more she looked around the more she was witnessing a home that contained a family. Leena felt like an intruder. She felt her throat close up and she had to choke down the desire to cry.

"Alice definitely gave it the right touch," Michael said, confirming Leena's thought. "Come on let's finish the tour." Michael led her into the new room she had just seen from the outside. "This is the new room." Leena looked around. It was empty except for a cherry dresser and a rocking chair. "This is the new bathroom. This is coming in handy."

"I see," she said.

"I just wanted to expand what we've got. The way it was, it was a two-bedroom, one-bathroom house. You had to go outside to change your mind." Michael laughed as if he had invented the old joke. "Seriously though, it's a guest room. Alice's parents come a lot, my parents, her sister and family come, you know. And having another bathroom? What a luxury!"

Leena was speechless.

Michael took her by the hand and started to lead her away from the new room. He opened a basement door, flipped a light switch on the wall, and brought her down to a dark room. It was definitely Michael's touch: It was painted both red and gray with a dark brown area rug on a cement floor. There were two small windows high up near the ceiling. On one side of the room, there was a sofa and a table with a bookshelf above it. There were guitar and car magazines all over the table. Two guitars were propped up on stands, one acoustic and one electric, and there was a third one in a case. On the opposite side of the room, there was a television on a small table.

"This is my room in case you couldn't tell," Michael smiled sheepishly.

"I love it. It's you," Leena lied.

"I come down here to play and just be me, I guess," Michael stood looking around with his hands in his back pockets.

"It's important to have a place to go and be alone." Leena looked at the guitars. "Play something for me, please!"

He picked up a steel string that had been sitting in its stand. He sat down on the couch. "Let me see." He strapped on a capo, put his fingers on a D chord, and started to pick. She recognized it immediately as *Here Comes the Sun* by the Beatles.

Leena's eyes filled with tears. "I *love* this song! It's one of my favorites."

Leena sat in the chair and gave Michael her full attention. Michael sang the first verse and then they sang together. Leena stopped singing and let Michael finish the song.

Leena got up sat next to him on the couch and hugged him. He was still holding the guitar.

"You have a nice voice," Michael commented.

"Well, so do you," She said and paused then added, "I play guitar too, only not that good."

Michael looked at her in awe, "So you've told me. Play something." He handed her the guitar.

"Oh boy, what have I gotten myself into?" She took the guitar from Michael. She strummed *Across the Universe*, singing along to it cautiously and a bit self-consciously.

"That was good."

"Yeah, right."

"I'm serious. That wasn't bad at all. And besides," he said incredulously, "I don't know that Beatles song! Damn, you're going to have to teach it to me!" He laughed. "I mean it!"

They played and sang for the rest of the afternoon. Waning sunlight poked through the tiny window on top of the room signaling the end of the day. They didn't notice they had not eaten a thing.

"Wow, it's almost five-thirty. Let's take a break and get something to eat," Michael said standing up and stretching out with a yawn. He carefully placed his guitar back into its case. Leena put the guitar she had been using on its stand. They went up to the kitchen.

"Do you want to go out to eat or something?" Leena asked.

"No, let's stay in. I'll cook some omelets, how does that sound?"

"Sounds good."

Leena walked around looking at the contents of the house more closely while Michael cooked. She tried not to be obvious. She walked up to a table that had a handcrafted needlepoint, framed picture of a barn. On the mantle, there were many framed photographs. She stopped dead in her tracks. There she was: Alice. For the first time Leena got a chance to see Michael's wife. In the picture with her was Tommy as a toddler of about three years. They both had warm smiles and beautiful blonde hair. She was pretty and petite. Tommy resembled Michael. There wasn't much doubt about his paternity. There was another picture of the three of them. Michael had a huge smile and was holding Tommy's hand. Alice was up against him. His arm was around her shoulder. It must have been taken fairly recently. Tommy appeared to be around five or six, his present age.

Michael didn't notice what Leena was doing. He was busy cracking eggs, toasting bread, and flipping omelets. Leena had another sudden attack of *what am I doing here*? She was feeling like a home-wrecker. Being down in the gray and red room allowed her to be in Michael's world, without feeling like an intruder.

Leena turned toward the kitchen still standing in front of the fireplace. She had to admit to the feelings she was having. "This is wrong isn't it, Michael?"

He was not paying attention and turned around and said, "Don't you want an omelet?"

"No, I mean, yes that's fine. I said what we're doing is wrong, isn't it?"

Michael turned around, seeing that she had been looking at the photos and understanding what she meant, he gave her a dismissive glance.

"I'm serious. I need to be real here. I have been a distraction to you and some kind of good time, going down memory lane. But you belong here with," she paused to avoid names, then realized they deserved recognition, "with Alice and Tommy."

Michael finished up the omelets and put them onto two plates, then turned off the stove. He put the plates aside and walked over to her. "Look, I *know* that if I were standing in your kitchen with your life all around me, I would be feeling the same way. Maybe coming here was not a good idea. Why don't we head out somewhere tonight?"

"I don't know. Maybe I should go back to Wendy's."

"No, please don't go." He turned to her and their faces were a few inches away. "The couch downstairs is a pullout bed. We'll stay down there."

Leena thought about it and didn't like the idea of leaving him and ending their weekend together. She didn't like the idea of another motel either. "Ok, I guess."

"Good, then it's settled. Now sit down and eat. You're going to need all your strength." He sat in front of his plate and winked at her. Leena sat down and picked at the omelet.

When they were done, they cleaned up the kitchen together. Michael washed the dishes and put them into the dish rack. Leena dried and put them into the cabinet.

While Michael was in the bathroom, she went into their bedroom again to look at it. She sat on the end of the bed and felt how soft and comfortable it was. She turned around and looked at the center of the bed and imagined Michael making love to his wife. She laid her hand down on the bed as if to reach out to the invisible couple. Her other hand went up to her mouth to stop the sound of a whimper. It was a small room with a small bed. She and Bruce shared a king-size bed. His house was a small house, so much smaller than hers. *To live together so closely you must really get along well.* Then she tried to look for a silver lining. She thought *The fact that they put an addition onto the house must indicate a serious need for more elbow room.*

She went over to the night stand and looked down at a romance novel under the lamp. Leena opened the drawer. She lifted a notepad and some blank envelopes to look underneath. There was a crossword puzzle book, pens, hair barrettes and hand lotion. She quickly shut the drawer and felt disgusted with herself for snooping. She went back to the living room to wait for Michael.

MICHAEL GOT SOME SHEETS from the linen closet to make up the pullout bed in the basement. They worked together tucking in the corners. When they were done Michael turned back the top sheet. He lay down on his side, propping himself up on his elbow. He patted the mattress, inviting Leena to join him. She did. They didn't leave the bed until hours later when hunger brought them back upstairs.

Leena was in a strange state of mind. She was happy and sad at the same time. Spending so much time with the love of her life was a dream come true. Being in his house was surreal. She had to constantly stop herself from thinking about Michael's wife and Michael's wife's house. Her selfish need to be with him canceled out all the moral dilemmas when they popped into her head.

"It's weird now, Michael," Leena said. They sat at the kitchen table nibbling Fig Newtons. "I wish we had stayed together after high school. But at the same time, it's hard to say that because I love my kids. I mean, I wouldn't have those kids. But you and I would have had kids, I'm sure. Our kids. I like the sound of that. But it wasn't meant to be, I guess."

"Can't go back, only forward," Michael said so matter of fact. "Can't really let yourself go there, babe. It's impossible to think about life without our loved ones. It's like some other force leads you a certain way, and you have no control over it. Fate is a funny thing."

"Fate brought us back together."

"Yes it did," he said, nodding and chewing.

"I still get sad thinking about how it ended for us. I mean, you got over me just fine when you got to college," Leena said, letting her bitterness show. "You found that girl, Sybil!"

"Oh, Leena! Think about it. I was eighteen. I go off to college, away from my girlfriend, and the opportunity for sex is *right* there. You can't blame me. Sybil made herself so available. I was a horny teenager for Christ's sake."

"We were so young," Leena lamented. "I wish I could go back and do it all differently."

"I won't say that I didn't get married until thirty-three because of you, but I think I got pickier about who I dated and I didn't want to settle." Michael thought this was a compliment.

Leena thought about what he said and she had a sinking feeling in the pit of her stomach. *Did this mean that it was the real deal for him when he met and married Alice?* She had to ask.

"So Alice was 'the one?'"

"Uh oh, I'm getting myself into troubled waters, aren't I?"

Leena waited for him to talk.

"Yes, if you must know, I thought Alice was 'the one' and I love her." He knew right away he hit a nerve, but he couldn't un-ring the bell.

Leena got very quiet. The last thing she wanted to hear was anything the least bit positive about the wife. She saw their new relationship as having a future.

He continued, "I don't want to lie to you. I don't feel like I've hit that dead-end that you and Bruce seemed to have hit. But sometimes I think Alice and I don't have as much in common as you and I do. I think that is the glue you and I have. I feel so comfortable with you now, like I did back then too. I can be myself with you. But I feel like you are going to want a major decision soon, and I don't blame you at all. But there is a boy involved in all of this. I'll tell you right now, I am not ready for that decision. It's not the right time."

Leena nodded, "I know, I know." This was not what she wanted to hear.

"I know I'm sounding like I want my cake and eat it too. I suppose that's true," Michael continued. "But I hate to rock the boat. I don't know what to do. I don't know what I want." Michael got up and paced around the room.

"I just want to be with you, Michael. I have some of the same feelings about not wanting to disrupt my life. I like my life at the inn, and my life with my kids and everything else that goes along with it. Bruce is not a bad guy, actually. I shouldn't paint him to look like the bad guy here. But I am feeling like we've hit that dead-end, like you said. He's not my soul mate, that's for sure. I don't think I ever really loved him. Not the way I should have, anyway."

"That's a real shame," Michael concluded. "You weren't in love when you married him?"

Leena said, "I don't think so. I was pregnant with Becky when we got married. I think we did 'the right thing' more than coming together out of true love."

"How sad." Clearly, Michael didn't relate.

"You've found your soulmate in Alice?"

Michael paused and looked at Leena, and not knowing how to answer her question, he shrugged and said, "Maybe. I mean, what's a soulmate anyway? Some Hollywood ideal?"

Leena was not hearing what she wanted to hear. "I need some air." She went outside.

Michael came out a few minutes later with Harvey who ran around the yard, sniffing. Michael went up to Leena and hugged her from behind. They both looked up at the stars as if to find the answers to such hard questions. He kissed her neck and she moved her head as if to get away from him.

"Leena, you make me very happy."

She turned around and buried her head on his shoulder and cried.

"Let's go back inside," he said. "It's getting cold."

They went back down to the room with the red and gray walls. They spent their first night together. Leena and Michael finally found sleep well after midnight.

SUNDAY MORNING, LAZY AND free, they lay together in jumbled up bed sheets down in the room which separated them from Michael's real life upstairs. Leena looked at the dark and uninspired walls of his basement, and saw the irony in the colors: red and gray. Light did not shine into the room this time of the day. She could have used some. It was within strange and unfamiliar walls where pleasure was fleeting and her soul was wearing down.

"We need to get up and straighten this place out, I hate to say it," Michael said.

"I know, of course. Let's clean up, do the laundry, and get it all out of the way."

Michael was relieved by her willingness to cooperate.

They stripped the sheets off the bed. Michael folded the bed back into a sofa and moved the table back in front of it. They brought the sheets over to the washing machine across the room behind slatted doors. Michael put the sheets in with a few other items of clothing and started the machine.

"You want some breakfast?"

"Not really, just coffee."

He made coffee and put a few slices of wheat bread in the toaster. They sat down together at the kitchen table. Harvey was still curious about the new visitor, and made sure she didn't forget he was there. His tail swept the floor again.

The telephone rang. Michael jumped up to answer it. Leena could tell it was Alice by Michael's demeanor. He turned away from Leena and looked out the window as he spoke. "So how did it go? Uh-huh, yeah?" He did more listening than talking. "Oh not much, just hanging with Harvey." Silence as he listened. "No, Pete wasn't around after all. But, you know, I'm getting a lot of much-needed practice done."

Leena felt disgusted by his ability to lie. *Yeah, practice having sex,* she thought

"Uh-huh, okay. When do you think you'll head back? Good. I know." Michael lowered his voice, but Leena watched him and listened as if her life depended on it. "He did? Aww, how cute. Yeah, put him on." There was a pause. Michael turned back around to look at Leena and made a face, pointing to the receiver he nodded his head and smiled. "Hi ya honey. I know, Mommy told me. You'll have to tell me all about it when I see you later. Okay, put Mommy back on. I know. Love you honey." Michael was still looking at Leena, smiling. When Alice returned to the phone he turned his back again. "I'll see ya later then. I know, yeah, me too. I do too. Yup, bye."

Michael hung up the phone and turned self-consciously around to look at Leena. "She's leaving around two to come home, so she should be here by three-thirty or so." Leena was silent and had a face a mile long. "What?"

"'Me too' what?"

"Huh?"

"You said 'me too.' What was that?"

Michael sighed and for the first time acted annoyed with Leena's possessive side and answered her curtly, "I don't remember."

"How could you forget? You just had the conversation a few seconds ago!"

"I don't think it's any of your business, okay?"

Leena was furious. She stood up abruptly and went outside. Harvey followed her to the door with anticipation of a game with his favorite ball. He remained behind the glass door. Leena went out into the yard. He stood and wagged his tail, watching her.

Leena stayed outside thinking Michael would follow her and comfort her again. She was wrong. She came back inside after five minutes. He was at the table with a cup of coffee and eating some toast.

"Coffee's ready. You want some toast?" he asked.

Leena went to the cupboard and found a mug and poured her coffee, put the cream and sugar in, and sat down with him at the table. She sipped it in silence.

"We went over this already," Michael said, laying down the unwanted ground rules again.

Leena looked into her coffee and up at Michael's face when she knew he was looking away. He finally caught her looking at him and he took her hand in his and gave it a squeeze. "Can't I love two women at the same time?"

Leena didn't like being lumped in with Alice. "I love you, Michael. Too much, I think. It's sort of scares me." She was crying now. "I *hate* sharing you with *her*."

"*Her* has a name and she's Alice. And whether you like it or not she exists. We exist and Tommy exists. I'm sorry that I got on with my life!" Michael's voice went up. He stood up and leaned against the counter.

Leena cried. "You went on with your life, didn't you? If you loved me so damn much why didn't you fight for me?" Michael asked.

"Foolish pride I guess. Being young and stupid?" Leena sniffed.

"It *is* what it *is,* and we were lucky to come together now, don't you think? Let's enjoy what we have and not make every little thing a big fat drama or a major competition." Michael wanted to change the subject. "You want to go somewhere or do something?"

Leena sat and cried. She got up and went to the bathroom. When she came out she said, "I guess I should get going. You probably want to clean up or something."

He agreed quickly. "I'll bring you back to your car." Michael left the dishes in the sink but she watched him wash her coffee mug, dry it, and put it back into the cabinet, erasing her presence in his house as quickly as possible.

Without much conversation, they got into Michael's van. Michael put the van into reverse and looked over at Leena. He hoped she'd remember without him telling her but she didn't. She looked at him, puzzled. "You gotta duck down, remember?"

Leena was humiliated again and realized her stay at Michael's house had not been worth it. The emotional toll was high. She ducked down onto the seat and watched the trees go by out the window.

"You can get up now," Michael said after a mile. "I'll bring you by my store if you think you'd like to see it."

"Sure," Leena said as she sat up and put her seatbelt on.

They drove into North Stonington and Michael pulled up to the curb. He pointed across the street to his antique shop. She looked over at the storefront. The sign said *Ever More Antiques.* Leena started to open the door to get out. "What are you doing?" Michael asked.

Leena looked over at him.

"I don't think we should go in. Someone I know might be around here."

Leena shut the door and sat silently looking at the storefront. She finally spoke in a monotone. "Cute name."

Michael explained how he named the store using his last name, Everly. Then he went into detail about receiving antiques from Europe. Leena had stopped listening.

Michael brought her back to her car at the Seven Eleven. "Email me this week, okay?" Michael asked.

Leena nodded and started to get out of the van.

Michael took her hand and kissed it, then pulled her to him and kissed her. She raised her hand and stroked his bearded face. Stealing one more kiss, one more intense hug and one more longing glance she got out and got into her own car. They stared at each other through their windows.

Michael backed out and left.

Leena headed to Wendy's. Michael went back to his small, cozy house with the friendly dog, to finish drying the sheets, putting them away, and covering his tracks.

CHAPTER 23

Jason, Andrew, and Jeremy ran through the yard and through the chairs set up for the guests. The boys stopped in front of the ice sculpture and rubbed their hands on it. Michelle shooed them away.

Wendy had insisted on an ice sculpture for her wedding day. Leena tried to talk her out of it due to the forecast for very warm weather. The heart-shaped ice wreath sat on a table under the tent in the backyard of the inn. Even though it was September twenty-eighth summer was still apparent, taking its toll on the sculpture.

"You were right about that sculpture, Leena," Wendy said staring at the water that had accumulated in the dish.

"Stop worrying. It only has to last for a few more hours. It's designed that way," Leena assured her.

"Andrew, come over here!" Wendy snagged her son when he tried to run by. "Where's Jeremy?"

"He's over there with Jason."

Wendy looked across the yard. She spotted her soon-to-be stepson lifting a rock and looking under it. Jason stood over him. Jeremy was on his hands and knees. Wendy groaned. "Can you and Jason please try to keep Jeremy just a little bit clean?"

"I guess."

"Okay, sweetie. Thanks." Andrew walked over to the two boys.

"They'll be fine. They're boys. They're supposed to be dirty. Come on." Leena led her friend down the hallway to the room where Wendy had spent the night. Wendy sat down in a chair in front of the mirror while Leena helped her with some final touches on her hair and makeup.

"I'm feeling so nervous," Wendy said. "Why is my hair doing this?" Wendy asked as she fiddled with a few strands that seemed out of place to her.

Leena gently took her hands from her hair and guided them down to her sides. Leena put her hands on Wendy's upper arms and said, "Stop. You look fantastic! And of course, you're nervous. You're getting married!"

"That doesn't help," Wendy said.

"Today is going to be perfect. The weather is perfect. You look smashing. Frank looked so cute. I just saw him a little while ago."

"You did? What did he look like?"

"A little nervous too," Leena said as she gently combed Wendy's hair into place and added more hair spray. They both looked into the mirror together. "How's that?"

Wendy inspected her hair. "It'll have to do. What time is it?"

Leena looked across the room at the clock on the dresser. It's quarter to one."

"Fifteen minutes. It feels like an eternity," Wendy said.

"It'll be over sooner than you want it to be."

"You're right. I'm going to enjoy every minute, starting right now." Wendy took in a big gulp of air and exhaled.

"It's your day," Leena said.

They spent a few more minutes primping and preening. "Ready?" Leena asked.

"As ready as I'll ever be."

A few minutes later, out on the lawn, under a trellis of roses, Leena was standing next to Wendy. Frank's brother, Barry, was the best man.

The marriage officiant spoke. "We are gathered here today to join this man, Frank William Snowden, and this woman, Wendy Pulford Lassiter, in matrimony. The bride and groom have written their own vows." He looked at Frank and nodded his head for him to speak.

Wendy, I found love again when I met you. Your presence in my life has centered me and it keeps me standing tall. I am blessed this day to receive your hand in marriage, a marriage that will bring us together and bring our sons Andrew and Jeremy together. I look forward to the future as a loving couple and a loving family. I Frank, take you Wendy to be my wedded wife to have and to hold from this day forward, in sickness and in health, until death do us part.

Frank placed the ring on Wendy's finger. It was Wendy's turn.

Frank, we came together when neither of us expected to find love. Your son, Jeremy, brought us together, and I will be forever grateful. Andrew is lucky to have a new brother. I am blessed this day to receive your hand in marriage, a marriage that will be full from the first day, with love and compassion, until the end of time. I Wendy, take you Frank to be my wedded husband to have and to hold from this day forward, in sickness and in health, until death do us part.

Wendy placed the ring on Frank's finger.

"You are now joined together by love. I now pronounce you husband and wife. You may kiss the bride," the marriage officiant proclaimed.

They kissed. Everyone clapped and cheered.

Leena stood in front of the small congregation beside her best friend and tried not to let everyone see how much she was crying. She quickly wiped tears away with her fingertip before turning around to walk down the aisle. Leena saw a few guests in the audience wiping their eyes, especially Wendy's mother.

A gentle breeze came through under the canopy making Wendy's veil flutter like wings, then resting again around her neck. They walked down the aisle as a quartet played the conclusion to the Wedding March. They stopped near the doorway to the inn. Leena and Frank's brother Barry walked back and stood next to them. All the guests came up and congratulated them.

THE WEDDING RECEPTION WAS a very low-key affair. The four-piece ensemble played classical music to the small group of thirty-eight. Hal had prepared all of the food and Michelle and her niece Carly helped serve. Leena had insisted that Jackie be a guest at the wedding: a decision that didn't sit well with Bruce.

"Don't you embarrass me today," Leena muttered under her breath to Bruce. His drinking commenced immediately after the ceremony.

"Stop nagging me," he said to her and walked away.

Leena tried to keep her distance from him. From across the room, Leena watched Bruce. To someone who was practically a non-drinker she could not understand the need to keep drinking until inebriated. Bruce drank defiantly. That was Leena's take on it. Or he was an alcoholic, which was a definite possibility.

Observing Wendy and Frank made Leena jealous but she did not show it. On one side of the room was her best friend totally in love and enjoying her day. On the other side of the room was her getting-drunker-by-the-minute husband.

This day seemed to be a crossroads for Leena. She wanted what her friend had: a second chance at love. She didn't want anything more to do with the man across the room. At her own wedding nineteen years ago, she recalled how things had not changed.

Leena danced with her new husband. Looking over his shoulder she observed her parents looking on with such glee. Leena had married well. This up-and-coming lawyer, son of a lawyer, had what it took to go far. There was never any doubt about his ability to support his new wife and a family someday.

Into the early evening hours, their reception continued. The band played all their favorite songs. Leena danced with her friends from high school and college. Bruce spent time with his buddies drinking at the open bar, getting progressively drunker. His ability to drink a lot when they went out with friends should have been a red flag. Leena had always overlooked it.

At the age of twenty-two and a baby on the way, only Bruce and Wendy knew about the pregnancy. Leena suspected that giving birth only seven months after her wedding was the reason Bruce's parents never warmed up to her.

In their honeymoon suite, the night before they would leave for the Bahamas, the disappointment of having her new husband say not a word, lie down on the bed and fall asleep immediately, was a crushing blow. Leena sat in a chair by the bed and watched Bruce sleep. He never stirred until the alarm went off at nine the next morning. Bruce didn't talk much that morning. She suspected that talking, or even thinking, was probably a painful thing to do.

They consummated the marriage once they got to their hotel in Nassau. Leena recalled it was just a "quickie" before they went down to the bar before dinner.

Leena's eyes filled with tears as she watched Wendy and Frank slow dance. Frank was so attentive and gentle. Leena glanced over at Bruce and caught sight of an upside-down glass in front of his face. She turned her head quickly and walked out to the kitchen.

Jackie was in the kitchen with Becky. They stopped talking when they saw Leena enter the room. "What's the matter, Mom?" Becky asked. Leena was visibly shaken.

Leena was caught off guard. She attempted to gloss over her feelings. "Oh, nothing sweetheart."

"It doesn't look like 'nothing,'" Becky said.

"It's just an emotional day. I'm very happy for Wendy."

"You don't look happy, Leena," Jackie added.

"Well, I am happy!" Leena got defensive. "I'm not too thrilled with your father's drinking, that's all, if you must know."

"That's what I thought," Becky said. "What else is new?"

"He just broke off part of the ice sculpture," Jackie said.

Becky nudged Jackie with her elbow.

"What?" Leena said.

"It's nothing," Becky assured her. "Come on Mom, you can hang with us, Okay?"

THE MEAL WAS SERVED and Leena was seated next to Bruce. They were also seated next to Wendy and Frank and Barry and his wife, Cynthia. Leena was thankful that Wendy and Frank were so caught up with each other that they were not aware of Bruce's unsteady demeanor.

Half way through the meal Bruce took his fork and started tapping on the side of his water glass a little too hard. Leena thought the glass would break. Bruce stood up.

"I would like to propose a toast," Bruce started out. All eyes were on him. "To the happy couple." Bruce swayed slightly and he put his hand down on the table to steady himself. He raised his champagne glass. Leena watched him, dreading every word. "I propose a toast," he repeated. "To two of the nicest people in the entire world. This happy couple found love after divorce. The divorce rate for second marriages is quite a bit higher than first marriages, and even *that* is fifty-fifty. So I hope this works out. If it doesn't, they know where to find me." Bruce laughed at his own joke. Leena glared at him and kicked his foot. He looked down at this foot but didn't seem to make the connection with his wife. He continued. "But I have faith that they will not become a stas-tis-tisk," he mispronounced the word.

"That's enough!" Leena said to him. She looked around at the guests and they looked uncomfortable.

Barry stood up and saved the day. He put his arm around Bruce's shoulder and spoke clearly and loudly. "What he's trying to say is we raise our glasses to the new couple and wish them every happiness for their future together." Barry raised his glass high and all the guests followed suit.

"Hear hear!" Bruce yelled, raising his glass and gulping down the entire glass of champagne. He sat down heavily.

"Thanks a lot!" Leena snarled. Cynthia could only stare. She kept quiet.

Bruce did not pick up on the sarcasm. "You're welcome."

Each table was round and allowed the guests to mingle easily. Bruce's mouth was still running, but the food seemed to sober him up. He managed to behaved through the rest of the meal.

The wedding cake was distributed and coffee was served. By six o'clock Wendy and Frank got ready to leave. Some of Wendy's coworkers tied a few ribbons onto the back of Frank's car and "Just Married" was written on the back window. Wendy and Frank seemed genuinely surprised by it.

Wendy and Frank took their sons aside and said their goodbyes. Andrew and Jeremy would stay with the Frazers that night. Jeremy's mother and Andrew's father would pick them up the next day. It took the boys no time flat to follow Jason up to his room to play video games.

After the guests said their goodbyes and gave lots of hugs to the new couple, Leena took Wendy aside and said, "I am so sorry about Bruce. He makes me *so* mad!"

"You don't need to apologize for him, Leena. It's not a problem," Wendy knew how bad Leena was feeling.

Leena gave Wendy a big hug and said, "Have a great time! I'm so happy for you. A little jealous, but you know I am so happy for you Wen."

"I know you are. Things will work out for you. Hang in there."

"The boys will be just fine," Leena said.

"They've been looking forward to staying here. It's all they've been talking about." The two friends hugged again. "We'll see you in a week." Wendy got into the car. Leena gave Frank a hug and he walked around to the driver's side and got in.

Leena and the rest of the guests watched as their car drove off, ribbons flailing behind with the forward momentum of the car.

CHAPTER 24

Jackie walked into Becky's dorm room and took it all in. She noticed the walls were adorned with posters of some of her favorite rock bands. Original sketches and paintings were leaning against the wall, her way, Jackie figured, of remaining humble in the face of true Monet-like talent.

The room, although small, was cozy, but according to Becky the novelty of being away from home and living with another artist roommate had worn off just one month into her college experience. She had never had to share a room before. Now she was faced with listening to the nonstop stream of consciousness from her roommate, Katie. Jackie met her briefly as she was heading out the door. She heard just enough to understand Becky's position.

Becky cleared away a pile of clothes and books at the end of her bed for Jackie. "See what I mean?" she said after Katie was half-way down the hall.

"Really! Does she always talk that much?"

"Pretty much."

"So do you miss home?" Jackie asked sitting down on the bed.

"I miss having my own room."

"I know what you really miss, I mean who," Jackie said.

Becky blushed. "Yeah, my Chris." She picked up his picture she had in a frame by her bed and stared at it. "We'll see each other at Thanksgiving." Jackie watched Becky as she carefully placed the picture of Chris back where it belonged. Jackie looked at his picture. Chris stood leaning against his car with his arms crossed. He had a big smile on his face.

"I can't say I miss home too much because I went home twice already, once for the wedding. I'm coming back for our Halloween party."

"Halloween Party?"

"Yup. It's sort of a tradition. Ever since I, and now Jason, outgrew going trick or treating, my mom throws a party for us and our friends."

"Cool. You mean you all dress up in costumes and stuff?"

"Yes! And my mom always dresses up in a costume too. It's pretty wild." Becky said. "One year she dressed up as four-star General. She had a moustache and the whole getup. My friends thought she was my father! It was weird."

"Does Bruce, I mean your father, dress up? I can't picture that."

"Neither can I. He doesn't do it. He says it's 'not his thing." Becky shrugged. "What are ya gonna do?"

"So who comes to this party?"

"My friends, Jason's friends, some parents: the ones my mother is friendly with at the school."

"Your mom is cool." Jackie paused. "Do you think I could dress up and come?" Jackie already knew the answer but wanted to hear Becky tell her she was included.

"Well, of course!" Becky laughed and shook her head. "Hello? Girlfriend, you can come as anyone or anything you want." Becky got up from her desk chair and went to the closet to hunt for a different outfit.

"I think I'll be a witch. No, maybe a vampire," Jackie didn't hesitate. "What are you going to be?"

"I'm not sure yet. Maybe Britney Spears. You know, I'll dress up in the schoolgirl outfit?"

"That's a good idea."

"What do you think of this?" Becky held up a yellow chiffon shirt."

"Put it on. Let me see you in it."

She made a quick switch. "So?"

"Nice. How do I look?" Jackie asked, now doubting her choice. She looked at Becky nervously. "You think Rick will like this?" Jackie stood up giving Becky a better look at her low rider black jeans and a shirt that was too short to cover her belly button.

"Are you kidding? It's awesome. Very sexy."

"Yeah?"

They both heard Katie's voice as she approached the room.

"Let's go before she starts bending our ears again," Becky said.

Jackie smiled and nodded. "We should get going anyway if we want to get a table before eight. Rick's band goes on at nine."

JACKIE PULLED UP OUTSIDE *Mayfield's* in Providence, a restaurant where Rick and his father's band would perform. They got out of the car that Jackie had borrowed from Leena and walked toward the building.

"Can't miss that sign," Jackie observed. The neon sign that spelled out the name of the establishment lit up the street and reflected in nearby windows.

The place was filled up to capacity by the time they arrived. Jackie was close to tears when the hostess told her there would be a half-hour wait for a table. When she learned the tables in the same room as the band were all reserved, she did cry.

"We need to sit in that room," Jackie pleaded with the hostess, pointing to the room with the stage. "Rick told me I could sit up front."

The waitress looked down at her book. "Are you a special guest of the band? What is your name?"

"Jackie Furth."

"You should have told me. Right this way."

Jackie looked at Becky and her smile returned. Her spine straightened with pride as the two of them followed the woman to a small table for two in the front.

"Thank you," Jackie said to the hostess. "Can you believe this? So that's what Rick meant when he said I could sit down front," she said to Becky. "He could have been more specific."

A waitress came to the table to bring menus and ask for their drink order. They ordered sodas. A short time later they ordered some dinner.

Backlash came out a little after nine. A light spattering of applause filled the air. Jackie clapped and yelled "Oooh" the second the light hit the stage. Becky felt a little embarrassed by the attention she had brought to their table.

Throughout their first set, Rick smiled and winked at her as he plucked away on his bass guitar. Jackie was mesmerized.

They finally took a break after playing for forty-five minutes. Rick disappeared briefly and then reappeared in front of Jackie and Becky's table. Jackie stood up immediately when she saw him walking toward her. He gave Jackie a quick embrace and a peck on the cheek.

"You were awesome, Rick," Jackie cooed.

"Thanks. Hey Becky, good to see you again."

"Hey Rick. How long you playin' for tonight?"

"We take about a fifteen-minute break now and then we'll play 'til eleven or so."

"Sit. Stay a few minutes." Jackie demanded.

Rick looked around for a chair but there were none. He shrugged. There were a few moments of awkwardness.

Jackie broke the silence. "I think Becky's mom has some party coming in November. Maybe she can hire you again."

"That would be cool," Rick said.

Rick took Jackie's hand and said to Becky, "Will you excuse us?" He led her away from the table. "I'll bring her back in a few minutes."

"Where are we going?" Jackie asked him. She looked at Becky as they left the room.

"I just want you to myself for a minute. I missed you," Rick said.

"Me too," Jackie said.

"Here, follow me." They walked through the back of the restaurant, through the kitchen and stepped out to the back alley where they found they were sharing it with a restaurant employee having a cigarette break. They both looked over at the man as he stood dragging in the smoke. He nodded his head to acknowledge them and they nodded back and then turned to each other. Jackie giggled for no apparent reason. Rick bent down and kissed Jackie. They did not care that the man was still there. Rick said, "I have an idea. You drive Becky back to the doom at eleven and then come back to my place. Let me give you directions. Got a pen?"

Jackie pulled the directions to the restaurant out of her purse along with a pen. She turned the paper over and handed it to Rick. He wrote directions to his apartment on the back. By this time the man had put out his cigarette and had gone back inside. They were alone in the alley.

"I thought he'd never leave," Rick said. Jackie shoved the directions into her purse. He leaned against Jackie and kissed her, grabbing her around the waist and pulling her close. His hands explored starting with her bare belly and moving up under her top. Their kissing became more intense. He pulled away.

"I better stop. I need to pull myself together," Rick said, laughing. "You're making me crazy." He turned his back on Jackie and made an adjustment with his right hand on the outside of his pants.

Jackie realized what he had done and giggled softly to herself. "You'll just have to get yourself out of those confining pants later, that's all there is to it," she said coyly.

"Whew, give me a minute." Rick laughed and put his hands on his hips and walked in the alley in a wide circle. "I better get back."

They went inside and Jackie followed behind him watching the way he walked. He turned briefly to throw her a smile from across the room and then disappeared, coming out a few minutes later to play with the band.

SHE DROVE ACROSS TOWN, following the directions Rick had given her and found the apartment complex, no problem. *Building 2 apt 3D* it said on the paper. The guest parking area was on the side of the building and Jackie walked around to the front entrance. She pushed button number 3D.

"Who is it?" Rick said in a sing-song voice.

"It's me," Jackie mimicked him. She pulled the door open after the buzzer sounded.

She climbed the stairs, heading for the third floor. She felt so alive and happy, happier than she had ever been, content as she had ever been.

"I think I'm in love, Becky." Jackie had just told Becky when she drove her back.

"You do? He's the real deal?"

"I'm pretty sure. No, I am sure. He's so nice to me and gentle, and he treats me with respect. Kevin wasn't so nice come to think of it. I mean, he used to put me down and shit. Makes me mad to think about it now. But, hey, some other girl can put up with his crap. Not me. I've got Rick."

Jackie found door 3D and knocked. Rick opened the door and Jackie entered. He removed her purse from her shoulder and tossed it on the couch. From behind he kissed her neck as he slid her jacket off her shoulders. It landed on top of her purse. Just like in the restaurant, Rick took her by the hand and led her away, this time, to his bedroom.

She did not notice one single thing about his place until the next day. She observed just how much of a guy's place it was: Dirty dishes in the sink, a pile of clothes on the floor of his bedroom and bathroom. His guitar was in its case, in the corner near an amp. "I see you fixed up the place since you knew I was coming."

"Sorry. I haven't had a chance to clean. Can't afford a cleaning lady."

"I think you need a wife," Jackie said. She didn't plan the comment, but being his wife was in the back of her mind.

"I don't know about a wife. That would be a long ways away."

"You don't see yourself getting married?"

"I'm only twenty-four. Not gonna think about *that*."

At nineteen, Jackie did think about it. She had been told by Leena that she was too young to have those thoughts, and that she needed to experience life a little more before the thought of settling down crossed her mind. This advice was a carbon copy of Leena's words to Becky, Jackie would find out weeks later when the two girls compared notes.

"What do you say we get something to eat? I'm starving," Rick said to Jackie, propping himself up on his elbow in his bed. Jackie lay next to him with the sheet covering her up to her armpits. She held onto the sheet, crossing her arms across her chest. She stared relentlessly into his eyes. Rick let his head fall back down to the pillow and he stared up at the ceiling. "I could get used to this," he said.

Jackie smiled. "Me too."

"So let's eat!" Rick leaped out of bed. "Come on girl, now don't be lazy." Rick yanked the sheet off of Jackie and she laughed with a scream. He started to pull her by the ankles.

"Okay, okay," she giggled. She got to her feet.

THE WAITRESS AT THE local breakfast place called Rick by his first name. Many patrons nodded as they passed. A middle-aged woman wearing her Sunday best passed by the table and then backed up. "Rick?" she said.

"Hey, Mrs. Brown."

The woman glanced quickly at Jackie. Her lip curved slightly serving as a greeting. She turned back to Rick. "Your mother tells me your sister is engaged."

"That's right," Rick confirmed. "Next year some time."

"Wonderful news. To the Goodwin boy, right?"

"Right." Rick straightened up from his slouching posture. "Oh, this is my friend Jackie, Mrs. Brown."

"How do you do," she said formally.

"Hi," Jackie said.

"I just ran into your mother at the store. I guess we had the same idea: to go shopping after church," she said.

"No doubt," Rick said. "She had to pick out her Sunday roast, I suspect."

"Please give Sally my best. Good to see you." She looked at Jackie. "Nice to meet you."

Jackie smiled. "Same here."

"You seem to be popular around here," Jackie said after she left.

"Me and my family have lived here forever. I didn't exactly move far away from my folks when I moved out, you know. As a matter of fact, I told the old man I would help him load some stuff into the back of his truck today. He's renovating the garage and he's throwing stuff away. You need to get back or do you want to come with me later?"

"I'll come."

They spent the rest of the day together. First, they took a ride over to Home Depot to get items for his father. Then they stopped at a guitar store where Rick knew the fellow behind the counter. They commiserated over faulty amp plugs which caused some reverb. Rick stood with his hands halfway into his back pockets, elbows poking out, as he swayed and talked and laughed.

Jackie walked around the store, letting them talk. She pretended to know what she was looking at. The sound of the cash register turned her head. Their conversation was over and it was time to leave.

"What'd you get?" Jackie asked in the car.

"A new cable for my guitar and amp. Something's a little screwy with mine."

"Seemed like you knew that guy pretty well."

"Darnell? Oh yeah, he and I went through school together, since Kindergarten.

THEY PULLED INTO HIS parents' driveway. "Hey Old Man," Rick said with a grin as he got out of his car.

Jackie recognized Rick's father as his bandmate. "Hey, Rick."

"You remember Jackie? She came to watch us last night."

"Hi again. You guys were awesome," Jackie said politely. She observed his father's receding hairline and wondered if Rick's beautiful dark blonde hair would eventually disappear with age.

"Well thank you. I do remember. How could I forget such a pretty girl," his father said. Jackie blushed. "Rick, it's this stuff here I've put aside for the dump and this stuff is for charity or whatever." His father pointed to the piles in the garage. "It's amazing what you accumulate over the years," he directed the comment to Jackie. "Then there's that stuff up in the rafters that need to come down. That can all go to the dump I suppose, unless you see something you want."

Jackie watched while Rick filled up his father's dump truck with miscellaneous planks of wood, strips of metal, a rusty hammock and boxed up books that mice had nested in. Rick laid out a separate pile for unwanted junk that must have been important in its day. Now there was no use for it – only the memories they held. An old pair of hockey skates and a beat-up stick; an older model turntable; fishing gear; a camping lantern, sleeping bag and backpack, all remnants of a normal childhood. She wondered how he could part with them.

"The dump's open tomorrow so I'll take the truck then. I'll bring this stuff to the church that's having the tag sale. You mentioned I was coming?"

"That's right."

"Then I'll load this up after the dump run." Rick wiped the sweat off his brow by lifting his arm and wiping his forehead on the sleeve of his t-shirt.

"Come on inside and get a cool drink. Your mother has some iced tea, I think, or a soda." Rick's father said.

They stood outside on the porch and had some iced tea with Rick's parents. It was unusually warm for the first week in October. Rick's mother stared at Jackie. Jackie became self-conscious as she sipped her drink.

"Jackie, it's Jackie, right? Is that short for Jacqueline?"

"Yes, it is."

"What is your last name, dear?" she asked.

"Furth."

"Do you live around here?

"No, I'm living down in Weekapaug."

"That's were Dad and I went a few weeks ago to play at the inn, remember? She works at that inn. That's how we met." Rick reminded his mother.

"Oh I see, yes I remember you telling me that," his mother said.

"I was up last night to visit my friend at Risdee and we all went to see *Backlash.*

"How thoughtful of you. You are a pretty girl. Don't you think she's a pretty one?" Rick's mother directed the question to both Rick and his father.

Jackie blushed and dipped her head down. Rick said, "She Da bomb, Ma."

"The what?" Her face scrunched up.

"I think that means she's The Best," Rick's father interpreted the lingo.

"You both might as well stay for dinner. I've got a roast in the oven," Rick's mother said.

Rick and Jackie looked at each other and smiled at her predictability.

"Is that okay with you, Jackie?" Rick asked her.

"I'd love to," Jackie replied. Any opportunity to spend time with families in their homes was something that filled the void of her upbringing. Jackie had become used to feeling envious about other people's good fortune. She was becoming acutely aware of his normal parents. "Who's this?" is what Jackie's father would have said to Jackie's friend when she still lived at home. Awkward moments like that kept most of her friends away in her early teen years.

As Jackie glanced around the back yard she noticed a beautiful garden with lots of roses winding all around on a trellis. Some of the flowers in the beds that surrounded the trellis were fading, some were still in full bloom. It was obvious someone cared enough to keep the garden flourishing well into the fall. The yard itself, though small, was meticulously cared for. Inside the house was as neat as a pin. This did not rub off on their son.

Jackie observed Rick's parents, saying very little. By degree, the longing for a family rose in Jackie. It was just behind her eyes; it settled in her bones; it called to her in her sleep. Unresolved emotions regarding her mother fluttered inside her stomach. Being with Rick's parents fueled her desire to find her own mother.

"You're awfully quiet," Rick said when they had a moment to themselves, sitting on the sofa in his parents' living room.

"Am I?"

"My mother can be a bit of a noodge."

"Don't be silly. She's great. This is great."

"If you want to leave, speak now. I can make some excuse." Rick laughed and whispered to her, "She hasn't set the table yet so we can still escape."

"I really want to stay."

It was decided. Mrs. Diamen fed them until they felt like they would burst. Pleasant conversation without conflict passed between them. Rick's father was so laid back and funny. Jackie eventually found herself laughing and joining in the conversation.

Jackie offered to help his mother take the dishes off the table and load the dishwasher, but Mrs. Diamen wouldn't hear of it. Without a word Mr. Diamen and Rick cleared the table and the three of them had everything cleaned up in no time.

JACKIE WAS QUIET IN the car on the way back to his apartment. Deep sadness started to replace her happy mood.

"What's the matter? Did my mother ask you some nosey questions?"

"No, not at all. You're mother's great!"

"Then what is it?"

Jackie looked over at Rick as he drove. Her eyes filled up with tears.

"You gonna tell me?" Rick asked.

"It's just that I never had that growing up, and when I see it I miss it. No, wait, how could I miss it when I never had it? I mean, I wish I had had it." Jackie said with a suppressed cry in her voice.

"You want to talk about your parents?"

Rick had no idea what box he had just opened up. Jackie spilled her heart to him: The mother who gave up on her, the sister she hadn't seen in over three years, and the abuse from her father were the three things that dragged her heart down. There was just so much she could give herself that she didn't receive from childhood. There would always be a void.

"Maybe you should try to find your family," Rick suggested. Now they were parked in Rick's parking space in front of the apartment building.

"I've been thinking about it. But then again I don't want to. Why should I care about someone who stopped caring about me?"

"Wow, my parents have always been there for me and my brothers and my sister. And that's the house I grew up in. I feel spoiled now."

"Nah, you're lucky, that's all."

"You wanna come up?"

Jackie shook her head. "No, it's late. I better get back."

"Okay." Rick walked her to her car. He leaned down and kissed her. She threw her arms around his neck and squeezed. "Whoa," Rick laughed.

"Thanks for so much fun," Jackie said.

"Let me know if you can come next weekend."

"I can't come next weekend. Maybe you can come down during the week?"

"You betcha. I'll call ya. We'll make plans."

CHAPTER 25

Leena sat on the edge of her bed, rising early for her morning jog. She turned and looked at her sleeping husband. He lay on his side with his left arm stretched up straight under his head touching the bedpost. His mouth was open and a low snore filled an otherwise silent morning. Leena felt angry. Another Sunday morning he'd sleep in nursing an all too familiar hangover. He didn't stir at all as she moved around the room to get dressed. She left quietly and headed down the stairs and out to the street.

When Leena returned to the inn Jackie was standing outside on the porch. She watched Leena. "Whatcha doing Jackie?"

"You going on your morning run?"

"Yeah, well I just finished." Leena was panting. Her hands were on her hips.

"I thought I'd catch you before you went. Was gonna ask if you wanted company."

"Well, you're welcome to join me tomorrow morning."

Jackie was silent. Leena suspected she wanted to say something. Leena started to ask her what was on her mind but they both spoke at the same time. "Sorry," Leena said, "you first."

Jackie paused and said, "I was just going to say that I have breakfast ready. That is, the bacon and sausage are done. The French toast and eggs are ready to go."

Leena nodded and started to head inside. "Great, let's go," Leena led the way to the kitchen.

They entered the kitchen and Jackie still had a troubled look on her face.

"Is there anything wrong, Jackie," Leena asked.

Jackie stood like a statue. She took a deep breath and said, "I've been thinking about trying to find my mother."

"Really?" Leena was surprised.

"It's been on my mind. I don't know, lately, it's been more on my mind, I guess. I, like, never considered actually doing it, until now."

"What made you change your mind?"

Jackie waited momentarily before saying, "Rick."

"Rick said you should?"

"Not exactly, I mean, sort of, but, I don't know." She let out a long sigh. "I met his parents this weekend."

"Oh, I see."

"They were so nice, you know. I got thinking, maybe my mother is nice. What if she's been looking for me? She only did what she did to save her own life. Maybe I've been mad at her long enough."

"That's a lot to think about. Maybe you should pursue it."

"You think?"

"Sure."

"Where would I start?"

"Do you have any guesses what town she might be in?"

"Not really. I was thinking she's probably still in Connecticut, but for all I know she's in California."

"You want some help?"

"Would you?"

"Of course. After we finish breakfast here, why don't we do some investigating. We'll look online. Sound like a plan?"

Jackie sighed deeply, "Okay!"

"What about your father?"

"No. Just my mother."

After morning chores were done Leena and Jackie went upstairs to Leena's office. She dragged a dining room chair down the hall and the two of them planted themselves in front of the computer. "The internet is amazing. I don't know what we did before we had it," Leena laughed. "Okay, what's your mother's first name?"

"Addy, well, Adeline. She went by Addy."

She did a search for "Adeline Furth," her mother's married name, and did not come up with a hit. "The good news is," Leena said, "is that Adeline is an unusual name, and so is Furth. What is her maiden name?"

"Carter."

Leena plugged in "Adeline Carter" and also Connecticut and got nothing. She tried the same name without Connecticut and got a few hits, but Adeline was a middle name. No hits for Adeline Furth, or Carter.

"Where was the last place you lived with her?"

"East Hartford."

"Nothing. We could hire a private investigator," Leena said as she leaned back in her chair.

Jackie's eyes widened with disbelief. "That would be expensive!"

"Well, if you're serious about finding…"

"I know!" Jackie interrupted. "Let's call my neighbor Mrs. Barber! She might still live there. She might know!"

"Great. What's her first name?"

"Francie, uh, Francine, I think."

"I think we've got her." Leena smiled when she found a landline for Francesca Barber. Jackie looked nervous. "Should we call her?"

Jackie looked stunned. "Uh, yeah, I guess." She shook her head as if to rid herself of cobwebs and said emphatically, "Yes!"

"So you'll talk to her, okay?" Leena asked.

Jackie looked scared but nodded yes.

Leena punched in the numbers, heard it ring, and handed the phone to Jackie. Jackie stared at Leena until a voice on the other end caught her attention and she looked down.

"Hello?"

"Mrs. Barber?"

"Yes?"

"Um, this is Jackie." Jackie stopped her introduction thinking that was enough information. With the silence on the line, she realized she would need to say more. "I mean, Jackie Furth, your neighbor from years ago? Do you remember me?"

"Jackie?" the woman yelled. Leena heard it from the earpiece. "Jackie Furth?"

"Yeah," she laughed and finally looked up at Leena, smiling.

"Oh for God's sake. How are you dear?"

"I'm good, really, how are you?"

"Fine. What a nice surprise, Jackie! You must be twenty by now."

"Nineteen."

"Nineteen! Well, I'll be."

"So how are you, Mrs. Barber? I mean what have you been doing?" Jackie asked nervously.

"First of all, call me Francie. You know we're not formal. I been doin' okay. Earl passed away last year, though."

"Oh, I'm so sorry to hear that."

"Cancer. It was awful. But thank the Lord it was quick. So where you at now, hon?"

"I'm living in Rhode Island, working at an inn. It's a bed and breakfast, and I get room and board here too."

"How nice. You like it?"

"Uh-huh, I like it a lot. I live with a nice family. Well, I have my own apartment, you know."

"I'm so happy for you, Jackie. Wow, Jackie, I can't believe it's you! You must have a reason you calling me. Is something wrong?"

"Oh no, nothing's wrong. I, uh, decided to try and find my mother and I thought you might know where she is." Jackie took the phone away from her ear and pushed the speaker button.

"Your mama, huh? You mean you never seen your mama since back then?"

"Nope. Not since she walked out when Jess and I were twelve and fifteen. I know you remember that."

"Mm hmm!" she acknowledged. "Horrible. What she done was downright neglectful. Your father wasn't no better. If you don't mind me sayin,' your parents were bad. Not at first. I liked your mama *at first*, but they just let all hell break loose, didn't they. I just hope God can have mercy on their souls."

"I know." Jackie looked at Leena to get her reaction. Leena's brow was furrowed. "You have no idea where I might find her?"

"Lord, no! Nope, no idea."

"I see," Jackie nodded to Leena.

"Wait a minute. There's a woman that I know was pretty friendly with yo' mama. She lived in Manchester and she worked as a hostess or waitress at a restaurant in town here called *Fly By Night*. Her name was Jeanie Sampson or Simpson? They was pretty tight, you know. I wouldn't be surprised if she knew about your mama. But I think the restaurant has a different name now. Let me think. It's something like *The Slammer* or something. Hold on, let me think." There was silence for a moment. Suddenly Francie yelled, "*Slam Dunk*. That's the name. It's a sports bar and restaurant now."

Jackie wrote again on the notepad.

"You gonna try and find her?" Francie asked.

"I'm thinking about it."

"Well that's up to you, dear, but I say she don't deserve that."

"Probably not." Jackie looked at Leena and Jackie looked stuck. "Well, I appreciate your help."

"What about Jesse? What's she up to?"

"I haven't seen Jesse either."

"Now that's just not right, child." Francie said "child" with an exaggerated letter I, and a silent D —with a mild southern drawl.

"Have you heard anything about my sister, Jesse?"

"Lord no child. You ain't seen your sister neither?" she asked incredulously.

"Fraid not."

"Lord, have mercy. Maybe Jeanie can tell you 'bout Jesse too. That is, if you find Jeanie."

"Maybe," Jackie sounded defeated.

There was an awkward silence.

Francie finally said, "Now, sweetie, you come by and see me one of these days. Will ya? I'd love to see you again. Promise me you will!"

"I promise."

"You just holler if you need anything, dear. You like family."

Jackie said goodbye promising to stop by the next time she was in her town.

Jackie and Leena stared at each other for many seconds. Finally, Leena said "I'll look up the number for *Slam Dunk*, ok?"

"Ok."

"Do you want to make the call or would you like me to call?"

"I gotta think about it. Let's talk about it tomorrow. Ok?"

"Ok, sweetie. Let's talk tomorrow."

WHEN LEENA MADE THE call to *Slam Dunk* she asked for Jeanie Sampson or Simpson. Jackie had decided she didn't have the stomach to make the call. Leena offered. She talked to a manager who told her she had quit but said she might be working at a bar down the street called *Meetinghouse Café*. Leena found a phone number.

"I might as well, right?" Leena said. Jackie shrugged anticipating a dead end.

Leena's head popped up and her jaw dropped, making eye contact with Jackie when the person who answered at *Meetinghouse Café* told her a Jeanie Sampson did work there, but would not start her shift until five o'clock that evening. It was three.

"We'll call later," Leena observed Jackie's expression and saw dismay or fear. "We've gone this far, right?"

"Right."

It was the same Jeanie Sampson who knew Jackie's mother. Jackie got up the nerve and made this call. Jeanie told her she was fairly certain her mother lived in Willimantic. She had visited her a few times over the years but she had not been in touch with her for over nine months. Her mother had remarried. She couldn't remember the name of the street she lived on but she recalled that the house – a red house – was down a side street off of Church Street and it was about four to six houses down on the right. There was a rose trellis in the side yard next to a detached garage. Jackie wrote furiously on a notepad. Leena looked over her shoulder.

Jackie hung up after saying thank you to her many times.

"Well?" Leena asked.

"She gave me a description of the yard and said the house was red," Jackie said, pointing to the illegible writing on the pad in front of her. "She might be in Willimantic."

"Yeah? Let me see if she comes up in a search now." Leena typed. Nothing. "What do you want to do?"

"I don't know. I could just go there."

"You could."

"If I decide to go, would you come with me?"

"Yes, of course."

"Can I let you know? I gotta let this all sink in. I gotta think about it."

"Of course. When you decide, let me know."

Jackie gave Leena a hug, "Thanks, Leena."

"You are very welcome. Glad I could help."

"I'll listen for the dryer. I'll be in my room," Jackie said.

"Thanks."

NOW IT WAS ON her mind constantly. The image of her mother flashed across Jackie's mind throughout each day. She couldn't seem to shake it. She had not gotten up the nerve to make the trip to find her yet.

Many of her tasks reminded her of her mother or their home when she was little. The smell of bacon and eggs filled the air on a Sunday as she and Leena worked side by side cooking for and feeding the guests. The memory of her own Sunday mornings returned each time she prepared breakfast at the inn. Sunday was the one morning a full breakfast was cooked. Jackie was allowed to stand on a chair at the stove and stir the scrambled eggs. She and her sister ate breakfast with their parents. Her father usually hid behind the Sunday newspaper. After breakfast, she and Jesse went to church with their mother. Her father stayed home.

Some of the guests at the inn went to the church up the street after breakfast. The bells in the tower rang for a good fifteen minutes every Sunday morning after the last service. In the last few weeks, Jackie was tempted to go to the church each time she heard them. She hadn't gotten the nerve to go.

After the bells stopped ringing the following Sunday, Jackie came out of her room and found Leena in the kitchen. A full week had elapsed.

"Leena?" Jackie said.

"Yes?" Leena said. Leena was squatting down on the kitchen floor searching for a serving dish. "Have you seen that green dish with the butterflies on it? It didn't get stolen did it?"

"It's over here, Leena." Jackie walked across the room and pointed to a cabinet above the refrigerator.

Leena walked over and opened it, finding the dish. "What on earth is this doing here?"

"I think Michelle put it there. I'll tell her not to if you want me to."

"No, don't bother. That's okay."

"So, I was thinking," Jackie started again. She watched Leena search through cabinets for other items. "I think I'm officially ready to go find my mother."

Leena closed the cabinet and turned around to pay attention to Jackie. "Really?"

"I think so. I've been thinking about it lately and I want to do it. So let's do it."

"Great. Let me go get my calendar book and see what day is good." Leena walked across the kitchen to the area near the phone where she kept it. She came back and sat down at the table. "How about either this Tuesday or Thursday? I have a lawn guy coming on Wednesday and I think I want to be around for that."

"Either day is fine with me."

"How about Tuesday?

"Sure."

There was no specific incident that started the decline of her family, Jackie explained to Leena. As Jackie got older, she learned that money was tight. Her father did a bit of gambling and her mother liked to shop for pretty clothes. By the time she reached the age of ten their arguments over spending escalated into a never-ending battle. Her mother resorted to hiding her purchases in boxes under Jesse's and her bed. Her father would come home late from work bringing with him a very long face and a need to medicate himself with alcohol.

Her mother eventually took a job as a waitress. Jackie tried to explain it to Leena. "I think it was when my mother got a taste for the world outside that things really changed drastically," she continued. "She went from waitressing in a local diner to waitressing at a bar at night. That was it. She started meeting men that actually paid attention to her. She was pretty as I recall. I mean we needed the money desperately at the time and my father was all in favor of her 'getting off her dead ass' as he so eloquently put it."

"My mother never worked after she had me and my sister," Leena recalled. "I have an older sister too. I sometimes wonder if my mother had gone out and gotten a job when Nancy and I were older if that would have changed her for the better. You know, getting her out of that house, away from my domineering father. Maybe it would have given her some much-needed confidence. Maybe that's why they remained married until death do they part. She knew nothing else. I've always wondered about that."

"So what's worse? Staying married out of some kind of habit? Or leaving, breaking up a family, to find some happiness before you die?" Jackie waxed philosophical.

"That is the question, isn't it?" Leena responded. "I don't know. I guess if you're unhappy you should get out. But when there're children involved then it's a more complicated concept. It would certainly be a dilemma for me."

"Why, are you unhappy in your marriage?" Jackie boldly asked.

"Oh, I don't know. It's okay. It's no worse than anyone else's marriage after eighteen years." Leena said. "I think most women fantasize about some other life they don't have."

"I get the feeling you aren't that happy with Bruce. I can see why. He sort of reminds me of my father sometimes, when he drinks, I mean."

"I'm not too thrilled with the drinking. I'll admit that. I could have clobbered him at Wendy's wedding." Leena shook her head and said, "What an ass he is sometimes."

"My father got drunk at my aunt's wedding – about a year or so before my mother left. He got good and drunk. It was my mother's sister's wedding. Oh my God." Jackie paused to remember the fallout. "My new uncle ended up punching him in the jaw because my father and mother were making a scene. My mother left early, during the reception, and no one knew where she went. The rumor was she had been flirting with one of the ushers and might have left with him. He wasn't around either. She came home in the middle of the night." Jackie shook her head in disgust.

"What a mess!" Leena said, picturing the scene. "So, what about your father? Any thoughts about looking him up?"

Jackie's face dropped. "I have no intention of talking to my father ever again. He had his chance to do right. He didn't." She waited and thought about her statement and amended it. "My mother didn't do any better, did she? But I reached the end of my relationship with my father and I don't have much curiosity about him, really. He took up drinking in a major way after my mother walked out on us. Me and my sister were just in his way from that point on. He didn't have my mother to knock around no more so we were his punching bags. I'm not ready to forgive him."

Leena wasn't sure what to say, "I see. So things became physical."

"Way physical. So when my mother'd be out late, they'd fight like cats and dogs when she came in. She denied stuff but I think he knew the truth. One night he called where she worked and she had left there hours before. Whew, did all hell break loose that night. He ended up smacking her around. My sister and I climbed out the window and ran over to Francie's house. You know, the one we called last week? We did that a lot."

"Right."

"The physical stuff started to become a habit. He knew he was getting away with it. He was a big guy. Very intimidating figure. Not only was he tall, he was kinda big. You didn't mess with him if you could help it. My mother never reported him. If I had to guess I think she figured she deserved what he did to her because she was going out with other men."

"What a mess," Leena said. "So tell me about the night your mother left for good."

"It wasn't much different than other nights. She came in late. He suspected she was not telling the truth and he pushed her around, bloodied her lip. But this fight was bigger than usual. He kicked her and knocked her around, threw her clothes out on the lawn, stuff like that. I think she just couldn't take it no more and never came back." Jackie fought back tears.

"So my sister and I had to fend for ourselves, really. She's older than me, and when she got out of there after finishing high school, I was left alone with him."

"How old were you when she left?"

"Who my mother or sister?"

"Well, both, I guess."

"I was twelve when my mother left us and I was fourteen when my sister left. Shortly after that things really went downhill with my father and me and they took me out of the home and put me into a foster home for a while, but I ran away from that place when *that* father decided he liked me *too* much."

"Oh dear, Jackie." Leena paused. "Things *have* been tough for you."

"I don't know why I tried to off myself. None of these people, including the cheating boyfriend, Kevin, was worth dying over! I realize that now."

"Of course," Leena agreed. "Where did you go after the foster home?"

"The state put me into a group girl's home which was no picnic, but at least there weren't no men around to beat me or molest me."

Leena was surprised by her frankness. "Well, you've put it all behind you, and moving forward is best. If it helps you to find your mother and you either try to have a relationship with her or, I don't know, tell her off maybe, then that's what we'll do. I don't know how this will turn out. Are you prepared for anything?"

"Yeah, I am. My expectations are low. Anything good that happens will be a bonus, I figure.

"So it's a date. Tuesday, right?"

"I'm ready."

CHAPTER 26

It wasn't a long ride to Willimantic but it seemed that way. Rain was coming down in sheets. Leena suggested postponing the trip but Jackie wanted to push forward. The windshield wipers needed replacing and the sound of the radio didn't quite drown out the squeaking sound they made. Jackie fidgeted with the radio dial stopping when she found what seemed like the most annoying hip-hop song Leena had ever heard, although she had not heard many.

"Are you hungry? You want to stop and get a bite?" Leena asked Jackie.

"I couldn't eat a thing. If you want to you can."

Leena looked over at her and laughed a little. "I couldn't eat a thing either."

"I just want to get this over with," Jackie said.

"Are you having second thoughts?" Leena asked.

"I don't know. Yes and no. No, I guess not. I like the thought the element of surprise will bring. If showing up unannounced will rock her world it'll be a small price to pay for walking out on me seven years ago." Jackie and Leena exchanged glances. Jackie went back to listening to the radio. Her head bobbed slightly to the beat of an angry rapper. When the song was over and a commercial came on Jackie turned the volume down. She looked over at Leena again and said, "I just want you to know that even if things don't go good with my mother, I won't blame you or nothing. I'm not gonna be disappointed if she turns out to be, I don't know, a bum, a hooker or... hey, maybe she won't even remember me."

Leena shook her head, "I'm sure she'd remember you, Jackie."

"I don't know. It's been a while. She might be dead, you know."

"There is the unknown here. She may not even live there, you know."

"I know. This could be a dead end." Jackie paused. "I know!" They exchanged another sympathetic glance.

"Let's not have any expectations, that way you won't be too disappointed," Leena said.

Leena changed the subject. "Maybe we could get you enrolled in some classes, maybe art classes up at the University of Rhode Island. It's only a hop, skip and a jump from the inn, really. You're such a talented girl. You should do something with your art."

"I can't afford that!"

"I'm sure we can help you out with some of that. That could be our next road trip. We'll go visit the school. What do you say? Get you in there for January?"

"I don't know *what* to say. You've been so kind to me, I just can't believe it."

"Is that a yes?"

"Yes, it's a yes!"

"Good." Leena smile.

They arrived in Willimantic a little after eleven in the morning. The rain had let up and a fine mist had taken its place. They navigated their way around the back streets of the State University. Willimantic, Leena had read somewhere, had earned a reputation as a haven for drug addicts.

They found Church Street. Leena said, "We'll just drive down each of these streets slowly and look for a red house. I'll look on the left, you look on the right."

"She said it's on the right," Jackie said.

"Yeah, but that depends which way we enter the street. What else? A trellis?"

"Yeah, the trellis is next to a garage, a detached garage," she said.

Two streets into their search they did not find a house matching the description. The neighborhoods were fairly quiet. There were a few mothers out with young children. They stared at them as they drove by slowly.

"What about this one," Jackie said pointing. Leena slowed way down. "It's red, but no trellis or garage. Never mind. Keep going."

On the third street, Jackie blurted out, "Stop! This must be the house." Leena pulled over to the curb and looked out Jackie's window and saw a dilapidated red house with peeling paint. Next to the driveway and detached garage was a rose trellis, as described by Jeanie Sampson. There were no roses, nor any flowers on it, only a potted plant hung on it with dead leaves hanging over the edge. The garage was an eyesore. It was open and clearly full of junk. Jackie stared at Leena and sighed loudly, turning away to look toward the house again. Beside the front door was the number 128.

"This might be it. Are we sticking to the plan that you will go to the door alone? I'll go with you if you want me to," Leena said.

Jackie didn't respond right away as she looked over the yard and the adjoining yards carefully. The lawn had more dirt than grass and there were miscellaneous toys strewn all over it. There was a beat-up, red car in the driveway and another car on blocks around the corner of the house next to the trellis. The neighborhood was a mixture of nice houses and houses in disrepair. This one was the latter. A dog was barking from the direction of the back yard. She turned around to Leena and said, "You mind coming with me?"

Leena took Jackie's hand and squeezed it and smiled. "Of course I don't. Let's go. You ready?"

"Ready as I'll ever be."

They both walked up to the front door and stood silently for a few moments. Finally, Jackie knocked. They heard the voices of young children from the other side of the door.

"I don't think this is her house," Jackie said, puzzled by the presence of children.

"We've come this far. Knock again," Leena said.

Jackie knocked and still no one opened the door. Leena stepped forward and spoke loudly, "Is anyone home?" The door suddenly opened and two young children stared up at them. "Hello," Jackie said nervously to the children, "Is there anyone home with you?"

"Someone's at the door!" the girl yelled as she walked away. The boy stood and stared at them, saying nothing. His face was dirty and so were his clothes. Jackie felt a huge wave of anxiety. A very thin woman wearing a bathrobe appeared looking as though she had been woken from a deep sleep. What little sunlight there was made her face scrunch up and recoil. They all stared at each other for a few moments. Leena hoped Jackie would remember to speak.

Finally, Jackie said, "Mother? Is that you?" A look of anguish washed over Jackie's face.

The woman rubbed her eyes, squinted, and said, "What? What do you people want? What'd you say?" She slurred and coughed and simultaneously reached for a cigarette in her bathrobe pocket. She put one in her mouth and felt around for a lighter. Jackie and Leena remained still. The woman stepped away from the door and into the room to the right. She returned holding a lighter. She lit up her cigarette.

Jackie's nerves were visible at this point and she reached behind her back for Leena's hand which Leena gladly took. She forced herself to speak again. "Mother? It's me, Jackie." She waited for a response of recognition. Leena squeezed her hand.

The woman took a long drag and squinted through the smoke to have a better look. She opened the screen door which had further obscured her vision and stepped out onto the rickety porch and examined this person who claimed to be her daughter. She looked a long time at Jackie and then looked at Leena to try to put the puzzle together. The children came to the woman's side and started to quarrel with each other. She snapped at the boy who looked to be about four. The girl was around six years old. "Knock it off Caleb! You'll be sorry later for all this racket! Christine, bring him to the TV room!" The two children left on command. The woman seemed to have forgotten what Jackie had originally asked her. "What did you say your name was?"

"It's me, it's Jackie. You don't recognize me, do you?"

They examined each other. Her mother squinted to look at them, even though there was no undue light. When her mother squinted her lip went up in a snarl. Jackie observed her bad teeth. "Jackie? Oh my God. What on earth…" She tried to concentrate. "Is that you Jackie? What are you doing here? Oh my God! I must be dreaming." She didn't smile. She was truly perplexed.

"I wanted to find you." Jackie didn't know what to say.

Her mother shifted her attention to Leena and bluntly asked, "Who are you? Do I know you too?"

"No ma'am. I'm just a friend." Leena smiled politely.

She stared at Leena with an eerie glare as she sized her up, then turned back to Jackie. Jackie and Leena waited to see if she would invite them in. She appeared to be falling asleep on her feet. Her head jerked and then she said, "Come in, come in for Christ sake." She mumbled, "Jackie."

Leena and Jackie entered the house stepping over toys and a chewed dog bone. Jackie quickly wiped her eyes. Her mother pushed some toys and mechanic's magazines off a ripped sofa indicating where she wanted them to sit. The cats they saw scurrying when they entered the room had gotten the best of the furniture, using them as scratching posts. Apparently, they had the option of relieving themselves inside the house. The smell of cat urine could be detected through the thick fog of smoke. Leena and Jackie picked two open spots on the same sofa, sitting down gingerly as if sitting slowly would keep whatever was on the sofa from merging with their clothing.

Leena had an immediate reaction of utter disgust as she viewed the surrounding squalor. Each way she turned there were dirty dishes, overflowing ashtrays, and miscellaneous toys. The carpet was completely worn out and filthy. The visit felt like a huge mistake. This meeting could not be over soon enough.

Jackie's mother sat on a chair that was adjacent to the couch. She smoked her cigarette. She squinted through the smoke that curled up and across her face. "What did you say you were doing here?" She directed her question to Jackie. Jackie's face said it all.

"I just wanted to look you up after all these years." Jackie avoided saying "Mother" again. "You left home when I was twelve and…"

"Please, Jackie. Don't rehash that. Your father was too much to put up with." She said as she blew her smoke up toward the ceiling.

"So you left us with him?" Jackie looked angry. "You left for a better life, right? Didn't you leave us to be with Aaron?"

"Who?" she asked, sounding annoyed.

Jackie couldn't believe she didn't remember the name of the man who took her away from her two children. "Aaron something, he was a musician."

"Oh, him!" She thought for a minute, inhaling smoke. She let the ash fall to the floor. "I guess. Aaron. Wow, now that's a blast from the past. I don't know where he is neither. Probably playin' the blues in some smoky bar somewhere." She laughed and shook her head.

"You left us with Dad. He didn't smack you around no more, so he smacked me and Jesse instead."

The woman said nothing.

"So is your life better now?" Jackie asked as she looked around the room. Only Leena picked up on the sarcasm.

"Life is just fine, Missy," she said defensively.

"Who are those kids?" Jackie asked.

"What do you mean 'who are those kids?' You mean those kids in there?" She gestured toward the muffled sound of the TV coming from the next room. "Why, they're my kids. Whose did you think they were for Christ sake? You think I'm a God damn babysitter?"

"I," Jackie stumbled and forced her question, "I didn't know I had a brother and another sister."

"That's right. They're your kin. That's Caleb and Christine. Caleb's father lives here. Christine's father didn't stick around. See, everyone leaves everyone eventually, kid. That's life." She stopped and searched for another cigarette after putting the butt she had into a beer can on the table next to her chair. "So get used to it. You were full-grown, for Christ's sake when I left. I don't know why you're pissin' and moanin' *now!*"

"I was twelve!" Jackie said, crying.

Her mother looked at Leena again. "Who did you say you were?"

"My name is Leena. I'm a friend of Jackie's."

"You look too old to be a *friend* if you don't mind me saying so." She looked down and lit her cigarette.

"I don't mind." Leena deliberately kept her response short. Leena had to bite her tongue.

"Well, what a shock, Jackie. Jackie. Wow." She sucked on a cigarette. She studied Jackie's face and then pointed at it, bringing the cigarette up with her fingers toward Jackie's face. "You're a pretty girl. You can thank me for your good looks, not that good-for-nothing father of yours. How old are you now, twenty-something?"

"I'm nineteen." Jackie looked over at Leena. Any questions she had rehearsed left her mind.

"And so you wanted to find me, eh?" she said. "How come?"

"Geez, I don't know maybe 'cause you're my *mother*?" Jackie yelled the last word.

"So does Jackie have other siblings she should know about?" Leena asked.

She didn't pick up on the sarcasm and said, "Well, Jackie knows her older sister Jesse." She looked over at Jackie to verify that she remembered her own sister by raising her eyebrows. Deep wrinkles lined her forehead making her look older than her forty-three years.

"Have you been in contact with Jesse?" Leena asked.

She took a drag off of the cigarette and dunked her head down until her chin touched her chest, then she shook her head from side to side while flailing her free hand. "Heavens no."

Jackie had decided she would not offer any information about herself unless her mother asked her. It was a test. If she cared, she'd ask. Her mother had no questions for her daughter. Jackie had one: "Are you high, Addy?" She used her name this time.

Addy made a strange sound of disapproval with her lips as if the mere notion were unthinkable. She shook her head the same way she did to the question about Jesse. Her eyes closed quickly then opened in a jerk.

"Are you on state aid or do you work?" Jackie asked.

"What? What kind of question is that? I got my man supporting us here." Addy got up without warning and went to the bathroom.

Leena leaned to Jackie and whispered, "Do you want to leave, Jackie?"

Jackie looked at Leena. A tear fell down onto Leena's hand as she grasped Jackie's hand. She nodded and said, "Soon. When she comes out, we'll leave." Leena took a tissue out of her purse and gave it to Jackie.

A loud truck pulled into the driveway. Leena and Jackie stood up and looked out. A tall, thin man with a goatee and a cigarette hanging out of his mouth got out of his truck. He wore filthy jeans and a T-shirt that had an unidentifiable emblem on the front. One large tattoo took up most of his upper right arm. He was looking at Leena's car as he walked toward the house. He entered the house and they all stared at each other.

"I keep telling you bitches to stay the hell away from my house," the man snapped at them. Before they had a chance to respond he said, "We had an inspection last week and this is too fucking soon, so you can get the hell outta here."

"We're not..." Leena started to talk.

"Where the hell is Addy? Addy!" he yelled. The two children ran into the room, saw the man, and ran back into the room they came from. He didn't say a word to them.

Addy came back to the room and greeted the man in an obviously phony way. "Hi, honey, you're home early."

"Who are these people?"

"You won't fuckin' believe it, Randy, this is my daughter, uh, Jackie." Addy was still as nonplused as she had been from the start and turned her back to Leena and Jackie looking for something on a table that was not where it should have been.

"You're what? Oh for Christ's sake! Are you shittin' me? This is your daughter?" Randy said. He looked Jackie up and down. "Well aren't you a hot little piece of ass." He glared at her face but longer at her body. "Who are you?" He looked at Leena like the devil would look at an angel. Shivers went down Jackie's and Leena's spines.

"I'm a friend," Leena said.

He turned back and faced Jackie. "What do you want? You must have come here for something. You lookin' for money?"

"No. We've got to go, right Leena?" Jackie turned to Leena. She was frightened.

"Everything's cool." Addy shot Jackie a phony smile. "We're just vistin' that's all, Randy. Chill." She made a motion with her hand as if to soothe him.

"Well make it snappy. We gotta go somewhere soon."

Leena and Jackie looked at Addy and she looked confused. Then she said, "That's right, we've got an appointment." She looked over at Randy and he had turned around and headed for the kitchen.

"What's your name now? You're married to that guy, right?"

"Well, right. I'm married to Randy. My name is Page now. Better than that awful Furth name, now ain't it?"

"I just wanted to see you again. See if you were okay," Jackie said.

Addy stared at Jackie with a puzzled look.

"Never mind. This is dumb." Jackie said. "I'm glad I know more about you. I'm glad your life looks miserable. You deserve it. But what do you care that my life sucked living with my father, and then foster care!" Her voice escalated. "Do you *care* that it *sucked* for me?" she yelled.

"Are you sassing me, girl? 'Cause if you are…'"

Randy walked back into the room holding a beer. "Are they still here?"

"They was just leavin,'" Addy said. "Great to see you, Jackie."

With their not-so-subtle hint, they headed toward the door and went out onto the porch, Addy followed them outside. Jackie turned around one last time. "Nice to see you, *Mother*," Jackie said in a nasty tone. She turned heel and walked swiftly to the car.

Leena and Addy maintained eye contact briefly. Leena gave her a look of disapproval but she doubted she interpreted it, and if she did, she didn't care. Leena said to Addy, "Sorry we bothered you, Mrs. Page." Addy didn't say a word as she watched Leena get into the car and start it. Addy was walking back into the house before their car had left the curb. They heard yelling coming from the house the second her mother walked back inside.

They drove down the street in silence. She navigated out of the neighborhood as quickly as she could. Jackie didn't speak. She was crying. She kept her head turned looking out her window. Leena didn't know if she should talk to her but she gave it try. "I am so sorry Jackie," Leena said, looking at Jackie and then back at the road. "I don't think we should be too surprised though. Now you know why she never contacted you after all these years." Jackie remained silent. "You'll see, when the dust settles, you'll be glad you did this, even though it doesn't seem like it was a good idea right now." She waited for a response. "Are you okay Jackie?"

"I'm fine, Leena. And you're right. I needed to get this wake-up call." Jackie sniffed and wiped her nose with the tissue she still had clutched in her hand. "I had my memory of her. I remembered her as sweet and loving. It's good to know she doesn't give a crap about me. I feel bad for those kids."

"Oh, those kids! Me too." Leena agreed. "Nothing we can do about it. I bet DCF is on their butts about the conditions those kids are living in."

"DCF?"

"Department of Children and Families?" Leena said.

"Right, I should have known that. That's probably who took me out of my father's house."

"I think that's who Randy thought we were."

"He was way creepy, don't you think?" Jackie asked.

"Very." Leena paused and thought about what she'd say next. "Jackie, it was obvious your mother was either on drugs or drunk."

"Yeah," Jackie sighed and leaned her head back on the headrest. "I just need to shake this creepy feeling I have and move on. I know I'll be glad we did this. I'm just not feeling it yet."

"The good news is that you're nineteen and you are starting a brand new life. If you didn't get what you wanted growing up you should focus on giving yourself what you want now." Leena tried to be philosophical.

Jackie nodded. She went back to staring out the window.

CHAPTER 27

Leena got into Michael's van and immediately his hands were all over her.

"Can't we wait until we go to the motel?" Leena asked.

Michael ignored her.

"Michael!" Leena said, pushing him away.

"I missed you," he said, backing off but holding her hands. "Don't you think it's getting kind of expensive, paying for a motel every time?"

"Well, it is, but that's the way it is," Leena said. "We split it."

"I know but it adds up. Why don't we, you know, here," Michael said motioning with his head and eyes to the back of the van. "No windows."

"Michael!" Leena was surprised. "Someone might see through the front."

"No one's gonna see. Besides, look. There's no one around."

Leena looked around the parking lot of the park.

"You know, we don't stay at the motels very long. Just long enough." He smiled wryly and started to unbutton her blouse and kiss her neck.

"But Michael," Leena protested. She noticed the junk in the back had either been rearranged or removed. He had planned ahead.

Michael ignored her again. She pushed him again. He said, "Look, we're in a deserted parking lot in the middle of the workday. It's raining and it's cold. No one's coming out to a park today."

"Maybe a cop will." Leena sighed. "What's up with this Michael?"

"You know what's up." He fondled her and kissed her until she gave in. He guided her to the back. Their lust played out quickly.

Leena snuggled up to Michael. "You're a bad influence. I can't believe you talked me into this."

"I think it's more exciting when it's sort of wrong, don't you? Remember the library?"

"Yes, you're right, I guess," Leena said, but missed the romantic aspect of it. "There's something to be said about relaxing too."

"We're relaxing right now. What did you bring for lunch today?" Michael asked.

"Roast beef sandwiches and some homemade cookies."

"Did you make the cookies?"

"I did."

In the front seat again, Michael devoured his food quickly, Leena picked.

"I hate all this sneaking around, Michael," Leena said, wanting to talk future.

"We won't sneak around forever, hon," Michael said. "I don't think talking about it, at least for now, will do us any good. Let's get through the holidays."

"I know."

"I don't know about you but I worked up an appetite." He took another huge bite.

"When all this gets resolved, when we finally can be together-together, I'd love to take a trip somewhere, wouldn't you?" Leena nibbled her sandwich.

"Sure, that would be nice. Like where?"

"What do you think of Ireland?" Leena asked.

"I don't know. I hadn't, but I will now. Why, that's your first choice?"

"I think so. Or maybe the Grand Canyon. Can you believe I've never been to either?"

"I went out to the Grand Canyon about fifteen years ago with some buddies. It was awesome. We hiked all the way down and camped. Hiked all the way back out the next day."

"You did? I'd love to do that. At our age, we'd probably have to train ahead of time." Leena laughed. "Get a Stairmaster or something."

Michael smiled and nodded in agreement. "Why Ireland?"

"I don't know. It's so beautiful there. All my ancestors are Irish. It's not that I have any big connection to them but it might be cool to go to the place where my great grandparents came from. Did you know I had an ancestor who survived Titanic?" Leena asked.

"You told me."

"Oh. So anyway, I tried to get Bruce to take me there a few years ago, but being the procrastinator that he is it never panned out. Then we got the inn, and, well, we never found the time or the money."

"Well, we'll go to Ireland, just you and me."

Leena stared at Michael with much hope and smiled.

THE FOLLOWING THURSDAY THEY met at the same location. The weather cooperated this time and they were able to walk around the park that they were only able to see the week before through drippy windows. They walked along the path that eventually led to a duck pond. There were many people out enjoying a crisp October day. The ducks waddled in and out of the water accepting a steady diet of bread from young children and elder folk. The trees were letting go of their leaves; there were still enough remaining to make the branches sway with a just a gentle breeze.

They stood at the edge of the pond and looked out with little to say. Leena suspected Michael was sulking. She had insisted they just spend time together and not resort to anything physical. "We're building our relationship this way," Leena had told him.

They found an empty bench and sat down. Michael sat with his legs apart and with his hands buried inside the front pouch pocket of his hooded sweatshirt. He had the hood up. Leena looked at him and could only see the tip of his nose behind the fabric. She dug one of his hands out of his pocket and took it out and held it. He looked at Leena and smiled.

"How's business?" she asked.

Michael seemed surprised by the question. "Oh fine. Same shit, different day. How's the inn?"

Leena laughed and mimicked him. "Same shit, different day." She turned smiling and nodding, looking out at the pond. "But these meetings are what I look forward to," she said looking back at him.

Michael nodded. "It's nice."

"How are you and Alice getting along?"

Michael's head turned quickly. "We're not going to get into that are we?"

"I'm just asking."

"We get along okay, I guess. So this is your idea of improving our relationship?"

"I just want total honesty, that's all." Leena wanted to hear him complain about her, say something negative. "I'm so sick of Bruce I could spit. I told you about the wedding. He drinks and then his lips flap."

"I know what that's like. My father was pretty much that way. He finally stopped drinking. Well, now his ticker isn't so good. People like that, they don't seem to care that they are hurting the ones they love. They're selfish. When they get sick, that's when they stop. For themselves, not for their family."

"It can be a toxic situation," Leena added. "I see that it can't be good for the kids either, or should I say it hasn't been good for them. They're getting so old now. What's done is done. But I think what we have is making me realize what I don't have, or never had, with Bruce. It's been an eye-opener. I guess I am feeling more ready to take a step toward something new. You know what I mean?"

"And like I said last time, let's be patient."

Leena knew she had to back off. She changed the subject. "How's that addition coming? You haven't mentioned it lately, or at all."

"Oh, it's pretty close to finished. The rest of the bathroom went in this past weekend. The tile was done, and the tub and toilet, they were done, but the counter and sink were put in the other day. Now Alice is picking out wallpaper. Now comes the fun part for her. She loves the details. That's not my thing. You're like that, right? You've got a lot of rooms to decorate."

"There're lots of rooms. A lot of detail. I like that."

"She's got carpet and wallpaper sample book things all over the place and paint swatches. She's like, 'Which one do you like?' and I'm like, 'I don't care, you decide.'" Michael laughed a little. "I'm glad she's like that, 'cause I would pick something hideous, or they'd just be white walls."

Leena had become quiet. Michael looked at her. "What?"

She wiped one eye and sniffed.

"What's wrong?"

"It's hard," she said wiping the other eye, "hearing about her and your life in that house. I shouldn't have asked."

"I'm sorry. You asked about the addition. I didn't mean to hurt you." Michael said hugging her with an arm across her shoulder.

"I know. It's not your fault. I asked."

"So how's that girl Jackie working out," Michael asked, changing the subject.

"Oh, Jackie! Where do I begin? She's been major league moping around the past week. I told you we went to find her mother right?"

"Hmm, not such a good idea."

Leena looked at him sternly. "Thanks for reminding me."

"Sorry. You know what I mean."

"It was quite a blow for her. I wish I could take it all back. I wish I had the foresight, but that's the way it played out. I feel kind of guilty about it all. I can't help it."

"I told you, you shouldn't feel guilty. She was pretty determined to find her, as I recall."

"I know, but I still wish I had checked out her mother on my own. I could have avoided that whole scene." Michael was quiet. "Maybe someday this will actually be a good thing that happened to her. Finding her mother again, I mean."

"Things have a way of working themselves out," Michael concluded.

"Rick's been great. He comes around a few times a week and so that lifted her out of her funk, anyway. She met his folks which is what whet her appetite to find her mother.

"You're doing a good job," Michael said.

"Thanks. I appreciate that."

Michael got up off the bench and led her by the hand. They walked around the pond again, heading back to their cars.

"You sure you don't want to hang out together inside the van?" he asked, as they headed toward his van.

"Hang out? Don't you mean have sex? No!"

"If it's that time of the month, maybe you could just do *me* a favor," Michael said under her hair as he kissed her neck and collarbone.

"Michael! Geez!"

"We've got time. Come on. You said you didn't have to leave today until one. It's not even noon." He had a way of convincing her.

"Alright," Leena gave in and they got into the van. She still wasn't into it. "So we'll just 'hang out' as you put it. We'll talk," she said sternly.

"Okay. What do you want to talk about?" he asked.

"I don't know. How about old friends we both knew from high school?"

"Boring." Michael leaned over and kissed her. When they stopped minutes later Michael had his pants unzipped and he was ready for whatever favor Leena would do for him. She obliged.

"I better get going," Michael said immediately after.

"You said we had until one. Why don't we take another walk."

"No, I should be heading back, really. Same time, same place?"

"Okay."

With a peck on the lips, he was gone. Gone from her life for another week. Leena went home feeling let down. She knew Michael went home happy.

THE NEXT WEEK WAS the same only Leena partook equally in the sexual activities in the back of his van. Michael was fulfilling a need, no doubt, but the most important need was not being met. This drive-by companionship couldn't begin to fill the void she had in her life with Bruce. What was just a fissure in her marriage was now a chasm. There was no jumping back over to the old, familiar side.

As she drove home, she realized she was crying. Jackie popped into her mind. She recalled the conversation they had at the kitchen table when she first started seeing Rick. Something she said kept repeating in Leena's mind all the way home: "I didn't want it to happen in a car. I want it to be more special than that." And this coming from such a confused young woman.

CHAPTER 28

Jackie didn't even look both ways when she crossed the street. She ran to the car and got in quickly. It wasn't the rain that made her run, even though it was coming down in buckets, but rather the profound loss. Sitting in the driver's seat she stared straight ahead and tried to take in what she had just seen.

A few minutes later Becky came out and got into the car.

A gasping choke emerged from Jackie's throat bringing up with it a sob. She asked, "Why?" but knew there was no answer for such a simple question.

"What happened?" Becky asked.

Jackie sat in silence and didn't answer her. She looked over at the front of the bar. The neon lights that spelled out *Mayfield's* wobbled with the raindrops through the windshield. They saw a man come out of the building with a jacket draped over his head. He looked up and down the street and then crossed. Rick recognized the car. He tapped on the glass and motioned for Jackie to put the window down. She ignored him.

"Come on Jackie, open the window, or let me get in the car," Rick said loud enough to be heard through the glass.

Jackie ignored him. She looked up at his face and it triggered her mouth to quiver and more tears to fall. "Go away!" She screamed.

"Would you open the window, please!"

She opened the window an inch. "What?"

"Jackie, I can explain."

"I saw you. I saw *her*! What is there to explain?"

"Look, I like you a lot. More than a lot, but I never said we were exclusive. I'm sorry you had to see that, I truly am." Rick said rather matter of fact. Jackie said nothing and Rick continued. "I didn't know you were coming tonight."

"Obviously!" she screamed.

"Can I get in? It's kinda like pouring out here?" Rick asked. He stood for a minute and realized he was getting nowhere. He nodded and said, "I'll call you."

"Don't bother." Jackie shut the window.

Rick stared at her and then turned around and ran back inside.

"What's going on? What happened?" Becky fired off her questions.

Jackie told her.

JACKIE WANTED TO SURPRISE Rick. She and Becky arrived late only catching two songs from *Backlash*'s first set. The girls stood in the back of the room. The band took their break after Rick's father announced that they would return in fifteen minutes.

Jackie stopped dead in her tracks as she rounded the corner on the other side of the stage, down a dark corridor. A pretty blonde girl wearing a small halter top and a short skirt had her arms around Rick's neck, kissing and hugging him. At first, Jackie didn't realize it was Rick. As she went further down the hallway the reality of what she was seeing sunk in. She saw a girl running her fingers through Rick's dirty-blonde hair. Rick's arms were around this girl's tiny waist. Suddenly Jackie felt paralyzed and sick. She watched Rick's gestures that were familiar to her now. She heard him say to the girl, "You're coming over later after we're done, right?" She heard the girl's reply, "Of course."

When a waiter came through the hallway and asked Jackie if he could help her, Jackie said "No, I was just leaving."

Rick and the girl looked her way when they heard the voices. Rick saw Jackie. The last thing Jackie saw was the utter shock of discovering her presence in the hallway. "Jackie, wait!" he yelled out to her but Jackie was already running out of the building.

BECKY HAD SUCH EMPATHY for Jackie that she was crying too. "He's a schmuck! You don't need some two-timing ass hole like that in your life. Musicians are the worst!"

"Don't I know *that* already. My mother left me and my sister for one. God, how ironic!" she screamed and cried.

They both cried. Becky said, "Let's go back to my dorm. You want me to drive?"

Jackie nodded without looking at her.

Jackie and Becky got out of the car and switched sides. Becky got behind the wheel.

As they drove back to Becky's school Jackie stared out the window crying and sniffing. Becky pulled into her dorm parking lot.

Jackie asked, "Does anyone ever stay together?"

Becky replied, "Sure. Someday you'll find someone who will be loyal to you."

"That'll be the day. It's just not meant to be, for me!" She looked at Becky through eyes filled with tears. One blink sent them streaming down her cheeks. "I thought he was the one Becky. I loved him!" She sobbed. Becky dug around in her purse and handed her a tissue.

Becky hugged her and pulled her head down on her shoulder and stroked her hair. "Come in for a little while. You're in no condition to drive. You can stay here for the night if you want."

"No, I promised your mother I'd work tomorrow's breakfast shift. I gotta go. I'll be fine."

"No, you're not. Come in."

Jackie agreed.

Becky's roommate was gone. Jackie plunked herself down in a chair and Becky sat on the edge of her bed and watched her cry.

"Do you think your parents still love each other?" Jackie finally asked.

"I guess so. Why?"

"I don't know. I mean, it doesn't seem like they do. Feels like they just tolerate each other. That's the way it is for any relationship. They're all doomed!" She cried some more. "Why bother!" she said angrily.

"Well, my parents do fight sometimes, but they work it out. I know my dad drinks and that infuriates my mother." Becky said. "Hey, one time he was really drunk and he came down to the dining room, with a room full of inn guests, in his *underwear*. Can you believe it?" Becky laughed a forced laugh. "My mom was *pissed*!" Becky figured the story would make Jackie laugh. It didn't.

"When was that?"

"About a year ago." Becky said.

"Maybe everyone gets sick of everyone eventually and then they leave. Everyone leaves," she whimpered.

"Not everyone. I know this sucks, but don't get too negative about it. Not all guys are like that."

Jackie grunted a laugh. "Right. Chris is probably getting it on with some chick right now." Jackie looked at Becky and caught her look of disapproval to her comment. "I'm sorry Becky. Really I am. I didn't mean that." She started to cry again.

"I know you didn't. I understand." Becky struggled with what to say. "And you know, this doesn't mean it's the end with Rick."

Jackie looked at her like she was crazy.

"You two can get beyond this. You're both young and, I don't know, shit happens."

"You'd take Chris back?"

"I hate the thought of it, but I suppose I would. I would consider it. If it were just a one night stand I might. I don't know. I hope to never find out."

"I hope you don't either. It sucks."

They sat together in silence. Jackie was calmer. "I should get going," Jackie said.

"No, stay the night."

"No, I'm gonna go."

"I insist Jackie! I'll call my mom and explain that..."

"I'll be fine." She got up off the chair and Becky stood up. "Your mom is expecting me."

"You're staying. Please. Blabbermouth is gone for the weekend. You can sleep on her bed. I'll call Mom."

"Alright. Thanks, Becky. You're the best."

"It'll be okay, you'll see," Becky put her arm around Jackie's shoulders.

SUNDAY MORNING LEENA SERVED breakfast by herself. With leaf viewing season in full swing the inn was close to capacity. She managed alone but did receive a few complaints about slow service.

Leena was not the least bit mad. Jackie returned to the inn around eleven. Leena made it a point to be hanging around the kitchen when she knew, from Becky's call, she was on the way.

Jackie entered the kitchen. She could have gone directly into her apartment from the outside but didn't. Contrary to her body language and what she said when asked if she wanted to talk, Leena knew she wanted a shoulder to cry on. "No, I don't want to talk about it," and "What's there to say?" were her auto-responses. Jackie sat down with a big sigh. She finally made eye contact with Leena. The tears began all over again.

Leena took her hands in hers and gave them a squeeze. "I know there's really nothing I can say that's gonna make you feel better. Time will heal. That's not just some bull people say. Think of this as a rite of passage. Every girl gets her heart broken at least once."

"I've had my share, don't you think? And I'm only nineteen!" She took her hands back and leaned against the back of the chair, slumping, knees coming forward. She put her hands into her jacket pockets.

"But you're young and you do have a long life out ahead of you. You're a beautiful girl. Has anyone ever told you that?"

"Rick did," she cried. She took her hand out of her jacket pocket and wiped her cheek with her fingers.

"Being so pretty has its upsides and its downsides. You're not going to have any trouble meeting guys. You'll get more opportunities than a lot of girls out there. You can be pickier. That's the good news. But there will be a learning curve. You'll just have to learn how to tell the bullshitters from the sincere ones."

"Rick *was* sincere. I don't know," she sobbed. "He wasn't, was he – sincere? He seemed like he cared." She put her head down on the table on top of her folded arms. Leena stroked her silky, long brown hair. She sniffed and wiped her nose on her sleeve.

Jackie lifted her head. "I'm gonna go take a hot shower and try to wash this feeling off me."

"You need to 'wash that man right out of your hair,'" Leena sang from *South Pacific*.

Jackie looked completely puzzled. "Huh?"

"Never mind. I'll see you later. I'll be baking today so if you want to join me, please do, okay?"

"Maybe." She went into her apartment.

CHAPTER 29

Disappointment and loss were powerful mood-altering forces. Leena thought Jackie handled what her mother dished out fairly well, but when Rick didn't work out, she worried about her. She saw the despair in her eyes. Her attitude was weak at best. Knowing her history made Leena nervous. She never regretted taking Jackie in and giving her a new home, but she was feeling the burden of responsibility now. Leena was kicking herself for how she handled the search for her mother.

"I don't need you until four. Anything you feel like doing until then? We could go shopping or something?" Leena asked Jackie.

Jackie shifted in her seat at the kitchen table and without looking at Leena put her head down on the table on top of her crossed arms. "Mmmm," she muttered.

Leena tried again. "You know, our Halloween party is this Thursday. I have some ideas for you. Becky and I got our costumes at a store up in Westerly and…"

Jackie stood up, and as if Leena had not been speaking, walked away and went outside. Leena went to the window and watched her walk down the street. Jackie walked slowly without looking up from the road. She disappeared around the bend. Leena worked in the kitchen but kept an eye on the street waiting for her return.

Later, Leena went out front to wait, using the excuse of pulling weeds out of her chrysanthemum beds. She heard voices coming from down the street. Jackie was walking back toward the inn and she wasn't alone. A young man accompanied her. Jackie was laughing and that surprised Leena. The two of them walked up to Leena and stood right next to where she was kneeling on the ground. "Hey Leena," Jackie said.

Leena looked up, using her hand to shield the sun from her eyes. "Jackie, hi."

"This is Garrett. Garrett this is Leena."

Leena stood up. The young man nodded, smiled, and said, "Yo."

"Hello Garrett, nice to meet you." Leena pushed her hair out of her eyes with the back of her hand and squinted with one eye to get a good look. He looked older than Jackie but didn't act it. He wore an oversize T-shirt and long shorts that hung low on his hips. The pant legs ended way below the knee. She could see that he had a big, black tattoo that wrapped around his right calf. His hair hung in his face, almost completely obscuring his eyes. It didn't look clean.

"I'll see ya," Jackie said. They continued to walk down the street around to the other side of the inn. Leena watched.

Leena went upstairs to get ready for the evening. She first went to the TV room where she had a better view of the other side of the road. She watched as Jackie laughed at some silly moves Garrett was making: some kind of punk-style moonwalk, Leena surmised. Leena showered and changed and went back down to the kitchen. Hal had arrived and was organizing his work area. Leena stepped outside to look for Jackie again.

"She's out on the front porch," Hal said. He knew she had been concerned all week.

Leena came back inside. "Oh, okay," Leena said.

Minutes later Jackie entered the kitchen. "I'll be right back. Gotta change." She left and went to her apartment and returned a few minutes later. "Told you I'd be ready at four," Jackie said, pointing at the clock that showed four o'clock exactly.

"I didn't have a doubt," Leena said. "Who was that?"

"I told you, Garrett. I met him down at the amusement park just now. Kinda cute, heh?"

"Kinda. You're not jumping right into something are you?" Leena said noticing the sudden change in her mood.

"No, I just met him, Leena! Sheesh."

Jackie's mood elevated back to normal, but Leena knew it was artificial.

THE HALLOWEEN DECORATIONS HAD been up for two weeks. When Halloween day arrived, Jackie and Jason helped Leena get ready for the annual Frazer Halloween party. By late afternoon Becky arrived home with her friend Cheryl.

Jason got into his hobo clothes, making his face dirty with some of Becky's charcoal pencils.

Jackie's idea of participating was to wear all black clothing; more black eye makeup than usual; and black nail polish.

Becky dressed up as Britney Spears. Cheryl was a playboy bunny. Leena dressed up as a 1920s flapper. Mothers, neighbors, and friends came dressed up. Quite a crowd had gathered.

Bruce came home from work and stopped to look around. Leena, Becky, and Jason crowded around him laughing and talking at the same time.

"Why don't you come to the party this year Dad," Becky said.

"No, it's not for me. You have fun, though" he said. He walked over to the door to the upstairs.

Jason said, "Come on Dad, you can put on that baseball jersey and cap and come as Derek Jeter."

He turned and looked at Jason and said, "Tell me all about it later, sport." He entered the code and disappeared behind the door. Leena had a momentary feeling of sadness as she watched Bruce leave. She looked over at Jason who had disappointment written all over his face.

Trick or Treaters came up onto the porch and to the door which was adorned with a plastic skeleton. Two carved pumpkins, containing candles, sat on either side of the front door. Leena had purchased a pumpkin carving kit. She had chosen the template for a witch on a broomstick. Jason carved the other one following the pattern for a cat with an arching back. A tape machine, hidden under the hay that served as a chair for the stuffed jack-o-lantern-headed person, played spooky music. Fake spider webs were all over the porch.

The din of talk and laughter filled the front room of the inn. The doorbell rang consistently during the party. Leena offered a huge bowl full of assorted candy. She encouraged each kid to take a big handful. When a child was too polite Leena took more candy out of the dish and put it into their bags.

Jason and his friend, Ryan, worked the CD changer. He was officially too old to go door to door. A decision Leena and Jason argued about three years ago when Jason was in seventh grade. She had told him, "You're getting too old for Trick or Treating. You'd only be going out looking for trouble. If it's not about getting the candy anymore, you're not going. Perfectly nice and honest kids turn to vandalism at this age. The answer is No!" That was the year Leena started throwing parties for her kids and others. She gave them an alternative to mischief.

Leena went to the door to greet the next visitor and a young man stood there looking like a punk rocker or a biker, it was hard to tell. Leena recognized him. It was Garrett, the young man Jackie had brought back to the inn a few days before. He was not in costume. "Is Jackie here?" he asked.

"Oh Garrett, right? Yes, she's right over there," she said pointing across the room.

Garrett made a beeline to Jackie. She was delighted to see him. She clung to his arm and he playfully pulled her hair.

The time came to judge the best costume. Leena and Becky were the judges. Leena announced to the group that two winners would be picked in five minutes. They decided on two of Jason's friends. One wore an alien costume and the other wore a Frankenstein costume. The prizes were two twenty-dollar gift certificates, one to the local video game store, and one to a music store.

Before the announcement, Leena went to find Jackie. She was missing. Leena walked into the kitchen and heard a sound coming from the pantry around the corner. She poked her head around and saw Jackie and Garrett kissing. They were standing up but were all over each other. Garrett's hands were up under her shirt. Leena was startled. "Oh, I'm sorry, I didn't know…" Jackie looked at Leena and smiled at her. Garrett had a look of lust on his face. He glared at Leena waiting for her to leave so he could go back to what he was doing. Leena turned around immediately and walked back into the kitchen. She momentarily forgot why she had come out to the kitchen and went back into the front room to join the party.

"Mom, you ready?" Becky asked.

"What? Oh, yes."

"What's wrong?"

"Nothing. Let's announce the winners.

JACKIE AND GARRETT JOINED the party a little while later but eventually disappeared before the party ended at eleven. Becky, Jason, and Cheryl helped clean up as did some of the mothers and neighbors. With so many helpers it was done quickly. Jackie was nowhere to be found. Leena asked the girls, "Do any of you know where Jackie went?"

"No," Becky said. Cheryl shrugged.

"She was hanging around with that guy and, well, I was just wondering if…" Leena found it hard to concentrate. She changed gears. "When are you going back, girls?"

"Tomorrow morning," Becky said. "Cheryl has an 8:45 class and I have a ten o'clock class. We're leaving around 7:45."

"You want to drop Jason at school on your way tomorrow morning, that is, if you can leave around 7:30?"

"Sure," Becky said.

"Well, you'd better get to bed then. Thanks for helping girls."

"Ok, goodnight Mom."

"Night, hon. Night Cheryl."

"Good night Mrs. Frazer," Cheryl said.

Before Leena went upstairs, she heard music and laughter from Jackie's room. She also heard a deeper voice and it was easy to put two and two together: she had invited Garrett into her room. Leena stood for a moment at her door, not listening in, but simply feeling disappointed about Jackie's choice.

SOMETHING WOKE HER UP. The clock displayed 3:11. Squinting and feeling confused Leena had no idea why she woke up. Then she heard something rattling outside below her window. Leena thought it might be a raccoon getting into a garbage can. She saw a garbage can on its side but it was no raccoon. It was Garrett walking away from the inn. He had come from Jackie's outside entrance. He staggered away, across the Miller's front lawn and down the street.

Leena went back to her bed and sat on the edge for a minute. She turned to look at Bruce. He was sound asleep. She decided to go down and check on things.

Only two couples were staying at the inn that night. The inn was quiet. She heard the faint sound of snoring coming from one of the rooms. Leena went out on the front porch to see if Garrett was coming back. He wasn't. All the doors were locked. She walked by Jackie's door and it was quiet so she decided to go back to bed.

AT 7:00 A.M. LEENA was preparing breakfast for one of the couples. Becky and her friend, Cheryl came down not looking very rested. They helped themselves to some coffee. Leena talked them into eating some French toast. Jason joined them.

"Isn't Jackie helping this morning?" Becky asked.

"No. I didn't need her this morning. Only four guests. She lowered her voice and said, "That guy she was with spent the night. Well, part of the night. He stumbled out of here around three o'clock." Leena showed her disgust.

"You're kidding!" Becky said. "Oh my God." She made a face to Cheryl.

Leena shook her head as she kept her eyes on the French toast she was turning over in the pan. "I hope she knows what she's doing."

"She didn't waste much time finding a new boyfriend," Jason said.

"Is Rick out of the picture for good?" Becky asked her mother.

"Apparently so. I thought he would call her but so far he hasn't." Leena put the slices onto two plates and added bacon and started to head toward the dining room.

"That's so sad. She was crazy about him," Becky said. Leena nodded in agreement.

Leena brought plates out to the couple in the dining room. She chatted with the couple for a few minutes and then returned to the kitchen. The girls and Jason were getting ready to leave.

"We gotta go. Thanks, Mom. And thanks for the party. Awesome as usual," Becky said.

"Thanks, Mrs. Frazer," Cheryl said.

"You are very welcome. Did you leave your costumes out where I can find them? I'm gonna return them all today."

"Yeah, they're on my bed."

"Okay, email me when you get there?"

"Yep." Becky gave her mother a hug and a kiss on the cheek and left.

"Be careful," Leena called out to the girls as they got into Cheryl's car. "Jason, you ready?"

Jason followed his sister to the car. "See you later, Honey," Leena called out to Jason.

Leena went back to the dining room to offer the couple a coffee refill. "What else can I get for you today?" Leena asked.

The man said, "Everything was perfect. You want anything, Mary?"

"No, I'm fine." She sipped on her coffee. "So you had a Halloween party here last night?"

"Yes, I've been doing that for the kids for years. We have so much fun. I hope it didn't disturb you."

"Oh no, not at all. I love kids. I'm a retired school teacher. Retired last year."

"You don't say. My best friend is a teacher. She's lives in Connecticut."

The conversation paused and Leena took her cue to head back to the kitchen.

"Oh, excuse me, one more thing," Mary said. Leena turned around and returned to their table. "I hope I don't sound nosey, but I heard something last night in that room out in the back and…"

She trailed off and Leena was immediately interested. It was Jackie's room. "Yes?"

"I heard some commotion and I thought I heard some yelling."

Mary's husband interrupted, "Mary, please."

"I want to tell her, Richard." She turned back to look at Leena. "I heard someone yelling and it woke me up. It startled me a little. It sort of sounded like a woman screaming. Then I heard a garbage can fall over outside. I hope everything is alright."

Leena thought of Garrett stumbling out after three. She tried to recall what it was she heard before the garbage can was knocked over. "I heard the garbage can too. I have a tenant that lives in the room. She works here." Leena paused and thought about it, still holding the coffee pot. "I'm going to go check on her right now." Leena turned to leave and stopped and turned around to face Mary again. "Thank you."

She approached the door and knocked on it. There was no answer. She knocked harder and still harder. "Jackie, you awake? Open up hon."

Mary and Richard stood outside the kitchen door in the hallway on their way back to their room. Mary stopped and peered through the crack of the kitchen door to find out the outcome despite her husband's request to mind her own business.

"Jackie, open up. I want to talk to you."

Still nothing.

Leena went to get her master key. She knocked one more time before she used it.

Leena opened the door. Jackie was lying on the floor, naked. Leena screamed. In a déjà vu moment, she fell to her knees to see if she was alive. The irony of this repeated scene shook Leena to her core. "Jackie!" she screamed. She couldn't wake her up. She was beaten and bloody. Leena screamed again, "Jackie!" Mary and Richard charged through the kitchen and stood at the entrance to Jackie's room. Leena grabbed a blanket off the bed to cover her body. She stood up and ran to the kitchen intercom and called Bruce. "Bruce, are you there? Are you there?" No answer. "Bruce," she screamed, "Where are you?"

"What?" he finally said.

"Bruce something's wrong with Jackie," she said frantically. "Jackie's been attacked! Get down here, hurry!" Leena looked at the couple who were now standing in the kitchen.

"What can we do?" Richard asked.

Leena stared at them blankly. She stood up. She put her hand to her forehead to think. Leena was crying hysterically. She said through her sobs to the couple, "I'll call an ambulance. You make sure there's a pillow under her head." They started to walk into her room. Leena yelled. "No! Don't touch her. Oh my God! You shouldn't touch an injured person." She dialed 911 and panted out the crisis to the operator.

Bruce rushed down the stairs and into Jackie's room. Leena was huddled over Jackie trying to rouse her gently by patting her cheek and saying her name over and over.

The couple remained in the kitchen, not knowing what to do. "Richard go out and flag down the ambulance," Mary said.

"She's breathing, but it's shallow," Leena said.

Bruce was down on his knees saying, "Jackie, can you hear me? Can you hear me?"

Jackie moved her head slightly and opened one eye very briefly. The other eye was swollen shut. Her lips moved to say something, but then she was quiet.

Leena started to cry. "Jackie, honey, can you speak to me?" She cried and mumbled, "Why didn't I check on her when I got up. Oh my God!" Leena looked around the room. There were beer cans strewn all over the floor, a bottle of Jack Daniels sat on a table, and the lamp Leena had bought years ago for her mother was broken, lying on the floor. Leena walked into the kitchen and paced around the room mumbling to herself. Bruce knelt by Jackie, talking to her and rubbing her hair.

The ambulance arrived. A man and a woman came in with the backboard and medical bags. Richard led them through the inn to Jackie's room.

"I know who did this Bruce."

"Who? Rick?" Bruce asked.

"No, no, a guy she just met. He came to the party last night. I should have gone into her room last night when I heard the noise. Damn it!"

"What noise?" Bruce asked.

A police officer walked in. "What happened here?" he asked.

"My tenant, Jackie Furth, was attacked," Leena said breathlessly.

"Let's start from the beginning," the police officer said. "Do you know what happened?"

"Not really. I heard something."

"What did you hear?"

Leena watched the paramedics from the kitchen working on Jackie as she lay on her bedroom floor. They checked her vitals and put a neck collar around her neck.

"Ma'am, tell me what happened."

Leena finally looked at the officer. "I woke up around 3:00 but I don't know what woke me. Then I heard some noise out back. It was the garbage can. From my bedroom window, I recognized that boy that Jackie met. Garrett something. He had come out of her room and walked up the street. He came to our Halloween party last night. All I know is his first name: Garrett. She met him down at the amusement park. Why didn't I do something right then and *there*?" She cried.

Leena turned suddenly toward Mary. "What did you hear? You said you heard screaming?"

"Your name ma'am?" the officer asked Mary.

"Mary Carnaroli. This is my husband, Richard. We're guests. I woke up because I heard some yelling, maybe someone screaming. I'm a light sleeper. Then I heard the garbage can fall over, like she did. I feel terrible that I didn't do something. I mean whatever I heard wasn't something that lasted long. It was quiet right afterward. I guess that's why I ignored it. Richard here is always telling me to mind my own business." Richard stood, looking sheepish.

"Is that all you heard?" he asked.

Leena and Mary nodded. Bruce and Richard did not hear a thing. The officer told Leena not to disturb her room until he got a team over to investigate.

"Do you have any other guests?" the officer asked.

"Yes, just one couple. They're upstairs."

"Could I talk to them?"

"Do you want me to knock on their door?"

"Yes ma'am."

That wasn't necessary. At that moment the couple came down the stairs and headed toward everyone.

"What's going on?" the man asked.

The police officer questioned the couple. They had not heard anything.

The paramedics lifted the board Jackie was strapped to. She had the blanket on her. Leena rushed in and removed Jackie's bathrobe off of the hook of her bathroom door. She handed to them and they placed it over her and put her arms into the sleeves.

"I'll take care of the guests, okay?" Bruce put his arm around Leena's shoulder. "You go with Jackie. Everything'll be fine." Leena started to sob all over again.

"Thanks, Bruce. Thanks, I need to go, you know?" Leena said. She hugged Bruce and followed the paramedics out to the ambulance. "I'll call you when I know something."

JACKIE HAD A CONCUSSION, a cracked rib, and quite a few bruises. Her right wrist was sprained but not broken. She needed three stitches on her upper lip. The tests showed that her blood alcohol was very high. Jackie needed to stay overnight for observation.

Leena called Bruce. "They're going to let me see her in a few minutes." She told Bruce of her injuries. "Don't forget to pick up Jason from school. And can you and Jason keep an eye out for the new arrivals later? I think there are, I don't know, seven or eight people coming later today. Look at my book near the phone in the kitchen."

"I will. Don't worry. Jason and I will handle it. Don't rush back."

"Hal can call his nephew, and I think Michelle can call Carly, or whoever, to help if I'm not back."

"We'll manage. Stop worrying. See you later," Bruce said.

"Thanks. Did you feed the other guests?" Leena asked.

"We're all fine here. I had a nice visit with them."

"I appreciate it, Bruce. What about work?"

"I'm going to go to the office for a little while before I get Jason."

"Can you put out the sign out front that says 'Back at 3:00'? Sometimes people show up early, you know."

"Sure thing," Bruce said patiently. They hung up.

Leena walked into Jackie's room. Jackie turned to Leena and smiled when she saw her. Leena gently asked, "How are you feeling? You gave us all quite a scare."

"I'm feeling pretty stupid at the moment, and pretty sore."

"I bet. What happened, Jackie? I told the police officer it was that Garrett person. I saw him leave. You'll have to give a statement when he comes."

"I don't even remember that much. I'm so stupid. We got drunk. I let him talk me into…" Jackie trailed off.

"He talked you into what?" Leena asked.

"Nothing. Shit, I'm so stupid!"

"Would you stop saying you're stupid. Are you saying that he forced himself on you?" Leena tried to say it delicately.

Jackie looked down, avoiding eye contact. "You mean did he rape me? No, at least I don't think so. We had sex. I didn't really want to. I didn't say no, you know? And, well, he did it." Jackie looked up at Leena started to cry. "Kinda dumb. I guess that wouldn't count as rape would it?"

Leena said, "Before you leave here, I want you to talk to someone about it. Let's find out for sure what it was. You came in unconscious. We'll ask if they did a rape test on you. Is there any possibility that you might be pregnant?"

"No. I went back on the pill when I was with Rick." She started to cry again. She put her hand up to her new stitches on her mouth when she felt a tug. "I figured Rick would come back to me." She shook her head and turned toward the window. Her sobs were barely audible.

"What on earth made him beat you up?"

Jackie turned around to face Leena. "We were both drinking. We were listening to music. We were drunk. *Damn it all*," Jackie yelled. Leena was startled. "I *hate* drinkers. So why would *I drink*? So stupid. I'm no different than my father!"

"Calm down. Then what happened?"

"I think I yelled at him after he had sex with me. He thought I was accusing him of rape, so he smacked me in the face. I called him something like a 'gutless coward' for hitting a woman and he went psycho on me."

Leena took her hand. "This is very distressing that you resorted to this behavior, behavior that got you into trouble a short time ago, Jackie. This is not a good sign."

"I didn't try to kill myself. Is that what you think? Or you think I wanted him to try and kill me?"

"No, but you let some stranger take advantage of you. Didn't that happen after Kevin? The night you tried to kill yourself? I wouldn't exactly call you lucky, but next time you might get killed by the guy you let take you off to some secluded spot." Leena was tough but she knew she had to be.

Jackie knew she was right. She turned her face to the wall and didn't respond.

"This isn't teaching Rick a lesson. It didn't teach Kevin a lesson."

"I don't need a lecture right now, Leena! *I* learned a lesson!"

"Apparently not!" Leena's voice went up. She lowered it. "I'm just concerned for your well-being."

Leena stayed when the doctor came in to talk to her about test results. She stayed when the counselor, Susan, came in to see her. Leena recognized Susan immediately from the first visit regarding Jackie and her suicide attempt. Between Susan's visit and a visit from the police officer, they got all the information they needed.

CHAPTER 30

Leena crawled into bed with the covers up to her chin and a pillow down the middle of the bed sandwiching her in like a cocoon. The TV remote lay on her stomach at the ready. Dateline NBC had a segment about insurance fraud. Leena watched but did not pay attention.

Bruce came in and got ready for bed. "You're in bed early."

"I know. Glad today's over. I'm whipped."

"Long day," he said.

"You said it. Not one I would want to repeat any time soon."

"They'll release her tomorrow?"

"That's what they're thinking. I hope so." Leena sighed and looked at Bruce. "So, you think I should kick her to the curb now?"

"I didn't say that! No, I don't think that at all. She's been through hell," he said, being more sympathetic about Jackie than usual. "I truly feel sorry for her. She didn't deserve that."

Leena looked at Bruce with gratitude and smiled at him.

Bruce crawled into bed next to her. "So are you too exhausted for this?" He leaned over and kissed her on the cheek, although he aimed for her mouth, she moved to avoid him. He reached his hand up and brushed her hair from her face.

She looked at him, puzzled. Leena still felt something for him she thought she had lost, or had dismissed. He leaned over again and kissed her. She didn't move this time. He removed the pillow that separated them. She allowed him to move up against her body. His breathing accelerated. He felt around for the remote control and shut the television off.

Michael flashed across her mind momentarily, but she put him out of her mind. Bruce's large frame was upon her in a short amount of time. She was surprised to realize she wanted him there.

Afterward, Bruce lay with his arm across Leena's belly. Leena pulled the blankets up over them both. She didn't know how she felt. Was it still love? Or was it just sex? She was very confused. Leena felt guilty about being with Bruce and, at the same time, guilty about her affair she was having with Michael. She thought of how Michael had told her he had not given up his marital relations, so ultimately, she felt justified.

"That was nice," Bruce said to her. Leena remained silent. "Wasn't it?" He asked.

"Yes." Her feelings for Bruce didn't seem to compare to how she felt about Michael. If she hadn't found Michael again this feeling would have sufficed.

"It's been a while hasn't it?" Bruce asked.

"Yes it has," Leena said, staring up at the ceiling. "Quite a while."

"We shouldn't let so much time go by," Bruce said. He took his arm off her stomach and turned over facing in the other direction. He was asleep within minutes.

LEENA WAS ABLE TO pick Jackie up by mid-afternoon the next day. She moved slowly getting out of the car. Her ribs were quite painful. Leena led Jackie up to Becky's bedroom.

"You can stay here for now. You're going to have to take it really easy this week. Just let me wait on you, okay?" Leena told her.

Jackie liked the idea of being pampered by Leena. She looked at this incident as a good thing. Her ribs made sitting up straight painful. Leena fluffed her pillows to accommodate the angle that felt most comfortable.

"I've got chicken pot pie for dinner later. How does that sound?"

"Whatever you have would be fine, thanks," Jackie said. "I was going to work the dinner shift tonight. I feel so bad."

"Well, it looks like you won't be doing any of that for a little while." Leena smiled. "Don't worry about it."

"I feel bad about messing up your schedule."

"Why don't you concentrate on getting better and not worrying about things you can't control. Michelle said she can get her niece to come tonight and Hal's son is coming in to do some housekeeping. They're willing to work in a pinch. So no need to worry about it." Leena started to leave.

"I'm so lucky to have met you," Jackie said.

Leena stopped and turned around and said, "I know." She smiled and left and went into the kitchen. She came back a few minutes later with some juice and a straw. "Here. Just holler if you need anything else."

LEENA COULDN'T HAVE TREATED Jackie any better than if she had been her own daughter. The care she took was something she was willing to do. But her ultimate sacrifice, however, was canceling her next meeting with Michael. She felt a twinge in her stomach when she sent off the email that explained it all to him.

Leena heard Jackie call her name from Becky's bedroom. Leena went to the doorway and stood to see what she wanted. "Could you go down in my room and get my sketch pad and pencils? There on the dresser."

"Sure." Leena went down and retrieved the items and returned to her side. "Why don't you go out on the deck to sketch. It's not too cold. I brought your coat too." Leena placed it on the foot of the bed.

"Yeah, maybe. Okay, why not." She got up and Leena helped her on with her coat. They walked out onto the front deck off of the TV room, above the main porch. Jackie settled herself onto a lounge chair. Leena went back inside.

The gentle breeze that kicked up the dry leaves, making a swirling sound on the ground below was a reminder of the changing season. It was mild for the fifth of November.

Twenty minutes later Jackie came back in and stood in the doorway of the office. "It got cold out there." She stood silently, watching Leena work at the computer. "Whatcha doing?"

Leena looked up from the screen and said, "I'm updating the website. I want to announce our holiday hours and availability. Also, I'm offering a Christmastime package."

"You're open for business on Christmas?"

"Well, not *on* Christmas, but right before and right after. I usually shut down the week of Christmas through the new years, but I think I will make the inn available for some more holiday stuff." Leena typed and then continued. "This place needs the steady income to keep it afloat. I have to think of ways to get people to come."

"Oh," was all Jackie said. "I'm gonna go rest now. Call me when dinner is ready?"

"Okay." Leena looked up and watched Jackie walk slowly down the hall to Becky's room.

LEENA INVITED JACKIE TO join the family for dinner. Her face was not swollen anymore. Her black eye was now a shade of brown. The large scratch across her cheek, likely caused by a ring, was no longer bright red. The stitches in her lip had been removed earlier that day.

Jason and Bruce stared at her as she entered the dining room. Jackie looked at Jason as she sat down. She noticed his curiosity and said, "I'm quite a sight, ain't I?" Jason quickly looked down at his plate.

Jackie picked up her fork with her left hand and started to eat. Her right wrist although out of the splint was still a source of pain when she tried to twist it around to eat. Leena watched her struggle and said, "I took the liberty of cutting up your meat for you. But you are doing really well with your left hand, isn't she?" Leena looked up at Bruce and Jason. Observing Bruce's expression, she could read him like a book. He didn't approve of Jackie's presence at the table. Bruce's intolerance came sooner than she had expected.

Everyone started to eat. There was silence at the table until Bruce spoke. "So, what's the plan now, Jackie?" he asked her.

Jackie looked up from her plate over at Bruce and said, "About what?"

"Do you have any plans for, sort of, living your life a little more carefully?"

"Bruce!" Leena scolded.

Jackie looked at Leena and then back at Bruce. "Well, this taught me a pretty big lesson if that's what you mean." Then she muttered, "I was pretty stupid."

"I'd agree with that. You're not a cat, young lady, with nine lives, you know."

"No sir, I know."

"My wife can't be there to save you every time you make a bad decision. Your luck will run out eventually."

Leena looked over at Bruce. She was annoyed but tried to let the conversation burn itself out. She knew his lips were loosened by the fourth beer that he had brought to the dinner table.

"Without a plan, you're bound to falter," He continued.

Jackie said, "Yes sir."

Leena came to her rescue. "I think she's been through enough and she's coming along just fine, getting stronger every day." She quickly changed the subject. "Is it this weekend you are playing in that golf tournament?"

"Yes, that's right." Bruce's mind was on one track. "I knew a girl in college that slept around and didn't give much thought to her own welfare and you know what happened to her?" There was silence. "Well?" he asked as if Jackie actually would know the answer.

"No, I don't," she said.

"She slept around and…"

"Do we have to discuss such things at the dinner table?" Leena butted in looking at Bruce, getting his attention and motioning toward Jason indicating how he shouldn't tell the story in front of his son. Jason looked back and forth at his parents and Jackie as if he were at a tennis match.

Bruce ignored her. He didn't care that Jason was there. He continued, "She slept around and got AIDS. She's dead now, you know."

Jackie had stopped eating. Bruce frightened her and it wasn't the first time. He had been polite to her all weekend, but now he was turning on her. She looked at Bruce and nodded and looked down at her plate.

Leena couldn't take any more. "Would you shut up, Bruce! I'm sick of your comments, and if Jackie dared say it, she'd say the same thing. So *can it*!"

"Fine. I was just trying to help. Someone needs to wake this girl up. She's not doing it herself." He got up from the table abruptly and took his beer bottle and left the room. He walked down the hall to the TV room.

Leena and Jason watched him walk away. When they turned their heads back around, they saw Jackie with her head hanging down and she was crying.

"Don't listen to him," Leena said. "You know he can be a jerk sometimes."

"I got a similar lecture the other day from my dad, Jackie, only it was about a bad grade on my paper," Jason told her, trying to make her feel better.

Jackie looked over at Jason and smiled, acknowledging his empathy.

Jason continued but in a whisper. "He said that people who get bad grades will more than likely turn into homeless bums or something. I ignored him." Jason seemed older than his fifteen years at that moment.

"Thanks, Jason," Jackie said. "Thanks, Leena. And thanks for dinner. It looks great. I'm not hungry right now. I think I'm going to go to my room now, downstairs."

"You are not!" Leena said. "I said you can stay in Becky's room and I meant it. At least for a few more days."

"Whatever, I think I'll go now if you don't mind." Jackie got up and moaned as she straightened up and steadied herself with her good hand on the table.

"Alright. I'll check in on you later," Leena said. "Why don't I bring your meal to you."

"Maybe later. I'm not hungry. Thanks."

After Jackie shut the door to the bedroom Leena went down to the TV room. She stood in the doorway debating whether she would confront Bruce now or later. She stared at the balding spot on the back of his head. She turned and went back to the dining room realizing he had spoken under the influence. She and Jason finished eating in silence and then cleared the table together.

"I didn't know Daddy said that to you. He shouldn't scare you like that," Leena told Jason in the kitchen.

"It didn't scare me. I'm used to it. He was drunk so I ignored him." Jason left and went to his room.

Leena sat down at the stool at the kitchen counter. Tears filled her eyes. She hated Bruce at that moment. His getting drunk was so accepted, so matter of fact, to her children. She thought about their encounter a few nights earlier and it made her feel sick. She was mad at herself for falling for his false concern about Jackie. She was vulnerable and she let him come to her. She sat and drummed her fingers on the counter thinking of how much she wanted to tell him off.

Leena left the dishes and pans in the sink and went to the office to check her email. There was nothing there from Michael. She was disappointed. From the TV room next door, she heard her husband snoring. Leena shut the computer off and went to her bedroom to watch TV.

Later, Leena went through her normal routine of nagging Jason to shower and get ready for school the next day. Then she finished cleaning up the kitchen.

She stopped and poked her head in to check on Jackie. She was asleep with the television on. Leena tiptoed in and shut it off. She pulled a blanket up over her chest.

Then she turned off the television in the TV room where Bruce had also fallen asleep. She looked over at him. He was sitting up but his large frame was leaning to the right. His chin was almost on his chest. She hoped his neck would be stiff the next day. She went to bed alone.

THE NEXT DAY, AND the rest of the week, Jackie stayed upstairs while Leena waited on her. She was getting around better. She would spend hours in the TV room lying on the couch watching talk shows and soap operas and snacking on food that always seemed to leave crumbs.

They both agreed that she shouldn't have dinner at their table when Bruce was there. Leena hated giving in to his selfish drunkenness but it was necessary since Jackie was in no shape to be experiencing any more negative events.

Leena spent a lot of time with Jackie during her convalescence. She learned more about Jackie's parents and their poor choices.

Jackie and her sister, Jesse, sat together in the living room watching the Miss America Pageant together on a Saturday night. Their mother was out for the evening and they were home with their father. Jackie was nine and Jesse was eleven. Her father came to the doorway to see what the girls were watching. He had heard them laughing and talking.

"What's this crap you're watching?" he asked. The girls looked up and didn't say a word. He yelled, "Answer me! What's this crap?" Jesse told him. "Well, you're done watching this shit. A bunch of hookers is what they all look like, parading around in their underwear. Shut it off!"

"But Dad, it'll be over soon. Please let us watch it. We want to see who wins." Jesse pleaded.

"I gave you an order and you have the nerve to backtalk me? Shut off that fucking boob tube or I'll kick it in, so help me!"

Jackie and Jesse got up and shut it off and walked quickly toward their room. Without warning, he swung his arm around and slapped Jesse upside her head. She was knocked to the floor. Jackie turned and screamed, "What are you doing?"

"You're next if you backtalk me," He hollered.

Jackie watched as her father went back to Jesse and slapped her again – this time across the face. "Please stop, Dad!" Jackie cried.

In a liquor-induced rage, he turned and slapped Jackie. Both girls were crying and they scrambled to get to their room. He blocked the way. "You two sons of bitches are not going to watch so much trash on TV. It'll turn your minds to mush and turn you into a couple of whores!"

He walked over to the television set and without stopping he kicked the television so hard his foot broke the glass. It made a loud popping sound as it imploded. Sparks flew out of the set onto the floor.

Frightened, the girls managed to get to their room and shut the door. They both stood by the unlocked window – an escape hatch they had used many times before. This night they didn't wait for the punishment the broken television would bring. They fled out the window to the house of their neighbor, Francie Barber. She willingly put them up for the night in her living room on her pull out couch. This wasn't the only time Francie helped the girls.

Jackie retold the story with much clarity. "Bruce scares me. He reminds me of my father sometimes."

"I'm so sorry, Jackie," Leena said, reaching across the kitchen table and taking her hands. "Bruce can be a jerk when he's had a few drinks. He's never struck any of us. I'm not trying to justify his obnoxious behavior but you don't have to worry about that. Best to keep out of his way around here, though. I mean, who needs to hear his mouth running?"

"My father didn't hit us that often. He did it just enough to scare us every time he yelled because you never knew if that would be the day that he did decide to smack us." Jackie started to cry as she recalled his intimidation tactics.

Leena rubbed the tops of her hands. "You are safe here, Jackie, I assure you."

"I know," she said, sniffing. "My dad was tall too."

Leena nodded. "Where was your mother? She didn't leave home until years later, right?"

"Right. When I was really young, he wasn't a problem. We'd get a smack on our butt from time to time, but no big deal. But when she got a job and was out a lot, that's when he was on our asses. She was probably fooling around for years. She came home when she felt like it. I mean, my father got drunk a lot. His love affair was with the bottle. But man did they fight when she got home."

"Sounds like it was a pretty toxic environment," Leena said.

"Oh yeah. The night she left for good, well I told you that story, her dresser drawers were not only dumped out but the drawers were thrown around the room and one was out on the lawn. He threw it right through a closed window, breaking it, of course. I remember my mother with shopping bags out on the front lawn gathering up her stuff." Leena was shaking her head in disbelief. "She came back in for something and I think that's when he struck her and more hell broke loose. I jumped out my window and went to Francie's house. That was the last time I saw her, well until last month."

"I feel bad about getting you involved with finding her," Leena said.

Jackie shrugged. "There wasn't no way you coulda known what she was like. Her addiction *was* men. Now it's something else: booze or drugs or something."

"Or something," Leena nodded.

WITH THE WEEKEND APPROACHING, and a luncheon to organize, Leena was grateful for being busy. With Jackie underfoot, Leena wasn't getting much time to herself. Jackie would get bored and, at times, follow Leena around talking to her. Leena found herself saying, "uh-huh," a lot. Between waiting on Jackie and learning more about her miserable childhood Leena felt exhausted.

Leena went upstairs to change. She walked back to the TV room and noticed Jackie was asleep in front of the television. Leena watched her sleep. The girl whose blood was not the same as hers had insinuated herself into her life and home. She didn't mind taking care of her but she was starting to feel smothered. It had only been two weeks since she went to the hospital and Leena tried to tell herself to be patient.

In the hallway, her cell phone rang. It was Michael. "Hey, what's up?" Leena said. "This is a nice surprise." She went to her bedroom and shut the door.

Michael said, "I miss you. I'm at my store today and it's pretty quiet at the moment so I thought I would give you a call. Is this a good time to talk?"

"It's perfect. I'm upstairs in my bedroom. I was about to get ready for a bunch of old ladies and their historical society guests. Bruce is at work."

"Sounds exciting," he said sarcastically. "How're things working out with Jackie and Bruce?"

"Not good. He's a jerk. You know, he's not here that much and when he is, he thinks it's his way or the highway. He's not very nice to Jackie. He was at first when she came home, but he's mostly just cool toward her. Sometimes he makes comments."

"Is he being mean to you?"

"Oh, no it's mainly Jackie. I mean, I told him to shut the hell up the other night and he left in a huff and he wasn't exactly nice about it, but he's harmless."

"How's she doing?"

"She's doing much better. Her arm was just sprained, thankfully. Her bruises are almost gone. She's moving around much better. At this point, her sore rib is the main thing."

"You've been awfully nice to that girl. I think you've gone above and beyond. I'm not siding with Bruce, but you're in up to your eyeballs with her."

Jackie woke up and headed for the bathroom. She heard Leena's voice in her bedroom. She stood by the door and listened in on Leena's side of the conversation.

"I know. I've been feeling a little smothered lately. She's been sort of needy and I think she's milking it to a certain extent. Hey, I'm enabling her too, it's my fault."

"Can she work yet?"

"With her ribs, I don't think so, I don't know, maybe. I haven't asked. She's sort of taken up residency on my couch in the TV room. I've been her maid all week. My vacuum has been getting a lot of use, let's just say that."

"You're a good person," Michael said. "This will be over soon and everything will be back to normal."

"What *is* normal around here? I really don't know. Jackie is becoming a bit of a couch potato. I know she needs to rest but she's lying around like a bump on a log and frankly, it's getting to me. She's enjoying my waiting on her a little too much. I don't mind up to a point, but she can get up and she can bring a dish to the kitchen, it wouldn't kill her."

Jackie assumed Leena was talking to her friend Wendy. She knew she shouldn't be listening but she couldn't help it. She was glued to her spot, careful not to make the floor creak.

"I miss you so much, Michael. I want to be with you. It almost killed me to cancel our meeting last week. When can we get together?"

Jackie's mouth dropped and her eyes bulged.

"It's a little slower at the inn during the week, and Jackie's been following me around like a puppy. Kind of driving me a little crazy. I need a diversion. I need you!"

"Let's make plans right now. How does Monday sound? Too soon?" Michael asked.

"No, Monday would be fine. Where?"

"Where do you want to meet?"

"How about Watch Hill? That way I don't have to go too far from home."

"Yeah, I can work that out. Alright," he said.

"There's a place there called *Point of View*. It's on the water, of course," Leena told him. "Call me on my cell when you're close and I tell you how to get there."

"Okay," He said.

"What time?"

"Ten?"

"Ten sounds good to me."

"I wish we could just stay the night down there, but that's not the way it is," Michael said.

"Stay the night? That sounds wonderful. I wish we could just run away together and spend every night together. That's how I'm feeling right now."

Jackie listened to every word Leena said. Tears filled her eyes at the thought of Leena leaving.

"My band is playing in West Hartford tonight," Michael said.

"You're playing tonight? Oh, I'd love to come to a show again."

"You'll be able to come again eventually. We'll figure something out."

"I love to hear you guys play. And, of course, I love to hear you sing. Don't you dare play *Brown Eyed Girl* without me there."

"I wouldn't dream of it."

"It's going to be a looooong weekend. But the anticipation will be part of the fun. That's how I'll think of it."

"Here comes a customer. I better go." Michael said. "See you Monday?"

"Okay, Monday. Can't wait. Love you."

"Love you too. Bye."

"Bye."

A tear ran down Jackie's cheek, but she didn't know it until it tickled her lip. She quickly wiped her face and tiptoed back to the couch in the TV room and lay down.

Leena finished getting ready. She changed and put on some makeup and took a curling iron to her hair.

Before going back downstairs she poked her head into the TV room and saw Jackie still lying on the couch. She went downstairs.

As soon as Leena was gone Jackie started a massive cleanup campaign.

AFTER THE LUNCHEON, LEENA came back upstairs. Jason had returned home from his friend's house and was in his room playing a video game. Jackie was not on the couch in the TV room, she wasn't anywhere upstairs. The TV room was immaculate. She had vacuumed, wiped down the coffee table, and brought all her dirty dishes and snacks back to the kitchen. The kitchen was also cleaned up and everything was in its place.

"Do you know where Jackie is, Jase?"

"No, I haven't seen her. I thought she was with you."

"No." Leena left and went downstairs. She went to Jackie's door and knocked.

"What?" Jackie said.

"Can I come in?"

Leena heard footsteps and Jackie opened the door for her.

"I couldn't find you. How come you're down here?"

"I think it's time I moved back down, don't you? I don't want to be around when Bruce stumbles in."

"I see. Okay, so you are fine with that?" Leena asked.

"I'm fine. Thanks for asking."

"Is everything alright Jackie?"

"Everything is fine. Couldn't be better."

"Well, thanks for the cleanup up there. That was a nice surprise."

"It was the least I can do," Jackie said.

"You're staying in, right? You wouldn't go anywhere would you?"

"No, I'm not interested in getting into any more trouble. I'm just going to lay low."

"I'll see you tomorrow." Leena left.

For the first time in two weeks, Leena had her home back and felt the relief that Jackie's absence brought. She hadn't realized how much she had missed her time to herself. She checked on Jackie from time to time by knocking on her door throughout the weekend. Every time she would come to the door and tell Leena everything was fine.

The weekend brought many guests to the inn, mostly leaf watchers. The busy schedule was what Leena needed.

Michelle's niece, Carly, was Jackie's replacement all weekend. At one point, Jackie emerged from her room during the busy dinner rush on Saturday night. She stood back and watched Carly interact with Leena as she ran her tight ship. She laughed at something Leena said. A moment of jealousy followed a feeling of being cast aside. Jackie went back into her room for the rest of the night. She didn't know what to do with herself, cooped up in her tiny apartment. She didn't know what to do with her newfound information about Leena's indiscretion.

Leena had turned into the mother Jackie lost, in more ways than one; Becky, the sister she once had. She thought about the conversation she heard Leena having behind her closed bedroom door, about leaving her life and running away with her lover – a musician. She kept going over what she heard in her head. *I miss you so much, Michael. I want to be with you. When can we get together?*

How ironic, Jackie thought, *another musician*! She sat and cried.

CHAPTER 31

With a serious case of cabin fever, Jackie wanted to attend her painting class on Sunday despite still being sore. Leena helped Jackie pack up her supplies and brought her down to the community center.

In the car, Jackie wasn't talking. "Is there anything bothering you, Jackie?" Leena asked.

"Well, being stupid enough to get wasted, then beat up and screwed kinda bothers me."

"I realize that Jackie, but…"

"And sitting around with nothing to do, afraid of who'll see me all messed up if I do go out, that bothers me too. Stupid questions bother me." Jackie stared out the window to avoid seeing Leena in her peripheral vision shooting her looks back and forth as she drove.

Leena got the hint to leave it alone.

"Anything bothering you?" Jackie asked, turning to look at her.

"Like what?" Leena was confused.

"You asked *me*, so I'm asking *you*."

"Everything's fine. We'll drop it," Leena said, but couldn't drop it. "Because if it's about Bruce, I've told you a million times that he…"

"So this is dropping it?" She snapped. "I'm so over Bruce!"

Leena stared straight ahead. She pulled up to the curb and helped Jackie bring her supplies and easel inside. As she left the building she said, "I'll pick you up at one, is that right?"

"Yep," Jackie said. She turned and walked away.

There were a few new participants, but Jackie was still the youngest one there. Most were senior citizens. She really missed Becky at times like this.

At the end of the class, she was glad to be packing up. The side of her abdomen was still sore. Even with a stool to sit on she was uncomfortable. Her wrist was still stiff. Jackie brought her supplies out to the curb at the front of the building to wait for Leena.

Patrons from the restaurant next door were coming out after a Sunday brunch. Jackie watched the well-dressed men and women exit the establishment. Gloria Miller, Leena's neighbor, walked out as if she had stepped onto The Red Carpet.

The plow was Gloria and the freshly fallen snow was Jackie. Her approach was no approach, only ambush. What was water under the bridge turned out to be fodder for a cruel woman's entertainment and self-aggrandizement.

"You're Jackie aren't you?" Gloria said as she approached Jackie.

Jackie turned toward the voice and instantly said, "Yes." Jackie did not know her.

"Aren't you the girl who works for Kathleen Frazer?"

"Who? Leena? Yup."

"The girl that *Leena* took under her wing? You're a lucky girl from what I understand," she said, smiling, showing her capped veneers and bright red lipstick. "Your bruises are almost gone."

Gloria's husband Ashton walked out and stood at her side. "I'll bring the car around, dear."

"I'm Gloria Miller, your neighbor." She did not offer her hand to Jackie. Both hands clutched her tiny sequined purse. "This is fortunate that I bumped into you today," she continued. "I've been meaning to talk to you. I guess you've been in the hospital again. How are you feeling?"

"Fine."

"Good. Kathleen has invested quite a lot in you, dear."

Jackie started to realize the conversation was not going to be pleasant.

"I should think you would be more careful, make better choices."

"Have you been talking to Bruce?" Jackie asked.

"I was there that day, you know, at the beach last spring. It wasn't a pretty picture."

Jackie was becoming annoyed and couldn't understand why this woman was talking to her in the first place. She began to fidget. She looked up and down the street as she waited for Leena. She looked down at her feet.

Gloria continued. "So am I to understand that Kath, that Mrs. Frazer found you in the same predicament the other morning? Half dead?" She didn't give Jackie a chance to answer. "There's a drinking age of twenty-one and there's a reason children, like yourself, shouldn't be 'experimenting' with alcohol." Gloria made the sign of the quote marks with her long, red fingernails. "That scoundrel you picked up walked right through my peonies and knocked over a lawn ornament that night. He broke it! He trampled all over my flowerbeds after he visited with you."

"Oh," was all Jackie said. She looked around for an escape.

Gloria was enjoying her cat and mouse game. Her arms were crossed, her penciled eyebrows remained stationary. She was seeking an answer to a question even though she hadn't asked one.

"What's your question?" Jackie asked.

"My question, young lady, is what are you going to do about it? Your friends come over and hang out with you and the result is property damage.

I don't need my property value to go down just because Kathleen decides to take in a stray cat."

At first, Jackie didn't make the connection that she was the cat in question. She looked up the street for Leena's car. Jackie responded to her with her head turned away. "He wasn't my friend." Jackie turned back around to face her. "What makes you think he was my friend?"

"Well the other boyfriend of yours, one of many I'm sure, left his car running so long that the fumes came into my home. It gave me a headache."

She assumed she was now talking about Rick, but it could have been Chris. Jackie had had enough. Game over. "I already got attacked, physically, lady. I don't need no verbal attack, so tell your story walking. I'm just waiting for my ride."

Gloria's nostrils flared and her face turned red. "You haven't got the class or the upbringing to realize to whom you are speaking."

"And to 'whom' am I speaking to?" Jackie asked. "Some royalty or something?"

"You, young lady, are speaking to an adult, first of all. I am your elder," she snarled.

"Well, yeah! I mean, that's obvious." Jackie smiled.

"And I am your employer's neighbor."

"So? And that makes you special?"

"You should address me in a polite manner."

"What the hell are you talking about?" Jackie's anger was full-blown. "You're not being polite to me. Why should I be polite back?"

For the first time, Gloria looked embarrassed. "I'm talking about your manners, or lack thereof."

"You want to talk manners? Yours *suck!*" Jackie yelled loudly.

"Well, perhaps you'll be hearing from my lawyer. You don't think you can destroy someone's property and get away with it, do you?" Gloria asked her.

"Lawyer? I got a lawyer in case you didn't notice. I *live* with one! So bring it on lady!" Jackie snapped at her with her hands on her hips.

"Is that how you've been staying out of jail? Is Mr. Frazer representing you?"

"In case you didn't notice *I* didn't touch *your* property. That creep that attacked me did. So go find him and sue him."

Ashton pulled the car around. Gloria looked at her car and back at Jackie. "What goes around comes around young lady." Her husband got out and opened the passenger side door for his wife. Gloria stepped down off the curb to get into the car.

"I hope so," Jackie responded.

Ashton closed her door and walked around to the driver's side. She and Gloria exchanged one more look before their Cadillac pulled away from the curb.

Tears filled Jackie's eyes. She walked in a circle trying to shake it off, sniffing and wiping her face on her sleeve. She waited another five minutes before Leena finally showed up.

"Where the hell have you been?" Jackie snapped at her when she opened the door.

"What?"

"I've been standing here for a long time. You got better things to do with your time then picking me up on time?"

"What on earth has gotten into you?"

"Seriously, where do you go, Leena? I'd love to know. You were supposed to be here at one. It's, what, ten after?"

"I'm sorry I'm late. You're in a real mood today, Jackie. I don't understand."

"You'd be in a mood too if you just got the third degree from your friend Gloria."

"What do you mean? Gloria Miller was here?"

"She came out of that restaurant." Jackie pointed to the door. "She has it in for me. Does she and Bruce have their heads together about me or something?"

They loaded Jackie's supplies into the car. "What? No! What did she say? And she's *not* my friend by the way!" Leena insisted.

"She's a fucking asshole. She's mad about some flowers or something that that creep Garrett walked on that night." Jackie said. She slammed the car door getting in.

Leena looked over at Jackie. "She's an awful person. She's a bored, busybody housewife with way too much time and money on her hands. I had an encounter with her at that party a few weeks ago. I sort of told her off." Leena smirked with pride. "She's a sorry excuse for a human, so don't insult me by saying she's a friend of mine."

Jackie looked over at Leena. "You told her off? What did she say to you that got *you* mad?"

Leena didn't want to tell her the comments were about her so she fluffed over her response. "I don't really remember. Something about someone she didn't like on the cheerleading squad or school play, I forget exactly. She also made a comment about someone being Jewish. It was uncalled for."

"It must have been more than that." Jackie insisted.

"No, but it was enough. She's a piece of work, Literally. She's had *a lot* of plastic surgery. She's a freak. She's nosey and she's mean."

Jackie was quiet for a moment. "Man, who does she think she is anyway? Some queen or something?"

"I'm sorry you had a run-in with her."

Jackie sighed and leaned her head back on the headrest. "I must be a magnet for lousy people lately."

"Does that include me?"

They exchanged glances. She waited for her response. Jackie realized Leena would be terribly hurt if she had said "yes." She shook her head and said "no" and turned forward.

CHAPTER 32

Leena knocked on Jackie's door Sunday night.

"Jackie, can I come in?"

Jackie opened the door and stood out of the way to allow Leena to enter. Leena looked around and noticed her apartment was a mess.

"You need help cleaning up here? I could help you." Leena asked.

"Is that why you came down here?" Jackie asked.

"No, actually I came down to tell you that I need to go out tomorrow morning, maybe before you get up, I'm not sure. I mean I'm sure when I'm going out, but not sure when you'll be getting up, you know, before or after I leave." Leena laughed nervously realizing she was babbling. Jackie let her do the talking. "I'll be cooking breakfast for those three couples that are still here. Then I'm going out around 9:30 or so to do some errands. So I was wondering if you could just be around when they check out. Also, I think we're going to have an intake tomorrow around 3:00. Could you be around for them as well?"

"Sure, no problem," Jackie said.

"I was hoping you were feeling up to slowly getting back to work. Just some light duty stuff, that's all."

"Sure," Jackie said.

"Great. Not vacuuming or any lifting yet, but maybe a little waitressing, a little spit and polish in the rooms, you know, laundry?"

"Okay."

"Great. I've left you some leftovers in the frig downstairs here and I put your name on them. It's just some baked ziti and meatballs. There's enough for lunch."

"When are you coming back?"

"Not until 3:45 or so. I'm picking Jason up at school after his Newspaper club meeting around 3:30. He's on the school newspaper now," Leena said redundantly.

Jackie asked, "Cool. Where are you going?"

With the possibility of being asked this question, Leena's answer was well-rehearsed. "I'm going to Mystic to meet with an event coordinator for a charity auction I'll be having here the first week of December. Just another use for the inn, you know, renting it out for different events."

"I see." Jackie knew she was meeting Michael at ten o'clock down at Watch Hill. *What an elaborate lie,* she thought.

"I thought that you and I could go out on Tuesday, maybe go shopping? Would you like that?" Leena asked.

"Sure." Jackie grew weary of her condescension.

Leena sensed Jackie's mood was not up to what it should be so she didn't push any issues. "Okay then, so I'll see you tomorrow and have a good evening."

"Thanks."

"Good night," Leena said.

"Night," Jackie said.

Leena left and Jackie closed the door behind her. Leena stopped and looked back at the closed door and wondered about the girl behind it.

Jackie sat in her room with nothing to do but feel sorry for herself. She sunk into her loveseat and allowed the past to wash over her. She thought about her mother who abandoned her. She compared her situation then with her situation now. The parallels were strange.

Jackie stood in the doorway of her mother's bedroom watching her put on makeup and brush her hair. Jackie's right arm was in a cast and in a sling, the result of falling out of a tree while playing in the neighbor's yard. Only one day after this incident her mother was leaving for the evening, telling her she would have to prepare her own dinner. "There's a TV dinner in the freezer." Her mother told her that she was going out to a Mary Kay party. Her father was in no shape to cook. He was already drunk and asleep on the couch. Jackie only had the use of her left hand, her non-dominant hand. She went to bed hungry that night. It was not worth the effort. Jesse was at her friend's house, somewhere she went frequently. When her mother got home after two o'clock in the morning, she thought she was sneaking in but she was too drunk to be quiet. Her father woke up and didn't like the hour she rolled in on. It was not possible to sleep through the argument.

MONDAY MORNING JACKIE HEARD voices in the downstairs kitchen. She cracked her door to listen. She heard Jason saying something about his Parent Night at the high school on Thursday and Bruce saying something about his Mercedes going into the shop. She heard Leena tell the same lie about meeting an auctioneer.

She heard Bruce say, "Are you putting Jackie back to work today?"

"Yes. I talked to her last night and it's all set."

Jackie felt betrayed that Leena had asked her to go back to work because Bruce had told her to. Jackie thought Leena could stand up to him. *I guess not.*

"It's bad enough we support her. She needs to pay her way around here. For all intents and purposes, we've been paying for most of her medical crises."

"We're all set. Go to work. Go!" Leena sounded annoyed with him.

Bruce said to Jason, "You ready?"

"Goodbye honey," Leena said to Jason, "Have a nice day at school. I'll pick you up at 3:30."

Jackie noticed Bruce and Leena did not say goodbye to each other. She quietly closed her door.

A few minutes before she was to leave Leena knocked on Jackie's door. "You up?"

"Yes," Jackie said from behind the door.

"I'm leaving soon." Jackie opened the door and walked out, closing her door to her apartment behind her. Leena continued, "One couple just left. The other two are still here. Only one of the couples hasn't eaten yet. You're prepared to cook for them? They've only got 'til ten. That's the rule."

Jackie nodded. "I know the rule," Jackie observed Leena's appearance. She seemed to be wearing a little more makeup than usual. The top she was wearing looked new. Jackie said, "Have fun today."

Leena made a face as if she had a big job to do and was dreading it. "Oh, right, I'll try." She managed a smile mixed with a grimace. "Okay, see ya later." Leena paused and looked back. "You sure you're up to this today?"

"Yes."

Leena nodded. "Oh, I think I hear them coming," Leena referred to the guests.

"I'm on it." Jackie entered the kitchen.

"Thanks, Jackie." Leena left.

A couple entered the dining room.

"Hello there," the man said.

"Hi, have a seat and I'll get your breakfast," Jackie said. Jackie led them to a table.

"We come up this way every year to see the leaves. We usually stay at a place up in northwestern Massachusetts first, and, depending on our schedule, we come down to the coast, spending the night in a few different locations. Sometimes we stay in Newport, but this inn, this area, is not at all commercial. It's quieter here," the woman said to Jackie.

"Yes it is. You both ordered the eggs and toast but no bacon, right?" Jackie asked.

"That's right," The woman said. "Do you have marmalade?"

"It's in the bowl on the table."

Jackie left and returned with a basket of muffins. She returned with their breakfast and refills of coffee.

After both couples checked out Jackie went down to their rooms and stripped the beds and changed them. She brought their sheets and towels to the laundry room, combined the other sheets and towels from the other couple, and started a load of wash. She cleaned the sinks and toilets and sprayed down counters and tables. She normally would have vacuumed and cleaned the showers. After she put the wash into the dryer her duties were done. It was 11:45.

Jackie walked around the three entertainment rooms. She straightened salt and pepper shakers on the tables in the dining room, repositioned a vase on a table, and straightened an already straight framed picture on the wall. Everything was so tidy. There was nothing to do. She found a book in the library on the history of some New England lighthouses. She brought it over to the cushion on the window seat in the front room and leafed through it. She got bored soon after, replaced the book, and paced around some more, observing all the attention to detail Leena had taken to make the inn what it was – a very homey and cozy place to stay.

Jackie couldn't help thinking about where Leena had gone. Watch Hill was only a few miles away from the inn.

Suddenly she had a plan. Jackie went to her room and got a jacket. She packed her backpack with a sketch pad and pencils. She remembered the name of the place they were meeting was called *Point of View*.

She locked up the inn and put the "Open at 3:00" on the front door. She drove down to the Watch Hill area looking for *Point of View*. She wasn't sure if it would be a restaurant or a motel. She found it, no problem. It was a restaurant situated at the end of a line of shops. She saw Leena's car in the parking lot. *That was easy,* Jackie thought.

Suddenly she felt butterflies in her stomach. *So she's not in Mystic on business after all. She is having an affair,* she thought. "Now what?" Jackie said out loud. *I wait.*

She knew she didn't want to just walk into the restaurant and confront them. Jackie was determined to see who Leena was with. She zipped up her jacket and found a secluded spot up on a knoll against the wall of a restroom building which shielded her from the wind whipping off the ocean. She was close enough to the restaurant so she could see Leena when she came back out to her car. She took her sketch pad and pencils out of the backpack and started a drawing. *If Leena sees me here, I have my excuse. I came down to sketch,* Jackie thought. *I came here all the time with Becky.* "What are *you* doing here, Leena?" Jackie asked out loud to no one. "Why aren't you in Mystic?"

Around 1:30 a van pulled in and parked next to Leena's car. Leena was in the passenger seat. Jackie watched through some sparse brush. She saw Leena lean over and kiss the driver of the van for rather a long time. Leena put her head on the man's shoulder and he stroked her hair. Leena looked up at him like he owned the sun and the moon. They sat for a good ten minutes in the car, talking. There was no room for doubt this was her lover. It seemed apparent that they had just come from a more private meeting place.

They finally got out of the van and went into the restaurant. They walked without touching. Perhaps she was trying to be discreet in case she ran into someone she knew. Jackie laughed out loud.

Jackie couldn't get over the level of affection Leena displayed for this man. She was shocked and sad. Leena, a person she thought was her friend, lied to her. Jackie had confided in Leena about many personal things, yet Leena kept this secret. Jackie felt entitled; indignant. *Family and marriage should matter*, she thought. *Leena's just another selfish woman who gets sick of her family and finds something outside the home. It won't be long now until she leaves it all behind for this man.*

Jackie sat for quite a few minutes taking it all in. She wondered how long this affair had been going on. She packed up her stuff and decided to go back to the inn. Jackie's fact-finding mission was complete.

LEENA AND JASON ARRIVED home and they saw Jackie sitting on the front porch with her sketch pad as they pulled in the driveway. Leena came out to the porch to see her.

"How was your day?" Leena asked.

"Fine, and yours?" Jackie said without stopping her sketching.

"Okay. Did everything go okay this morning?"

"Like clockwork."

"Did the couple from New Jersey get here yet?" Leena asked.

"No. I'm just sitting here waiting for them."

"Okay, you want to wait for them? I'm going to go start some dinner. You want to join me and Jason tonight? Bruce has a meeting and won't be home."

"No thanks. I ate. You were right. There was plenty of leftovers." Jackie said. Leena started to walk away. "How was your meeting?"

"Oh, okay. Looks like that guy is going to have his auction here. That'll be weird, huh? I've never had an auction here before."

"What's his name?"

"Carl Schroder. It's a luncheon and they'll auction off arts and craft items for charity which benefits Alzheimer's disease."

"Hmm," Jackie said. She continued to sketch.

Leena looked down at Jackie's sketch. She almost looked away but didn't when she recognized the building: it was *Point of View* in Watch Hill. She said nothing and just stared down at it. Jackie felt her staring and looked up at her. Leena looked Jackie in the eye. Jackie knew by Leena's expression that she was burning to ask about her sketch.

"I'll be upstairs if you need anything," Leena said suddenly and turned and went into the inn.

Jackie watched Leena as she scurried inside. Jackie turned back around and stared out at the ocean. The three different sketch pencils she had used were clasped in her right hand. She massaged her kneaded eraser with her left hand. She flipped the sketch pad cover over and continued to look out at the water and wait for the guests.

CHAPTER 33

The guests from New Jersey turned out to be the guests from hell – not the first time guests at the inn would make unreasonable demands or leave a room turned upside down. From the start, there was no pleasing the couple. Jackie quit trying right after she was ordered to dust behind a lamp as the wife looked on.

Jackie had deliberately failed to forward a special request to Leena that a table be brought into the room for the man to "spread out on." Instead, she kept on walking as he and his wife barked orders at her.

Jackie stormed into the kitchen and walked right by Leena, heading straight to her room. "Your guests in room three would like *a word.*" She disappeared behind the slam of her apartment door.

Leena looked up from her food preparation as a blur that was Jackie was gone before she could say, "What? The new guests want to talk to me?"

"You deal with them. I'm not paid enough!" Jackie yelled from behind her closed door.

BRUCE CAME HOME IN a mood. Right away Leena knew he had lost a case. The only thing on Bruce's agenda was getting liquored up which he proceeded to do straight away. He passed through the downstairs kitchen and went upstairs.

Hal walked toward the back door. "See you Friday," he said as he put on his coat.

"Thanks so much for everything. Drive safe," Leena said.

"Goodnight," Hal said.

Jackie and Leena served the dinner crowd with very little conversation between them. Inside the kitchen Leena finally vented. "Did you hear that guy try to pronounce the name of that French wine?" Jackie didn't respond. "And his wife was so condescending!" Leena sputtered around the kitchen shaking her head.

Bruce came into the kitchen. Leena and Jackie looked up as he made his presence known. "I'm going out. We ran out of gin."

"Don't you mean *you* ran out of gin? It's certainly not *my* gin." Leena stood with one hand on her hip, the other leaning against the counter.

"I'm just telling you I'm going out. I'll be right back."

"That's your idea of fun? A night of drinking?" Leena couldn't leave it alone.

"Why do you talk to me like that in front of the hired help?" Bruce said.

Jackie watched them spar. She then said, "I've seen pretty much everything at this point, *Bruce.*"

"Who said you could talk to me like that, *Jackie?*" Bruce spat back.

"Stop it, both of you. It's true, Bruce, she's been around long enough to witness you making an ass of yourself when you're drunk! You've walked down here in front of guests in your underwear, for Christ's sake!" Leena said angrily, not letting Bruce live down the incident from a year ago.

"Nice, Leena, very nice." Bruce stormed toward the door, opening it. "Like anything I've ever done has compared to what this girl has done, and all within seven months! I mean, who's been causing bigger scenes?" He didn't wait for a response. He left, slamming the door.

Leena and Jackie looked at each other. Jackie shrugged and looked down at the floor. They heard the tires squeal as he left.

"He can be the biggest ass. Sometimes I wonder what I ever saw in him." Leena confessed. "You stood up to him, good for you."

"You don't want to be married to him anymore?" she asked.

"At times like this? Not really. I'd like to just kick him right in the rear end."

"I try not to let it get to me but I can't figure out why he hates me so much. He ever tell you why?" Jackie asked.

"Honestly? No. But I think he suffers terribly from S-S-S." Leena said.

"What's that?"

"Status Symbol Syndrome," Leena said with a smile. Jackie finally smiled. "He's a snob and I guess he sees you as someone who didn't grow up with advantages and so you couldn't have any social redeeming value. His snobbery and his drinking are what's driving us apart." Leena got quiet. She realized she was getting into territory she wasn't going to be comfortable with. "I just get frustrated sometimes." Leena changed the subject. "You doing okay? Are you still having some pain?"

"No, not too much. A little on this side," she put her hand on her left side.

"I'm sorry about those guests. It's to be expected. Not everyone's gonna be as pleasant as that sweet couple we had last week," Leena said referring to an elderly couple. "The week before last I was wet-vacing a room 'cause someone's kid threw up! It's times like that and people like that couple today when I'd like to walk away from this whole bed and breakfast thing. I mean I love the idea of having an inn on the water, but think about it, I cook and clean for people, and listen to their *shit*. What was I thinking?"

"It's not all bad," Jackie said. "Your meeting this morning went really well, right? You looked pretty happy after that." Jackie wanted to see how Leena would react.

"Yes, it went well," Leena said, turning her back as she spoke. She didn't want to pile more lies on top of her lies. "I don't know. Sometimes I'm sick of it, sick of Bruce, sick of picky guests." She let out a big sigh and concluded. "I'm just tired. Don't listen to me."

"Me too. I'm gonna turn in," Jackie said.

"Good night."

LEENA WENT UPSTAIRS AND spent the rest of the evening in front of the TV. She worked on a pile of sewing repairs as she watched a show. As she sewed, she went over the good part of her day in her mind: her encounter with Michael. She didn't pay attention to the television.

She was brought back to reality when she heard the door to the stairwell open. Bruce was back. She heard him clinking ice cubes in the kitchen, a sound that annoyed her tremendously. Bruce fixed his drink and went straight into the bedroom and shut the door. Leena continued sewing. A wave of depression swept over her as she thought about her situation. *Why can't that be Michael coming home to me? Michael wouldn't drink alone in the bedroom!* She thought.

THE NEXT DAY LEENA served breakfast to the two ungrateful guests who had nothing nice to say. At checkout time they questioned the bill and complained about the size of their room.

Jackie walked by holding an armful of sheets and towels. She heard the commotion.

"This girl was not helpful at all. She has a bad work ethic," the woman said, pointing at Jackie. Jackie stopped briefly and then kept walking.

"Let's go, Patty," the man said. They left in a huff.

Leena watched them walk out. She couldn't hear them but they seemed to be arguing with each other right outside the door. Leena stood and shook her head.

Leena joined Jackie down at their room where Jackie had already started to strip the bed. The room was a total mess. Empty soda cans and water bottles were on the dresser, bed, and floor. Papers overflowed from the wastebasket. A very wet towel was on the wood floor. Leena leaned over and picked it up noticing a slight watermark. She sighed and said to Jackie, "You want help in here?"

"Sure. It's not the first time someone's trashed a room."

Leena stood and looked around the room. Something caught her eye in the far corner. She walked over and found a used condom. Leena laughed out loud and shook her head. Jackie came over to see what she was looking at. They looked at each other. There was nothing left to say. Leena got some tissues from the bathroom and picked it up and placed it in the trash. Before she left the room, she said to Jackie, "Bring their wastebaskets to the laundry room, okay? I'll clean them. And bring the bedspread too."

By now Jackie was back on full duty. She was able to push the vacuum and do all her usual chores. She brought their sheets, towels, and the bedspread to the laundry room where she met up with Leena again. "No surprise that they took a towel, is it?" Jackie said to Leena.

Leena sighed and rolled her eyes. "No, not at all. It could be worse. I once had someone steal a lamp!"

Jackie made a face. "No one saw them leave with it?"

"No. But thankfully stealing is fairly rare. I think the average person knows this is just a small 'mom-and-pop' operation, not a big chain, so they're usually more respectful."

"You getting' kinda sick of doing this? Being an innkeeper?" Jackie tested Leena.

"Sometimes I do. I never figured I'd be cooking and cleaning for a living."

"What do you think you'd be doing if you didn't do this?" Jackie asked.

"I have no idea. Something that involves using my brain," Leena chuckled. Jackie did not.

CHAPTER 34

More guests arrived throughout the week, but not enough to use the upstairs rooms. Leena finally took on her wallpapering project in one of the rooms. She had Jackie do some bank runs and other errands.

Bruce came home late the next two nights, opting to have dinner out with friends. When he called to tell Leena he'd be late again she couldn't hold it in.

"This is a habit now, you coming home whenever you feel like it," Leena said.

"All of a sudden you want me home?" he said, defensively.

"Last time I checked you were still a member of this family. Or has something changed?"

"No, nothing's changed with me, just you!"

"What's that supposed to mean?" Leena asked. Jackie was in the kitchen listening to Leena's side of the telephone conversation.

"You bitchin' all the time that's what I mean. You're just so much fun to come home to."

Leena started to cry. "I wouldn't be bitchin' so much if you weren't drinkin' so much!"

"I gotta go. Jim's waiting."

"Jim? I thought it was Mike?"

"I don't appreciate the third degree, Leena," Bruce yelled into the phone.

"Fuck you!" Leena slammed the phone down. The call was over. Leena looked over at Jackie and they stared at each other for a few seconds. Leena went back to the counter to finish a chore, only she had forgotten what she was doing before the call. She was flustered.

"He'll be late again, I take it?" Jackie asked.

Leena didn't look at Jackie but nodded confirming her question while staring blankly into space. She remembered, a few moments later, that she had been looking through her address book to find a number for her electrician. She picked up the phone to call him and then put the phone back down. "I can't deal with this now," She said, and left to go upstairs.

Leena had a chance to cool off and came back downstairs. She found Jackie in the library polishing furniture. "Sorry I stormed out earlier. I just needed some time to be alone."

Jackie nodded.

"I've got to call the electrician to work on the breaker. Something screwy's been happening to the upstairs rooms. It's always something with this inn," Leena said with a long sigh. "I suppose it would be no different with a normal house. The week after Thanksgiving I'm having a guy come over to look at the basement. It's been getting wetter as the years go by. What started out as some dampness in the corner has graduated to puddles."

"I remember, as a kid, we had a lot of water in our basement. It came up to the first step sometimes. My father was too cheap to have a pump installed," Jackie said.

"Oh yeah? I hope ours doesn't get that bad. When we got this inn, Bruce promised he'd do all the repairs. He's very handy when he wants to be. But he rarely lifts a finger now and I resort to calling repairmen. It's way more expensive than if he would just do it himself. If I go into the poor house it'll be Bruce's fault."

Jackie nodded again.

Bruce arrived home late. Jackie, from her room, heard him come in and go upstairs. Things were quiet for the first few minutes, but then she heard muffled yelling overhead through the floor of their kitchen. She couldn't quite make out what they were saying but Jackie jumped when she heard the sound of what must have been a pan dropping on the floor of the kitchen. More yelling. Jackie sat in a chair and waited for the next loud noise, not unlike the anticipation of thunder after the flash.

Jackie lay on her bed with her pillow on top of her head. She pressed the pillow harder to her ear but it didn't drown out the sound of her parents' argument. The bass of her father's voice penetrated right through the wall of her room and straight through the pillow. A dish hit the wall right outside her room. She jumped and sat up straight on her bed. Her sister was out that evening, studying at a friend's house. Without Jesse, she felt more vulnerable, more scared. The thud of her mother's body against the same wall where the dish had hit brought Jackie to her feet. She could feel her heart beating wildly.

"You're hurting me!" she heard her mother scream. "Let go!"

"Not until you tell me his name."

"No fucking way!"

"Tell me his name you slut!"

"NO!"

He struck her mother and she shrieked in pain.

Jackie was crying. She didn't know whether to try to help her mother or escape out the window like she had done before. She stood by the window. Jesse wasn't there to make the decision.

There was silence. Jackie felt relieved until she realized that silence could mean death and she felt panicked all over again. She heard footsteps and the front door open and close. She looked out the window and watched her father walk out, get into the car, and speed away.

Jackie opened the door to her bedroom and saw her mother lying in the hallway. She was moving slightly and moaning. Her eye was swollen and there was blood on the side of her mouth and on her shirt. "Mother!" Jackie yelled.

"Help me up," she said.

"Should I call an ambulance?"

"No! Just help me up."

They walked over to the couch in the living room and her mother sat down. Jackie went to the bathroom and got a facecloth to clean her mother's face. "Should we call the police?"

"No! Are you kidding? He'd really kill me then!"

Jackie dabbed at her mother's face and got her some ice in a plastic bag for her eye. "Maybe some neighbor will call the police when they see your eye. They probably heard the yelling." Jackie carefully placed the bag on her eye. Her mother winced.

"Would you mind your own business," she yelled at her daughter. "I'll just tell them I bumped into something."

Like so many altercations before, this was swept under the rug.

JACKIE SAT IN A trance. She was brought back to reality by another thump above her head. She couldn't stand it anymore so she left her apartment and walked down the street. As she walked, she was reminded of Rick and Garrett. She always figured Rick would have called her after she stormed out of *Mayfield's* that night. She would take him back in a minute. He never called. She walked, hugging herself in November's cold night air.

She found a spot on the beach to sit. Despair engulfed her as she recalled all the rotten things that had happened to her in such a short amount of time. She hadn't felt this down since before Leena found her on the beach. She tried to dismiss the feeling of utter hopelessness but couldn't. *I wish Leena hadn't found me that day,* she thought.

Tears flowed down and hit her legs. In her mind, she felt it was inevitable that Leena would leave the inn behind and run off with her lover to have a better life. She never figured Leena would be that irresponsible, but after the last couple of fights with Bruce, it didn't look good. *Would she be so mad at Bruce and so smitten with lover boy that she would just leave? What about me?* she thought.

When she went back to her room it was going on midnight. The kitchen above was quiet. She was dead tired and slipped into bed and fell asleep right away.

JACKIE FELT BETTER WHEN she woke up. Sleep had definitely helped her mood. It was Thursday. Leena had set out the chores she wanted to be done. They included cleaning up some of the mess Leena had made wallpapering in the upstairs guest room. Next, she had to work on removing mildew from some of the showers.

When she finished she started to go down the stairs. She heard Leena on her cell phone out on the front deck. Jackie slowly walked toward the window in the front room and listened to her conversation from the other side of the glass.

Leena's voice sounded different. Jackie realized she was crying. She heard her say, "It's all so endless, so futile. I get so sick of everything." Jackie was silent and stood perfectly still. She listened. "I know, *I know*, I shouldn't be so upset, but you don't know. Maybe it's because of us but Bruce's behavior is getting on my very last nerve. I find him intolerable!" There was a long pause. Leena sniffed and continued. "Maybe I'd feel differently if you weren't in the picture, but the way I'm feeling today I feel like I could just walk away from this place! I'm *sick* of it all. I'm sick of asshole guests and I'm sick to death of Bruce! I don't know, Michael." Michael was talking, and then Leena said, "I do feel something for her, but she's not my daughter, you know? What's next with that girl?" She sighed loudly. "So say you'll see me tomorrow, Michael, *please*, I *need* you right now." Long pause. "I know." She was crying more. "Then when? Don't make me wait 'til then! Alright, alright. Michael? I love you." She was sniffing. Jackie sensed the end of the conversation and went back up the stairs. She heard the front door open and Leena walked back to the kitchen.

Jackie went to the guest room and shut the door and sat on the bed. Her mood sank that much deeper where a deep sigh could not reach it.

Jackie avoided being around Leena for the rest of the day. She went to her room for a while and then later went for a walk down to the beach. This time she went down to the spot where she tried to kill herself. She felt that if she revisited it, it would force her to deal with the feelings she had the day Leena found her, and to conquer those same feelings that were creeping back. She wanted to make that spot no different than any other spot on the beach. She sat close to where she was that night. This time Leena did not come out to see where she was. *Maybe that's what Leena wants. Me out of her life,* Jackie thought.

LEENA ASKED JACKIE TO help her in the upstairs kitchen to reorganize the cabinets to accommodate the new set of dishes she had just purchased. They worked side by side for a better part of an hour, with few words spoken.

"You've been pretty quiet today," Leena observed. "Or should I say, all week."

"Have I?"

"You want to talk about anything?"

"You're pretty quiet too. You wanna talk?"

Leena sighed and gave a sideways smile. "I suppose you heard us arguing last night."

Jackie nodded without looking at her.

"I'm sorry about that." Leena dismantled the box and folded it up. "He pushes my buttons, I guess."

Jackie nodded again. They finished the dishes. Jackie stood and waited for Leena to give her another chore. "You need help with anything else?"

"Oh, actually there is another thing. Would you help me reorganize the pantry? There are boxes full of canned stuff, cleaning stuff, and whatnot. Come, I'll show you."

They walked around the corner into the pantry and Leena explained what she wanted to be done. "These shelves were a mess, so yesterday I took most everything down and, well, now it's sitting here in boxes," she pointed down to them. "And obviously it needs to be put back." She explained how she wanted them organized. She and Jackie worked side by side again.

"So I hired that DJ for the singles dance for Saturday night." Leena tried to make conversation. She laughed and said, "I had a singles' dance last year, and no one ahead of time reserved a room, but after the dance, I booked *five* rooms!" Leena was still laughing. She looked at Jackie to see her reaction. There was none. She continued, "So, it was a profitable event. I'm thinking I'll hold one every month. That DJ guy I usually get..." She stopped abruptly when she heard Bruce enter from the stairwell.

Leena walked out into the kitchen. Bruce looked annoyed.

"What's wrong?" Leena asked.

"Why do I get the third degree the second I walk into the house?" he asked.

"Sorry. You had a look." She started to walk back toward the pantry.

Bruce fired back, "If I commented on every sourpuss face you've had lately, I'd never stop asking you."

Leena turned to face him again. Her back straightened and her lips puckered. She waited before she spoke, trying to decide when she would bring up another sore subject. *It might as well be now*, she thought. "I called that guy to come over and check the breaker. I'm still having trouble with the upstairs rooms and..."

"God damn it, Leena, I said I'd do it! You act like I never do anything around here and then you act like a martyr when you *call* the plumber, when you *call* the electrician. You know what? If you want to handle it all yourself then *call them*! Just stop telling me you've done so!"

"How am I supposed to ask you? I don't know how to ask without feeling like I need to be walking on eggshells all the time. You blow up at everything!"

"Oh right, I'm the bad guy here. You never raise your voice. You never start an argument. I forgot. You're perfect!"

Jackie stood silently in the pantry around the corner out of their sight.

"Well maybe if you just did what I asked the first time you..."

"So now I have to jump when you say jump, is that it?" Bruce's voice went up. He walked over to the refrigerator and got himself a beer.

"Drink, that's always the solution for you, isn't it?"

"That's right. With a nag of a wife like you I *need* a drink!"

"You've got an excuse for every rotten thing you say and do," Leena yelled.

"And you've got an excuse whenever I ask you to do the simplest thing," Bruce yelled back.

"What the hell are you talking about?"

"I asked you to come with me to the Miller's dinner party and you refused. Remember that?" Bruce said

"As if I'd get stuck in that woman's house for one second! Please! She's a bigot and a phony snob! I won't lower myself!"

"Well, I was pretty embarrassed going alone. I had to make some sort of excuse about some headache you didn't have."

"How about being on my side for once and saying 'no' to that party? No! You're too much of a social climber to say 'no.'"

"A lot of my colleagues were there and I explained to you that I felt I should go."

"Look, I don't want to rehash that argument," Leena said.

Jackie stood behind the wall in a trance.

Bruce took a large gulp of his beer.

"Drink drink drink, that's all you do when you come home!" Leena yelled louder.

"I need to drink to make living here palatable." Bruce went up to Leena and bent over slightly and glared straight into her eyes. Jackie peaked around the corner and watched them. Bruce put his finger up to her nose, spitting as he yelled. "You fucking bitch, you don't even know what you've got. You've got it pretty good around here. You're just a glorified housewife with this inn."

Leena realized at that moment that Bruce had already been drinking before he got home. "Get your finger out of my face unless you want to lose it."

Bruce looked fierce. "You gonna bite me? Go ahead and try."

For the first time, Bruce scared her. "Quit it, Bruce," she said as she tried to move away from him. He maintained his stance and his glare, not blinking. He blocked her way. Bruce finally broke the stare and moved back toward the kitchen table. He saw a basket on the table full of pens and notepads and gave it a hard shove, sending it flying across the room, its contents scattering. Leena flinched and let out a scream.

Jackie jumped and ducked back into the pantry. She didn't know what to do. She should try to be brave this time and stand up for her mother? She put her hands up to her ears to block their words, but she could hear them anyway.

"Who's it gonna be tonight slut? Hmm?" Jackie's father spat in her mother's face.

"Stop it!" her mother screamed.

"Why don't you stop it! You want a man? I'm all the man you'll ever need." He slapped her across the face and she stumbled onto the floor. He stood over her as she cowered and said, "One of these days I'm gonna kill you!" He kicked her. She screamed again.

Jackie ran to her bedroom and shut the door. She stood behind her door and cried.

"What's his name, slut?" she heard her father asked her mother from the living room.

"No!" her mother screamed for dear life.

Jackie lay down on her bed and put her pillow over her head.

Leena screamed, "Get out of my kitchen you fucking drunken bastard!"

Bruce's face was red. He got in Leena's face again. "You've crossed the line, you bitch!"

At that moment Jackie walked out into the room. Tears streamed down her face. She looked up and through her tears saw her parents. She felt something come up from her gut. It came out as a guttural scream, "NOOO!" She was sobbing. Fear gripped the girl as worlds came together in an eerily familiar way.

Bruce and Leena stopped and looked toward the sound.

Jackie screamed, "Just tell him his name!"

Bruce and Leena stared at Jackie and then Bruce looked at Leena in total confusion.

"What?" Leena asked.

Jackie was clearly distraught. Her hands were still up to her ears. "Just tell him his name and he'll go! He'll stop!" she yelled.

"Who's name?" Bruce asked.

"Her lover, the musician," Jackie said looking at Leena. "Your *secret* lover. He knows already! So just tell him!" Jackie screamed. She backed up into the pantry again and leaned against the shelves. She whimpered,

and in a half-whisper she said, "Just tell him you'll never see him again."
She slid down to the floor.

"You're not making any sense, Jackie," Leena said. She and Bruce had
walked over to the pantry and were looking down at her.

Jackie looked down at her lap. Leena squatted down by her side. She
suspected Jackie was talking about Michael but her behavior was so
strange she really didn't know.

"What is this girl talking about? What are you talking about? Did that
bump on your head make you crazy?" Bruce asked.

Jackie kept her gaze down. She was muttering to herself and sobbing
uncontrollably.

Leena looked up at Bruce and said nervously, "I don't know what
she's talking about."

Jackie kept muttering incoherently. She had taken her hands down off
her ears.

"What's wrong, Jackie?" Leena asked calmly. She put one hand on
Jackie's hands. Jackie flinched, pulling her hand away.

"She's nuts!" Bruce said.

"Shut up! You're not helping!"

"Who's got a lover, Jackie?" he said. He raised his voice, "Leena?"

"Can't you see she's upset?" Leena tried to make eye contact with
Jackie. "Are you okay?"

Jackie said nothing. She finally looked at Leena, and then Bruce. She
realized who they were. She muttered, "Leena?" Jackie got up off the
pantry floor and ran through the kitchen and down the stairwell to her
room.

"What is with that girl?" Bruce asked. "What did she mean 'your
lover'? Is this true?"

Leena felt a wave of nausea as her moment of truth was right in front
of her. She knew she had to make a snap decision: to tell Bruce the truth or
to try to convince him that Jackie was having a flashback, which seemed to
be the case. Her thoughts were whirling.

"It's true isn't it?" Bruce pushed it. "That's why you're so different
lately."

Leena decided to lie. She did not want to tell him the truth while he
was under the influence of alcohol and during such a heated discussion. "I
don't know what she was talking about. Obviously, she was not in her right
mind. I think our fighting reminded her of something, something awful that
happened as a kid when her parents were fighting. She's told me some
stuff and it was pretty awful. Stuff about her father beating up her mother."

"I think there's more to the story." Bruce circled around the kitchen in
a rage.

"She's a troubled girl. Just drop it!" Leena yelled.

"So we should keep this nutcase in our house, why?" Bruce yelled. "You know what? You're both nuts!" He stormed out of the kitchen and into their bedroom and slammed the door shut.

Leena went to her office, closed the door, and sat down heavily on the futon. She needed time to think. *Jackie must know about Michael.* Leena thought. Eventually she fell asleep. Around six she was woken up by the phone. It was Jason.

"Mom, I'm waiting here. You or Dad were supposed to pick me up at 5:30 from practice."

With a half dozen apologies, she flew out of the house immediately. When Leena got back from the school she went straight to Jackie's room and knocked. *What if she's done something stupid again,* Leena thought.

Jackie came to the door wearing a bathrobe. "I wanted to check on you to see if..." She didn't know how to word it.

"I'm still alive. Don't worry." Jackie turned and walked away and sat on her chair.

Leena came into the room and closed the door. "I'm glad to see you're fine. You want to tell me what happened?"

Jackie sat with her arms crossed and looked down at her lap. She shrugged.

"You said some things in front of my husband and I think I deserve an explanation."

Leena sat down on the loveseat next to her chair. She waited for an answer.

"I'm sorry. I don't really know what I said." Jackie paused and looked at Leena. "I really don't." Tears began to fall, she started sobbing.

Leena sympathized. She sighed. "What's going on, Jackie?"

Jackie could only shrug and cry.

"I think you need help. I think you have to resolve your issues with your parents and get into therapy. It would be in the best interest for everyone, especially you. You've put yourself into some situations that..."

"I know about your boyfriend, Leena," Jackie blurted out. "I saw you together a few days ago."

"What? You spied on me?" Leena's voice went up. She was angry. "Well did you?"

Jackie nodded. She fished a tissue out of her bathrobe pocket and wiped her eyes. Her bottom lip was quivering.

Leena was incredulous. "Like this is any of your business!" Leena snarled. She bolted to her feet. "I've got you spying on me? That's just great." She paced around the room. She listened to Jackie sniff. "So, you *did* tell Bruce about it. Man!"

"I didn't!" Jackie cried. "I didn't mean to. I told you, I don't know what I said." Jackie looked Leena in the eye and said, "I didn't know,

Leena, honest!"

"So you followed me?"

"I went down to Watch Hill and I saw you go into that restaurant with him."

Leena turned away and mumbled, "The drawing." Leena spun around and looked at Jackie and said it more clearly. "That drawing. You were taunting me!" Leena was yelling.

Jackie was crying. "All I can say is I'm *sorry*."

Leena got up to leave. She walked toward the door.

"Does he know now?" Jackie said.

"Who? Bruce. I don't know. I told him you weren't in your right mind. I don't know what I'm going to do. You've put me into an awkward position." Leena opened the door and turned around before leaving. "I guess, thanks to you, I have a decision to make, don't I?"

Leena left the inn and took a walk. The fresh air wasn't clearing her head the way she thought it would. This was not the way she planned it. She realized that she never had a plan.

LEENA AND JACKIE AVOIDED each other as much as possible the next day. Leena had all day to decide whether to tell Bruce the truth. It was an opportunity.

Bruce came home from work at a reasonable time. At first, they didn't speak but walked around each other in the kitchen. His silence was driving her mad.

"You want to talk?" Leena asked.

Bruce looked at her and nodded. "Bedroom" was all he said.

Bruce came right out with it. "What was that girl talking about? What's going on?" Bruce stood at the window. Leena sat down on the bed.

Leena waited and thought carefully about her answer. From moment to moment she didn't know which way she would go. "Jackie had some sort of flashback and thought we were her parents. They argued in front of her a lot and, I don't really know, but she had some sort of episode when you and I were yelling that reminded her of a terrible fight her parents had." Leena chickened out and let the truth remain undercover.

"So this had nothing to do with you? Jackie *is* nuts?" Bruce said, lacking any sympathy for her as usual. "It's time for that girl to go! She's been nothing but trouble all along and quite frankly I don't trust her in this house anymore. She's brought a dangerous person into this house. What if he had done something to Becky!"

"We have the security door so that…"

"Jesus Christ, Leena, do you hear yourself? What if Becky were, I don't know, walking in from the driveway, and some maniac that Jackie brought here attacked her? Hmm? What then?"

Leena had nothing to say to that.

"She's nuts. She doesn't use good judgment."

"I don't think Jackie is 'nuts' as you put it. She has a few issues, but…"

"It's beyond 'issues' when she thinks you're running off with a lover," Bruce laughed.

"I'll have a talk with her," Leena felt the need to defend her.

"Leena, remember you told me to tell you when you were turning a blind eye to the problems with the hired help? Remember I told you I would tell you that you need to fire someone? Well, I'm telling you now. She has *got* to go. If you want me to do it, I have no problem with that. I've not liked her from the start. You know that."

"Bruce, that's irrational. She'll be fine, I'll just…"

"Consider it done. I'll have a talk with her. You get too emotional."

"You're enjoying this a little too much. You're being sadistic!"

"I'm enjoying this? I'm going to do what needs to be *done*." His voice was going up. "I'm the man of this household and I can't have some little waif bringing home rapists, endangering *my* kids, and then accusing my wife of having a lover. I'll talk to her." He started to walk toward the door to leave.

Leena hated him. She felt trapped. The thought of sacrificing Jackie only to buy time she didn't want made no sense. She took a deep breath, closed her eyes and said it: "It's true that I am seeing someone." The moment was surreal. She didn't believe her own voice. She opened her eyes to see his reaction.

Bruce stopped dead in his tracks. He turned to face her. What she said had not sunk in yet. He looked puzzled.

"Jackie found out about me and…I don't want to lie anymore." Her eyes filled with tears.

"What did you just say?" Bruce asked calmly.

"I'm seeing someone. It's true." She felt scared suddenly.

His mouth was slightly open. "You're having an affair?" He pounded his hand down on the dresser. He turned from her and walked to the window and said, "How did I not notice." He shook his head. His hand came up to his mouth. He turned back around and glared at Leena. "So you were lying just now about Jackie having some sort of episode?"

"No. She did think we were her parents, but she just found out about the…" she trailed off to avoid the word 'affair.'

"Affair?" Bruce yelled and rolled his eyes up to the ceiling. He fixed his gaze out the window again. He was nodding his head. Without turning around he said, "So which is it? Are you having an affair? Or is Jackie nuts? Or both?"

Leena said sheepishly, "I am having an affair. We can leave Jackie out of it."

"How long has this been going on?"

"Since May."

He nodded again. "Well, aren't you clever. My my," he said as he continued to nod his head. "How long would this lie have gone on if your crazy chambermaid hadn't had a meltdown?"

"I was about to tell you."

"Yeah, right!" he yelled. He walked toward her in an intimidating way.

"Can we talk about this calmly?" Leena asked.

Bruce backed away and put his palms up. "I'm calm, I'm calm." He drew a breath and asked, "Do I know him?"

"No."

"Well, who is he, God damn it?"

"You said you'd be calm," Leena cried.

"I'm calm." Tilting his head, his eyes asked the question again.

"My old high school boyfriend."

Bruce was shocked. "What?"

"I was researching bands on the internet for finding bands for events here, and I accidentally came across a website that was his. He has a band and…"

Bruce cut her off. "For crying out loud. He came here?"

"No, he's never been here."

"So go on."

"I was just curious about him, that's *all*. I saw where he was going to be playing at a festival in Connecticut and so I asked Wendy to go. The truth is that I had no intention of talking to him. I was just curious to see him, that's all. You can ask Wendy."

"I don't want to ask Wendy. That doesn't matter now, does it?" Bruce loosened his tie. "I mean obviously you did *see* him. You more than *saw* him!"

Bruce was very quiet. He looked down at his fingernails, and then without moving his head, just his eyes, he looked up at Leena. "What's his name?"

"Michael."

Bruce gestured with one hand and gave her a look by lifting his eyebrows that requested more information.

"Why? What are you going to do?"

He took in a gulp of air. "Is he married?"

Leena was frozen. She did not respond.

Bruce slammed his fist down on top of the dresser and yelled, "Well?"

Leena nodded and mumbled, "Mm hum."

"Nice, very nice." Bruce paced around the room. He ended up in front of the window again and looked out. A full minute of silence went by. He asked more calmly, "You love him?" He was still looking out the window when he asked. He turned to watch her expression when she answered.

Sheepishly Leena nodded her head and mumbled, "Yes."

Bruce went back to staring blankly out the window. Leena saw tears in his eyes. He rarely cried. He cried at the funeral of a good friend a few years ago. He looked utterly betrayed when he looked one last time at Leena and walked past her and out of their bedroom. Leena watched his car drive up the street and turn the corner. She lay down on the bed and sobbed.

CHAPTER 35

A ship pulled up to the curb of the inn and Bruce got out, and then Michael followed him. Leena was on her hands and knees looking for pots and pans in the pantry. Bruce said, "You keep looking while I cook without them for people who deserve it." Michael walked in and stood in front of Leena and said, "I need to go home now." He turned around and left. Leena stood up to follow Michael but her legs felt like lead. There was water on the street and lawn, right up to the door. Leena watched as Michael walked across a plank and got on the ship. He pulled up the plank and the ship drifted away. She tried to call to him but couldn't. From the doorway, she turned around and saw Bruce holding a pan. He had a big grin on his face and said, "Jackie's dead."

LEENA WOKE UP SUDDENLY with a start. Her heart was pounding and she was disoriented. She didn't know where she was. When she remembered Bruce had told her, in her dream, that Jackie was dead it made her head swoon. She went and got a drink of water. She looked at the clock and saw it was almost 7:30 p.m. Then she remembered that Bruce had left. She went downstairs to look for his car to see if he had come home. He was still gone. The downstairs was quiet as a tomb.

She made herself some tea, went to the window seat in the front room, and sat quietly. She moved to a chair to read a book, or go through the motions of reading - her concentration was shot. She lay the book down on its spine, got up, and paced.

She called Wendy when her self-control on her emotions started melting away again. She needed a shoulder to cry on. Wendy would process her claim and dispense the right balance of sympathy and logic. Talking with her friend, her catastrophe was downgraded to a dilemma. She knew Wendy couldn't tell her what to do. That would be something she'd have to figure out on her own. She reminded Leena about the three years that led up to her divorce and how they were very unhappy. "Happiness and peace of mind are worth something," she told her, "even if it means breaking up your family. You can sacrifice just so much for your kids, Leena, but it comes a to point that you have to take care of your kids' mother."

BRUCE EVENTUALLY CAME HOME around ten. Leena was in the TV room. She listened as Bruce walked up the stairwell. She heard the door shut and then she heard the bedroom door shut. She wanted him to come to her to talk and it hurt her feelings that he didn't. *I guess I want my cake and eat it too,* she thought.

She found some courage and she went to the bedroom to face him. "Hi. Where were you?"

Bruce said without looking at her, "None of your business, that's where."

"Do you want to talk?"

"No."

Leena choked back her desire to cry. She noticed Bruce was taking clothes out of the closet and drawers. "I decided to sleep on the futon in the office, Bruce, so you can stay in here."

"Oh gee, thanks, Leena. Thanks for permission to sleep in my own bed!" He looked over at her as he held an armful of clothes. "I wasn't going to move into another room, I was going to move into another *house*!" He went to the closet and took out a suitcase.

"That's a bit of a hasty decision, isn't it? Where are you going to go?"

"Like I said before, that's none of your business."

"Can't we just talk about it?"

Bruce stopped filling the suitcase and looked at her with incredulity and said, "What's to talk about? You're seeing another man and you *love* him! Is there something I'm missing?" He went back to packing his clothes. He walked into the bathroom and started to fill up a toiletry bag.

Leena followed him. "I just don't want to do anything too soon without a plan or talking about…"

"A plan? Don't make me laugh. It's done, Leena, *done*!" He placed his smaller bag inside the large suitcase. "Tell Jason I'll be at his game tomorrow."

"You could move into one of the guest rooms," Leena thought of this idea on the spot.

Bruce turned around and looked at her. "You're kidding, right?"

"No."

He turned back around and continued packing. "Why don't *you* move into one of the guest rooms?"

"I will if that's what you want."

He was unresponsive. He left the room hauling his suitcase. Leena was powerless and watched him walk out of their bedroom. She followed him down the stairwell and into the kitchen and then followed him to the door.

He turned around and said, "You made your bed, now you're gonna have to lie in it." Bruce stared at Leena long enough to see her eyes fill with tears. Gravity pulled the tears down her cheeks. He laughed a sad laugh and said, "A bed you'd rather be in anyway." He turned abruptly and left. He wanted to stay suddenly, but he had to follow through and make his point.

Leena watched his car disappear around the corner once again. She stood and cried as she looked out the window of the door for quite a few minutes. She finally turned and went back upstairs to the TV room.

Later, Leena got ready for bed and went to the office to sleep on the futon. She realized she didn't have to but she couldn't bring herself to go back to their bedroom. *You knew this would not be easy, you fool.* She hugged her pillow and cried. *Will Michael do the same thing? He doesn't have a snitch living with him the way I do. How long must I wait for you, Michael?* She drifted off to sleep.

LEENA WOKE UP WITH a headache. When she realized what had happened, she started to cry again. *Why did I go to see Michael that night?* She questioned everything she had done over the last six months. This was a difficult situation. Leena didn't do difficult well. The guilt and the shame came down on her like a suffocating blanket. She got up and took something for her headache and got back into bed.

Her eyes kept filling with tears. A quiet sob came out. She knew she'd have to pull herself together for the singles dance that evening. She had time. She fell back to sleep until after eleven o'clock.

Leena's hair was a mess. Her eyes were puffy and red. She threw on her bathrobe and slippers and went to the kitchen to get something to eat. She took an apple out of the bowl on the counter.

Jason walked into the kitchen and stared at her. "You look terrible," he said.

"Thanks, kiddo," Leena said.

"I need to go to my game today at 1:00. You remembered right?"

"Of course, honey. I remember."

Jason filled a bowl full of cereal and sat down at the table.

Leena watched him eat. He was oblivious about the situation she had created. *What should I tell him?* She thought. *One baby step at a time for a while, that's all.* The first step was a hot shower to clear her soul and conscience and to tame her bed-head hair. What followed would come to her when that task was done.

After her shower, she put on some clean clothes and she blow-dried her hair. She called Michael on his cell phone from her bedroom. He was at his store.

"Hey babe, how are you doing? I got your email." Michael said. His voice sounded so sweet and soothing to her.

"It's out."

"What? What's out?" Michael asked.

"Our thing, us, it's out. Bruce knows."

"What? You told him?"

"No, Jackie did that for me. Well, sort of."

"Jackie? She knew?"

"Apparently so. She went down to Watch Hill last Monday."

"She saw us? Oh my God, where? In the van?"

"No, at the restaurant."

"Oh."

Leena started to cry. "He left."

"Oh shit, I'm sorry, babe."

"I don't know what I want, Michael. I wanted our secret to be out. I wanted to tell Bruce. I wanted to get this over with, but not this way. I don't know. I'm feeling so confused today I can hardly think."

"So Jackie told him?" Michael said.

Leena told Michael everything. "You know, we didn't have a plan, Michael, but this is not the way I wanted to do it. I guess the way I pictured it was that I would eventually sit Bruce down and tell him. He and I, at some point, would separate. I have no idea what I will tell the kids. They don't know."

Michael got quiet and stuck to "uh huh," and "right" as his responses.

He finally said, "Is there a chance that Jackie knows my last name or where I live and she will call my wife? Or would Bruce do something like that? Did you tell him my name?"

After a long pause Leena said, "No, no one will call your wife. *Your* secret is still safe, Michael. No one knows your damn name!" Leena snapped.

"Come on, babe, you can't blame me for asking. If it weren't for Jackie, you'd still be lying to your spouse too."

"I'm sorry. You're right. I'm so on edge today. I just wanted to call you and tell you what happened, that's all. Things are changing around here. I thought I'd be relieved when the truth was out but I'm not feeling relieved at all. I feel very sad about it."

"We shouldn't see each other for a while," Michael said.

"No. I need to see you. Don't say that. I don't need to hear *that* right now."

"We need to lay low. Let things cool down. Seriously," Michael said.

"Bruce left! What more can happen? It would drive me nuts not to see you. Please say you'll see me." Leena didn't care that she sounded desperate.

"So what do you want to do?"

"Please say you'll see me. This Monday?"

"I don't think that's such a good idea."

"But I need to see you. I need to feel like something is stable in my life."

"Okay, Monday, I guess."

"Not in the van," Leena said quickly.

"No, not in the van. We'll get a room. How about the one in Charlestown?"

"Okay. What time?" Leena asked

"How about 10:30?"

"Yes. Thank you. Michael, I miss you. I can't wait!" Leena started to cry. "I'm so sorry."

"For what?"

"For coming into your life and complicating it. I wouldn't blame you if you wanted to just end this right now." Leena said the words but didn't mean them.

"Calm down, babe. You just need to hold it together."

"I know." There was a half a minute of silence.

Michael started to speak, "So I'll see you on…"

"Are you still sleeping with your wife?" She asked suddenly. "You know, having *sex* with her, I mean."

His silence said it all.

"You are, aren't you?" Her stomach filled with butterflies.

He sighed and said, "Yes."

Leena inhaled quickly and started to cry. "A lot?"

"What's a lot? No, not a lot." He heard her crying. "I'm sorry, babe. How would it look if…" Michael didn't know what to say. Saying nothing might be best. "I don't know what you want me to say. Do you want me to lie?" he asked.

"No. I don't know, maybe," Leena said.

"Really? So I should lie?"

"No," Leena concluded. "It's just that everything that has transpired in the last few days, and to learn that nothing has changed for you… I don't know. Uh, what have I done?" Michael was silent in the face of her rhetorical question. "What do *you* want to do, Michael? Where do you see us? My life is falling apart. Do *we* have a future? Was this all for naught?"

"Slow down."

"I can't Michael. I need some answers."

"I don't know. There's a lot at stake, you know. It's one day at a time."

"This joke of a marriage must end. It was doomed from the start."

"You're being hasty. You and Bruce…"

"Hasty? I've been married for over eighteen years! I think I've given it enough time. Enough time to know it's not working."

"Maybe a divorce will cost you your inn? Ever think of that?" Michael said meekly.

"What do you know about my business? Nothing!" Leena said angrily.

"I'm saying that divorce is a messy thing. A friend of mine just got one. One of the guys in my band as a matter of fact. He was miserable and it was for the best, but they had to sell the house and..."

Leena cut him off. "Do you really think I would allow Bruce to get me to sell *my inn*?"

"I don't know anything about it or Bruce, but sometimes it comes down to tough decisions. Then there's the custody thing. For me, a father, I might lose custody of Tommy! Maybe only see him every week or two. I'd probably lose our house too." There was no response from Leena. "Hey, it's harder on the man, you *know* it."

"Whatever," Leena said.

"Yeah, whatever. You know I'm right!" Michael said. "What we have is wonderful and you know it. What we *had* was wonderful. I know it's selfish, what we're doing, but why fix what isn't broken?"

"But it *is* broken, that's the point! You don't mind all the cheating and sneaking around?"

"I don't like it at all if you must know. It bothers me terribly. I have chosen not to bring this subject up for fear of this exact conversation. *It sucks*, ok?" Michael was angry.

"Do you still love her?" she asked.

Michael moaned. "Oh come on, that's not fair.

"I need to know." Leena clutched a tissue in her fist and kept it close to her nose. She dreaded his response.

"Do you still love Bruce?"

"No, I don't. Now answer me," Leena demanded.

"I don't know. I do, but it's not the same as what we've got. She's the mother of my son. She's a good person who really doesn't deserve this. Does Bruce deserve this?"

"Probably."

"What do you mean?"

"I don't think he loves me. I wouldn't even be surprised if he were doing the exact same thing."

"It makes this, what we're doing, easier for you, then," Michael said.

"I suppose." She sniffed. "Let's just forget I asked," Leena resigned her feelings, fearing a change of heart on Michael's part. She was willing to take what she could get. "I love you."

"I love you too. When we're together it's just you and me. It's our universe. How cool is that? No one knows about us, except Wendy, but it's like our secret little world."

"I want to be able to show you off. You want to hide me away?" Leena asked.

"That isn't what I meant. I mean I love that this is just our here and now, our special time, that's all."

"I want to plan ahead somehow, to a time where we don't have to sneak around."

"This is all one day at a time, babe," Michael repeated.

"I love you so much Michael." Leena was in tears again.

"I know. We'll see each other on Monday. I gotta go, okay babe?"

"Yes," she sniffed. "I'll see you on Monday. Can't wait," she added hurriedly.

"Same here. Bye."

They hung up and Leena cried.

JACKIE WALKED INTO THE downstairs kitchen at the same time as Leena.

Jackie started to talk. "Leena, I just wanted to ..."

"Not here," Leena said, motioning toward Hal who had just pulled in and was getting out of his car. "Let's talk in your room."

They walked into Jackie's room and closed the door. "You know Jackie, for the record, my life is totally none of your business," Leena started.

"I know but..."

"Don't interrupt me. I mean, I've been pretty good to you and have let you stay here like family, really. You've created all sorts of stressful situations. You brought that dangerous person into my house. I've saved your life, for Christ's sake, not once but *twice!*" Leena sighed and took a long pause. "Then I stuck up for you."

"What do you mean?"

"With Bruce. Because of your, I don't know, altered state, it would have been easy to put this all on you and not tell him about what's been going on with me, and at first, that's what I did. I told him you had some sort of episode. Well, he was hell-bent on getting rid of you, firing you. He was very insistent. So what do I do? I save your ass again."

Jackie looked puzzled.

Leena sighed quite loudly and looked up at the ceiling. "So I took the opportunity to tell him about my affair. He knows now."

Jackie's eyes widened. "Really?" She felt ashamed and looked down at her hands and muttered, "Thanks."

"Well, don't thank me too soon. I don't appreciate being spied on or eavesdropped on. I want to be able to feel comfortable in my own house. Do you go through my things too?"

"Oh, no, no, I would never do that, I swear. I am so sorry, Leena, about this whole thing."

"Here's the deal. I think you need some professional help. Sooner rather than later."

"Do you think I have some sort of psychological disorder? Am I a schizo or crazy or something?"

"No, I don't think you are a 'schizo' or crazy. But I think you need to go back to that hospital and get some more counseling."

The waterworks started. "You're not going to fire me and kick me out?"

"For now, no. I think you need a break. You're a good person who has had some rough times. I feel sort of responsible for some of this because of that fiasco with your mother."

"You've been like a mother to me Leena and I hope I haven't screwed up what we have, what I have here." She thought about it and said, "I guess I already did screw things up, didn't I? You hate me now, don't you?"

"No. I like you, Jackie." Leena stared at the girl and saw her heart and soul. She realized that probably no one else ever had. It made Leena sad. Tears came to her eyes too. "Taking you in was something I wanted to do. I saw the good in you and I wanted to give you a chance. I guess what distresses me is that it can all fall apart in an instant, and it can affect my family." They stared at each other for a moment. "So, we're going to look into counseling this week, alright?"

"Uh-huh." Jackie liked this alternative to being fired and nodded whole-heartedly.

Leena turned to leave.

"Leena?" Leena turned around. "I need to know. Would you leave, you know, with that guy? Leave the inn behind?"

Leena sighed. "I have no intention of leaving my inn, or turning my back on my kids and all the responsibilities that go along with it all. I don't know what the future holds for Bruce and me. But no, to answer your question, I'm not leaving."

Jackie smiled. Leena left.

CHAPTER 36

A gentle breeze was kicking up, blowing leaves down the street and across the well-manicured lawns of the upscale neighborhood. Leena sat out on the porch taking a break before her party arrived.

Bruce pulled into the driveway and walked around to the porch.

"This is a surprise," Leena said.

"Probably not as big a surprise as the one I got yesterday."

"Touché."

Leena watched as Bruce put his six-foot five-inch frame into one of the small chairs on the porch. He sat with his knees protruding way out. He put his elbows on the arms of the chair and his hands to his chin. He alternated between braiding all of his fingers together and balancing the tips of his fingers to the other hand's fingers. First, he stared at Leena, perhaps to see her the way her lover saw her. When he couldn't bear to look at her as his ex-wife any longer, he turned his head toward the water.

Bruce finally spoke. "I've had a day to let things sink in and now we need to talk."

Leena nodded and said, "Okay."

"Where's Jason?"

"He's sleeping over at Jeffrey's house tonight."

Bruce nodded. "I need to ask," He looked at her, then looked out at the water and then back to her again. He forced his question out. "Is this guy someone you are willing to throw away your marriage for? Or is it just a fling?"

Leena saw the compassion in her husband that she knew he had somewhere. She rarely saw it. He looked truly sad. She didn't want to hurt him more than she had to. "I'm tired of the lying and the secrets, Bruce. Maybe Jackie did me, did us, a favor. I don't know." Leena was putting off what she needed to say and what he needed to hear.

"And?"

"And I don't want to throw it away, I really don't, but I feel like our marriage has been over for a while. Emotionally it seems over. And I'm talking about before this thing happened. You've been pretty indifferent toward me for years now, maybe our whole marriage even, and I've been thinking you don't love me. Maybe you never did."

"Well, I do love you. I'm just not good at showing it."

Leena continued, "I've never really felt loved by you."

"You feel loved by him?"

Leena nodded slowly and said, "Yes."

Bruce clearly didn't want to hear an affirmative answer. His head bowed down and when he looked up, he didn't seem to know where to look. He finally asked, "So back to my original question. Are you going to throw our marriage away for this guy? Or are you just sewing some wild oats? I know we sort of got together right away in college and you never had much chance to explore and, well, motherhood followed soon after and…" He trailed off and realized he wanted her to answer the question. "So, what's it going to be?"

"I truly do have deep feelings for you, Bruce. You are the father of my children. We've been through everything together. We got this inn together. We went through those years when you went through law school. You were a *rock* when my mother died!" Leena's lip started to quiver. She turned toward the ocean. It was a magnet in times of trouble. She had to forge ahead. "The truth is that I *do* love him." Leena broke into an audible sob. Saying it out loud to her husband was too surreal and uncomfortable. "He was my first love and maybe that's why it is, well, special." She looked at Bruce. His head rested on his large hand supporting its entire weight. He was looking down at the floor. He endured what she was saying. "I loved him back then and he's been in my heart ever since if I am being truthful." Only Bruce's eyes moved. He watched her speak. "But I loved you too. I just think we are both guilty of letting it slip into disrepair."

"Should I try to fight for you? Would it do me any good? I mean, would you consider not seeing him and trying to make our marriage work?"

"I'm not interested in counseling if that's what you're going to suggest. And what do you mean 'fight for me'?"

"I'd like to punch this guy's lights out actually." Bruce moaned and shifted his weight in the chair. It squeaked under the stress. "I feel like this is all my fault now. I should have paid more attention to you. I shouldn't *drink* so damn much," he gestured with both arms as if he was waiting for someone to load them up with firewood. "But fight, you know, try to make what's wrong right."

"You have never really invested in this marriage emotionally. I think if I felt like we had a good marriage I never would have looked him up in the first place."

"So this is it for us? You're not willing to try?" Bruce lifted his head up straight.

Leena didn't answer him but her eyes said it all.

Bruce's face sank. He seemed to have aged five years in five minutes. Bruce was a man who was normally self-confident and well-spoken. His shrunken pride seemed to stunt him.

"I've got to go up and get changed for that party tonight. Why don't we agree to stay here in this house together, at least for now. I mean, Thanksgiving is coming up real soon. Your family is supposed to come. My sister's coming. Becky is coming home next Wednesday. Why don't we get through the holidays and see what happens." Leena got up and went upstairs to change.

LEENA WAS STANDING IN her bra and panties when she turned around and saw Bruce standing in their bedroom. "Bruce, I didn't see you." He had already shut the door and locked it.

Bruce walked over to Leena and put his hands on her bare shoulders. He caressed them and moved his hands down the length of her arms. Leena turned to walk away but he squeezed her arms and pulled her back into his body, with her back to his front. He wrapped his long arms around her waist and buried his head in her hair and neck.

"Bruce you really shouldn't…"

"Shhh," he whispered and kissed her neck. They stood in front of a full-length mirror and they both looked at their reflection. "We look good together," he said. He turned her around to face him and cupped her face in his hands and kissed her.

If Leena wanted to end it, she wasn't doing a very good job convincing him of it. "No," she said, but didn't mean it. She kissed him back.

Bruce kissed her neck and slowly removed her bra straps from both shoulders. He unclipped her bra and let it fall to the floor. He moved his head back to look at her breasts, not letting go of her arms. He moaned and walked backward over to the bed. She let him take her there. He sat on the edge of the bed while Leena remained standing right in front of him. He pulled her toward himself and put his mouth and hands on her breasts. Leena looked down and watched him caress and kiss her breasts hungrily and desperately. He stopped and quickly removed his clothing. His eyes remained fixed on her body. Leena's only act of defiance was not helping him take off his clothes. She stood with her arms at her sides. He made every move. Sitting naked on the bed he removed her panties. Bruce looked up at her face. They made eye contact. He held out his hand to her and guided her onto his lap. She straddled his legs, accepting what was waiting for her, willingly.

They shared the joy and pleasure of the moment in a sad and sensual ride. It was quite perfect in many ways. With such a dark cloud overhead, their lovemaking was like that of new lovers fulfilling their lustful desires.

When they finished they didn't speak. Bruce feared disturbing the momentum and Leena felt plain guilt and remorse alongside satisfaction.

"I need to get ready for that thing tonight, you know that."

"I know. I'll be here when you're done."

Leena got up and looked at Bruce as if he were a child. "Seriously, what are you going to do tonight?"

"Nothing. I know what I'm not going to do. Drink."

"Really? Well, that's good." Leena left and hopped into the shower.

When she got out and came back into the room with a towel wrapped around her body. Bruce was still reclining on the bed. "I'm not going to wash you off me," he said as he lay stretched out with nothing to hide.

"Now you're being silly." She went into her walk-in closet and put on an outfit. She walked out holding a pair of shoes in her hand. "Would you get dressed please!"

"Why? There's no one up here but me. I think I'll walk around this way all weekend."

"I wish you wouldn't." Leena looked a little annoyed.

Bruce grabbed the sheet and covered up. "Happy?"

"That's better." Leena smiled.

Bruce smiled too. "I'll see you later." His implication was for more of the same.

"Bruce," Leena started.

"What?"

"No promises." She quickly left.

Leena went down to the kitchen where Hal had all sorts of things brewing on the stove and in the oven. Jackie was fiddling with decorations in the front room. "There you are. I've been wondering where you were. I want you here to greet them. You're better at that. They'll be here any second!" Jackie said. She looked at Leena hopefully and said, "You still mad at me Leena?"

"No, I'm not." Leena gave her a quick hug and went out to the lobby area.

CHAPTER 37

The ride over to Charlestown on Monday morning was both nerve-wracking and exciting. Leena tried extra hard to be as casual as possible when she left. Jackie was up and hanging around in the kitchen. Leena had hoped she would have slept in. No such luck. She kept telling herself that she did not have to answer to her and that her life was her business. She simply told Jackie she was going out for a while. Jackie did not dare to question it.

Leena didn't regret her encounter with Bruce on Saturday but she knew it fueled his hopes for a normal existence. By giving in to him she only prolonged the inevitable. For Leena her relationship with Michael had reached a point of no return. This was her future. She didn't know how she'd eventually attain it. She only knew it was meant to be.

She managed to avoid another encounter with Bruce for the rest of the weekend. Saturday evening's singles' parties went up to 1:00 a.m.; seven couples booked rooms. Sunday morning was hopping busy with the singles who were now couples. The afternoon luncheon was full of old ladies talking about their rose gardens and eating finger sandwiches. Sunday night was tough. Bruce waited for Leena but Leena kept watching one TV show after another. Bruce finally fell asleep. Leena slipped into bed after midnight and was up before Bruce for her morning jog.

Leena headed to Charlestown after feeding two couples. Michael called her on her cell phone. "I'm here already, where are you?"

"I just got off the highway. Shouldn't be more than a minute or so. You sound anxious."

"Of course I'm anxious. Aren't you?"

"Of course," Leena said. "I'm looking forward to the privacy of a room this time."

"It is better, I'll admit that. You want to start now by talking dirty to me?"

Leena laughed. "Ugh! I'll see you in a few. Bye." Leena pulled into the parking lot of the motel. She parked around the back in front of their room on the end.

"Hey, babe, you're looking good." Michael leaned into Leena and gave her a kiss.

Leena put her arms around her lover and hugged him with all her might, putting her head to his chest. She let go and moved back to look at him. "I feel like I haven't seen you for a month!"

"It's been a week to the day, silly girl." Michael took both her hands and they stared at each other. "Shall we?" Michael motioned toward their room. He got right down to business by trying to remove Leena's clothing.

"Can we just sit for a few minutes? Talk? I need to unwind." Leena eyed the bed.

"Ok, what do you want to talk about?" He sat down on the bed.

Leena hated when Bruce did that – putting the conversation ball back in her court. She feared their relationship was only about sex and not about substance, so she found a topic. "Tell me about your Thanksgiving plans, Michael," Leena asked as she sat down in the chair next to the bed.

"Okay, we're going to Massachusetts to my sister-in-law's house. They have three kids. Her other sister will be there too. She has two kids. Alice has a lot of relatives. It will be a madhouse. Tommy will be ecstatic. How about you? What are your plans?"

"Bruce's parents are coming and his aunt, Marnie." Leena rolled her eyes at the thought of old, dour Marnie. "She's Bruce's mother's sister. She lives with them. She never married or had kids and so never had much tolerance for kids. Oh, and my sister and husband are coming. They live in New York. They have one kid, Brenna who's eleven now. She's an only child. It's not that much fun for Jason. Brenna is younger and she's a real girl if you know what I mean, not to mention a Mama's Girl. She and Jason have never really played together. Kinda too bad."

"Yeah, I see what you mean. It's kinda that way with my sister. She has an older son, he's seventeen now. He can't really relate to Tommy."

"So you only had one child. Did you ever want more?" Leena asked.

"Another would be nice. We tried, but you know, it didn't work out. One's okay. Besides she teaches full time and when Tommy was a baby, I stayed home with him. I was a Mr. Mom. I never told you that."

"You were? I love that. You're amazing," Leena beamed.

"Oh yeah, that's me, I'm amazing. I hated the idea of putting him in daycare and so I used to take him to the store with me. I even had a crib and playpen in the back. He's my special little guy."

Leena watched Michael's expressions intently while he talked about his son. He was beaming. "That is so wonderful, Michael. Bruce was never there too much when I raised the kids." She laughed, "Well, he was there, but he didn't do diapers and he didn't babysit much. I made sure I was around most of the time. It's not that I didn't trust him with them as young children, but I sort of didn't trust him." She smiled at the thought she conjured up in her mind: "Like he might have driven off with the child in the car seat on top of the car." She laughed. "That's not nice, is it?"

Michael laughed too. "No, but I know what you mean."

They crawled onto the bed together and chatted about their kids.

Family was not often the subject that arose, more a subject avoided. If felt good to make it more real.

Leena's truth-telling that past weekend was not as cathartic as she thought it might be. "My head's still spinning over what Jackie said and what happened. I guess it's the next step we've talked about." Leena paused. Michael didn't comment. "Whoever said 'the truth shall set you free' didn't know what they were talking about. I thought I would feel relieved but I feel worse," Leena said.

"That's from the Bible."

"Oh," Leena said.

"It sucks - the whole thing. Is Bruce like accepting of it all? I don't get it?"

"Sort of. He was upset, don't get me wrong, but he still thinks there's a chance for us."

"Maybe you *should* give him another chance."

Leena looked at Michael like he was crazy. "What's that supposed to mean?"

"Maybe you still love him, babe."

"You know what? I don't want to talk about *them*, okay? I didn't drive all the way here so I could hear you tell me that I should stay with Bruce."

Michael reclined on the bed and stared up at the ceiling. "I could think of something else we could do instead." He looked at her with a devilish grin.

"I bet you can," Leena smiled and took his lead. She snuggled up close to Michael. Their lust had not subsided one bit. It always progressed so easily.

There came a knock at the door. They stopped and looked at each other. Not wanting to believe they could be interrupted, they continued. The knock was louder the second time. They stopped again.

"Who the hell could that be?" Michael whispered.

"How should I know? Ignore it. They've got the wrong room obviously."

A third knock.

"Should I go see?" Michael asked. Another knock.

With the next knock a male voice with a southern accent said, "Excuse me sir but I think your car was just stolen. I thought you should know."

Michael got up and put on his jeans and went to the door. He checked to see where Leena was. She had grabbed her clothes and slipped into the bathroom.

Michael looked out the window and saw his car where he left it. "You've got the wrong room, pal," he said through the door. Then he realized he could have meant Leena's car. He looked out again and it was true. Leena's car was missing. Michael went over to the bathroom door and said, "I think it's true, your car's not there."

Michael went back to the door and opened it up. A tall man wearing a plaid shirt and black jeans and sneakers stood in front of him. "Did you see the person who…"

The man burst into the room shoving Michael so hard he stumbled and fell onto the bed. "Where is she?" he said.

"What the fuck?" Michael yelled. "Get the hell out of here!"

Leena poked her head out of the bathroom door and saw Bruce. She only had her underwear on. She went back inside the bathroom and threw her clothes on.

"Come on out, honey. No matter you're not wearing much. I've seen you naked plenty of times."

Leena came out. "Bruce, oh my God! What are you doing?" she screamed.

"Shouldn't I be asking you what you're doing?" He looked at Michael and said, "Ya know, I saw every bit of her just last Saturday." He looked at Leena. "Isn't that right sweetie? Man, she was on fire. Couldn't get enough of me," he said looking at Michael again.

"Are you insane, Bruce? Are you drunk?"

"I'm as sober as a judge."

"You bastard!" Leena yelled.

Michael didn't know what to say. He stood and looked up at this man, this towering, jealous husband. He didn't want to resort to the line "It's not what you think" but, of course, it was. But what he did say, "Let's talk," earned him a sock in the jaw, laying him out flat on the floor.

"Michael!" Leena screamed again. She was crying. She bent down to Michael's side.

Michael tried to get up and Bruce said, "You can stay down there little man. You coming?" He addressed Leena. Michael cringed when he thought Bruce was about to kick him.

"I'm not going *anywhere,* especially not with *you*! Get out of here!"

"So this is the guy," Bruce said more calmly staring down at Michael on the floor. "I just had to see him." He stepped back and circled one time, rubbing the top of his head and then letting each hand rest on his hips.

Leena looked at her husband with total hatred. "Well, aren't you so clever finding me here, Bruce. Very good. You win. Is that what you wanted? What did you do hire a private investigator?"

Bruce laughed. "I didn't need to waste money on that. It was too easy."

"So now what?" Michael finally spoke. He was angry. "You gonna kill me?"

"Please, and ruin my life? Hardly. But it's tempting. You're married too, right pal?"

"Don't answer him, Michael," Leena said.

Michael had sat down on the corner of the bed. He looked defeated and pretended to ignore Bruce by looking at the floor.

"You're married too. I know." Bruce said with glee. "You're ruining your family too. Does your wife know what you're doing today?"

"I see you're wearing a disguise." Leena tried to say something hurtful. She looked at Michael and said, "He'd never be caught dead in plaid."

Bruce walked out the door and turned around. "I guess I needed to see it for myself you lying *bitch*." He started to walk away and said without turning around, "She's all yours pal. I'm done with her."

Leena ran to the door and watched him as he walked to a car she did not recognize, a black mini SUV. She looked around for her car. "What did you do with my car?" she yelled to him.

"It's around somewhere, you figure it out." He got into the car and sped off, tires kicking up dust behind.

Leena and Michael stood there trying to take in what just happened. They went back inside the room. Michael put his shirt and his shoes on.

Leena sat in the chair. "I'm *so* sorry. I had no idea."

"I know." Michael stood up. "I gotta get out of here. I can't handle this."

"Please, Michael, don't let this get to you. Let's look at this as a good thing, okay?"

"How are we going to do that?" Michael raised his voice to her. "He's probably calling my *wife* right this minute!"

"Okay, so if he is, wouldn't it hasten things along and we could just get on with *our* lives together? I mean what happened with Jackie is not what I wanted either, but it happened."

"I *have* a life!" Michael yelled. He saw Leena's face turn to horror.

"I'm not part of your life? What are you saying?" Leena cried.

"You are but… all you can think about is yourself!"

"That's not true."

"I don't want to get into this now." Michael walked out the door and stood by his car. Leena quickly gathered up her purse and jacket and stood beside him. "I gotta get outta here. I'm sorry. I'll talk to you later."

"Michael please don't go like this. Don't let Bruce win."

Michael looked her in the eyes and said, "So you slept with him right after he found out about the affair? Interesting." He turned and unlocked his car.

Leena looked away in shame. "I'm not proud of that. I don't know what I was thinking. I think I was feeling sorry for him and…"

He turned around quickly. "Please!"

"And you're not sleeping with Alice? *Please*," Leena copied Michael.

"And what if I am?"

"Nothing I can do about it. I know you are, and regularly! I guess that's the reason I did it last Saturday."

"Whatever. I gotta go." Michael was disgusted.

Leena started to cry. "Can we please just hug for a second?"

Michael reluctantly gave her a weak hug with one arm. Leena kissed him on the lips but he didn't react. She started to cry again.

"Are you going to be okay when you go home? He's not going to do something crazy is he?" Michael asked.

"I doubt it. I'll face whatever it is," Leena said.

"He wouldn't knock you around would he?"

"No, I really don't think so. He's never done anything like that."

"How do you know? This is a first, isn't it? You having an affair?"

Leena looked at him, puzzled. "You have to ask me that? You know it is."

"He looked pretty mad."

"I'll be fine."

Michael turned and got into his car and started the engine. "Get in. Let's find your car." First Michael stopped at the lobby and returned the key. They drove around the corner of the building and found the car parked in an adjacent parking lot. "I'll wait to make sure it starts." Leena looked at Michael and knew she would have to let everything sink in and leave him alone.

"I love you." Leena waited for his response.

He nodded, still looking ahead. Leena got out and got into her car. It started right up. Leena looked up. Michael glanced one last time at Leena and then drove away.

CHAPTER 38

Leena returned to the inn and went straight up to her room. She passed Jackie without saying a word. Jackie watched her breeze through. She knew something was up.

Leena came back down carrying something. She went out to the front door flipped the closed sign around. She walked down to the end of the property where the Vacancy sign stood and inserted the "NO" into the sign. She walked back into the kitchen and saw Jackie sitting at the table. Leena stopped abruptly and glared at her. "The inn is closed if anyone asks."

"How come?" Jackie asked.

"'Cause I said so, that's how come. Any more questions?" Leena said, full of anger.

"I thought you were gonna stay open more around the holidays."

"Well, it looks as if I changed my mind." Leena's head was tilted. "Maybe I'll change my mind about other decisions I've made around here this year. Like who I hire and who I *fire*!" Leena's voiced went up. She stared directly into Jackie's eyes like a predator seeking its prey. "Any *more* bright questions?"

"No."

"Good. There's one couple here, right?"

"Right."

"You're gonna handle it tonight. You figure it out." Leena turned abruptly and went back upstairs.

LEENA TOOK A SHOWER and then put on her pajamas. It was the middle of the afternoon. She dreaded Bruce's return, although she didn't know if he would return at all.

Leena tried to work on the computer on some miscellaneous business but she could not concentrate. She heard Bruce's car pull in around five-thirty. She got up and looked out the window and saw his Mercedes. She went back to sit at the computer. He came up the stairwell and walked right into their bedroom, closing the door. She heard the television a few minutes later.

Leena sat and fumed over her situation. She contemplated going in and confronting him. She decided not to.

Fifteen minutes later Bruce came out of the bedroom and down the hall to the office where Leena was sitting in front of her computer. He stood in the doorway with his hands on his hips. Leena looked up at him. She waited for him to speak. At first, he seemed to be at a loss for words, but, like the lawyer he was, he found his breath and began his opening statement. Leena had daggers in her eyes.

"I'm not going to apologize for what I did today. You probably thought I would, but I'm not."

"I didn't. So get the hell out of here."

"You do not want to take that attitude with me. I'm in no mood for any of your bullshit."

"Did you come in here to pour salt in the wound?" Leena snarled.

"It's already a gaping sore. You've done the damage already. All I did was confirm it."

"You've got *all* the answers, don't you?" Leena said, standing up. Her voice was getting louder.

Bruce shut the door and put an index finger to his lips and said, "Shh."

"Don't you shush me! You got something to say then just spit it out."

Bruce took a long breath in and let it out to calm himself. He began. "You said 'no promises' the other day right after we made, right after we had sex. I felt pretty betrayed at that point and figured you would go right back to him. I felt like such an *idiot!*" Bruce crossed his arms in front of himself. Leena remained quiet and let him talk. "I took the morning off and rented a car and waited for you to leave. This was not my proudest moment, but I felt I needed to do it."

"You're sick!" Leena sniped. "You rented a car and waited in ambush?"

Bruce looked at her with anger curling up around him. "That's right. You're the sick one!" He pointed in her face. He walked over to the window. Bruce put one hand on his hip and the other landed on top of his head. He took it down to gesture. "I bet I interrupted you right in the middle of it didn't I?" Bruce glanced out of the corner of one eye. He had a sly smile on his face.

"You sick *bastard*! What, were you watching? I hope you got off if you did!" Leena screamed at him. "Get out!"

"I wasn't *watching*. You're the one running around like a slut and you have the nerve to be angry with me?"

"Get *out!*" Leena's screeched. "How *dare* you call me that!" She walked up to Bruce and pushed him on his chest. She didn't budge his 260 pound, six foot five body. "Get to the part where you say you want a divorce and that, you being a big-shot lawyer, you're going to rake me over the coals. Go on!" Leena screamed.

Bruce stepped toward Leena and she backed away slightly. He put his index finger to his lips. "Shh, you want Jason to hear this?"

"I don't care at this point. He probably already heard you call me a slut."

"Here's the deal," he said wagging his finger in her face. "You and I live under this roof for the holidays. You sleep in here and I sleep in the bedroom," he said pointing to the futon and then gesturing at the door. "We'll figure something out after the first of the year."

Bruce changed gears. "So you two think you're sparing my feelings, her feelings, by lying to us? It hurts more I'll have you know. Why didn't you just tell me?"

"Tell you what? 'Bruce, I'll be out today, I'm having an affair. I'll be home in time for dinner'?"

"Don't get flip! Why didn't you tell me last May?" He looked on the verge of tears.

"Did you contact his wife?"

"No. How would I do that? Why you want me to? That would make it easier if I did, wouldn't it? No, I'll let the two of you figure that one out. You two can wallow around in the muck and mire that you've created."

"You really think any of this is easy? It's not. I hate it," Leena cried. "I've been miserable with you for a long time. *Years!*" she was crying now. "I finally have a shot at some happiness and…"

"And what? I ruined it for you? Sorry lady. I'm sorry if I don't want a wife that sleeps around!"

"I bet you've had affairs."

Bruce looked at her with such anger. He puffed up his chest and took one step toward her. For a moment she feared he'd strike her. "You listen to me and you listen good." He moved in toward her face and had to bend down to get eye to eye. "I've never, ever cheated on you. We took vows nineteen years ago and I have not broken them."

"Sure you have!" Bruce looked at her, enraged. Leena continued. "You promised to 'love, honor and cherish,' remember that? And you haven't." Leena was sobbing. Tears streamed down her face. "You've *never* loved me, nor honored me and you certainly don't cherish me! I just keep the house you live in comfortable. You get freshly ironed shirts, hot meals and everything is in its place for you. Why would you want to give that up? It's quite a good deal."

"I do love you," he became vulnerable. "I did love you," he corrected himself.

"Well getting drunk every night and being an asshole most of the time is a funny way of showing it. You don't give a shit about me, or where I go, for *years*. You come and go as you please around here. You're out with friends *a lot* during the week. You're watching football all the time. You drink as much as you want and see whoever you want."

"Are you still accusing *me* of having an affair?"

"It would make sense. You go out, or you're late, and you ignore me for months and months. Do you ever try to cuddle up to me at night? Rarely. Tell me about your day? No! Hmm, interesting. Sounds like an affair to me."

"I said I'm not and never did. I don't like you accusing me."

"Too fucking bad if you don't like it. Whatever it is, another woman, maybe it's another man! Maybe you're gay. News Flash: Husbands, normal husbands, want to have sex with their wives!"

"You are so treading on thin ice, you bitch!" He lowered his voice. "How *dare* you call me gay!"

"Whatever your deal is, I haven't liked it for years, Bruce. What did you *expect*?" Leena yelled and cried. "And I can't believe you fucking spied on me."

"It was the only way," he said. "Amazing. It doesn't matter if this eventually tears our family apart. You don't think beyond some itch you need to scratch. You're a mother, for Christ's sake! You shouldn't be out doing," He paused, "whatever you're doing." His hands rose in a gesture like a conductor.

"And you should be home where you belong, you hypocrite. Not out so many nights having business dinners with colleagues since you say it's all so innocent. And you shouldn't be drinking. You're a shining example for your kids. You're the one who ruined this marriage as far as I'm concerned. And you know what? I don't need a lecture from *you*. I devoted my *life* to you, since college, and our family. I *was* faithful, and I stuck by everything you did and everything you decided about our future. I supported you for a time and now, I think it's time for you to support me."

"You want me to give you my blessing so you can carry on seeing this guy?"

"No, but you need to stay out of my way. It's *my life* Bruce!" She yelled.

"Would you stop seeing him if I asked you to?"

Leena was shocked at the question. "No! So deal with it!"

Bruce stared at Leena, only this time with sadness, not anger. Leena sheepishly stared back with eyes full of tears. They stared for a full minute. He walked away, down the hall to the kitchen.

She heard ice cubes clinking in a glass. Her stomach churned. Anger seethed inside her. The sound of the removal of the liquor bottle cap seemed amplified as if he were in the same room with her. She listened to the liquid being poured into the glass, the sound of the ice moving. Leena stood still like a statue staring down the hallway toward the sounds in the kitchen. She heard the ice swirl as he stirred the drink, probably with his index finger. That was it. She walked down the hallway and entered the kitchen. Bruce turned suddenly as she entered. Leena walked up to Bruce, without hesitation, and knocked the drink out of his hand. It crashed to the floor and the glass broke into a few large shards.

"You have really crossed the line," Bruce yelled at her.

"No, *you've* crossed the line with your drinking. Now you know the reason for what's happened around here."

Jason walked into the doorway of the kitchen and asked, "What's going on?" Neither one had seen him enter.

"Do you want to tell him or should I?" Bruce asked.

Leena was silent for a moment. "It's nothing, Jase, Dad just dropped his drink that's all." Leena looked at Bruce and with as much scorn as she could muster, she said, "I'm sure he'll just fix himself another one right away."

Bruce didn't say a word. He turned and left, walking down the stairwell and out to his car. Jason and his mother remained in the kitchen and listened to him speed away.

"Just go to your room, Jason. I'm not in the mood for any questions." Leena walked back to the office.

Leena felt very depressed about her situation. For the first time, Leena related to how Jackie's mother must have felt before she abandoned her family. Stuck in a loveless marriage with her lover on the outside of her prison, she must have taken flight when the man she loved showed her a more pleasurable existence. But Leena knew she didn't have it in her to just up and leave her home, her business, and her kids. Jason still needed her. And for the first time she realized that Jackie needed her too.

LEENA HUNG AROUND THE office for most of the afternoon hoping to see Michael's screen name on her buddy list activate but she never did. She wrote Michael an email.

Michael, I am so very sorry about today. Bruce rented a car and waited for me to leave. Can you believe that!? I'm as shocked as you are. He just came home. And no, he did not get physical. We had words though. He just left. He said we should try to live under this roof through the holidays for the sake of the kids and then we'll take it from there. I guess I agree with that. That doesn't mean I'm NOT going to see you! We'll figure something out!! He doesn't know your last name, so no need to worry about getting a call. I know you were wondering. Please know how much I love you and please tell me you love me back. Write back and let me know where we stand. Love, Leena

Leena didn't hear from Michael, by phone or email, all the next day. It was torture. She checked the computer off and on all day long. Not hearing from Michael was driving her mad. She decided to call his cell phone. She got his voice mail. "It's me. I haven't heard from you. Call me." She hung up. Leena watched television to pass the time.

Leena checked her email and finally there was a note from Michael.

Sorry I didn't call or write. I have needed a few days to process what happened and to think about what I want to do. I really don't know what I want to do. I feel that what we are doing is very wrong. I've been feeling that way for a while, but at the same time I am selfish and I wanted it both ways. I don't want to "let Bruce win" as you said, but sneaking around is probably not the way we should be handling this. I don't have any answers. I know you want them. Let's see how Thanksgiving goes and then we'll decide what to do. Love M

Leena cried as she read Michael's note four or five times. She wrote back.

Michael, I want to talk to you on the phone tomorrow. Not sure you'll see this note before then. I need to talk to you. I need to hear you. Til then, Love forever, L

By the end of the day Leena called Michael after not hearing back from him.

"Hey," Michael greeted Leena's phone call. "How're you doing?"

"Alright, I guess. Did you get my email? I miss you more than I thought it was possible. This whole thing just makes me want to see you all the more," Leena said. Michael was quiet. "Say something."

"I know what you mean. Not a pleasant thing, what happened."

"Let's meet soon, just for coffee or lunch, anywhere you say. We won't do anything else. We'll meet at a restaurant or something. We'll just get together to talk and just be together. What do you think?"

Michael paused. "I hate to admit it but Bruce made me feel pretty guilty about this whole thing. It really brought everything into focus for me. Let's just wait and get through Thanksgiving, okay? I'm not asking for much here."

"I guess, but can we call each other?"

"I don't know. I'm not sure that's best. Give me 'til after Thanksgiving. Gotta go. Got a customer. I'll be in touch. Bye."

"Love you," Leena said. He had already hung up.

CHAPTER 39

Emotions were spinning in a swirling haze mimicking the lights on top of the ambulance. The flashes of light hit the faces of the EMTs as they tried to keep a poker face.

Michael hovered over his son. Sweat beaded on his brow and dripped down, merging with his tears. "You're going to be just fine, Sweetie, just fine!" Michael was trying to convince himself as he spoke to his unconscious son.

Tommy was loaded into the back of the ambulance and Michael and Alice got in with him. "Mommy's here honey. We're right here baby doll." Alice was hysterical. She yelled, "Why aren't we moving yet?"

The doors of the ambulance were shut and the driver started to pull out of Michael and Alice's driveway. One EMT stayed by Tommy's side keeping his eyes on the child and the monitor. "Sit back sir," the man said to Michael.

Michael was cursing the driver who ran Tommy down and cursing himself for not watching him closely enough. He hung his head down and cried, looking up again to stare at Tommy. There was blood on his head and on his dark green shirt. *He shouldn't have been wearing such dark clothes at this time of year,* Michael thought to himself.

"It was a freak thing, that's all," Michael cried. "Our dog ran after a ball," Michael said to the EMT. "He just ran out! Oh my God," he sobbed. Alice kept her head hanging down, sobbing quietly.

Michael looked over at Alice this time and reached for her hand. Alice looked up at Michael. His gesture made her cry more. She flopped her head down onto Michael's chest and sobbed. Her head was almost in his lap. Michael caressed her hair.

The ambulance pulled into the hospital's emergency entrance and the EMTs moved with precision, wheeling Tommy inside. Michael and Alice walked by his side telling him he was going to be fine up until he was whisked away behind a curtain. Michael and Alice were asked to wait outside in a waiting room.

Alice had trouble supporting herself and leaned on Michael. After several minutes, exhaustion crept up on them. "Let's sit," Michael suggested. They sat down and held hands tightly.

Michael was sobbing. Alice remained silent. "We need to be strong for Tommy," Michael said, stroking her hair.

It seemed like an eternity before a doctor came over to the Everlys. "Are you the boy's parents?" They nodded and stood up immediately. "He's stable for now. It's wait and see right now. I know the waiting is rough. He has a concussion but the CAT scan showed normal activity and I am extremely hopeful for a full recovery. He'll have to be monitored for swelling on the brain." Michael and Alice looked at each other and then back at the doctor. The doctor continued. "His right arm is fractured. It's in a splint at the moment. He'll be getting a cast."

"When can we see him?" Alice blurted out.

"The nurse will come out to let you know when you can go in. It won't be much longer. Okay? I'll talk to you later." The doctor left.

"It sounds like he'll be fine," Michael said, sighing. He felt Alice nodding her head on his chest. They both sat back down in their seats. Michael rested his head up against the wall and shut his eyes.

Eventually, they were allowed to see their son. Michael and Alice walked up to either side of Tommy. The nurse informed them that he would be moved shortly to his own room. Michael stood on Tommy's left side and stroked his good arm. Alice didn't dare touch him. The sight of the bandages and tubes made her queasy. Michael didn't take his eyes off Tommy. He was bending down talking into his ear. A commotion made him look up. Alice was being helped into a chair across the room by a nurse. She had started to faint. The nurse by her side saw the signs and assisted her by making her put her head on her knees. Michael ran over to her and squatted down beside her.

"Babe, you okay? Alice?"

"I'm fine." She looked into Michael's eyes and sobbed. They embraced and cried.

"Shh. It's okay, sweetie. He'll be fine." Michael put both hands up to her face and kissed her gently on the lips.

The nurse came into the room and said, "We're going to be bringing him up to the pediatric ward now."

Michael and Alice waited again in the waiting room until they were given the go-ahead to go to his room.

Up in his room, Michael brought two chairs to Tommy's bedside. They dozed off from time to time. His nurse came in frequently to check his vitals.

When morning arrived, it was a huge relief. Something about the sun coming through the window helped them to feel refreshed. "I'll go to the cafeteria, get some coffee. What can I get for you," Michael asked Alice. "You should eat something. You need to eat!"

"Crackers. Just crackers, I guess. Some juice too?"

"Okay. I'll be right back with it." Michael leaned down and kissed Alice's forehead. "I won't be long."

Michael returned with food from the cafeteria. They both nibbled. They had to bide their time.

Michael looked at Tommy who lay motionless in the bed. He stroked his forehead gently and said, "I love you, little tiger." Alice's tears started to flow again. Michael settled back into his chair. "So we wait," Michael said to his wife. "There's nothing more we can do but sit here and wait."

"I should call my parents and my sisters. Oh my God, what am I going to tell everyone?" Alice was sobbing all over again.

"Do it in your own time," Michael said. "We can deal with that tomorrow. It doesn't have to be today."

"We should call them today, Mike. When are you going to call your parents?"

"I don't know," Michael's look of dejection said it all. "I'll deal with that later. Oh shit, I'll make calls soon."

The nurse came in and switched Tommy's IV bag. She injected something from a syringe into the bag and pushed a few buttons on the automated IV machine. She went to the other side to adjust his sheets. "Hi Tommy, can you hear me?" the nurse said in a loud voice. Her name tag said Erica.

Michael said to Erica, "When will we be able to speak to the doctor again?"

Erica consulted her watch. "Dr. Bernstein will be coming in, oh I'd say within the next half hour or so."

"Shouldn't he wake up already?" Alice asked the nurse.

"Not necessarily. It's always a big relief when a patient wakes up, but it's the body's way of healing when they don't wake up right away. It's like the body knows when it should wake up and not before. I know it's tough. I'll be right down the hall if you need anything." She left them standing there, staring at their son and listening to the sound of his life beeping rhythmically on the monitor.

Dr. Bernstein entered the Everly's room on his rounds and examined Tommy. "We want to set up another CT scan. That will tell us if there is any swelling around the brain."

"What if there is?" Michael asked.

"A shunt would be inserted to relieve the pressure." Dr. Bernstein pointed to the location where it would go.

Alice gasped at the thought. She brought her hands up to her mouth and cried.

"Kids bounce back so quickly. A lot quicker than adults do in similar situations," he concluded.

Michael asked, "When do you think he'll wake up?"

"Don't know. We'll know more after the results."

THE AFTERNOON DRAGGED BY slowly. Michael found pacing in the hallway and back and forth into his room was better than sitting in the chair. "I think I better make some calls," he said. I can't use the cell phone here, so I'll go down to the lobby or outside. I'll call your folks."

Alice nodded. "Oh good."

Michael called his parents and he retold the story. He and Alice didn't blame the driver – a woman, about thirty, a mother herself. She had been visiting her parents who lived on their road. He told them how Tommy had been playing with Harvey and how he ran out from behind the large rock at the end of their property. Tommy followed him. Michael said, "The woman said she jammed on the brakes when Harvey ran out, so when Tommy ran out, she was going that much slower, thank God."

He repeated the story to Alice's parents. Her mother became completely hysterical. She told him they would be at the hospital as soon as possible.

TOMMY'S RESULTS WERE GOOD. There was no swelling. His eyes opened that afternoon.

"Tommy honey, it's Mommy. Daddy's right here."

"Hi sweetie," Michael said.

Tommy blinked and tried to focus. Michael called the nurse. Tommy started to cry. He was confused.

"You're alright honey," Alice said. "You just got a little boo-boo and you'll be fine. You need to rest for a few days."

Tommy's little face looked so sad, but he adjusted to his circumstances quickly.

Michael and Alice and their parents spent the rest of the evening doting on Tommy. Their dark cloud had lifted.

THE "CLOSED" SIGN WOULD hang in the window of *Ever More Antiques* for the days that Tommy was in the hospital. Michael and Alice took turns staying overnight by Tommy's side. A cot was set up beside his bed.

By this time, he had accumulated four new stuffed animals and other miscellaneous gifts from family, friends, and neighbors. He was beginning to think that getting hurt was a cool thing. His cast went up and over his elbow. The doctor explained to the child that he needed to get everyone he knew to write on his cast before it got removed. This challenge appealed to Tommy.

CHAPTER 40

Leena did not hear from Michael all week. She had left him voice mail messages and had sent him emails. Patience and understanding were turning into fear and frustration. It was torture.

Tension between Bruce and Leena around the house had subsided. Becky was expected to return from school any minute. Jackie was anticipating having her sister-friend back.

Leena tried one more time to contact Michael on his cell phone on her way to the store for last-minute items on this the day before Thanksgiving. She got him this time. She knew right away that something was wrong. "Michael, what is it? Something's wrong."

"It's Tommy. He had an accident and he had to go to the hospital. It was horrible."

"What? Is he okay? What happened? Tell me!"

"He was struck by a car!"

"Oh my God, Michael, is he okay?"

"He's okay now, thank God. The woman who hit him was beside herself. I realize now she wasn't doing anything wrong. Tommy darted out after Harvey."

"What are his injuries?"

"He got a concussion and didn't wake up until the next day. He has a fractured arm. What a week!"

"Michael, I am *so* sorry. Why didn't you call me? When did this happen?"

"Saturday."

"Saturday?" Leena felt her heart sink when she realized he had not called her. "Why didn't you call me, Michael?"

"Things have been crazy. I'm sorry. It's been non-stop pandemonium. Our parents have been here and we've been staying at the hospital most of the time. Tommy came home this morning."

"He did? He's home?"

"Yeah."

"Wonderful! Where are you now?"

"I'm in my car. I'm running some errands."

"Me too." There was a long silence.

"Well, I gotta go. I'm at the store now," Michael said.

"I am so sorry you've been through all this, Michael. So Tommy's gonna be alright?"

"He's fine now. Well, I'm here, so I'll talk to you soon."

"Okay. You call if you need anything," Leena said, knowing it was just the right thing to say and that he would not be calling. She started to cry, but she hid it from him.

"Of course, thanks. I'll talk to you after Thanksgiving some time. Have a nice day tomorrow."

"You too. Love you."

"Later," he hung up.

Leena felt sick thinking about Tommy being injured, but selfishly, she felt worse about the feelings that rushed to the surface. Suddenly she realized something: This was the end of her relationship with Michael. The logic of it filled her senses to a drowning height. She tried to catch her breath. Her heart started to beat wildly. She pulled the car to the side of the road. "Oh my God," she said out loud, crying. "This is the straw. This is the straw!" The tears flowed like a faucet. *You're overreacting. He said to wait until after Thanksgiving,* she thought. *Pull yourself together.*

CHRIS' CAR PULLED UP in front of the inn. He and Becky got out. Bruce came outside to greet them.

"Hi, Dad!" A big smile lit up Becky's face as she headed toward Bruce who was standing on the porch at the railing.

Bruce gave her a hug. "Hi, honey. We missed you." He let go of his daughter and extended his hand to Chris. "Chris, good to see you, young man." They shook hands.

"Thank you sir. Same here. It's good to be back in town."

"How's school?"

"Fine. Goin' really well."

"Good. Come on inside." Becky and Chris went inside. Bruce started to follow them.

"Bruce!" Gloria Miller yelled.

Bruce turned and saw Gloria and Ashton walking along the road at the edge of the Frazer's property. Bruce walked back to the railing of the porch. "Gloria, Ashton. How are you? You ready for Thanksgiving tomorrow?"

The Millers approached the porch. "As ready as we'll ever be." Gloria was now face-to-face with Bruce. Ashton stood to the side. "Doesn't seem like the help one gets these days is as good as it was years ago, but I'm hoping for the best. Against my better judgment, I'm trying someone new tomorrow. My fingers are crossed. How's that girl working out?"

"Jackie? Fine." He turned his attention to Ashton. "So when are you and I going to get out on that golf course?"

"Say the word. We're flying to France next week but we'll be back the week after next. We'll make a date."

"Sounds good."

"Bruce, I wanted to ask you if you had given any more thought to joining the Board of Directors as we discussed at our party a few months ago," Gloria asked.

"Oh Gloria, I don't think so. I'm sorry. I appreciate the vote of confidence but I'm stretched too thin as it is. I'm on the board of the Rhode Island Bar Association so I don't need more nights out and more meetings. And work is crazy, besides."

"That's a shame, Bruce. You'd be a great addition."

Leena returned from her last-minute errands and parked in back. She walked toward them. "What's going on?" Leena asked, not caring how accusatory she sounded.

Bruce put a false smile on his face. "The Millers were just walking by and came to say 'hi.'"

"Leena," Gloria greeted her cautiously. Ashton did the same.

"Are we discussing the hired help?" Leena leered at Gloria.

Bruce spoke before Gloria could confirm Leena's query. "She was asking me about joining the Board of the Historical Society."

Leena nodded. "I could use some help Bruce. Would you excuse us?" Leena motioned to Bruce.

Bruce said under his breath, "I'll be in in a minute. Becky's here. She got here a few minutes ago."

This news diffused Leena's rocky state of mind. "I see." Leena abruptly turned and went inside.

Bruce offered an explanation. "She's feeling a little under the weather. We've got a lot of company coming tomorrow." The moment was awkward.

A car pulled up in front of the inn. Loud music seemed to shake the bushes until the engine was cut. A young man got out and approached them.

"Can I help you?" Bruce asked. "We're not open at the moment."

"I know you," Gloria said to him. "Your Jackie's boyfriend, well, ex-boyfriend."

"Yes, ma'am,"

"And you are?" Bruce asked.

"I'm Rick, Mr. Frazer, Rick Diamen."

"Oh Rick, right. I'm sorry. I didn't recognize you. It's been a while hasn't it?"

"Yes, sir, it has. I was wondering if Jackie was still living here."

"Yes, she's still here. Let me go find her for you. Why don't you wait right here." Glad for the excuse to leave, he said, "Gloria, Ashton, as always, it's great to see you. Have a great day tomorrow. I'll call you about that golf game." Bruce directed his last comment to Ashton.

"You bet," Ashton said. "Gloria, come on."

Bruce went inside.

"You're not the boyfriend that Jackie had so much trouble with, are you?"

"Gloria, let's go," Ashton sensed the inquisition was about to start.

Gloria pointed her index finger toward the sky to shush her husband but looked as if she were checking wind direction. She kept her sights on Rick. "The one she, well, made a very foolish decision to date?" Rick looked puzzled. "I'm not so sure the Frazers would want you to be here at all. I don't think *we* want you here." She looked at her husband. "Maybe we should call the police."

"What are you talking about?" Rick asked.

"On Halloween? She was left a bloody pulp!"

"What?" Rick's voice went way up. "What happened on Halloween? What the hell?" Rick was angry.

"She was near death, although maybe that's what she wanted. She tried to kill herself before that. But property was damaged that night. My garden…"

"She tried to *kill* herself?" Rick started to shift his weight back and forth, he paced, dispelling energy. His arms went up in the air in a gesture.

"Gloria!" Ashton pleaded again.

"Mrs. Frazer found her. Right down there as a matter of fact." Gloria pointed to the water. The three of them looked in the direction of her gesture. "I thought she just liked to party a little bit too much but I found out she tried to kill herself. When was that Ashton? March? April?" Ashton didn't respond. "April, I think."

"I didn't know," Rick said. His pacing stopped. He had gone white.

"Anyway, that other boyfriend beat her up after the Halloween party. Probably, she finally told a boy 'no' and he didn't like that answer so he, well, you know."

"No, I *don't know*. Tell me!" Rick started to walk toward the door, too impatient to wait for her to answer him and for Bruce to summon her.

Jackie came out at that moment. "Rick!" She was utterly shocked. Bruce had not told her who was outside.

"Jackie, I…" Jackie looked at the Millers.

"What are you doing here lady?" Jackie snapped at Gloria.

"I was just…"

Jackie yelled. "Get outta here!"

Finally, the gentle tug of her husband's arm guided her from the Frazer's porch. Jackie watched them walk to the road. She turned back to Rick. "What are you doing here, Rick?"

"What was that woman talking about? Were you attacked?"

Jackie looked down at her feet. She nodded. "She's so nosy! It was something stupid, but that's over and I'm fine now." She looked back up at him. "What are you doing here?"

"I've been thinking about you and so here I am. I was in the neighborhood," Rick laughed a little. "I went about twenty miles out of my way to *be* in your neighborhood, but I ..." He cut himself off and approached her. He slowly held out his hands and took Jackie's hands. "I've missed these hands." He raised them to his mouth and kissed them. Jackie did not take her eyes off him. "Can I hug you?"

Jackie gasped. She shyly nodded her head. Rick drew her to his chest and they held on to each other for dear life. He caressed her head and her hair. Jackie's ear was over Rick's heart.

Leena stood at the window looking out at Jackie and Rick. She had just left her daughter in the kitchen fawning over Chris. Eventually, they left the porch and walked down the steps to the street. She watched them until they turned the corner, out of sight. Leena was consumed with jealousy. Her lip quivered and she sniffed trying to hold back the hysteria that lurked just behind her eyes. *Tomorrow is Thanksgiving. Chris came back to Becky. Rick came back to Jackie. This can't be happening again!* Leena's thoughts went back and forth from 1980 to the present and the conversation she just had with Michael on her cell phone. An inevitable tear fell quickly down onto her shirt. She wiped her cheek and turned when she heard someone behind her.

Bruce stood silently staring at Leena. They exchanged cold glances. Without speaking, blame for their lot was placed on the other. Words were at the surface. Trouble was brewing.

Jason walked into the room and unknowingly diffused a fight.

CHAPTER 41

A thick fog rolled in early in the morning and burned off by noon, but not before a few accidents on the highway delayed Bruce's family from arriving. The tension between Leena and Bruce was as thick as the fog. Leena didn't let it burn off. The residual effect of her conversation with Michael the day before, and her seething jealousy over Jackie's and Becky's luck in love, turned her into what could only be described as a bitch. She saw the fracture with Michael as a direct result of Bruce's and Jackie's actions. Her resentment toward everyone involved, including Tommy, increased tenfold.

Leena's demeanor had changed. Her silence raised suspicion with Jason and Becky. Upstairs in Leena and Bruce's bedroom, Becky cornered her mother. "What is going on with you and Dad?"

"Nothing, honey, we're going to have a nice day with Gramma and Grampa."

"You can't fool me. What is it? I mean, you're not speaking to Dad, like, at all. Jason said you guys were fighting like crazy the other day. What gives?"

Leena sat at her dresser in front of the mirror and fiddled with her hair. "Your father and I haven't been getting along lately. You know how we fight." She looked at her daughter in the mirror. "Can we just have a nice day?"

Becky stood watching her mother in the mirror as she tried to clip a barrette in her hair. "So isn't it great that Rick came back to Jackie?"

Leena's hand came down hard and fast, holding the barrette that wouldn't cooperate with her hair. She continued to look at herself in the mirror. "Hmm, yeah, great."

"I mean what a shock! I sure did feel bad for her before though."

Leena didn't respond. She brushed her hair out.

"Chris is coming at four. You said that's alright, right?"

"Yes I did."

"He's eating at home around two, but he said he could join us too."

"Whatever."

"Is Rick coming here too?"

Leena turned quickly to look at Becky and said in a most exasperated way, "No!"

"Why, you tell her he couldn't?"

"No, he's going somewhere with family. Long Island, I think. Okay?" She said curtly.

"Okay! Geez!" Becky left the room.

THE TRAFFIC JAM FINALLY eased up. Bruce's family members arrived first. They gave a blow by blow description of the multi-car accident on the highway, and then they went on to the weather report. Leena's sister and family arrived shortly thereafter.

Bruce's mother, Virginia Frazer, or Gini as she was known, the long-suffering wife of Harold Frazer brought her long face with her, along with a casserole with aluminum foil draped over the top. Her purse, ever-dangling off her right arm, never left her side. The wrinkles on her face mapped out her disappointment in Bruce's father.

But not getting married was no better solution for Gini's sister, Marnie. She found the downside of most everything in life and usually blamed the faults of the world on the liberal Democrats and the slanted mainstream media. The fact that there was a Republican president in the White House quelled her comments somewhat. But she did enjoy reminiscing about the downfall of the American morals due to Bill Clinton – a subject she never tired of. The only consolation Leena had at this visit was that Marnie would not grimace at her children's every move and see it as bad parenting, now that they were older.

Gini and Marnie had identical hairdos. There must have been a two-for-one special on their blonde hair color. Gale-force winds could not have moved a single hair. Perfume permeated each room they occupied.

Bruce wasted no time taking drink orders. They weren't in the house for more than ten minutes. "Mom, Dad, can I get you a drink?" Bruce offered. He knew better not to ask Aunt Marnie.

"Not yet, dear. Maybe some wine with dinner," his mother said.

"I'll take a gin and tonic if you've got it," Harold Frazer said.

"I think we can find some gin, Harold," Leena said. *Gin and tonic. This acorn didn't fall far from the tree,* Leena thought. Bruce gave her a scolding look. She gave it right back to him.

Shortly thereafter, Leena's sister Nancy and her husband Al Harmon arrived. Al was the brother Bruce wished he had. He never got along very well with his own brothers. Al was a financial adviser with a firm in New York City and doing very well for himself – a millionaire now. Not only did Bruce look up to Al on a social level but they had become drinking buddies.

Nancy found Leena in the kitchen. Her daughter, Brenna, was in tow. "So, there you are. What have you been up to? The inn is looking just beautiful," she said.

Leena was looking under the aluminum foil of the dish Bruce's mother brought. "Oh, thanks. Not much. Same ol' same ol.' Guests come and guests go. I could show you a few of the upstairs rooms if you want." She sniffed the dish and replaced the foil, and then made a questioning face. "I redecorated some of them since last time you were here. Come on."

Leena led her sister and Brenna upstairs to show them some of the rooms. "By the way, I thought you guys could have this room." Leena inserted her cardkey and showed her the largest guestroom. It faced the ocean. "Here. Keep this key for later."

"Oh, Leena this is wonderful," she said, smiling widely.

"I'll put Bruce's folks downstairs. They're not too keen on the stairs anyway.

LEENA HAD NEVER BEEN jealous of her daughter before but watching Becky and Chris made her stomach churn. The uncertainty of her relationship with Michael together with the memory of her own Thanksgiving break-up in 1980 forced her to suppress the desire to cry throughout the day. There was a foreboding of another Thanksgiving break-up, and by the look of things, it wasn't going to be Chris and Becky, or Jackie and Rick. *Was history repeating itself?*

Becky's giggle, that of a young girl in the presence of her beau, was musical. But to Leena, it was like the sound of a child's first violin lesson. Leena became quieter. All she could think about was Michael. All she cared about was Michael. Her heart was aching for Michael and the life she was gypped out of. She felt trapped once again.

Leena watched the clock, celebrating the minutes that were over and done with. The conversation was predictable if nothing else. She swung her leg to fight boredom and put on a smile to feign delight over some recipe Gini said she had concocted. Harold was on his third gin and tonic and it was only four-thirty. She figured Bruce and Al were on their fourth drink.

Leena rarely got a word in edgewise and no one ever asked her anything about herself – no one cared, so she didn't care about them. They were all too consumed with their own problems and ailments to realize they didn't know much about her at all. Their indifference suited her just fine. Usually it was an insult, but on this day, it was a relief.

"Who is that girl I keep seeing walking in and out? I assume that's some friend of Becky's?" Gini asked.

Leena looked at her mother-in-law and replied, "That's Jackie. She works here and lives in the apartment. She's a year older than Becky and, yeah, they're friends now."

"I see. You didn't introduce her to us," she said.

"I'm sorry, Gini, I will when we eat later. Will you excuse me?" Leena got up and found things to do in the kitchen. She intercommed Becky in her room. "Could you and Jackie come down and start helping with some things? Tell Jason too."

"Okay," they both said together.

With the help of her sister, Nancy, they all kicked into high gear and managed to get everything on the table at the same time, and served hot. All congregated around the beautifully decorated table around five for a turkey dinner with all the fixings and more.

For a few minutes Norman Rockwell would have had another subject for a painting, but before the stuffing made its way around the table Harold was off and running with old war stories and work anecdotes. Aunt Marnie proceeded to dispense her complaints and prejudices one by one. Gini passed the platter and dutifully sat silently while her husband talked. After all, he was the breadwinner and he was the one who made all the decisions. Telling him no, or telling him to shut his big mouth would never happen in her world. She knew her place.

Leena recalled her own parents and how they would argue at the table. It was usually her father who started it by finding some small thing to pick at, and then, quite often, it escalated. Leena's mother was shushed into submission. *It must be a generational thing,* Leena thought as she listened to the conversation. *Women stuck by their men letting them do or say whatever they wanted. Not this woman!*

Jackie sat with the family at the Thanksgiving table. A decision to include her met with expected opposition from Bruce. Becky insisted on seating her at their table and Jason shamed his father into dropping his complaint. Leena remained neutral.

"So you are the tenant who works here?" Gini asked Jackie.

"Yes, ma'am."

"I don't remember you last time I was here."

"That's because she wasn't here, Gini," Leena said.

"Well isn't that nice of my son and daughter-in-law to invite you to dinner. Where is your family, dear?"

"They don't live around here so they invited me today. I'm real grateful." Jackie looked up from her lap and made eye contact briefly with Bruce and then Leena. Her eyes returned to her lap where she stared at her folded hands.

"Where do they live?"

Jackie looked uncomfortable and looked to Leena for an escape. "Well, my mother lives in Connecticut."

"That's not too far, dear," Gini said.

"No, ma'am."

"And your father?"

Without hesitation, Jackie said, "He's dead."

"I'm sorry to hear that."

"Jackie's been a great help around here," Bruce said.

Leena was suspicious of a compliment about Jackie coming from Bruce.

"She's been very helpful with certain things. She has brought enlightenment."

Leena recognized the dig in reference to what had been recently revealed. Most certainly, Jackie did too. Before Bruce was able to expound Leena diverted the conversation. "So how's it been being retired, Harold? Are you driving Gini crazy yet?" Leena laughed a little. She looked around the table: no one was smiling.

"Retirement is just fine. I served my community for forty-three years, and now it's my time to relax," Harold said, referring to the law practice he had, much the same as his son's. Bruce worked for his father right out of college. Their relationship became strained, and after three years, Bruce broke free. His father didn't take it well. Leena recalled, with great clarity, the Thanksgiving the two of them ruined that same year Bruce left his firm.

"He worked like a slave all those years," Gini chimed in. "Just like our Bruce." She patted her son's hand.

"At least he worked for a living," Marnie snarled. "Not like some of these ne'er-do-wells you see on the dole. Why don't people try getting a job and stop waiting for Uncle Sam to give them a handout? Too many bleeding heart liberals out there for my taste. I had it tough but I worked my whole life, worked hard."

"Let's not forget about us stay-at-home mothers," Nancy said meekly. "That's work. I'd like to see a man do what we do all day, right Leena?"

Leena looked up from her plate. "Oh, right."

Bruce announced from his position at the head of the table, "Al, you and me, we go down to the beach after dinner and we'll hit some golf balls into the water. What do you say?"

Leena stared at him in disgust. He was visibly drunk. She looked back down at her plate and ate without much interest. She heard, but didn't listen to, Marnie and Gini argue over some trivial incident involving a telemarketer. Al and Bruce were talking about golf but their conversation had moved into something involving women with tight T-shirts. It caught Leena's attention. She saw that Jason was fixed on the two men and their opinions about legalizing prostitution. Becky and Chris were wrapped up in each other, not noticing anything else. Leena tried to tune everyone out.

A loud laugh filled the room as Al roared over some off-color joke Bruce had told. Leena caught a few words from Bruce's conversation with Al. He was still on the subject of women. She heard the word "pussy" and a moment later heard him say "piece of ass." Jason hung on every word.

"Bruce!" Leena finally yelled from the other end of the table. Everyone was quiet suddenly. All eyes were on Leena. "That's enough of that talk!"

Bruce looked at her and he looked around the table at all the faces. In front of family he needed to show that a woman must be put in her place. "I'm talking here. Can't you see I'm having an important discussion with Al here and I don't need *you* to tell me what to do in *my* house!" He looked at Al and laughed, looking for support. Al suppressed a chuckle.

Everyone was quiet. Leena's heart was pounding. She knew this grandstanding was for his father's benefit. Bruce spent his entire life trying to live up to Harold's standards. She was certain that if this had not been a family gathering Bruce would have been wearing the gravy or the mashed potatoes, or both. She stood up and went into the kitchen and stood against the sink and stared out the window. How she wished she could just go upstairs to her room and be alone. She knew she couldn't. *I am not going to cry,* she thought.

A hand came to rest on her shoulder. Leena turned to see who it belonged to. It was Jackie's. "I understand completely how you feel. I know exactly what you're going through."

Leena was in no mood to be charitable. She snapped at her. "I'm really not interested in hearing about your rotten childhood right now if you don't mind!"

Leena went back into the dining room with Jackie following behind her. Everyone watched Leena walk to her seat and sit down.

"Everything okay, dear?" Marnie asked.

"Fine, great. Let's eat."

"So, honey," Bruce began, "tell everyone where you were the other day. You know when I walked into that room and found you."

Leena was incredulous. She furrowed her eyebrows and stared, unblinking, at Bruce. Her heart raced at the thought of any revelations being exposed at her Thanksgiving table. She scrambled to think what her reaction would be if he spoke of it. She could turn the table over, spilling all the food, breaking all the dishes. She could run out of the house and drive off somewhere. She was prepared to flee.

"Well?"

"I don't know what you mean?" She looked at Bruce who was clearly enjoying the hunt.

"Well, I'll tell them." He turned and looked at individual faces, one at a time, "Leena was in this room, see, in a bedroom, and I walked in and found her, ah, wallpapering one of the rooms. She's quite a gal. She did a great job. So professional. The person that occupied that room must have been very impressed with her talents – being a return customer and all. You'll all have to see it." Bruce looked back at her, knowing he had taunted her like a cat playing with a mouse.

Leena sat stone-faced. Plots of revenge blocked any other thoughts for several minutes.

Nancy vouched for Leena's work as she had seen the newly decorated rooms upstairs. Oblivious to Bruce's taunts she said, "It's true she's got quite the knack for decorating."

Leena stared at her sister in disbelief.

All eyes watched the exchange between Bruce and Leena.

Leena went back to picking at the food on her plate. She pretended Bruce's comments were nothing more than small talk. The conversation went right back to politics, sports, money, illness, and self-aggrandizing. She was relieved the focus was off her once again.

ALL THE WOMEN CLEARED the table while the men went to the library to have their after-dinner drinks. This day couldn't be over soon enough for Leena. She endured more socializing with the women in the front room. Bruce's mother started dozing off in a chair. Leena and Nancy were stuck listening to Marnie rant and rave about the welfare case that lived down the street and how she should be "fixed" so she would not be able to have any more children.

Nancy went upstairs to put Brenna to bed around nine and never came back down. Leena figured Brenna didn't want to sleep alone so Nancy went to bed too.

Marnie got up and shook Gini's arm. "Come on old gal, Leena's going to show us to our room."

Leena brought them down the hallway and gave them both a cardkey. "We don't need to lock the door, dear," Gini said.

"I know, but it doesn't work any other way. Don't you remember that each room needs a cardkey to open the door?" Leena explained.

"I don't remember, but, okay, if you say so," Gini laughed and looked at Marnie as if Leena were being silly.

Leena left and went to the library and said to Harold as she handed him a cardkey, "Here is your cardkey, Harold. Gini is in room number one. See? It says it right here," she said pointing to the card. "I put Marnie in room number four." She turned to Al and said, "You and Nancy are upstairs in room five. Here you go. I'm turning in. Good night."

"Good night dear," Harold said. "Dinner was wonderful."

"Yes, super!" Al said.

"Thanks. I'll see you in the morning."

"I'll be up soon, dear," Bruce said with a sly smile.

Leena shot him a look and then turned and left.

She heard Al say as she walked away, "What crawled up her butt?"

Leena kept walking and went upstairs. Jackie and Jason were playing video games. Becky had left after dessert with Chris and wasn't home yet.

Leena went right to bed in her office on the futon.

THE NEXT MORNING LEENA cooked breakfast for everyone. Jackie came in to help.

Bruce's parents had a long ride back to upstate New York and left by ten. Bruce took Al to the golf course and they played a round of golf. Leena was left with her sister and niece.

"Why don't you and I take a walk along the beach. It'll give us a chance to chat." Leena hoped she could connect with her sister.

"Okay, I'd love that," Nancy said.

"Brenna why don't you go play a video game with Jason," Leena suggested. "I think Jackie will play with you too. They'd love to show you how it works."

"I don't want to. I'll stay with Mommy."

"Well, Mommy and I are going to go for a walk. I can get you some games to play up in the TV room? Or a video to watch?" Leena hoped Nancy would pick up on her cue.

"No, I'll go for a walk too," Brenna said.

Nancy did nothing to discourage her. She stroked Brenna's hair, going along with the young girl's decision. Leena didn't get to see her sister very often and she was feeling like she could use her sister right about now. With Brenna in tow, it was pointless. But she couldn't renege and so off the three of them went, down to the water. The entire holiday was a huge disappointment. Leena tried to look forward to seeing her sister but since Nancy became a mother her priority was Brenna, and so it should be, but Leena became a casualty of Nancy's motherhood. Their conversation didn't stray beyond how lovely a spot they had and what a good job Leena had done on the inn's upkeep. Brenna talked to Leena for most of the way back about her horse collection, her riding lessons, and how much she wanted her own horse. Leena listened patiently. Nancy indulged every word. She stroked the girl's hair every chance she got. It was almost more than Leena could take. She suppressed the desire to start a fight, or cry. Nancy never picked up on Leena's low mood. Even if she couldn't talk to her sister about some of her issues, she wished her sister had noticed she was troubled. Leena couldn't wait for her sister and family to leave.

After Al and Bruce got back from their golf game they showered and then found Leena, Nancy, and Brenna upstairs in the TV room. Brenna's TV watching was discretionary so the three of them sat for the rest of the afternoon with the television off talking about things such as Brenna's special private school and her teachers. Nancy had become one of those mothers who made reservations for a specific nursery school when she was five months pregnant.

Nancy never had any interest in Leena's children. After a few years of not being able to conceive Nancy finally had Brenna at thirty-six. Her jealousy was apparent back in the days when she was not having any luck and Leena, her younger sister by six years already had two children. Nancy had had very little tolerance, like Bruce's aunt, for Becky and Jason. Now, with Brenna, Nancy not only expected Leena to fully embrace her daughter, but listen to every word she said and to indulge every request. At every visit since Brenna's birth, the conversation was all Brenna and not much else. Nancy never carved out a life for herself beyond motherhood. *That will come back to bite her on the ass*, Leena thought. Initially, Leena was elated when her older sister conceived and subsequently gave birth at full term. No miscarriages or false alarms. It was a happy time.

The disappointment Leena felt multiplied as the years went on. The only sister she had was no more than a guest at the inn now. Leena just waited for check out time.

By four o'clock they left to go home to their two-million dollar estate in Westchester County, New York. Alone, at last, Leena retired to her office. She told everyone they were on their own for dinner and that they'd have to help themselves to the leftovers.

CHAPTER 42

The sound of laughter drifted up from the front porch below the office. Leena got up from her futon and looked out and saw Jackie and Rick. Leena grunted and went back to her futon and lay down again. She propped her arm under her head and turned up the volume on the television.

LEENA HAD NO CHOICE but to attend her meeting on Wednesday morning with her auctioneer and coordinator for the upcoming auction at the inn, to take place in a little over a week. After they left, she walked into the inn kitchen and found Rick and Jackie sitting at the table holding hands. She stopped dead in her tracks. They looked up at Leena.

"Hey Leena," Jackie said. Rick nodded hello. Jackie let go of his hands.

Leena stared at the two of them. "Hi."

"I did those errands you asked me to do," Jackie said.

"Good, good." Leena nodded and shifted her weight contemplating what her next move would be. She smiled weakly and said "Well, I'll see you later," and went upstairs. She changed back into her sweatsuit and found her place on the futon.

THE "CLOSED" SIGN REMAINED on the front door. Leena had no intention of attracting any new business. As it stood, she had three upcoming commitments: the auction luncheon, and two office Christmas parties the week after that. They had all been booked months in advance and she knew she'd have to suck it up. Leena didn't have the mental strength to deal with much of anything beyond her own upkeep. Plans to try to book the inn during the holidays were discarded. She had no motivation.

Four days after the holiday weekend and still no call from Michael. Pacing and watching television to kill time between checking her email was driving her mad.

She could stand it no longer. Leena nervously picked up her phone to call Michael several times. She kept pushing "End" before completing the series of numbers. After this ritual repeated itself for a good ten minutes, she let the call go through.

He answered. "Michael Everly."

"Hi. It's me."

"Hey me."

"How was your Thanksgiving?"

"Good, it went well. How about yours?"

"Eh, alright, I guess. I wasn't really into it. How's Tommy?"

"He's doing great, really great. It was a fantastic Thanksgiving. I mean talk about being thankful!"

"I hear ya. I'm so relieved to hear he's making a full recovery."

"Yeah, he's a real trouper, that kid. He got all his classmates to sign his cast and they made a really big card for him, you know, a get-well card."

"That was a thoughtful idea."

"He's been worried about Harvey because when I let him out he's afraid he'll run out into the road. He sits at the window yelling 'Harvey, come back here!'"

"How sweet," Leena listened patiently. "He sounds like a real cutie. I wish I could meet him."

"It was a crazy and hectic and *stressful* week, let me tell ya." He let out an audible sigh.

"I'll bet." By now Leena was feeling more comfortable: Michael sounded himself.

"So you stayed home right? Who came?" Michael asked.

Leena had already told him, but she repeated it. "Bruce's parents and aunt, and my sister, husband, and their daughter." Leena was tempted to get right into complaining about the whole lot of them but decided to leave that for another day.

"Great. Listen I was going to call you. You beat me to it."

"I figured you would. You busy at the store?"

"Yes, pretty busy. There're a few people walking around the store right now. So, can you talk now?" Michael asked.

"Yes, of course. I called you, remember?"

"We've gotta talk, about us." He paused. Leena let the silence pass and waited for his next remark. "You there?" he asked, stalling.

"Yes, I'm here."

"Hold on. Let me call you back. Someone's at the cash register."

"Okay, call me right back."

Leena sat and waited with the phone by her side. Finally, a half-hour later, he called her.

"Sorry about that. Some people were purchasing some stuff. Then someone else came in. Anyway, no one's here now, so let's talk."

"Okay."

"I've had a while to think about this and I think I have made a decision."

Leena's heart skipped a beat. She instantly had butterflies in her stomach. "Think about what, Michael?" she asked.

"About us."

"And?"

"And I think we need to stop seeing each other. I didn't come to this conclusion easily though," he said quickly. He said the words that Leena dreaded all week. There was silence on the other end of the phone. "This is not working out the way I thought it would. Actually, I had no idea how it would work. I never thought beyond the next meeting and…"

Leena started sobbing and sniffing. "What are you saying?" she yelled.

"I'm saying that we need to stop seeing each other. This is not working out…"

"Yeah, you said that already," Leena yelled at him. "You don't even have the balls to say this to my face? You're doing it over the *phone*?" Her anger was boiling over. "Fuck!" she yelled.

"Calm down, babe," he said.

"You want me to be calm? I thought we were trying to make plans to be together. I could have patched up the lies when Jackie went psycho on me, you know. But *NO*! I decided to take advantage of it and tell Bruce the *truth*. It was really dumb for us to get together so quickly after I told him. I mean in hindsight it was *so stupid*!" She cried and coughed and blew her nose.

"I don't see a solution I can live with," Michael said very coldly.

"So you're choosing *her*?"

"I'm choosing my *family*, Leena. And you should too. I mean, Bruce must love you to do what he did. If he didn't care he would have let you go."

"I don't give a shit about Bruce. He can rot in hell for all I care."

"Well, maybe you should patch things up with him. He is the person you chose all those years ago. It wasn't me!"

"You broke up with me, remember?"

"I tried to get back with you. Eh, let's not dredge up the past. The past is past. We're in the present now."

"Say you'll think about what you're saying, Michael! Don't make any decisions before Christmas. Promise me! You said 'the holidays.' A lot has happened very recently so you haven't had enough time to process it! Please, don't do this to me! I love you, Michael, *please*!" she begged.

There was a long pause. Michael listened to Leena sobbing into the phone. "I've made my decision. I've got to work on my marriage and be a better father to Tommy. He deserves that. I mean, he could have died! I need to commit to my little boy and his mother. My marriage was pretty good before you came along," Michael said defensively. "I love her."

Leena was hysterically crying. She could tell he meant it. "Michael, don't say that! Please Michael you know that's not true. I'm the one you love. You told me that."

"I did tell you that, but I love her too." He took a deep breath. "I love you, but I love her too and I need to be with her right now. Home is where I need to be!"

"This can't be happening. Oh, that little bitch, Jackie. I ought to kick her ass out of this house! All the things I did for her and look what she did to me!"

"You can't blame Jackie for something that was doomed from the start."

"You *bastard*! How can you *say* that to me?" she sobbed more. "You never *once* gave me the impression this wasn't the real deal. We talked about being together. We talked about traveling together. Ireland? Grand Canyon?"

"I'm not saying it wasn't real or that I didn't love you, 'cause I did."

Leena observed his use of the past tense. "Did? So you don't love me anymore?"

"I do love you, Leena, and I did love you long ago. It was great, what we had, and what we had more recently. I'll never forget it. I've been leaning toward this decision for a while. The encounter with Bruce was a huge wake-up call. But when Tommy's accident happened, forget about it. That was it. It was getting to me for a while. The guilt was eating away at the feelings I have for you, and I didn't want to jeopardize those good feelings. You don't deserve that. You'll always be in my heart, you know that. You'll always have a piece of my heart."

Leena was lying on her futon, curled up with the phone to her ear. She sat up to blow her nose again. "What am I going to do? Oh my God." She sobbed and gasped. "So was this just about sex?"

"No, it wasn't 'just about sex.' The sex was great. I don't deny that. It's just that I was in a different place in my life than you were when this happened."

"We can make it work. It's just going to take some work and some real planning this time. We didn't plan it at all, Michael. Don't make a hasty decision, Michael, *please!*" she begged.

"I've made up my mind. I'm so sorry," Michael's voice cracked with emotion.

Leena sobbed some more. "I'm not going to push you." She took a deep breath. "You're free, Michael. You're free!" She paused and said, "Just think it over and let the holidays go by. I won't call you before then, I promise." She paused and took another deep breath waiting to hear if her suggestion would fly.

"Okay, I will let the holidays go by, and I will think about it. I guess I at least owe you that." He heard her sigh. "I don't want to dismiss what we've had. So, yeah, I'll let everything sink in. Fair enough."

"Thank you, Michael. That's all I'm asking."

"Don't get your hopes up, babe." Michael heard more sniffing. "Okay?"

"Okay," She longed to hear him tell her he loved her, and everything would work out fine. She lay back down on her pillow. They said nothing for a minute. Her face contorted with silent sobs. Tears drenched the pillow.

"So, I'm gonna go now," Michael said. "Please try to have a good holiday. Enjoy your family. Bye, Leen."

"Bye." She took the phone away from her ear, moved it back, and looked at the buttons. She pushed the button and disconnected the call. She let the phone drop to the floor. She remained on the futon and cried for a solid hour.

Realizing she had to pull herself together she went and got in the shower. The warm water pouring over her body made her tears flow again. She resigned that they needed to come out. She had to tell herself that it was not over with Michael and that he was just confused because of Tommy's accident and the incident with Bruce. The feelings of doom concerning her own marriage returned and made more tears flow.

After she finished, she rubbed the condensation off the mirror with the towel to check out her face in the mirror. She grunted when she saw how puffy her eyes were.

Jason came home from school and Leena put on a front. He sensed something was wrong and he asked her, "What's wrong Mom?"

"I'm just not feeling all that great today, honey. Would you help yourself to the leftovers or a frozen dinner tonight? I'm going to go to bed early tonight."

"Okay," Jason went to his room.

BRUCE RETURNED HOME FROM work promptly at 5:30. Leena could not bear to see him. She stayed in the office with the TV going and the door shut.

Bruce came right into the room without knocking. "What's with the 'Closed' sign still up?" He looked at her sitting on the futon, watching TV. "What's your problem? You look horrible."

"Thanks, so do you," she said.

"I'm serious, what's wrong?"

"It's none of your business. Why don't you get out and start your night of drinking your beer or your gin and tonics."

"So answer me about the sign. I have the right to know why you're going to turn away business."

"What? I'm not entitled to a vacation? That's all it is, it's *my* vacation time. If you want to deal with guests, by all means, turn the sign around."

"You're mad at me 'cause you thought I was going to tell the family about your little indiscretion at the love nest motel, right?" He taunted her.

Leena glared at him. "You're so astute. The ravings of a drunken madman out for vengeance sort of ticks me off, you're right."

"Well, I wanted you to know how I felt moments before that guy opened the door. The panic and stress, it was awful."

"Then you should have spared yourself the anguish and not done it at all."

"I told you I had to."

"You do what you gotta do. Now leave me the hell alone. I'm trying to watch something."

Bruce looked at the TV and there was some Hollywood insider show about an actor he had never heard of. He doubted she cared. He made a face of disapproval and left. Leena got up and slammed the door.

CHAPTER 43

Fall used to be Leena's favorite time of year. The bright colors that normally delight were now a reminder that natural beauty would soon die and fall to the ground in a blur of mud-colored death. She came to realize that her relationship with Michael was no different than the summertime flowers: beautiful while they lasted but destined to die at the end of the season. Leena knew, in her heart of hearts, that it was over.

Leena had no plan, no escape hatch. "I shouldn't feel so trapped, or unfortunate, but I do. I'm living here in my dream house on the ocean. And I have two wonderful kids," she told Wendy. Wendy tried to assure her that time would heal her broken heart. But soon the calls to Wendy dried up. It was hard to take having a friend who was a happy newlywed. She had what Leena longed for: a second chance at love. Wendy checked in on her friend from time to time but there was never anything she could say to repair the damage.

A week had passed since Thanksgiving and the "Closed" sign remained. This was normally a time of year Leena enjoyed. She was always one of the millions of shoppers out to snag the first of the Christmas sales. Leena remained secluded.

SUNDAY MORNING, THE DAY after the charity auction, Leena, once again, could remain in her pajamas the entire day. She went down to the basement to fill up her grief bucket some more. Leena spent the morning going through her storage area digging out old photographs of old friends, family pictures of the kids, her parents, and pets they no longer had.

Memory is a harsh mistress. Favorite photos of loved ones, smiling, filled precious boxes. The mind holds onto the good and bad memories forever, editing the past to fit perception, not reality.

What Leena was really looking for were her senior yearbook and two separate photographs of Michael. She picked up the book and opened up to the page that had Michael's senior photograph and his blurb underneath it which contained silly inside jokes and memories. She moved on to the two photographs which were carefully placed in an envelope where she also kept her one and only love letter that he wrote to her when he first went off to college. It read:

Dear Leena, I've only been here a few weeks and miss you terribly. What are you doing? Are you behaving? I know I don't have to ask you that. I'm just kidding. My classes are tough but I don't mind the challenge. I've met a few nice people. I'll call you and we can make plans for you to come up and see me here. You think your parents will let you come? Well, I better go. I've got class in 20 minutes and it takes almost that long to walk across the campus. Did I say that I miss you terribly? Oh yeah, I did. But I didn't say I love you yet. So here it goes... I love you my brown-eyed girl. Love me back!! xxxooo Love always, Michael.

Leena cried and brought the letter up to her chest and pressed it against her heart. She leaned her head back against the wall and looked up at the ceiling. She looked down again and took out the two photographs of Michael. One was of Michael standing at the edge of a pool when he was on the swim team. The other, Wendy had taken of the two of them when they were all at a friend's house. They were sitting close together on a sofa. She instantly remembered the evening.

There was a light on the back porch that made the moths dance around it haphazardly. From the sofa in the basement, they could see the others outside smoking cigarettes and laughing. They didn't join the group. In the dimly lit room where the music originated, their hands entwined. They kissed. They parted and then touched foreheads and talked about their future together.

Wendy entered the room. They looked up and a flash captured the moment.

She stared at the photograph of their moment frozen in time. *If the universe could stop at just one moment it would have been that one*, she thought. She let the photograph fall to her lap in her hand. *Why didn't I take a recent photo of you?* She thought. A cold chill went through to the bone when she thought of the finality of it all. Another tear fell. "Why have you forsaken me, Michael?" She said out loud.

LEENA WAS FILLED WITH self-doubt and self-loathing. She could no longer use tactics like book clubs or shopping to occupy her unsettled and distracted mind. She felt the need to resolve and put her emotions into action.

With little forethought, Leena went upstairs, got dressed and left the inn. She got into her car and drove up to Michael's house in Voluntown. She didn't know what she was doing. Something pushed her in that direction.

She had to use a map to find his house since she had ducked down in his car the day she went there. Leena drove by his house slowly enough to look up the driveway. She saw Michael's van. They had no garage so it was apparent that Alice's car was not there. She noticed the large rock that sat at the edge of the property near the road. She could see why Tommy was not seen right before he was struck.

Leena contemplated pulling into the driveway and having it out with Michael but something stopped her. She had another idea.

She left Michael's street and headed down to his antique store in North Stonington. She pulled up to the curb across the street in front of the store and shut off the car's engine. She sat and stared at the store, studying it. The name of the store, *Ever More Antiques*, was spelled out in large gold letters. She had not noticed the first time that his store was next door to a bakery. Large stones made up the façade of both stores, with large picture windows on either side of their front doors. Different size cakes for different occasions were on display in one window, chocolates in the other. Christmas garland wound around the display shelves. Michael's store windows contained items that were made up to look like rooms in a house: one was a kitchen, and the other a cozy living room with a tiny, fully decorated Christmas tree. A "Sale" sign was in the window. She watched as a customer went into the store. Tears rolled down Leena's cheeks. "This is his store," Leena mumbled to herself through the tears. She watched another stranger emerge from his store.

Then she saw a woman inside the store walk up to the front window and remove a small object from the kitchen scene. She handed it to a man who was standing next to her. They talked for several minutes. The woman returned the object to the window where she found it. Leena's heart raced as she realized it must be Alice. She took a deep breath and looked down at her lap. She closed her eyes as if to decide on her next move.

The sound of a tinkling bell caught her attention. The man she had seen at the window left the store. He was carrying a small bag. Leena got out of her car and approached the store. She could feel her heart pounding. She was on autopilot.

The same tinkling sound alerted the store owner. Leena immediately looked around as if she were shopping. She didn't have the nerve to go right up to the woman she believed was Alice.

As she slowly walked around the store the woman came up behind Leena and asked, "Are you looking for anything in particular?"

Leena was startled and jerked her head around to see her face. There before her was a very pretty woman whom she knew to be thirty-two years of age. She had straight, shoulder-length, blonde hair that was parted on the side. Bangs adorned her oval face. She had a perfectly upturned nose. She was smartly dressed in modest pumps and a light magenta scarf around her neck which matched her skirt and lipstick perfectly. Leena did not expect her to be so pretty. The photograph she saw at Michael's house did not do her justice. "Oh, I'm just looking," Leena said. Instantly she had her usual feeling of not being dressed appropriately.

"Okay, if you need any help just let me know." She started to walk away but Leena desired more from this woman.

"Oh, yes, one thing," She blurted out.

The woman turned around and said, "Yes?"

"Um, are you the owner of this store?" Leena asked.

"Yes, yes I am." Leena didn't say anything and looked at her up and down. The woman felt her eyes on her and said, "Why do you ask?"

"Oh, no reason. My husband was here before and he was talking to someone about a set of fireplace irons. Not sure who he talked to."

"Well, it may have been me, although I don't recall," she paused and said, "Or perhaps he talked to my husband, Mr. Everly?"

"Perhaps that was the person." Leena's heart jumped at the sound of his name.

"Would you like me to show you some fireplace irons?"

"Okay." She followed Alice across the store. As she walked Leena stared at her and sized her up. *So this is the woman Michael had chosen to stay with. Of course, he chose her. She's so much prettier than I am*, she thought.

"Could this be what he saw?" Alice asked her pointing to fireplace irons leaning against the wall.

"Oh, Um, let me see," Leena studied them. "Might be. I'll have to think about it and ask him."

"Okay, well if you need any help, give a holler." Alice started to walk away.

Leena blurted out, "How is your son?"

Alice stopped abruptly and turned around, staring right into Leena's eyes. "Excuse me?"

"Your son, I heard he was injured the other day. I was very sorry to hear that."

"Oh, he's much better, thank you." Alice looked uncomfortable and puzzled.

"I only ask because a similar thing happened to my niece a few years ago," Leena lied.

"How do you know about my son?"

"Well, my friend has a fourth-grader at your son's school. It's a small community you know. Anyway, I was sorry to hear about the accident." Leena continued her lie.

"Is your niece alright?" Alice asked.

"My what?" Leena had forgotten already what she told her.

"Your niece, the accident?"

"Oh, yes, she's fine now. Thank God." Leena turned her back on Alice and looked at some nick-knacks on the shelf behind her.

"So what happened to your niece?"

She remained with her back to Alice and said, "She was struck by a hit and run driver almost eight years ago. But she pulled through." Leena turned around. "Her mother, my sister, she stuck by her side like glue. I think she even slept in her room with her for months. She's quite a woman. She was always a stay-at-home mother, you know. Very devoted. The whole thing was quite a shock, very upsetting. It tears a family apart and all." Leena was rambling and suddenly felt the urge to escape.

"Well, our son is going to be just fine too. He's getting around well now. Thanks for asking." Alice said. She stood, graceful and poised, with her fingers braided, and her feet neatly together.

"Well I should be going. I'll think about those fireplace irons. It was nice to meet you. What is your first name?" Leena asked. For some reason, she needed to hear it.

"Alice, Alice Everly. It was nice to meet you too. Have a nice day."

"You too. Goodbye." Leena left and made the door jingle, announcing her departure from Michael and Alice's store, and her departure from Michael's life. She barely made it to the car when the tears rolled down her face once again.

Leena sat behind the wheel of her car and waited until she could pull herself together enough to drive away. Right before she started the engine, she saw an all too familiar van pull up in front of the store. It was Michael. Leena's heart pounded and she felt butterflies in her stomach. *What a close call,* she thought. Sitting as still as a statue all she could do was watch as Michael got out of the van. He went around to the passenger side and opened the door. He helped Tommy out of the van. This was the first time Leena had ever seen Tommy, except in the two photographs on his mantle. The boy had a sling over his shoulder holding his right arm which was entirely encased in a cast up to his bicep. Michael gently took Tommy's left hand and they walked into the store.

Leena's eyes filled with more tears. "Oh my God, what a close call!" she said aloud. *I should just go in and confront him. I should show her that he's not the man she thinks he is, pretending to be a good husband and a good father,* she thought. "What bullshit!" she said out loud, angrily.

Leena kept her left hand on the handle of the door, contemplating opening it again. She watched the front of their store for another fifteen minutes. She spoke out loud again, "What am I doing here?" Leena started the engine and looked over at the store one last time, trying to memorize it. Right before she pulled out, she saw the three of them in the window. She watched as Alice pointed to something up on a shelf and Michael reached up and took it down and handed it to Tommy. Tommy walked out of

Leena's sight. The last thing she saw was Michael putting his arm around Alice's waist. She leaned into him and kissed his cheek. Then they both walked away from the window out of Leena's sight, deeper into the store.

Leena couldn't have tortured herself any more than if she were on a rack and her body was being stretched beyond its capacity. She stared at the spot they had occupied behind the glass for another minute. "Enough already!" She pulled out and left.

CHAPTER 44

Each day crawled along much the same as the one before. Leena moped around in her pajamas, most days. With Christmas approaching, Leena and Bruce managed to be civil to one another. Their bickering had subsided. Leena was broken. Bruce didn't kick her when she was down.

Jackie had not only learned the ropes out of necessity but was taking over for Leena on many occasions. The year before Leena enthusiastically organized parties with live music and sing-along Christmas carols on two consecutive weekends. She had hired a Santa Claus for a few hours for children to visit, attracting a good-sized lunch crowd. This year, nothing. Jackie, Michelle, and Hal ran, from start to finish, the two office Christmas parties that had been scheduled. Leena appeared briefly and then disappeared when she saw they were running smoothly.

She spent most of December lying around watching TV on her futon in the office which was now her bedroom. As the weeks pushed toward the holiday it became more difficult to function. Depression had a strong grip on her. Leena had to fight the urge to call or email Michael. She was still clinging to the hope that he would contact her in January. Her hope was fading with the sun, heading toward the shortest day.

One evening, in particular, Bruce and Jason sat in the kitchen eating dinner together. Leena walked in and saw takeout containers on the counter. She went to the refrigerator and looked for a minute and then shut the door. She looked at the empty fruit bowl.

Bruce watched her walk around the kitchen. He said, "Yep, there's not much to eat around here. Time to go shopping."

Leena gave him a dirty look and went back to the office.

BRUCE CAME TO LEENA a week and a half before Christmas. "We need to talk."

Leena sat on her futon watching TV. She didn't turn to look at him or acknowledge is presence. He entered the office and closed the door. He sat down on the chair in front of the computer.

"I wanted to take advantage of Jason not being home." He paused and stared at his wife. Leena finally looked up at him briefly, and then turned back to the television. "Can I shut this off?" He asked. Holding the remote, he waited for Leena's approval.

Leena nodded.

Bruce shut it off. "We should talk."

"You're here to tell me you're leaving me, right?"

"Well, we do need to talk about it," Bruce was patient, not angry. He knew it was a delicate situation. "It won't be long before the holidays are over and..."

"So you're leaving, yes I know," Leena said angrily.

"I think it's best."

Leena sat up straight and looked at Bruce. "Would you consider staying? Staying and working it out with me?" Leena started to cry. Her anger dissipated. She looked pathetic. Her hair was a mess and she was wearing the same pajamas all week.

"You want me to stay? You want to work things out now?"

"Yes, that's what I'm saying." Leena leaned over and picked up her box of tissues and blew her nose.

"Wow," Bruce said. He was surprised. "It's over between you and that guy, isn't it? That's why you're," he thought for a moment, "such a mess."

Leena looked at Bruce like a lost puppy. She shrugged and cried some more.

Bruce couldn't help feeling sorry for her. "Well, I'm not so sure that's a good enough reason for me to stay. I mean, I'm your second choice, apparently. If he calls, you'd see him. Am I right?"

Leena knew he was right but said, "No, that's not true. I'm saying why don't we work it out? You said you wanted to work things out. So why don't we?"

"It's not that simple. Just because you're in a bad place doesn't mean I should allow myself to be such a chump."

"So what did you come in to tell me?" Leena turned on him.

"Let's not get yelling at each other. Let's keep this quiet and calm, okay?"

Leena looked down at her lap where her hand was clutching the tissue. She sniffed and then nodded in agreement.

Bruce got right into it. "I'm going to move out right after the first of the year. I've found a place up near work, a condo, and..."

"You bastard! You've already found a place to live?"

"I thought we agreed to be calm?" He continued. "I just signed a rental agreement for a condo up near work. I have an option to buy, but let's do it this way for now. Let's not make any major decisions. I move out, you keep the inn. It's your inn really, your business. And we'll see how things go. What do you think?"

"Do I have any choice?"

Bruce looked at her as if she were a child and said, "No, I'm afraid not. I've made my decision."

Leena burst into tears. Those were the words she heard Michael say a few weeks ago. It was more than she could take. She laid down on her futon and cried.

Bruce was tempted to sit next to her and comfort her. The memory of her standing in front of him screaming at him at the motel came to his mind. He resisted and told himself she didn't deserve comfort.

"We need to sit down and explain this to the kids. Becky will be home in a few days and we should do it before Christmas."

"No, Bruce. Let's wait until after Christmas!" Leena cried.

"I think sooner is better than later."

"Don't I ever get a say in anything?" Leena yelled.

He paused. His ire was up. "If you hadn't gone and had an affair, I wouldn't have to tell my kids I'm leaving at all!"

"Now look who's not being calm."

Bruce sighed. "I'm trying to be calm and I'm trying to do this as rationally and as painlessly as possible. I'm trying here."

Leena said nothing. She looked down at her hands again.

He got up and went to the door. He turned and looked down at his wife. All he felt was pity with a dose of disgust. "I'm sorry that it had to end this way. I was willing to work it out, as you know when I learned about it all. But only now, now that your relationship with him ended badly, you want to work it out with me, I don't want to be your second choice."

He waited for a response but didn't get one. He quietly left the room and closed the door.

LEENA'S INTUITION TOLD HER that she would never see Michael again, at first a hard concept to grasp. She knew she could never pick up the phone and ask him to lunch like an old friend.

The resentment toward Bruce and Jackie eventually subsided, but she was left feeling like a hollow, burned-out shell where nothing could reside or it would crumble to pieces.

The thought of Bruce leaving or finalizing their marriage was another weight that bore down on Leena. It was like waiting for the death of a parent: the inevitability of time bringing the last chapter to a close.

THE TRUTH WAITED IN the shadow. Leena wanted it to remain there but Bruce stuck to the plan to tell their children as soon as possible.

A family meeting was called and the Frazers met in the living room. It was a week before Christmas.

"Your mother and I have asked you both to come in here because we have something very important to discuss with you." Bruce looked over at Leena who was sitting in a chair directly across from Becky and Jason. He continued, addressing his kids. Bruce and Leena observed the looks of puzzlement on their faces. "Some things have changed between your mother and me and, as much as I, as we, hate to say it, we've decided to separate."

"What?" Becky said loudly, looking at her mother to see if it were true.

"No way!" Jason exclaimed.

"Your mother and I both feel it would be best for everyone if we didn't live together right now. We're not making any hasty decisions, but I have decided to move out after the first of the year to a place up near work."

"Mom, is this true?" Becky asked.

Leena nodded. She held a tissue up to her nose.

"It's 'cause you drink too much, isn't it?" Becky asked boldly, looking at her father. Jason looked at his sister, shocked at her bluntness.

"I have to own my part of this. I do drink too much sometimes and I am sure that it was a factor in this situation." Bruce looked at Leena and said, "Do you want to add anything here?" Leena shook her head. Bruce let it go.

"I know this sounds like a lot to deal with right now but we promise you both that we will try to *not* disrupt your lives as much as humanly possible. I chose a place up near work, very close to the inn. Becky, you're an adult now, honey. You're going to college and you're starting a new phase of your life. I know you'll handle this with maturity. You understand that these things happen, don't you?"

"Yeah, I guess," Becky said sadly. She exchanged looks with Jason.

"Jason, nothing has to change around here. You and I can still do the stuff we normally do. We can still go surfing. I told you I'd bring you to the club and teach you how to play golf. That's a promise I will keep. Okay, buddy?"

"K, Dad," Jason said quietly.

"We're going to have a fabulous Christmas, regardless. You'll see." Bruce tried to soften his announcement. "Okay, we'll see you at dinner in a little while."

They got up and left to go to their bedrooms.

"That went well," Bruce said to Leena.

"Yep," she said. She got up and went back to the office.

CHAPTER 45

Christmas morning's magic faded with each passing year as the children approached adulthood. It was sad to see Becky's and Jason's enthusiasm dwindling. The recent news of their parents' separation dampened it further.

Leena was content to have her family together for the holiday. Christmas day was a temporary fix bringing Bruce and Leena together in a fresh and positive way, even if for just one day. Smiles had been in short supply all month. This day brought them out of hiding.

Jason howled when he opened up the big, long box Bruce had wrapped. It was a new surf board. Leena was just as surprised.

Bruce had done most of the Christmas shopping this year. He was more generous than usual. The fact that they had just dropped a bombshell gave him the impetus to get more expensive gifts. Both Jason and Becky received new computers and monitors, and Jackie, who was invited to join the family that morning, also received a computer.

Bruce had done an about-face concerning Jackie. He knew Leena was going to need the girl more than ever in the near future, so he had been treating her with kindness and respect.

Jackie retrieved four wrapped gifts and handed them to each member of the Frazer family. "I hope you like these." Everyone got quiet. Bruce held the gift from Jackie and didn't know how to react.

Leena sat with a large package on her lap. "Jackie, you didn't have to do this." Leena laughed a little and said, "I don't think I pay you enough."

"I didn't have to spend much, and actually if it weren't for you, Leena, I wouldn't have been able to do this. You'll see. But it's just my way of saying thank you to each and every one of you for taking me in," Jackie looked at Leena, "and letting me stay," she looked at Bruce, "and being my friend. Jackie alternated her gaze between Becky and Jason. So open something!" she said. Her eyes glazed over. She quickly wiped a falling tear with one finger. She sat down on the floor.

"Let's take turns," Becky blurted out. She pointed to Jason. "You first."

Jackie's gift to Jason was a detailed pencil drawing of all his favorite video game characters put into one picture. One creature seemed to grow right out of another. It was rather creepy but much to Jason's liking.

"This is awesome Jackie," Jason said, turning it around to show everyone. "Cool! I love it! Thanks."

"Thanks for teaching me how to play," Jackie said. "Who knew I'd like it so much!"

"You next Becky," Leena said.

Becky ripped open a painting of a portrait of Chris. The likeness was uncanny. "Oh my God, Jackie. How on earth did you do this? This is so, I don't know, so *him*!" She turned it around and everyone cooed.

Jackie said, "I stole a picture from you. You have a million of him. You never missed it." They both laughed. "I took a chance you guys would still be together. I got lucky. I should say, *you guys* are lucky, to have each other." There was a moment of awkwardness and shifting of eyes as everyone realized the irony of her comment.

"Me next?" Leena broke the silence. Jackie nodded. Leena ripped the paper off a large oil painting of the inn. "Oh Jackie," Leena gasped. "I'm speechless." Her chin started to quiver. Everyone remained quiet as the back of the painting faced them. Leena studied it. She noticed that the point of view was from across the street right about where Leena found her that day back in April. It was no accident she chose that vantage point. There was undue sunshine coming from behind the inn, as if heaven were endorsing *Sunset Inn*. Leena's interpretation was that the inn was like a beacon that called out to this troubled girl.

"Come on Mom, turn it around so we can see," Becky said.

Leena turned the painting around. They all cooed and gasped. Leena got up and hugged Jackie. "I love it, Jackie. I'll treasure this always. I will find a place of honor to hang it."

"Come on there's one more from Jackie," Jason said. "Dad."

Bruce took his cue and took the paper off a smaller framed picture of the four Frazers. Jackie had taken individual photographs of each family member, including the cat, Jasper, and by using a Decoupage method made a colorful collage. "This is lovely, Jackie. Thank you very much. It's quite clever, actually. You really have an artistic eye."

Jackie blushed. "I hope you all like them."

Becky got up and darted down to her room and came back with a large present. She announced, "I didn't do something for everyone like Jackie did." She handed it to her mother. "But I made this for the whole family. Mom you open it."

Leena took the present from her daughter and ripped the paper off. Becky had also done a beautiful painting. The composition was comprised of boats at a dock in the background with a grassy and sandy hill with a broken fence in the foreground. Leena instantly recognized the area was down at Watch Hill with its lineup of stores and eateries behind the boats. "Oh, honey!" Leena stared at the scene. Leena looked at Jackie and they exchanged a knowing glance. This pushed Leena over the edge. She started to cry and got up and left the room. Everyone watched her run to the bathroom. It was an awkward moment.

Bruce tried to distract everyone by saying, "You both have a lot of talent. You did an amazing job. She's obviously very moved."

Leena returned and sat down in her chair still holding a tissue. "I'm sorry. I love your paintings. They are so great." She dabbed her eyes and said, "I have some redecorating to do, don't I?" She laughed, half crying.

They finished opening a few more gifts. Afterward, Leena went around picking up discarded paper and cartons. Jason was going over all the stuff he got, neatening up his pile, and taking inventory.

Jackie started to walk down the hallway with Becky. She was helping her carry her new computer equipment. Bruce called out, "Jackie?" Jackie turned around. "You're joining us for dinner later, right?"

"Uh, okay."

"Good. See you there." Bruce looked down at Jason. "What do you say we try out that surf board today, or this coming week?"

"Cool," Jason nodded.

"The waves are kicking out there," Bruce said. "I can't wait."

"Cool's a good word for it," Jackie said to Leena. "Won't it be too cold to go in the water? Hello? It's December."

Leena shook her head and shrugged and simply said, "Wetsuits."

THE FRAZERS' CHRISTMAS TABLE was impeccably set. But it was Becky and Jackie who put it all together. They had learned a lot from Leena who normally would take great pride to set her table. She left it to the girls gladly.

Normal described Leena's mood this day. Normal was a welcome relief. Bruce made a fire in the living room's fireplace. Leena appreciated Bruce's thoughtfulness toward Jackie that day and his decision to cut drinking out of the equation, and she told him so.

"Thanks, Bruce," Leena said when she entered the living room.

He looked up from the floor where he was stoking the fire. "Thanks for what?"

"For being so kind to Jackie today and, well, all this week."

"I've been wrong about her. She's a good kid." He stood up and wiped his hands together. "She deserves a break. You were right. I think the two of you are a good match, actually."

"What do you mean?" She thought it was a dig.

"You seem to get along well, and relate to each other, that's all. She's a hard worker."

"Yeah, you're right. I'm fond of her. If you could have seen her mother, Bruce," Leena said.

"She sounded dreadful." Bruce bent down and picked up another log to put inside the fireplace. He backed up to admire his work. He looked at Leena. "She's lucky to have you."

Leena sat down in the chair in front of the now roaring fire. Bruce sat down in another chair. They sat in silence and watched the dancing flames. It was a respite from what had transpired, and what was to come.

CHAPTER 46

Sleep was Leena's escape once again. Moments before waking all was fine, but when she stirred, opening her eyes to a new day, and in this case, a new year, the dream state hemorrhaged while reality filled the void. Leena's inbox was full of New Year's resolutions. Getting out of bed and cleaning herself up was on her shortlist. New Year's Day, symbolic of change for most people, brought reality to the Frazers, harsh and jarring.

It was moving day. Bruce kept his word and prepared to move out on January 4th. He had a few boxes packed up and ready for the mover on Saturday morning. He arranged for a small truck to come and remove a few pieces of furniture. Leena and Jason sat on the front window seat and watched as a burly man muscled Bruce's favorite armchair into the back of the truck.

Becky stood at the window, arms crossed. No one spoke. Leena held a tissue up to her nose. She looked at her kids through eyes full of tears. She watched Jason as he watched his father so intently through the window. He didn't seem to blink.

Bruce walked around the outside of the inn to the kitchen entrance and entered where he found Jackie sitting at the table with a magazine. She looked up but didn't speak. Bruce did. "So you're staying on, right?" Jackie nodded cautiously. "Good, good," he said, standing in front of her with his hands in his pockets. He paused to collect what he wanted to say. "You've been a big help to Leena. Big help. She's gonna need your support now more than ever." Jackie nodded again. "I was wrong about you Jackie. I apologize for the things I said to you. You didn't deserve them." Jackie's eyes lit up and she smiled a humble smile. "Okay, so, I'll see ya. If you need anything call. I'm serious."

"I will. Bye Mr. Frazer. Thanks. Thanks for letting me stay. Good luck."

"Please, call me Bruce."

Jackie nodded. They stared at each other for a few moments. Bruce nodded and the corners of his mouth curled up in a smile.

Bruce walked into the front room for his goodbyes to his family. He looked visibly shaken. Becky ran up to her father and threw her arms around his neck. Bruce wrapped his arms around her waist and kissed her on the cheek. Jason stood next to him with his hands in his pockets, looking down.

Leena looked on from the window seat across the room. Her guilt and shame consumed her. She wanted to run and hide but she knew this was music she had to face, however dissonant its sound.

"So listen, Kiddo," Bruce directed his comments to Jason, "You and I have a date tomorrow morning to go surfing."

Jason nodded and said, "Okay." Bruce gave him a hug.

"I'll be back later this afternoon to take you both up to my new place. It's nice, you'll see. I have spare bedrooms so you can come and stay anytime you want." Bruce observed the looks on his kids' faces and added, "I mean you could practically walk to my place from here, that's how close it is. Okay?" They both nodded. Bruce looked over at Leena who was crying quietly behind her tissue. Their silent exchange was not bitter or angry, just sad.

Bruce left and the three of them watched out the window again. The bitter cold January day kept them inside. Bruce said a few things to the driver of the truck and then he got into his Mercedes and pulled out with the truck following close behind.

Once he was out of sight Leena had no more energy to pretend everything was alright. She got up and went upstairs. Jason went up to his room soon after. Becky went into the downstairs kitchen where she saw Jackie sitting at the table flipping through a magazine. Becky sat down and joined her.

"I think there's more to this than what they told us," Becky said to Jackie.

Jackie looked up from the magazine and then back down without commenting.

Becky picked up on her demeanor. "You know something, don't you."

She looked up again and stared at Becky. She didn't know what to say.

"Tell me what you know, Jackie."

"I think your mother should do that, not me. Don't ask me, okay?"

Becky stood up and looked at Jackie and thought about it. "Okay, I will." She left and went upstairs.

Becky walked into the TV room where her mother was sitting on the couch. "So tell me, mother, why did Dad really leave?"

Leena turned her head quickly to face her daughter. Her comment took her by surprise. She turned back around and watched the television. Becky walked over to the table and picked up the remote and shut the television off.

"Well, I'm waiting." Becky leaned against the wall in the spot that used to be occupied by her father's armchair. She crossed her arms.

Leena stared straight ahead. Turning again to look at her daughter, she said, "There *was* more to it." The waterworks started again and she picked up the tissue box from the table and put it on her lap. She removed a fresh tissue and dabbed her eyes. "I was seeing someone and your father found out."

"Mother! No!" Becky rolled her eyes up to the ceiling and back to Leena staring intently into her eyes. "What were you *thinking*? Are you *nuts*?" Becky walked into the hallway and back into the room, dispelling energy.

"If you came in here to give me a hard time, to give me a lecture you can turn yourself around and get out!" Leena raised her voice. "It's been a hard time for me lately. I'm not asking for any sympathy. I only need some space."

"But Mom," Becky said with a calm voice. "Why?"

"It just happened, that's all."

"How can it 'just happen'? Did you meet some guest or something?"

Leena looked at Becky and shook her head and smiled a false smile. "No, I didn't meet *a guest*. He was someone I knew from high school."

"High school? What are you talking about?"

"Never mind!"

"You don't mean that guy? The one you told me broke your heart?"

Leena nodded and cried, bringing the tissue back up to her face. Her face made some contortions as she sobbed.

"How on earth?"

"I don't want to talk about it, okay? I don't mean to be rude about it, sweetie, but I just can't talk about it right now. Someday I will."

Suddenly Becky felt sorry for her mother. "So did you marry Dad because you were pregnant?" Becky blurted out. "You had to marry Dad, didn't you."

Leena looked at Becky and realized the math was easy. It was never something that was discussed.

Becky started to cry. There were many minutes of silence. She finally asked, "Did you ever love Dad?"

"Of course, honey. Did I feel like he was my soul mate? Maybe not, but I did love him. And I still do."

"Then why split up?" she cried.

Leena shrugged.

"Is it over with you and the high school guy?" Becky asked.

Leena nodded and cried. "I think so."

"You think so?"

"All I know right now is it's January 4th and your father just left, and I'm sitting here on this couch. I can't think much beyond that right now."

They spent the next few minutes not speaking. Becky watched her mother cry. Her tears seemed to have no end. "I'm sorry, Mom. I'm sorry you're in so much pain." She walked over and sat down next to her mother and offered her a hug.

"Thanks, Beck," Leena said through her tears. "I don't expect you to approve of what I did, but please let me work this out, okay?"

Becky nodded, agreeing with her mother. She took one of the tissues from the box for herself. She sat with her mother for a few more minutes. She got up to leave.

"Beck?" Leena said. Becky turned around. "I don't think Jason needs to know all this, do you?"

"No, I guess not. That's your call. See ya later." Becky left and went to her room. Leena turned the television back on.

AS PROMISED, BRUCE RETURNED later in the afternoon and brought Becky and Jason to his new place. Their mood lifted when they walked into his condo. It was new and clean. Sunlight poured into the living room through a large sliding glass door. Becky and Jason walked around quietly at first, observing.

"I call this room," Jason said as he entered one of the three rooms upstairs.

"And this room can be yours, Becky," Bruce said. Becky walked in and looked all around. They saw mattresses leaning against the walls of their bedrooms. "We had these two spare beds in the basement at home, so your rooms are practically ready. I'll have to order a mattress for myself, though." Bruce looked at his almost empty new bedroom. All that occupied it were his suitcases, his briefcase, and laptop and a folding table and chair.

"Dad, is this permanent?" Becky asked.

"I don't know honey. It's a separation for now, but I just don't know what we want to do. I don't know, and I don't think your mother knows right now. We both just need time to sort things out."

Bruce looked at Jason who wasn't saying much. "It'll be cool having two different places to go," Bruce said. Jason nodded. "You're real close to the school from here, Jason. You could ride your bike to school." Jason nodded again.

BY THE THIRD WEEK in January Leena brought Becky back to school. Leena and Becky filled up the car with bags of clean laundry, the new computer and monitor, some blank canvases and other miscellaneous things.

When they got to Becky's dorm, they had to make several trips bringing her stuff inside. Becky's roommate was already there. Leena was cordial, and then said she had to be heading back. Becky walked her mother to the outside of the dorm building. They stood and stared at each other. Leena envied her youth and her fresh start in life. She was proud of her daughter. She was a smart and talented girl with a good head on her shoulders.

"How did I get so lucky having you as my daughter?" she said with tears in her eyes.

"Mom," Becky said. "Don't look so sad." Becky knew there were no words to patch up her mother's life. That was something she would have to do on her own.

They hugged. "I love you Beck." Leena squeezed her hard. "I love you *so* much!"

"I love you too, Mom. I just want you to be happy. Please, Mom, get happy again."

"I will," she said. They parted and stared at each other. Tears streamed down Becky's face at the sight of her mother as she walked over to the car.

"I'll chat with you on IM once I get this computer hooked up," Becky called out.

Leena looked back and nodded. They waved one more time and Leena got into the car and left.

More profound sadness followed Leena all the way home. Becky was yet one more person leaving her life to move on to something else. Intellectually she knew that was how it worked, but she was feeling abandoned all over again. Leaving Becky this time was ten times more painful than when she and Bruce left her last September. Leena's emotions were raw. She drove most of the way home in tears.

CHAPTER 47

The conversation was the same from week to week. Wendy tried to be the voice of reason but Leena was still hoping that Michael would come to his senses and eventually realize they were meant to be together and come back to her; that he'd leave his wife and come back where he belonged.

With the new year getting older by one month, Leena had wanted desperately to make the call to Michael throughout January and get his answer. Wendy talked her out of it each time. She pointed out that he was showing how unreliable he was and how fickle. Wendy endured a few harsh words from her friend but let them slide.

Wendy had returned from a teaching seminar she had attended the previous week. She gave Leena a call. After listening to the usual litany of complaints about the inn which invariably would be tied to Michael's decision to leave her, and Bruce's desertion, Wendy waited for the right moment.

"So I went to my seminar in Norwich the other day," Wendy started out.

Leena was barely listening. "Oh yeah, how'd that go?"

"Okay. It was attended by the whole region, you know." She paused, but not for long. "Teachers from my area, teachers from Norwich were there. Just elementary school teachers." Wendy waited for that to sink in.

"Did you say Norwich?"

"Yes," Wendy knew what was coming. She wanted Leena to prompt her.

"Was *she* there?"

"Yes she was. I saw Alice. I met her. She was seated two tables away from my table. We all went to the luncheon after our morning workshop."

"And? Are you trying to tell me something, Wendy? Was Michael there, is that it?"

"No, Michael wasn't there! But I did learn some stuff." Wendy dreaded what was to come. She knew it had to be said.

"What did you learn? Wendy you're driving me crazy!"

"I wasn't going to tell you this but I think you need to know."

"For goodness sake, tell me. How bad can it be? I already know Michael chose to stay with her."

"She's pregnant," Wendy blurted it out. There was silence from the other end of the phone. "Leena, you there?"

"What makes you think that? I mean, are you sure it was Alice?"

"I'm sure it was Alice Everly, Leena. I'll just tell you how I found out. Are you there?" Wendy didn't hear anything. "Leena, are you there?" She finally heard sniffing.

With a choke, Leena said, "I'm here."

Wendy took a deep breath. "I was standing in line for the buffet table." Wendy sighed and said, "No, let me back up. When we arrived around 8:30 we all got name tags. I was looking for my table assignment and I passed a woman and I noticed her tag said 'Alice Everly' and under her name it said, 'Grade 2 Norwich.'" Wendy could hear Leena sniffing, an all too familiar sound of late. "I obviously realized who she was. So, leading up to the buffet table, she was ahead of me about like six feet or so, and she was talking to another woman. They seemed to know each other well. Anyway, I heard her say something about missing school due to her morning sickness. I heard her say something about the added stress of her son Tommy having his accident made it all worse."

"No, Wendy! No!" Leena sobbed. "Oh my God, no!" Leena screamed and dropped the phone.

"Leena, you okay?" There was silence. "Are you still there?" Wendy waited.

Finally, Leena picked up the phone. "How can you be sure she was *pregnant*?" Leena asked.

"Later, at a break around three, I saw her talking to the same woman. I was standing there near a refreshment table and I sort of insinuated myself into their conversation. I noticed she was rubbing her belly which did look like it was sticking out a bit. She's small so I think she looked sort of thick there. Anyway, she was talking about 'the baby.' So I said something like, "Oh how nice, when is the baby due?' and she said 'the middle of June.'"

There was a long silence as Leena counted backward on her fingers. "Oh my God, Wendy, she got pregnant in September! We were still together. We were two months away from breaking up!" Leena sobbed and mumbled. Wendy waited patiently.

"I've been contemplating telling you this, or not telling you this news, all weekend, but I think you had to know. The way you've been talking about Michael coming back to you didn't seem realistic to me. This sort of synched it for me. Anyway, don't be mad at me."

"I'm not mad at you. You're my dearest friend. If I found out and also found out you knew and didn't tell me, then I'd be mad at you." Leena waited a few moments. "Thank you. No, I mean it."

"I didn't get any pleasure out of telling you, you know. My gut was that Michael was not being straight with you about your future with him. Even last fall I felt that. I am so sorry, Leena. I wished and hoped against hope that he would choose you, I really did."

"I know you did. Oh shit, Wendy," Leena said suddenly, but then stopped talking. Wendy could hear her crying.

"What?"

"The addition, oh my God, the addition, that *bastard*!" she cried hysterically.

Wendy didn't know what she meant. "What are you talking about?

"He built an addition to their house, and when I went there in September, I saw it. That was probably right around the time she got pregnant. What do you bet the plan was to expand their *family*." Leena was crying uncontrollably. "And it must have been the plan the whole time. He started that addition in *the spring*! Oh my God, Wendy. They were trying to get pregnant the entire time I was with him! That *bastard!* What am I going to do?" She asked rhetorically.

"You need to move on. You need to find your own happiness. You *so* need to put this all behind you." Leena was quiet. "You know how rotten it was for me after my divorce, and before it, of course. I thought my world had completely ended. Remember the days our situation was reversed and I was crying in your ear? He cheated on me and we never got past it, even though we tried. I think a relationship that forms through infidelity is doomed. His fell apart soon after. But look at me now! I met Frank and we're so happy. Andrew and Jeremy are best pals, thankfully. Things will work out for you. You're still young and you're so pretty."

"Ha, young? I'll be forty in two months. I'll be shriveling up any day now."

Wendy laughed. "Well, so will I. Next month! We're in it together, girlfriend."

"Did she mention Michael?" Leena asked.

Wendy was silent.

"Well?"

With a sigh, Wendy completed the story about the encounter with Alice. "Sort of. Her friend asked her, 'Do you know whether you're having a boy or girl?' and she said to us, 'No Mike wants to be surprised, so we didn't ask even though I had an ultrasound.' Obviously the friend knew who Michael was."

"So he wants to be surprised. How precious. I should give him a surprise." Leena sounded calm all of a sudden.

"What's that supposed to mean?"

"I can fantasize about killing him, can't I? No wait, I'll kill her and then he would have to live with that."

"Stop talking like that. I don't like it."

"I'm not serious, but there's no law that says I can't *think* about it." Leena added, "And she called him 'Mike'?"

"Yeah, I think so."

Leena's crying picked up again. "He was always 'Michael,' always will be. I wonder when he started going by 'Mike'?"

"Is that important?" Wendy asked.

"No, I don't suppose it is. It makes him sound like someone I don't even know. Maybe I never did." She continued crying and said, "He started out as a cheater, remember? I should have known from the start."

Wendy tried to lighten it up. "So what do you say we get together soon? We'll go shopping. I could set you up with one of my friends or colleagues."

"No, I'm not ready for that. Jesus, Wendy, I'm not divorced. Not yet anyway. I gotta figure out what I want to do next."

Wendy heard more sniffing. "I'm so sorry I had to tell you."

"You did the right thing. I better go, okay?"

"You gonna be okay?"

"Yeah."

"I'll talk to you tomorrow. I'll check on you," Wendy said.

"I'll be fine. Stop worrying."

"I'll call you. Take care."

"I'll be fine. Bye. Thanks, Wen."

CHAPTER 48

Leena's moping and sulking did not let up. Jason and Jackie watched her walk as if she had weights on her ankles. Her hair was a perpetual mess and she wore the same stained sweat pants and shirt day after day.

Leena was taking very little responsibility for the inn. Without issue, Jackie picked up the slack. Jackie, Michelle, and Hal were running the inn. "I can't deal with them today," Leena would say to Jackie as her explanation for not stepping up to the plate. Jackie didn't question it. She just did what needed to be done.

Jackie had also taken on the responsibility of food shopping and preparing meals for Jason. She didn't tell Leena that was what she was doing. Leena was so far down in self-pity that she wasn't aware that the simplest and most basic tasks were not getting done.

Keeping her relationship with Rick on the down-low was yet another favor Jackie did for Leena. When she went somewhere with Rick she walked up the street to meet him, away from the inn. Leena had not asked her about Rick at all and Jackie knew she didn't want to know.

JACKIE WAS LEAFING THROUGH a cookbook, sitting at the kitchen table. Leena entered and walked past her to the coat rack. She took her coat off the hook and opened the door to go outside without saying a word to Jackie.

"Where are you going?" Jackie asked, looking up from the book.

"Just going for a walk," Leena replied.

"It's kinda late, isn't it? It's dark."

"No, it's fine."

"It's pretty cold out. That's a very light coat."

"No, I don't think so. It's fine."

"You want company?" Jackie asked.

"No, I'm going alone," she said and walked out.

Leena walked all the way down along the causeway toward the next town. She fought the sharp, dry air that pierced her face and made her squint. The moisture in her nose froze with each breath. The temperature had dipped down close to zero degrees. Leena turned her collar up to shield herself from the frigid air.

Leena's despair had caved in on her. What had been keeping her afloat, up until this point, was the hope of resuming her relationship with Michael.

With all her cards on the table, she concluded she didn't have a hand. As she walked down the street, she thought about all the people she loved and all the people who didn't need her anymore: Michael, Bruce, Becky, Jason, Wendy, her sister Nancy and even Jackie.

Jackie doesn't need me anymore, she thought. *She's become so independent. Becky's gone. She doesn't need me anymore either. When she's home she's off with Chris. Jason's fifteen. He barely talks to me anymore. I'm just an overprotective mother whose taste in music is old fashioned. Bruce never loved me!* Leena sobbed thinking of the wasted years with him. *Michael went back to his life. It was simple for him. He can just shut off his feelings for me like a light switch.*

On her way back to the inn Leena stopped in front of the spot where she found Jackie the year before. She stood and looked down at the waves hitting the rocks. Ice had formed on the tops of the rocks. She took the crooked little path that wound down and around and she sat down on the sand next to the exact rock where she had found Jackie's lifeless body. The February wind coming off the ocean was brutally cold - a wind-chill factor of minus 20 degrees - but she felt she needed the onslaught of cold air to punish herself for not handling things correctly. The tears flowed with ease. Her nose ran incessantly. She wrapped her jacket tightly around herself but still shivered in the cold. Her teeth started to chatter.

The thought crossed her mind to sit there all night. If she lived through the night it was meant to be, and if she died then that was meant to be. *If there is a God, he'll decide for me,* she thought. *Am I needed anymore? Am I wanted?*

Leena waited for the numbing cold to freeze her emotions and make her feel more normal. She sat there for close to an hour and started to fall asleep.

"Leena, wake up! Are you crazy? Wake up!" Jackie was squatting by Leena's side shaking her.

Leena's eyes opened and looked at Jackie as if she were a total stranger.

"Are you okay? It's freezing out here, come on!"

"Jackie?" Leena asked.

"Yes, it's me. Come on!"

"Jackie, what are you doing here?" Leena asked, still unclear.

"I was just going to ask you the same question."

"I'm just sitting here thinking, that's all. Just clearing my head."

"Well, this isn't a very good spot for that. I don't have to tell you that! And this isn't exactly the best season to be doing this either."

"Well it's the only season I've got at the moment. Summer might have been nicer."

"Why don't you come in before you freeze to death," Jackie said. "Or is that the idea?"

Leena looked around at her as if she knew her thoughts. She turned back around to look at the water.

"Come on Leena. This is silly. Come inside."

"No. I'll c-come inside in a little while. You go ahead."

"That guy, your boyfriend, he broke up with you, didn't he?" Jackie asked.

Leena turned around again to look at Jackie. Jackie walked around to face her and squatted down to her level. She waited for an answer.

"He did, didn't he?" Jackie asked again.

"Yeah," Leena cried.

"And you loved him *a lot,* didn't you?"

Leena nodded.

"If there's anything I've learned, or you taught me, is that no guy is worth dying for."

"I wasn't going to k-kill myself. I was just going to let f-fate s-step in, that's all."

"Well, this is dumb!" Jackie moved over and put her arm around Leena's shoulder.

"He decided to s-stay with his wa-wife," Leena admitted and started to cry.

"I'm sorry." Jackie rubbed her shoulder.

"They're g-going to have another b-baby!" Leena was sobbing. "How do you like that? He let on that we had a f-future together, and at the s-same exact t-time he was getting his wife p-pregnant! On purpose!"

"Oh Leena, that's horrible. I had no idea."

"Not so ha-horrible f-for him. He's happy as a l-lark," she sobbed.

"You're a strong woman and you'll get through this, I *know!* You're way stronger than I am." Leena listened and cried, resting her head on Jackie's shoulder. Jackie continued. "I am so very sorry about what happened when I said those things that night. Please believe I am sorry. I care about you Leena. You've been like a mother to me and you are the last person I would want to hurt."

"I'm not b-blaming you, Ja-Jackie." She sniffed and pulled her coat tighter. Her teeth were chattering non-stop. "I guess I d-did b-blame you at f-first. Everything th-that has ha-happened has ha-happened ba-because of m-my own actions. My lack of judgment. I blame n-no one but m-myself." Her teeth were chattering so much that it became difficult to talk.

"Please can we go inside? It's so cold out here! We'll talk about it inside."

Jackie helped Leena to her feet. They maneuvered around the rocks and found the path and crawled up to the road. Before they crossed back over to *Sunset Inn* Leena stopped for a moment to look at her inn in the moonlight. "It's a beautiful inn, isn't it?"

"It sure is," Jackie agreed.

Leena and Jackie stood there looking at the house. Leena said, breaking her gaze from the house and looking directly at Jackie, "I loved him so."

"I know." Jackie put her arm back around her shoulders and guided her into the inn. Jackie entered the code and they walked up the stairwell to her futon in the office. "Are you going to be okay?"

"Yes, thanks. I'll be fine."

Jackie left and returned a few minutes later with two mugs of hot chocolate. She handed one to Leena and sat down in the chair next to the computer. They sipped their cocoa. Jackie had wrapped a heavy blanket around her body. Leena held the mug tightly and close to her face. Leena's teeth finally stopped chattering.

"Don't feel bad about what you said in front of Bruce last fall," Leena said to her. "What happened with me and Michael was inevitable. Everything that happened played out exactly how it would have played out, with or without you." Leena said. "I know this now."

"I appreciate that."

"Please know you aren't to blame, Jackie. If anything, you coming here was a Godsend, to me and the inn."

They finished their hot chocolate and Jackie stayed by Leena's side until she fell asleep. She covered her with the blanket again and went to bed in Becky's room where she stayed right down the hall from Leena.

CHAPTER 49

It had been about two weeks since Leena's flirt with death out between the rocks. She had managed to get herself back to a place she considered normal. Her life was filled again with the details and chores that went hand-in-hand with running a successful inn. She couldn't indulge in self-pity any longer. Her goals were simple: Get up every day and figure out ways to fill the seats or rooms at the inn, or risk losing it to foreclosure.

Jackie had turned her own corner. She had self-confidence she had never had in her life. There was much distance now from her downward spiral of a year ago thanks in part to Rick but also Leena's commitment to her.

Leena could no longer justify mourning her husband's departure or Michael's change of heart. "Things have a way of working themselves out," Leena had told Jackie. "Things happen for a reason. I believe that you know. It was meant to be that Rick came back to you." Her jealousy was gone and Jackie was, once again, free to discuss her personal life with Leena.

LEENA AND JACKIE WALKED up and down the aisles of the fabric store, *The Print is Right,* in Westerly, looking for fabric for window treatments to go with the wallpaper she had put up months earlier. They were of the same mind for most of their choices.

"The bedspread has more earth tones with, sort of, springtime green flecks. That's why this one might be better." Leena said.

"I don't know, this green might clash a little," Jackie said. "We should have brought some here to hold up to it and compare."

"I couldn't just drag the bedspread here with me," Leena said.

Jackie laughed. "No, I meant the wallpaper sample."

Leena chuckled. "Of course." They both laughed.

"I might as well break it to you now. I'm gonna take down room two's wallpaper this year and replace it. It's peeling. It was the first wallpaper I hung when I first started renovating. I hate it now. But this time I'll pick something to go with the curtains. Smart, huh? Last year, not so smart. I just picked paper on an impulse." Leena had picked wallpaper in haste on the day she met Michael, to corroborate her story.

"I want you to teach me how to hang wallpaper," Jackie said.

"Sure. It's easy. Well, it's hard at first but, I don't know, there's something so rewarding about hanging paper. It's hard to explain."

"Well, I hope you don't go too paper crazy." They both laughed again.

Leena's cell phone rang. She dug it out of her purse. "Hello."

"Leena, it's me."

Leena was paralyzed. Her heart started to beat furiously. She went pale and her spine stiffened. Leena looked at Jackie and she mouthed to her, "It's Michael!" Jackie's eyes widened and her mouth opened slightly. They had no secrets between them anymore.

"Can you talk?" he asked.

"Michael?" Leena asked, still looking at Jackie.

"Hi. I know it's been a while. I'm sorry."

"I'm in a store at the moment. I must say, this is quite a shock. What do you want?"

"Can you talk?" Michael repeated himself.

"Wait a minute. I'm going to walk outside to my car, hold on." Leena put the phone down by her hip and said to Jackie in a whisper, "I'm going to see what he wants. I'll be right back."

"*Leena!*" Jackie warned. "*Don't!*"

"I'm fine! Believe me!" She walked out into the parking lot. "I'm walking to my car, hold on." She got into her car. "Okay, what's up?" she said casually.

"I told you I would call after the holidays and well, it's way after the holidays, isn't it," Michael said nervously. Leena was silent and let him talk. "So how are you?"

"Fine."

"Good. I wasn't sure I should call. But better late than never, as they say, you know, about calling you." There was a long pause. "So I'm calling." He laughed a nervous laugh.

Leena remained silent.

"I guess I wanted to apologize. I guess I wanted to just touch base, try to remain friends."

"Okay."

"I know I should have called in January. There were some issues with my father and a few other issues."

"I see." Leena was neutral.

"Oh, this is hard for me."

"So what is it you want, Michael?"

"Like I said, I promised I'd call."

"And I know how much you hate breaking promises," Leena said sarcastically.

"I didn't like leaving it the way we left it. But things have been crazy around here."

"Really? Crazy how?"

"Just busy. Like I said, my father, the store, the band, the usual stuff. But I knew you had some stuff to deal with on your end and I figured you'd need time to decompress from that." He sighed an audible sigh and continued. "I feel bad about everything and I didn't mean to hurt you, I really didn't."

Leena closed her eyes as she listened to his voice. She could almost feel him through the phone. She still craved him but had not allowed herself to for the last few weeks. She wanted to blurt out, "Please take me back! Please let's meet somewhere!" She held back. It was harder than raising a huge boulder above her head.

"You still there?" he asked.

"I'm here. You called and did the right thing, Michael. Now what?"

"I just wanted to, I don't know, keep in touch. Touch base?"

"How's your wife? Are you still married?"

"Yeah."

"You never told her about us, did you?" She knew the answer.

"No," Michael said.

"Why the call? I know, to 'touch base.' But why call now? What's the point, Michael?"

"It felt like the right thing to do."

"So you did your good deed. Anything else?"

"I see you're mad at me. I don't blame you. Oh boy, this is awkward."

"Is there anything new in your life, Michael?"

"Not much. Like I said, my father, he had an episode last month and had to have another heart procedure."

"Sorry to hear that. I hope he'll be ok."

There was a long pause. Leena waited to see if he would reveal his wife's condition.

"So what else is new?"

"Like what?"

Leena sighed, audibly showing her disgust. "Like why you put on that addition to your house?" There was silence. "Well?"

"I don't know."

"Isn't it for the new *baby*? Can you *ever* tell the truth?" Leena's voice went up. "You were planning another *baby* at the same time you were seeing me, Michael! What have you got to say about that? How low can you get? I mean you were *planning* that baby!"

There was more silence. Michael was caught completely off guard.

"Well? I'm waiting, Michael. Don't you think I *deserve* the truth?"

"Of course you do. How did you find that out?"

"It doesn't matter how I know. Oh my God, Michael. You weren't going to tell me! This is sickening. It's embarrassing, really. I must have been in a trance months ago. What kind of man does this to his family?

Why did you string me along? This wasn't fair to your wife either!" She heard him breathing.

"I'm sorry," was all he could say.

"You know what Michael? I am *so* done with you. It hurt for a while. I'll admit that. And from time to time it gets to me, but you know what? I'm over it. You need to stay out of my life. I'm very sorry I intruded into yours, I truly am. I mean, it wasn't at all fair what I did to Alice, even though she doesn't even know about me." Leena had no problem saying her name.

"No, Leena, don't be sorry. I'm not. I'm glad you came back into my life. I don't regret a single thing."

"You should! Go count your blessings before your wife realizes what a snake you are and kicks your ass out of that newly expanded house of yours. Go kiss her big belly."

There was much silence. They heard each other breathing.

"Are you still with Bruce?" Michael finally asked.

"Nope, he left. Some of us told our spouses the truth. And for what? You never had any intention of choosing me. You deliberately strung me along, I guess for the sex. I don't know for what else. We never really did much together besides that."

"That's not true. We did lots of fun stuff."

"Whatever!" Leena grunted.

"Are you divorced now?" Michael asked.

"You know what? My life is none of your business anymore, Michael, I mean Mike. It's Mike now, isn't it?" Leena removed the cell phone from her ear before she heard his response. She looked at the buttons and pushed the button to end the call. She put the phone into her purse and sat in her car staring straight ahead for several minutes. She surprised herself when she realized she was not crying.

Leena got out of the car and went back into the fabric store. She met up with Jackie. They stared at each other. Leena looked angry, not sad.

"Are you okay? What did he want?"

Leena shook her head. "He wanted to keep his promise about calling after the holidays. He wanted to '*touch base*.'" Leena sounded mad.

"Did he want to start seeing you again?" Jackie asked.

"I don't know. Maybe. Why else would he call?" Leena looked right at Jackie. "Not that I would! I'm done!"

"Are you okay, Leena?" Jackie asked again.

"I'm fine. More than fine. I'm glad he called actually. I said a few things I've been wanting to say to him. He didn't admit to the baby until I brought it up, then he had to admit it." Leena exhaled with anger and disgust. "What *nerve*! And what a fool I was to tangle up my life that way."

"So you're cool with everything?"

"Way cool."

Leena and Jackie continued their search for curtain fabric feeling each bolt. "What do you think of this one? This would go nicely with that bedspread."

CHAPTER 50

Leena looked out the window of the 747 and watched the city disappear behind the clouds. She laid her head back and looked forward to listen to the flight attendant give instructions on the oxygen masks and flotation devices.

This dream trip of a lifetime was bittersweet. It was the trip Bruce had promised her and they never took. It was the trip Michael promised a few short months before. Now, she made a promise to herself and she was keeping it.

LEENA WAS FEELING GOOD about how she left the inn behind. For one week, Jackie would be in charge. Jackie turned out to be a gem of sorts: A gem at the bottom of the ocean is worthless until someone finds it and realizes its worth. Leena trusted her completely now.

"Ireland? Really?" Jackie asked.

"I've always wanted to go there, my whole life. This is a birthday present I am giving myself." Leena responded.

"When is your birthday?"

"April first. I'm a real live April fool!"

"Stop, you are not," Jackie said. "Hey, we all make mistakes."

"I've not been very smart about the way I've lived my life this past year. And I was a fool when it came to Michael."

"I've been a fool for men too, as you know."

"Well, I should know better. I'm turning forty for crying out loud. You're supposed to be a fool for guys at your age."

"When are you leaving?"

"March thirty-first."

"What about Jason?"

"He'll be staying at Bruce's place. I asked Bruce to stop by a few times during the week to check on you. I'll give you all his phone numbers in case you need anything. He said he'd be available for anything. Of course, Hal and Michelle will be here too."

LEENA LOOKED OUT THE window again and saw only blue sky.

Five hours in the air and another hour at the airport in Shannon and Leena drove off in her rented car. She had no choice but to get used to driving on the other side of the road: the wrong side. Once she got out of the congested areas it was smooth sailing. Acres and acres of lush green sped by the car in repetitive motion. Sheep and cattle dotted the countryside. Not a traffic light stopped her but a herd of cattle did as they crossed the road to another pasture. *What could be better on that side? It only looks greener. Don't be fooled.* Leena smiled.

The stone walls created a labyrinth as far as the eye could see, delineating pastures created generations ago. It seemed every wall was connected to every other wall in the country, perhaps connecting every person to every other person.

Armed with a map she forged ahead with her plan to find the bed and breakfast where she had made a reservation in the small town of Doolin, in County Clare. She stopped at the end of a road and saw the usual jumble of stacked signs. Each board was appropriately sharpened into an arrow pointing either right or left. Third sign down from the top said *Doolin* and it pointed right. The one below it said *Cliffs of Moher* pointing in the same direction. Leena turned right.

A few miles down the road she came to the parking area for the Cliffs of Moher. She pulled in. Daylight was gone. Leena did not get out of the car. She decided to return the next day, on her fortieth birthday. "This is where I'll want to be," she said.

It took less than half an hour to find the ambitiously named *Heaven's Gate*. The abode itself was not impressive but location trumped all. Standing at the end of the lawn the Atlantic Ocean waved in the distance, inviting a soul, any soul, greeting her.

Leena walked up the driveway and knocked on the door. A middle-aged woman greeted her and then invited her inside as if she were a long-lost relative. She introduced herself as Katherine O'Malley, and out of nowhere her husband appeared with an outstretched hand to shake informing her of his name: Thomas. With an offer of tea and scones, Leena got comfortable in their living room straight away. She struggled to understand what they were saying. Their thick Irish brogue was inviting and soothing with its sing-song rhythm, but close to impossible to understand. She pretended to understand them at first by nodding her head, but soon she was able to latch onto it, like a moving carousel.

The inn was a simple place. It was their home that they opened up to tourists for the extra money. No one toiled over whether the curtains matched the wallpaper. There was no rhyme or reason to the art on the walls: not exactly eclectic. Dozens of knickknacks adorned almost every inch of tabletop and shelf. Shamrocks were big. Still, it felt comfortable.

The O'Malleys didn't charge anywhere near what Leena charged at her inn. She did not tell the O'Malleys she was an inn owner herself. It would have created inquiries and inevitable comparisons.

"So you come with us, eh? Down to the pub tonight, hear Johnny play," Thomas O'Malley said more as a statement of fact than a question.

"Who's Johnny?"

"Our son," Katherine said. "He's a master on the fiddle."

"That sounds nice but I was thinking of just settling in and ..." Leena started to explain.

"We won't hear of it, Mum," Katherine said. "You need to go. Get yourself a pint and relax. Nothing like it!"

"Okay, if you insist." Leena smiled.

"I don't insist dear. You make up your mind. We're leaving at eight."

Leena nodded and smiled.

"And so you're here all by yourself, love?" Katherine asked. "Don't you 'ave any family?"

"Yes, I've got two kids. My son is fifteen and my daughter is eighteen. And well, there's Jackie, she lives with us. They're back in the States."

"Eighteen! Goodness Gracious! You must have been a wee one when you had 'em. How old are you, dear?"

"I'm forty. Forty tomorrow as a matter of fact." Leena said. "It's my birthday."

"Dear Lord, Tom, did you 'ear that?"

"I 'eard it Mum."

"Actually, this trip is my birthday present to myself. I've wanted to come to Ireland since I can remember. So here I am."

"And ya wanted to come alone, did ya?" Katherine asked, truly in the dark.

"I did. I love my kids to death but this is what I wanted." She didn't want to tell them about all of the broken promises.

Katherine had to accept her answer. "I see."

"Have you lived here long?" Leena asked them.

"You could say that," Katherine said as she laughed, exhibiting her gapped, slightly buck teeth. "Me whole life. Me Mum lives down the street and me sisters live here too. Me other brother moved to Kerry, runs a tourist boat. Mc Da died last spring."

"I'm sorry. My mother passed a year and a half ago, my father several years ago."

"I'm sorry to hear that, dear. Me Mum, she's a feisty one, she is, at eighty-three, ya know. She still can drink any man under the table? I swear the beer preserves her." Katherine said. Leena laughed, and then realized Katherine was serious.

"So where do you plan to go on this vacation all by yerself?" Thomas asked.

"In the morning I'm planning on seeing the Cliffs of Moher. Later, The Burren. I want to go to Galway. Then I'll drive over to Dublin. Other than that, I'm really not sure. If I have time I'd like to drive south. I'll come around full circle, stopping in Limerick hopefully, and then fly out of Shannon again a week from today."

"Aye. Excellent choice, the cliffs," Thomas said. "If you hadn't said that I would have insisted you go there."

"You'll find God there," Katherine said with confidence.

Leena nodded but doubted it. "I can't wait to see them. That's why I wanted to come in this direction first. I know I should kiss the Blarney Stone, and maybe if I have time, I'll do that."

"You made a good decision," Katherine said. "The stone is overrated. Remind me, I'll hook you up with me son's tour boat if ya find yerself down Kerry way. It's very touristy but Dingle is a must-see too."

"Okay, I'd like that."

Katherine looked at the clock on the wall. "Thomas it's getting on eight? We best be goin' eh?"

The O'Malleys loaded Leena into their truck and they all headed down to the local pub. Experiencing their culture was just the therapy she needed. They were right. She enjoyed the people, the authentic Irish music, and she couldn't have gone home without having a pint of Guinness.

Leena laughed and sang - something she had not done in months. This was the best medicine. The O'Malleys introduced her to everyone in the bar. Everyone knew the O'Malleys. A local man grabbed Leena and danced with her – willingly, she kicked up her heels.

Maybe it was the fact that she was quite tipsy but she was sure she could understand the O'Malleys better on the way back to their inn. Leena nodded, saying "aye" instead of "yes."

She settled into her room around midnight. Back home it was only seven o'clock but Leena was exhausted and fell asleep right away.

THE O'MALLEYS PREPARED A huge breakfast. There was no way for Leena to eat enough to make a dent. One other guest, an older man, came out of the room down the hall from where Leena had stayed. She didn't know he had been there. The two of them ate breakfast together. The O'Malleys did not join them. Leena found out the man was an American on vacation, heading to Galway to visit relatives he hadn't seen in eight years.

Leena left by nine and thanked her hosts for a hospitable stay.

Katherine walked Leena to her car. She reached out and moved Leena's hair off of her shoulders with both hands, and then rested her hands on her shoulders and said as she looked deep into Leena's eyes, "I hope you find what yer lookin' for, dear."

Katherine's providence startled Leena. "Me too," she agreed. Her eyes got glassy. She gave Katherine a hug. "Thanks for everything."

"Goodbye, dear."

"Goodbye, Katherine." Leena waved to Thomas who was standing at the window in their living room.

LEENA JOINED THE MANY tourists who made the same journey to the Cliffs of Moher. Awesome was the view and breathtaking was the height. Her first glimpse brought her to tears. Standing with her arms crossed over her stomach, the Atlantic Ocean roared seven hundred feet below, a vertical drop. The cold winds, remnants of winter, were delivered with an unfaltering gust. Her hair flapped behind her head.

The rays of the sun were trapped on the surface of the water, flickering like Morse code. The seagulls soaring above the water's surface were far below any passerby up above. Their cries were drowned out by the tide's inevitable collision with rock.

On this clear morning, the first day of April and her fortieth birthday, Leena could almost make out her inn directly across the water. She conjured an image in her mind of Jackie tending to daily chores and greeting new arrivals with her beautiful smile and her new-found confidence.

Leena discovered a self-guided path at the very edge of the cliffs. There were quite a few people walking on it; many had cameras around their necks and Leena detected many nationalities. She took the path and followed it down. A tiny, low-lying fence separated tourists from peril. It was a mere suggestion and not a mandate. Some of the tourists ignored the danger signs and stepped over the fence and walked along the absolute edge of the cliff. Some lay down on their bellies and peered over the edge. Leena couldn't help but wonder how many people had chosen these cliffs as the last thing they'd ever see. She knew this ocean, like life's experiences, was deep, foreboding, and at times impenetrable, pursuant only to the rhythm of nature.

Leena stopped and moved aside to sit and rest. Without having to concentrate on her every step she was able to gather her thoughts. Leena's eyes followed the cliffs down to the water, and then she looked out to sea. She knew what the O'Malleys meant now. There was a sense of honor being at a place where God himself must have cleaved free this majestic piece of land, making it an island, sending it out on its own millions of years ago, only to end up here at a certain longitude. Leena felt like an island now, finally set free from what held her; set adrift.

There was no pull to finality, far from it. She could only hope there would be no more sad surprises on the other side of the Atlantic when she returned. Closure started here on the absolute edge of the world. She knew she had to find the strength to surrender the past and accept the future with open arms. She was ready.

ABOUT THE AUTHOR

This is Barbara Hawes' first novel.
Barbara lives in Connecticut. She is the
proud mother of two grown sons.

Made in United States
North Haven, CT
23 May 2022

19463621R00200